Lisa Kleypas is the author of a number of historical romance novels that have been published in fourteen languages. In 1985, she was named Miss Massachusetts and competed in the Miss America pageant in Atlantic City. After graduating from Wellesley College with a political science degree, she published her first novel at age twenty-one. Her books have appeared on the *New York Times* bestseller lists. Lisa is married and has two children.

Visit her website at www.lisakleypas.com

Praise for Lisa Kleypas:

'Each member of the family is a delight to meet…a spectacular story that continues the saga of the Hathaway family'
Romance Reviews

'Lushly sexy and thoroughly romantic…superbly crafted characters and an intriguing plot blend together brilliantly in this splendid romance'
Booklist

'Kleypas's effortless style makes for another sexy exploration of 19th century passion and peccadilloes, riveting from start to finish'
Publishers Weekly

Married by Morning

LISA KLEYPAS

piatkus

PIATKUS

First published in the United States in 2010 by St. Martin's Press, New York, USA
First published in Great Britain as a paperback original in 2010 by Piatkus
Reprinted 2010

A CIP catalogue record for this book
is available from the British Library.

ISBN 978-0-7499-5304-1

Typeset in Times by Phoenix Photosetting, Chatham, Kent
Printed and bound in Great Britain by Clays Ltd, Bungay, Suffolk

Papers used by Piatkus are natural, renewable and recyclable
products sourced from well-managed forests and certified
in accordance with the rules of the Forest Stewardship Council.

Mixed Sources
Product group from well-managed
forests and other controlled sources
www.fsc.org Cert no. SGS-COC-004081
© 1996 Forest Stewardship Council

Piatkus
An imprint of
Little, Brown Book Group
100 Victoria Embankment
London EC4Y 0DY

An Hachette UK Company
www.hachette.co.uk

www.piatkus.co.uk

To my dear, elegant, wise Connie
Because a good friend is cheaper than therapy.
Love always,
L.K.

Chapter One

Hampshire, England
August 1852

Anyone who had ever read a novel knew that governesses were supposed to be meek and downtrodden. They were also supposed to be quiet, subservient, and obedient, not to mention deferential to the master of the house. Leo, Lord Ramsay, wondered in exasperation why they couldn't have gotten one of *those*. Instead the Hathaway family had hired Catherine Marks, who, in Leo's opinion, cast an unflattering shadow upon the entire profession.

It wasn't that Leo found fault with Marks's actual abilities. She had done an excellent job of instructing his two youngest sisters, Poppy and Beatrix, in the finer points of social etiquette. And they had needed an inordinate amount of help, since none of the Hathaways had ever expected to mingle in the upper circles of British society. They had been reared in a strictly middle-class environment, in a village west of London. Their father, Edward Hathaway, had been a medieval history scholar, considered a man of good blood but hardly an aristocrat.

However, after a series of unlikely events, Leo had inherited

1

the title of Lord Ramsay. Although he had trained to be an architect, he was now a viscount with land and tenants. The Hathaways had moved to the Ramsay estate in Hampshire, where they had struggled to adjust to the demands of their new life.

One of the greatest challenges for the Hathaway sisters had been to learn the absurd multitude of rules and graces expected of privileged young ladies. Had it not been for Catherine Marks's patient instruction, the Hathaways would have rampaged through London with all the finesse of stampeding elephants. Marks had done wonders for all of them, especially Beatrix, who was undoubtedly the most eccentric sister of an already eccentric family. Although Beatrix was happiest romping through the meadows and woods like a wild creature, Marks had managed to impress on her that a different code of behavior was required in the ballroom. She had even written a series of etiquette poems for the girls, with such literary gems as:

> *Young ladies must display restraint*
> *When speaking with a stranger*
> *Flirtations, quarrels, or complaints*
> *Put our reputations in danger*

Naturally Leo hadn't been able to resist mocking Marks's poetic abilities, but he had to admit privately that her methods had worked. Poppy and Beatrix had successfully navigated a London season, at last. And Poppy had recently married a hotelier named Harry Rutledge.

Now only Beatrix was left. Marks had assumed the role of chaperone and companion to the energetic nineteen-year-old. As far as the rest of the Hathaways were concerned, Catherine Marks was practically a member of the family.

Leo, for his part, couldn't abide the woman. She aired her opinions at will and dared to give orders to him. On the rare occasions when Leo tried to be friendly, she snapped at him or turned away in scorn. When he stated a perfectly rational opinion, he could hardly finish a sentence before Marks had listed all the reasons why he was wrong.

Faced with the immutable fact of her dislike, Leo couldn't help but respond in kind. All during the past year he had tried to convince himself that it didn't matter if she despised him. There were many women in London who were infinitely more beautiful, engaging, and appealing than Catherine Marks.

If only she didn't fascinate him so.

Perhaps it was the secrets she guarded so zealously. Marks never talked about her childhood or her family, or why she had taken a position with the Hathaways. She had taught at a girls' school for a short time, but she refused to discuss her academic tenure or explain why she had left. There were rumors, passed on by former students, that she might have been a poor relation of the headmistress, or that she was a fallen woman whose loss of status had obliged her to go into service.

Marks was so self-contained and tenacious that it was often easy to forget she was still a young woman in her early twenties. When Leo had first met her, she had been the perfect embodiment of a dried-up spinster, with her spectacles and forbidding scowl and her stern hyphen of a mouth. Her spine was as unbending as a fireplace poker, and her hair, the dull brown of apple moths, was always pinned back too tightly. The Grim Reaper, Leo had nicknamed her, despite the objections of the family.

But the past year had wrought a remarkable change in Marks. She had filled out, her body slender but no longer matchstick thin, and her cheeks had gained color. A week and a half ago, when Leo had arrived from London, he had been absolutely astonished to see Marks with light golden locks. Apparently she had been dyeing her hair for years, but after an error on the part of the apothecary, she had been forced to abandon the disguise. And whereas the darker brown locks had been too severe for her delicate features and pale skin, her own natural blond was stunning.

Which had left Leo to grapple with the fact that Catherine Marks, his mortal enemy, was a beauty. It wasn't really the altered hair color that made her look so different . . . it was more that Marks was so uncomfortable without it. She felt vulnerable, and it showed. As a result, Leo wanted to strip away more layers, literal and physical. He wanted to *know* her.

Leo had tried to keep his distance while he pondered the ramifications of this discovery. He was confounded by his family's reaction to Marks, which amounted to nothing more than a collective shrug. Why weren't any of them even a fraction as curious about her as he was? Why had Marks deliberately made herself unattractive for so long? What the devil was she hiding from?

On a sunny Hampshire afternoon when Leo had ascertained that most of the family was otherwise occupied, he went in search of Marks, reasoning that if he confronted her in private, he would get some answers. He found her outside in a hedged garden filled with flowers. She occupied a bench at the side of a graveled path.

She was not alone.

Leo stopped at twenty yards' distance, drawing into the shade of a heavily foliated yew.

Marks was sitting beside Poppy's new husband, Harry Rutledge. They were engaged in what appeared to be an intimate conversation.

4

Although the situation wasn't precisely incriminating, neither was it appropriate.

What in God's name could they be talking about? Even from this remote vantage, it was clear that something of significance was being said. Harry Rutledge's dark head was inclined over hers protectively. Like a close friend. Like a lover.

Leo's mouth fell open as he saw Marks reaching beneath her spectacles with a delicate hand, as if to wipe away a tear.

Marks was *crying,* in the company of Harry Rutledge.

And then Rutledge kissed her on the forehead.

Leo's breath stopped. Holding still, he sorted through an emulsion of emotions and separated them into layers . . . amazement, worry, suspicion, fury.

They were hiding something. Plotting something.

Had Rutledge once kept her as a mistress? Was he blackmailing her, or was she perhaps extorting something from him? No . . . the tenderness between the pair was evident even at this distance.

Leo rubbed the lower half of his jaw as he considered what to do. Poppy's happiness was more important than any other consideration. Before he went dashing over to beat his sister's new husband to a bloody pulp, he would find out exactly what the situation was. And *then*, if circumstances warranted, he would beat Rutledge to a bloody pulp.

Taking slow, measured breaths, Leo watched the pair. Rutledge stood and went back to the house, while Marks remained seated on the bench.

Without making a conscious decision, Leo approached her slowly. He wasn't certain how he was going to treat her, or what he was going to say. It depended on which impulse leaped out most strongly the moment he reached her. It was entirely

5

possible that he would throttle her. It was equally likely that he would pull her to the sun-warmed grass and ravish her. He found himself stewing in a hot, unpleasant rush of feeling that wasn't at all familiar. Was it jealousy? Christ, it was. He was jealous over a skinny termagant who insulted and nagged him at every opportunity.

Was this some new level of depravity? Had he developed a spinster fetish?

Perhaps it was her very reserve that Leo found so erotic . . . he had always been fascinated by the question of what it would take to demolish it. Catherine Marks, his fiendish little adversary . . . naked and moaning beneath him. There was nothing he'd ever wanted more. And that made sense, actually: When a woman was easy and willing, there was no challenge in it. But taking Marks to bed, making it last a long time, tormenting her until she begged and screamed . . . now, *that* would be fun.

Leo walked toward her casually, not missing the way she stiffened at the sight of him. Her face became pinched and unhappy, her mouth strict. Leo imagined taking her head in his hands, kissing her for long lascivious minutes, until she was limp and gasping in his arms.

Instead he stood with his fists in his coat pockets, surveying her without expression. "Care to explain what that was all about?"

The sun glinted on the lenses of Marks's spectacles, momentarily obscuring her eyes. "You've been spying on me, my lord?"

"Hardly. Whatever spinsters do in their personal time doesn't interest me in the least. But it's difficult not to notice when my brother-in-law is kissing the governess out in the garden."

One had to give Marks credit for composure. She showed no reaction except for the tightening of her hands in her lap. "One kiss," she said. "On the forehead."

6

"It doesn't matter how many kisses, or where they landed. You're going to explain to me why he did it. And why you let him. And try to make it credible, because I'm this close"—Leo held his thumb and forefinger a mere quarter inch apart—"to dragging you bodily to the coach road and putting you on the next cart bound for London."

"Go to the devil," she said in a low voice, and sprang to her feet. She had taken only two strides before he caught her from behind. "Don't touch me!"

Leo turned her to face him, controlling her easily. His hands closed over her slender upper arms. He could feel the warmth of her skin through the thin muslin of her sleeves. As he held her, the innocent scent of lavender water rose to his nostrils. There was a faint dusting of talc at the base of her throat. The fragrance of her reminded Leo of a freshly made bed with pressed sheets. And oh, how he wanted to slip into her.

"You have too many secrets, Marks. You've been a thorn in my side for more than a year, with your sharp tongue and your mysterious past. Now I want some answers. What were you discussing with Harry Rutledge?"

Her fine brows, several shades darker than her hair, gathered in a scowl. "Why don't you ask him?"

"I've asked *you*." Met with her mulish silence, Leo decided to provoke her. "Were you a different kind of woman, I'd suspect you of casting your lures at him. But we both know you don't have any lures, don't we?"

"If I did, I certainly wouldn't use them on you!"

"Come, Marks, let's attempt a civil conversation. Just this once."

"Not until you take your hands off me."

"No, you'd only run. And it's too hot to chase after you."

Catherine bristled and pushed at him, her palms flattening against his chest. Her body was neatly packaged in stays and laces and countless yards of muslin. The thought of what was beneath . . . pink and white skin, soft curves, intimate curls . . . aroused him instantly.

A shiver ran through her, as if she could read his thoughts. Leo stared down at her intently. His voice softened. "Are you afraid of me, Marks? You, who bludgeon and cut me down to size at every opportunity?"

"Of course not, you arrogant ass. I only wish you would behave like a man of your station."

"You mean like a peer?" He raised his eyebrows mockingly. "This is how peers behave. I'm surprised you haven't noticed by now."

"Oh, I've noticed. A man fortunate enough to inherit a title should have the decency to try and live up to it. Being a peer is an obligation—a responsibility—but instead you seem to regard it as a license to engage in the most self-indulgent and disgusting behavior imaginable. Moreover—"

"Marks," Leo interrupted in a velvety tone, "that was a perfectly wonderful attempt at distracting me. But it's not going to work. You're not getting away from me until you tell me what I want to know."

She swallowed hard and tried to look everywhere but at him, which wasn't easy when he was standing right in front of her. "The reason I was talking privately with Mr. Rutledge . . . the scene you witnessed . . ."

"Yes?"

"It was because . . . Harry Rutledge is my brother. Half brother."

Leo stared at her downbent head, trying to absorb the information. The sense of being duped, betrayed, ignited a bonfire of rage. Holy hell. Marks and Harry Rutledge were *siblings*?

"There could be no good reason," Leo said, "for such information to have been kept secret."

"The situation is complicated."

"Why have neither of you said anything before now?"

"You don't need to know."

"You should have told me before he married Poppy. You were obligated."

"By what?"

"Loyalty, damn you. What else do you know that might affect my family? What other secrets are you hiding?"

"It's none of your business," Catherine shot back, now twisting in his grip. "Let me go!"

"Not until I find out what you're plotting. Is Catherine Marks even your real name? Who the hell are you?" He swore as she began to struggle in earnest. "Hold still, you little she-devil. I just want to—*ouch*!" This last as she turned and jabbed a sharp elbow in his side.

The maneuver gained Marks the freedom she sought, but her spectacles went flying to the ground. "My spectacles!" With an aggravated sigh, she dropped to her hands and knees and began feeling for them.

Leo's fury was instantly smothered by guilt. From the looks of it, she was practically blind without the spectacles. And the sight of her crawling on the ground made him feel like a brute. A jackass. Lowering to his knees, he began to hunt for them as well.

"Did you see the direction they went in?" he asked.

"If I did," she said, fuming, "I wouldn't need spectacles, would I?"

A short silence. "I'll help you find them."

"How kind of you," she said acidly.

For the next few minutes the two of them traversed the garden on their hands and knees, searching among the daffodils. They both chewed on the gristly silence as if it were a mutton chop.

"So you actually need spectacles," Leo finally said.

"Of course I do," Marks said crossly. "Why would I wear spectacles if I didn't need them?"

"I thought they might be part of your disguise."

"My disguise?"

"Yes, Marks, disguise. A noun describing a means of concealing someone's identity. Often used by clowns and spies. And now apparently governesses. Good God, can *anything* be ordinary for my family?"

Marks glared and blinked in his direction, her gaze not quite focused. For a moment, she looked like an anxious child whose favorite blanket had been set out of reach. And that caused an odd, painful twinge in Leo's heart.

"I'll find your spectacles," he said brusquely. "You have my word. If you like, you can go into the house while I keep searching."

"No, thank you. If I tried to find the house on my own, I'd probably end up in the barn."

Seeing a metallic glimmer in the grass, Leo reached out and closed his hand around the spectacles. "Here they are." He crawled to Marks and faced her in an upright kneeling position. After polishing the spectacle lenses with the edge of his sleeve, he said, "Hold still."

"Give them to me."

"Let me do it, hardhead. Arguing comes to you as naturally as breathing, doesn't it?"

10

"No, it doesn't," she said immediately, and colored as he gave a husky laugh.

"It's no fun to bait you when you make it so easy, Marks." He placed the spectacles on her face with great care, running his fingers along the sides of the frame, viewing the fit with an assessing glance. Gently he touched the tips of the earpieces. "They're not fitted well." He ran an exploring fingertip over the upper rim of one ear. She was remarkably pretty in the sunlight, her gray eyes containing glimmers of blue and green. Like opals. "Such small ears," Leo continued, letting his hands linger at the sides of her fine-boned face. "No wonder your spectacles fall off so readily. There's hardly anything to hang them on."

Marks stared at him in bewilderment.

How fragile she was, he thought. Her will was so fierce, her temperament so prickly, that he tended to forget she was only half his size. He would have expected her to slap his hands away by now—she hated being touched, especially by him. But she didn't move at all. He let his thumb brush the side of her throat, and felt the tiny undulation of her swallow. There was something unreal about the moment, something dreamlike. He didn't want it to end.

"Is Catherine your real name?" he asked. "Will you at least answer that?"

She hesitated, fearful of yielding any part of herself, even that scrap of information. But as his fingertips slid along her neck, the light caress seemed to disarm her. A bloom of color rose from her throat.

"Yes," she choked out. "It's Catherine."

They were still kneeling together, her skirts having billowed and settled everywhere. Folds of flower-printed muslin had been caught under one of Leo's knees. His body reacted strongly

11

to her nearness, heat sliding beneath his skin and gathering in inconvenient places. Muscles tightened, thickened. He would have to put an end to this, or he was going to do something they would both regret.

"I'll help you up," Leo said brusquely, making to rise. "We'll go inside. I warn you, however, I'm not through with you yet. There's more I—"

But he broke off, because as Marks had tried to struggle upward, her body had brushed against his. They went still, caught front to front, their breath mingling in uneven surges.

The dreamlike feeling intensified. The two of them were kneeling in a summer garden, the air weighted with the perfume of hot crushed grass and scarlet poppies . . . and Catherine Marks was in his arms. Her hair shimmered in the sunlight, her skin petal-soft. Her upper lip was nearly as full as the lower, the curves as delicate and smooth as a ripe persimmon. Staring at her mouth, he felt the hairs on the back of his neck lift in reflexive excitement.

Some temptations, Leo decided hazily, should not be resisted. Because they were so persistent that they would only keep returning, time and again. Therefore such temptations absolutely *had* to be yielded to—it was the only way to be rid of them.

"Damn it," he said raggedly, "I'll do it. Even knowing I'll be annihilated afterward."

"You'll do what?" Marks asked, her eyes huge.

"This."

And his mouth descended to hers.

At last, every muscle in his body seemed to sigh. At last. The sensation was so pleasurable that for a moment Leo couldn't even move, just felt her mouth with his mouth. Sinking into the feeling, Leo let it take him. He stopped thinking altogether and did everything and anything he wanted . . . tugging at her upper lip and then her lower one, sealing their mouths together, touching his tongue to hers, playing with her. One kiss started before another had finished, a chain of erotic strokes and skims and nudges. The delight of it went all through him, echoing in every vein and nerve.

And God help him, he ached for more. He was dying to put his hands inside her clothes, and feel every inch of her body. He wanted to drag his mouth over her in intimate trails, kiss and taste every part of her. Marks responded helplessly, curling her arm around his neck. She moved against him as if sensation were coming from all directions. And it was. They both struggled to press closer, tighter, their bodies pursuing a new and unsteady rhythm. Had they not been separated by so many layers of clothing, it would have been outright lovemaking.

Leo continued to kiss her long after he should have stopped, not only for the sheer pleasure of it, but also because he was reluctant to face what would happen afterward. Their cantankerous relationship could not resume as usual after something like this. It had been set on a new track with an unknown destination, and Leo was certain that neither of them were going to like where it led.

Finding that he couldn't release her all at once, he did it by degrees, letting his mouth nuzzle the edge of her jaw, following to the vulnerable hollow behind her ear. Her pulse was swift and vibrant against his lips.

"Marks," he said on a rough breath, "I was afraid of this. Somehow I knew . . ." Breaking off, he lifted his head and looked down at her.

She squinted through the mist that had accumulated on her lenses. "My spectacles . . . I've lost them again."

"No, you haven't. There's steam on the lenses."

13

As the fogged spectacles cleared, Marks shoved at him. She struggled to her feet, frantically swatting away his efforts to help.

They stared at each other. It was hard to say which one of them was more appalled.

But judging from her expression, it was probably Marks.

"This never happened," she snapped. "If you have the gall ever to mention it, I'll deny it to my last breath." She gave her skirts a few agitated whacks to remove the bits of leaves and grass, and shot Leo a fierce warning glance. "I'm going to the house now. And don't follow me!"

Chapter Two

Their paths didn't intersect again until dinner, a crowded affair that included his sisters Amelia, Win, and Poppy, and their respective husbands Cam Rohan, Kev Merripen, and Harry Rutledge. Catherine Marks sat with Beatrix at the far end of the table.

So far none of Leo's sisters had chosen conventional men to wed. Rohan and Merripen were both Romany Gypsies, which accounted in part for their ability to fit in easily with the off-kilter Hathaways. And Poppy's husband, Harry Rutledge, was an eccentric hotelier, a powerful man whose enemies reputedly liked him more than his friends did.

Could it be true that Catherine Marks was Harry's sister?

Leo glanced from one to the other of them at dinner, searching for similarities. *Damned if I can't see a resemblance,* he thought. The high cheekbones, the straight lines of the brows, the slight feline tilt at the outward corners of the eyes.

"I need to speak to you," Leo said to Amelia as soon as dinner had concluded. "In private."

Her blue eyes widened with curiosity. "Of course. Shall we walk? It's still light outside."

Leo gave her a curt nod.

15

As the two oldest Hathaway siblings, Leo and Amelia had had their share of arguments. However, she was his favorite person in the world, not to mention his closest confidant. Amelia had a great deal of common sense, and she never hesitated to say what she thought.

No one had ever expected the pragmatic Amelia to be swept off her feet by Cam Rohan, a dashing Romany Gypsy. But Cam had managed to seduce and marry Amelia before she had quite known what was happening. And as it had turned out, Cam was able to provide the level-headed guidance the Hathaways had needed. With his black hair worn a trifle too long and a diamond stud glittering in one ear, he was hardly the image of a staid family patriarch. But it was Cam's unconventionality that allowed him to manage the Hathaways so adeptly. Now he and Amelia had a nine-month-old son, Rye, who had his father's dark hair and his mother's blue eyes.

Walking leisurely along the private drive with Amelia, Leo cast a proprietary glance at their surroundings. In summer, the Hampshire sun lingered until at least nine o'clock, illuminating a mosaic of woodland, heath, and grass meadows. Rivers and streams scored the landscape, feeding bogs and wet meadows teeming with prolific wildlife. Although the Ramsay estate was certainly not the largest in Hampshire, it was one of the more beautiful, with an ancient timber forest and three thousand acres of arable land.

In the past year Leo had come to know the estate tenants, he had made improvements in irrigation and drainage, repaired fences, gates, and buildings . . . and the devil knew he had learned far more than he'd ever wanted to know about farming. All part of Kev Merripen's merciless instructions.

Merripen, who had lived with the Hathaways since child-

16

hood, had undertaken to learn as much as possible about estate management. Now he was intent on teaching this accumulated knowledge to Leo.

"It's not really your land," Merripen had told him, "until you've put some of your own blood and sweat into it."

"Is that all?" Leo had asked sarcastically. "Only blood and sweat? I'm certain I can find one or two other bodily fluids to donate if it's that important."

But privately he acknowledged that Merripen had been right. This feeling of ownership, of connection, couldn't be acquired any other way.

Shoving his hands in his pockets, Leo let out a taut sigh. Dinner had left him restless and irritable.

"You must have had a row with Miss Marks," Amelia remarked. "Usually you're slinging arrows at each other across the table. But tonight you were both quiet. I don't think she looked up from her plate even once."

"It wasn't a row," Leo said curtly.

"Then what was it?"

"She told me—under duress—that Rutledge is her brother."

Amelia glanced at him suspiciously. "What kind of duress?"

"Never mind that. Did you hear what I just said? Harry Rutledge is—"

"Miss Marks has been under quite enough duress without you adding to it," Amelia said. "I do hope you weren't cruel to her, Leo. Because if so—"

"*I,* cruel to *Marks*? I'm the one you should worry about. After a conversation with her, I usually walk away with my entrails dragging behind me." His indignation doubled as he saw his sister trying to suppress a grin. "I gather you already knew Rutledge and Marks were related."

"I've known for a few days," she admitted.

"Why didn't you say anything?"

"She asked me not to, and I agreed out of respect for her privacy."

"The devil knows why Marks should have privacy when no one else around here does." Leo stopped in his tracks, obliging her to stop as well. They faced each other. "Why is it a secret that she's Rutledge's sister?"

"I'm not certain," Amelia admitted, looking perturbed. "All she would say is that it's for her protection."

"Protection from what?"

She shook her head helplessly. "Perhaps Harry might tell you. But I doubt it."

"By God, someone's going to explain it to me, or I'll throw Marks out on her arse before she can blink."

"Leo," she said in astonishment. "You wouldn't."

"It would be my pleasure."

"But think of Beatrix, and how upset she would be—"

"I am thinking of Beatrix. I won't have my youngest sister being looked after by a woman with a possibly dangerous secret. If a man like Harry Rutledge, who has ties to some of the most nefarious characters in London, can't acknowledge his own sister . . . she may be a criminal. Has that occurred to you?"

"No," Amelia said stonily, beginning to walk again. "Honestly, Leo, even for you this is a bit dramatic. She is not a criminal."

"Don't be naïve," he said, following her. "No one is exactly who he or she pretends to be."

After a curtailed silence, Amelia asked warily, "What are you going to do?"

"I'm leaving for London on the morrow."

18

Her eyes widened. "But Merripen is expecting you to take part in the turnip planting, and the fertilizing, and—"

"I know what Merripen expects. And I do hate to miss his fascinating lectures on the wonders of manure. All the same, I'm going. I want to spend some time with Rutledge and pry some answers out of him."

Amelia frowned. "Why can't you talk to him here?"

"Because he's on his honeymoon, and he won't be willing to spend his last night in Hampshire chatting with me. Besides, I've decided to take on a small commission to design a conservatory for a house in Mayfair."

"I think you want to be away from Catherine. I think something happened between you."

Leo glanced at the last brilliant orange and purple vestiges of daylight. "The light is going," he remarked in a pleasant tone. "We should head back."

"You can't run from your problems, you know."

His mouth twisted in annoyance. "Why do people always say that? Of course you can run from your problems. I do it all the time, and it never fails."

"You're obsessed with Catherine," Amelia persisted. "It's obvious to everyone."

"Now who's being dramatic?" he asked, striding back toward Ramsay House.

"You watch everything she does." Amelia stubbornly kept pace with him. "Whenever her name is mentioned, you're all ears. And lately, every time I see you talking or arguing with her, you seem more alive than you have since . . ." She paused, seeming to think better of what she'd been about to say.

"Since when?" Leo asked, daring her to continue.

"Since before the scarlet fever."

It was a subject they never discussed.

The year before Leo had inherited the viscountcy, a fatal epidemic of scarlet fever had swept through the village where the Hathaways had lived.

The first to go had been Laura Dillard, Leo's fiancée.

Laura's family had let him stay at her bedside. For three days he had watched her die in his arms, hour by hour, until she had slipped away.

Leo had gone home and collapsed with the fever, and so had Win. By some miracle they had both survived, but Win had been left an invalid. And Leo had emerged an entirely different man, scarred in ways that even he couldn't fully catalog. He had found himself in a nightmare he couldn't wake from. He hadn't cared if he lived or died. The most unforgivable part was that in his torment, he had hurt his family and caused no end of problems for them. At the worst of it, when Leo had seemed bent on destroying himself, the family had made a decision. They had sent Win to recover at a clinic in France, with Leo accompanying her.

While Win's weak lungs had regained their strength at the clinic, Leo had spent hours walking through the heat-drowsed pantiled villages of Provence, up switchback footpaths scattered with flowers, across arid fields. The sunshine, the hot blue air, the *lenteur,* or slowness of life, had cleared his mind and calmed his soul. He had stopped drinking except for a single glass of wine at dinner. He had sketched and painted, and finally he had grieved.

When Leo and Win had returned to England, Win had wasted no time in achieving her heart's desire, which had been to marry Merripen.

Leo, for his part, was trying to make amends for the way he had failed his family. And above all, he was determined to avoid falling in love ever again. Now that he was aware of the fatal depth of feeling he was capable of, he would never give another human being such power over him.

"Sis," he told Amelia ruefully, "if you have some lunatic notion that I have any kind of personal interest in Marks, forget it at once. All I intend to do is find out what skeleton she has in her closet. Knowing her, it's probably a literal one."

Chapter Three

"I didn't even know about Cat's existence until I was twenty," Harry Rutledge said, stretching out his long legs as he and Leo sat in the Rutledge Hotel's clubroom. The quiet and luxurious spot, with its numerous octagonal apses, was a popular gathering place in London for foreign nobility, travelers of means, aristocrats and politicians.

Leo regarded his brother-in-law with thinly veiled skepticism. Of all the men he would have chosen to marry one of his sisters, Rutledge would certainly not have topped the list. Leo didn't trust him. On the other hand, Harry had his good points, among them his obvious devotion to Poppy.

Harry drank from a snifter of warmed brandy, considering his words carefully before he continued. He was a handsome man, capable of great charm, but he was also ruthless and manipulative. One would expect no less from a man of his achievements, among them creating the largest and most opulent hotel in London.

"I'm reluctant to discuss Cat for several reasons," Harry said, his green eyes guarded. "Among them the fact that I've never been particularly kind to her, nor did I protect her when I should have. And I regret it."

"We all have regrets," Leo said, taking a sip of brandy, letting the velvet fire slide down his throat. "It's why I cling to my bad habits. One doesn't have to start regretting something unless one stops doing it."

Harry grinned, but sobered quickly as he stared into the flame of a small candle lamp that had been set on the table. "Before I tell you anything, I want to ask what the nature of your interest in my sister is."

"I'm asking as her employer," Leo said. "I'm concerned about the influence she may have over Beatrix."

"You never questioned her influence before," Harry shot back. "And from all accounts she's done an excellent job with Beatrix."

"She has. However, the revelation of this mysterious connection to you has me worried. For all I know, the two of you have been hatching some kind of plot."

"No." Harry stared at him directly. "There's no plot."

"Then why all these secrets?"

"I can't explain without telling you something of my own past—" Pausing, Harry added darkly, "Which I hate doing."

"So sorry," Leo said without a trace of sincerity. "Go on."

Harry hesitated again, as if weighing the decision to tell him anything. "Cat and I had the same mother. Her name was Nicolette Wigens. She was British by birth. Her family moved from England to Buffalo, New York, when she was still an infant. Because Nicolette was an only child—the Wigens had her fairly late in life—it was their desire to see her married to a man who would take care of her. My father Arthur was more than twice her age, and fairly prosperous. I suspect the Wigens forced the match—there was certainly no love in it. But Nicolette married Arthur, and I was born soon after. A bit

23

too soon, actually. There was speculation that Arthur wasn't the father."

"Was he?" Leo couldn't help asking.

Harry smiled cynically. "Does one ever know for certain?" He shrugged. "In any case, my mother eventually ran off to England with one of her lovers." Harry's gaze was distant. "There were other men after that, I believe. My mother wasn't one for limiting herself. She was a spoiled, self-indulgent bitch, but very beautiful. Cat looks very much like her." He paused reflectively. "Only softer. More refined. And unlike our mother, Cat has a kind and caring nature."

"Really," Leo said sourly. "She's never been kind to me."

"That's because you frighten her."

Leo gave him a disbelieving glance. "In what possible way could I frighten that little virago? And don't claim that she's nervous around men, because she's perfectly amiable to Cam and Merripen."

"She feels safe with them."

"Why not with me?" Leo asked, offended.

"I believe," Harry said thoughtfully, "it's because she's aware of you as a man."

The revelation caused Leo's heart to jolt. He examined the contents of his brandy snifter with studied boredom. "Did she tell you that?"

"No, I saw it for myself, in Hampshire." Harry turned wry. "One has to be particularly observant where Cat is concerned. She won't talk about herself." He drank the rest of his brandy, set down the glass with care, and leaned back in his chair. "I never heard from my mother after she left Buffalo," he said, lacing his fingers together and resting them on his flat midriff. "But when I reached the age of twenty, I received a letter bidding me to

24

come to her. She had contracted a wasting disease, some form of cancer. I assumed that before she died, she wanted to see what had become of me. I left for England at once, but she died just before I arrived."

"And that was when you met Marks," Leo prompted.

"No, she wasn't there. Despite Cat's wishes to stay with her mother, she had been sent to stay with an aunt and grandmother on her father's side. And the father, apparently unwilling to keep vigil by the sickbed, had left London altogether."

"Noble fellow," Leo said.

"A local woman had taken care of Nicolette during the last week of her life. It was she who told me about Cat. I gave a brief thought to visiting the child, but I decided against it. There was no place in my life for an illegitimate half sister. She was nearly half my age, and in need of female guidance. I assumed she was better off in her aunt's care."

"Was that assumption correct?" Leo brought himself to ask.

Harry gave him an inscrutable glance. "No."

An entire story was contained in that one bleak syllable. Leo wanted very much to hear it. "What happened?"

"I decided to stay in England and try my hand at the hotel business. So I sent Cat a letter, telling her where to send word if she ever needed anything. Some years later, when she was fifteen, she wrote to me, asking for help. I found her in . . . difficult circumstances. I wish I had reached her a little sooner."

Feeling a tug of unaccountable concern, Leo found it impossible to maintain his usual veneer of carelessness. "What do you mean, difficult circumstances?"

Harry shook his head. "I'm afraid that's as much as I can tell you. The rest is up to Cat."

"Damn it, Rutledge, you're not leaving it there. I want to

know how the Hathaways got involved in this, and why I had the misfortune to end up as the employer of the most ill-tempered and interfering governess in England."

"Cat doesn't have to work. She's a woman of independent means. I settled enough money on her to allow her the freedom to do anything she wished. She went to boarding school for four years, and stayed to teach for another two. Eventually she came to me and said she'd accepted a position as a governess for the Hathaway family. I believe you were in France with Win at the time. Cat went for the interview, Cam and Amelia liked her, Beatrix and Poppy clearly needed her, and no one seemed inclined to question her lack of experience."

"Of course not," Leo said acidly. "My family would never bother with something so insignificant as job experience. I'm sure they started the interview by asking what her favorite color was."

Harry was trying unsuccessfully not to smile. "No doubt you're right."

"Why did she go into service, if she had no need of money?"

Harry shrugged. "She wanted to experience what a family was like, if only as an outsider. Cat believes she'll never have a family of her own."

Leo's brows drew together as he tried to make sense of that. "Nothing is stopping her," he pointed out.

"You think not?" A hint of mockery varnished Harry's hard green eyes. "You Hathaways would find it impossible to understand what it's like to be brought up in isolation, by people who don't give a damn about you. You have no choice but to assume it's your fault, that you're unlovable. And that feeling wraps around you until it becomes a prison, and you find yourself barricading the doors against anyone who wants to come in."

26

Leo listened intently, perceiving that Harry was talking about himself as well as Catherine. Silently he acknowledged that Harry was right: even in the worst despair of Leo's life, he had always known that his family loved him.

For the first time he understood fully what Poppy had done for Harry, how she had broken through the invisible prison he had described.

"Thank you," Leo said quietly. "I know it wasn't easy for you to talk about this."

"Certainly." And in absolute seriousness, Harry murmured, "One thing I should make clear, Ramsay: If you hurt Cat in any way, I will have to kill you."

Dressed in her nightgown, Poppy sat in bed with a novel. She heard someone enter the elegantly appointed private apartments, and she looked up with a smile as her husband came into the room. Her pulse quickened pleasurably at the sight of him, so dark and graceful. Harry was an enigmatic man, dangerous even in the view of those who professed to know him well. But with Poppy, he relaxed and showed his gentle side.

"Did you talk with Leo?" she asked.

"Yes, love." Harry shrugged out of his coat, draped it over the back of a chair, and approached the bedside. "He wanted to discuss Cat, as I expected. I told him as much about her past—and mine—as I could."

"What do you make of the situation?" Poppy knew that Harry was brilliant at discerning other people's thoughts and motives.

Harry untied his cravat, letting it hang on either side of his neck. "Ramsay is more concerned for Cat than he'd like to be, that's clear. And I don't like it. But I won't interfere unless Cat asks for help." He reached down to the exposed line of her throat, drawing the backs of his fingers over her skin with a sensitive lightness that caused her breath to quicken. His fingertips rested on the rapid tattoo of her pulse, and caressed softly. Watching a delicate tide of pink rise in her face, he said in a low voice, "Put the book aside."

Poppy's toes curled beneath the bed linens. "But I've reached a very interesting part," she said demurely, teasing him.

"Not half so interesting as what's about to happen to you." Drawing the covers back with a deliberate sweep that left her gasping, Harry lowered his body over hers . . . and the book dropped to the floor, forgotten.

Chapter Four

Catherine hoped that Leo, Lord Ramsay, would stay away from Hampshire for a good long while. Perhaps if enough time passed, they would be able to pretend the kiss in the garden had never happened.

But in the meantime, she couldn't help but wonder . . . why had he done it?

Most likely he had merely been amusing himself with her, finding a new way to set her off balance.

If life were at all fair, she thought dourly, Leo would have been pudgy, pockmarked, and bald. But he was a handsome man with a strapping six-foot build. He had dark hair and light blue eyes and a dazzling smile. The worst part was that Leo didn't look at all like the rogue he was. He looked wholesome and clean and honorable, the nicest gentleman one could ever hope to meet.

The illusion was dispelled as soon as he opened his mouth. Leo was a thoroughly wicked man, articulate in all circumstances. His irreverence spared no one, least of all himself. In the year since they had first met, he had exhibited nearly every objectionable quality a man could possess, and any attempt to correct him only made him worse. Especially if that attempt had been made by Catherine.

Leo was a man with a past, and he didn't even have the decency to try and hide it. He was frank about his dissolute history, the drinking and skirt-chasing and brawling, the self-destructive behavior that had nearly brought catastrophe to the Hathaway family on more than one occasion. One could only conclude that he liked being a scoundrel, or at least being known as one. He played the part of jaded aristocrat to perfection, his eyes glinting with the cynicism of a man who, at the age of thirty, had managed to outlive himself.

Catherine wanted nothing to do with any man, least of all one who radiated such dangerous charm. One could never trust such a man. His darkest days might still be ahead of him. And if not . . . it was entirely possible that hers were.

Approximately a week after Leo had left Hampshire, Catherine spent an afternoon outside with Beatrix. Unfortunately these outings were never the kind of well-regulated walk that Catherine preferred. Beatrix didn't walk, she explored. She liked to go deep into the forest, investigating flora, fungi, nests, webs, and holes in the ground. Nothing delighted the youngest Hathaway so much as the discovery of a black newt, a lizard's nest, or a rabbit warren, or the tracking of badgers' marks.

Injured creatures were caught, rehabilitated, and set free, or if they could not fend for themselves, they became part of the Hathaway household. And the family had become so accustomed to Beatrix's animals that no one so much as batted an eye when a hedgehog waddled through the parlor or a pair of rabbits hopped past the dinner table.

Pleasantly tired after the long ramble with Beatrix, Catherine sat at her dressing table and took down her hair. She scrubbed her fingers over her scalp and through the loose blond waves, soothing the little aches left from tight braids and hairpins.

A happy chatter came from behind her, and she turned to see Beatrix's pet ferret, Dodger, emerging from beneath her dresser. His long, sinuous body arced gracefully as he loped toward her with a white glove in his teeth. The mischievous thief liked to filch things from drawers and boxes and closets, and hide them in secret piles. To Catherine's frustration, Dodger especially loved *her* possessions. It had become a ritual humiliation to go through Ramsay House in search of her own garters.

"You overgrown rat," Catherine told him as he stood tall and braced his tiny paws on the edge of her chair. She reached out to pet his sleek fur, tickled the top of his head, and carefully pried the glove from his teeth. "Having stolen all my garters, you're moving on to gloves, are you?"

He regarded her affectionately, his eyes bright in the dark stripe that formed a mask across his face.

"Where have you hidden my things?" she asked, setting the glove on the dressing table. "If I don't find my garters soon, I'll have to keep my stockings up with pieces of old string."

Dodger twitched his whiskers and appeared to grin at her, displaying tiny pointed teeth. He wriggled invitingly.

Smiling reluctantly, Catherine picked up a hairbrush and drew it through the loose locks of her hair. "No, I don't have time to play with you. I'm getting ready for dinner."

In a liquid and lightning-fast movement, the ferret leaped to her lap, snatched the glove from the table, and streaked from the room.

"Dodger," Catherine exclaimed, dashing after him. "Bring that back!" She went out into the hallway, where maids were

31

rushing back and forth with unusual haste. Dodger disappeared around the corner.

"Virgie," Catherine asked one of the maids, "what is happening?"

The dark-haired girl was breathless and smiling. "Lord Leo has just come from London, miss, and the housekeeper told us to ready his room and set another place for dinner, and unpack the luggage when the footmen bring it up."

"So soon?" Catherine asked, feeling the color drain from her face. "But he didn't send word. No one expected him."

I didn't expect him, was what she meant.

Virgie shrugged and hurried away with an armload of folded linens.

Catherine put a hand to her midriff, where nerves were leaping, and retreated into her room. She wasn't ready to face Leo. It wasn't fair that he had come back so soon.

Of course, it *was* his estate. But still . . .

She paced in a tight circle and tried to marshal the chaos of her thoughts. There was only one solution: She would avoid Leo. She would plead a headache and stay in her room.

In the midst of her turmoil, there was a tap on the door. Someone entered without waiting for a response. Catherine nearly choked on her own heartbeat as she saw Leo's tall, familiar form.

"How dare you come into my room without . . ." Her voice faded as he closed the door.

Leo turned to face her, his gaze sweeping over her. He was travel-rumpled and a bit dusty. His hair wanted a good brushing, the dark brown locks disheveled and falling over his forehead. He looked self-possessed but cautious, the ever-present mockery in his eyes replaced by something she couldn't identify. Something new.

Catherine's hand drew into a fist against her midriff, and she struggled to catch up with her own breathing. She held still as he approached her, while her heart pounded with a dizzying mixture of dread and excitement.

Leo's hands went on either side of her shrinking body and gripped the edge of the dressing table behind her. He was too close, his masculine vitality surrounding her. He smelled like outside air, like dust and horses, like a healthy young male. As he leaned over her, one of his knees pressed gently into the mass of her skirts.

"Why did you come back?" she asked weakly.

He stared directly into her eyes. "You know why."

Before Catherine could stop herself, her gaze dropped to the firm contours of his mouth.

"Cat . . . we have to talk about what happened."

"I don't know what you mean."

He inclined his head slightly. "Would you like me to remind you?"

"No, no . . ." She shook her head for emphasis. "No."

His lips twitched. "One 'no' is enough, darling."

Darling?

Filled with anxiety, Catherine fought to keep her voice steady. "I thought I made it clear that I wanted to ignore what happened."

"And you expect that will make it go away?"

"Yes, that's what one does with mistakes," she said with difficulty. "One sets them aside and moves on."

"Really?" Leo asked innocently. "My mistakes are usually so enjoyable that I tend to repeat them."

Catherine wondered what was wrong with her that she was tempted to smile. "This one will not be repeated."

"Ah, there's the governess voice. All stern and disapproving.

33

It makes me feel like a naughty schoolboy." One of his hands lifted to caress the edge of her jaw.

Her body raced with conflicting impulses, her skin craving his touch, her instincts warning her to move away from him. The result was a kind of stunned immobility, every muscle drawing up taut. "If you don't leave my room this instant," she heard herself say, "I'll make a scene."

"Marks, there is nothing in the world I would enjoy more than watching you make a scene. In fact, I'll help you. How shall we start?" Leo seemed to enjoy her discomfiture, the wash of uncontrollable color over her face.

The pad of his thumb stroked the thin, soft skin beneath her jaw, a coaxing motion that caused her head to tilt back before she quite knew what she was doing. "I've never seen such eyes," he said almost absently. "They remind me of the first time I saw the North Sea." His fingertips followed the edge of her jaw. "When the wind chases the waves before it, the water is the same green-gray your eyes are now . . . and then it turns to blue at the horizon."

Catherine could only assume that he was mocking her again. She scowled at him. "What do you want from me?"

Leo took a long time to answer, his fingers trailing to her earlobe, massaging lightly. "I want your secrets. And I'll get them out of you one way or another."

That gave her the impetus to swat his hand away. "Stop this. You're amusing yourself at my expense, as usual. You are a dissipated scoundrel, an unprincipled cad, and—"

"Don't forget 'lecherous libertine,' " he said. "That's one of my favorites."

"Get *out*!"

He pushed away lazily from the dressing table. "All right. I'll go. Obviously you fear that if I stay, you won't be able to control your desire for me."

"The only desire I have for you," she said, "involves maiming and dismemberment."

Leo grinned and went to the door. Pausing at the threshold, he glanced over his shoulder. "Your spectacles are fogging again," he said helpfully, and slipped through the door before she could find something to throw.

Chapter Five

"Leo," Amelia said as Leo entered the breakfast room the next morning, "you have to get married."

Leo gave her a warning glance. His sister knew better than to start a conversation with him so early. He preferred to ease his way into the day, whereas Amelia liked to fling herself at it full tilt. Moreover, he'd slept badly the night before, plagued by erotic dreams involving Catherine Marks.

"You know I'll never marry," he said.

Marks's voice came from the corner. She was perched on a small chair, a sunbeam glancing off her fair hair and causing dust motes to glitter around her. "Just as well, since no rational woman would have you."

Leo took up the challenge without hesitation. "A rational woman . . ." he mused aloud. "I don't believe I've ever met one of those."

"How would you know if you did?" she asked. "You wouldn't be interested in her character. You would be far too busy examining her . . . her . . ."

"Her what?" he prompted.

"Her dress measurements," she finally said, and he laughed at her prudishness.

"Is it really so impossible for you to name ordinary body parts, Marks? Breasts, hips, legs—why is it indecent to talk about the human anatomy in a straightforward manner?"

Her eyes narrowed. "Because it leads to improper thoughts."

Leo smirked at her. "Mine already are."

"Well, mine aren't," she said. "And I would prefer them to remain that way."

His brows lifted. "You don't have improper thoughts?"

"Hardly ever."

"But when you do, what are they?"

She gave him an indignant glance.

"Have I ever been involved in your improper thoughts?" Leo persisted, causing her face to flame.

"I told you I didn't have any," she protested.

"No, you said 'hardly ever.' Which means one or two are rattling around in there."

Amelia broke in. "Leo, stop tormenting her."

Leo barely heard her, his attention fixed on Catherine. "I wouldn't think badly of you at all if you did," he said. "In fact, I'd like you much better for it."

"No doubt you would," Catherine shot back. "You probably prefer women with no virtues at all."

"Virtue in a woman is like pepper in the soup. A little makes for a nice seasoning. But overdo it, and no one wants very much of you."

Clamping her mouth shut, Catherine pointedly looked away from him, putting an end to the rapid-paced argument.

In the silence, Leo became aware that the entire family was staring at him with collective bemusement.

"Have I done something?" he demanded. "What's going on? And what the devil are you all reading?"

Amelia, Cam, and Merripen had spread papers over the table, while Win and Beatrix appeared to be looking up words in a massive legal tome.

"A letter was just delivered from our London solicitor, Mr. Gadwick," Merripen said. "It seems there are legal issues that weren't made clear when you inherited the estate."

"No surprise there," Leo said. He went to the sideboard, where breakfast had been laid out. "The estate and title were tossed in my direction like used fish wrappings. Along with the Ramsay curse."

"There is no Ramsay curse," Amelia said.

"Oh?" Leo smiled darkly. "Then why did the last half-dozen Lord Ramsays die in quick succession?"

"Pure coincidence," she replied. "Obviously that particular branch of the family was clumsy and inbred. It's a common difficulty for bluebloods."

"Well, we certainly don't have that problem." Leo returned his attention to Merripen. "Tell me about our legal issues. And use small words. I don't like to think at this hour of the morning. It hurts."

Looking none too happy, Merripen sat at the table. "This house," he said, "and the parcel of land it stands on—about fourteen acres in total—were not part of the original Ramsay estate. It was added later. In legal terms, it's a copyhold portion, which is a separate property within the main estate. And unlike the rest of the estate, the copyhold can be mortgaged, bought, or sold at the will of the lord."

"Good," Leo said. "Since I'm the lord, and I don't want to mortgage or sell anything, it's all fine, isn't it?"

"No."

38

"No?" Leo scowled. "According to the rules of entailment, the lord always retains his land and manor home. It's nonpartible. And nothing can change that."

"That's right," Merripen said. "You are entitled to the ancient manor home. The one on the northwest corner of the estate where two streams meet."

Leo set down his half-filled plate and stared at him blankly. "But that's a pile of rubble covered with scrub. It was built at the time of Edward the Confessor, for God's sake."

"Yes," Merripen said in a matter-of-fact tone. "That's your true home."

Becoming more and more irritated, Leo said, "I don't want that bloody wreckage, I want *this* house. Why is there a problem with that?"

"May I tell him?" Beatrix asked eagerly. "I've looked up all the legal words, and I know it better than anyone." She sat up with her pet ferret Dodger draped around her shoulders. "You see, Leo, the original manor home was left to ruin a few centuries ago. And one of the ancient Lord Ramsays acquired this fourteen-acre parcel and built a new home on it. Ever since then, Ramsay House has been handed down to each new viscount by special custom in the manor. But the last Lord Ramsay—the one just before you—found a way to leave all partible property, including the copyhold, to his widow and daughter. It's called an award of enfranchisement, and it's theirs for life. So Ramsay House and the fourteen-acre parcel it stands upon have been left to Countess Ramsay, and her daughter Vanessa Darvin."

Leo shook his head incredulously. "Why haven't we learned of this before?"

Amelia answered in a glum tone. "It seems that the widow had no previous interest in the house, because it was a shambles.

But now that it's been restored so beautifully, she has informed our solicitor that she intends to move in and take possession."

Leo was filled with outrage. "I'll be damned if I'll let anyone take Ramsay House from the Hathaways. If necessary, I'll bring this to chancery at Westminster."

Merripen pinched the corners of his eyes wearily. "Chancery won't take it."

"How do you know?"

"Our solicitor has talked to the copyhold specialist at his firm. Unfortunately, there was never an entail placed on Ramsay House, only on the original manor home."

"What about purchasing the copyhold from the widow?"

"She has already stated that no amount of money would induce her to part from it."

"Women's minds are frequently changed," Leo said. "We'll make her an offer."

"Very well. But if she refuses to negotiate, there's only one way for us to keep this house."

"I can't wait to hear this," Leo said.

"The last Lord Ramsay made a provision that you would retain the copyhold, including the house, if you married and produced legitimate male issue within five years of ennoblement."

"Why five years?"

Win answered gently. "Because in the last three decades, no Ramsay has managed to live longer than five years after receiving the title. Nor have any of them sired a legitimate son."

"But the good news, Leo," Beatrix said brightly, "is that it's been four years since you became Lord Ramsay. If you can stay alive for just one more year, the family curse will be broken."

"And furthermore," Amelia added, "you have to marry and sire a son as soon as possible."

Leo stared at them all blankly in the expectant silence. A disbelieving laugh escaped him. "You're all mad if you think I'm going to be forced into a loveless marriage just so the family can continue living at Ramsay House."

Coming forward with a placating smile, Win handed him a piece of paper. "Of course we would never want to force you into a loveless marriage, dear. But we have put together a list of prospective brides, all of them lovely girls. Won't you take a glance and see if any of them appeals to you?"

Deciding to humor her, Leo looked down at the list. *"Marietta Newbury?"*

"Yes," Amelia said. "What's wrong with her?"

"I don't like her teeth."

"What about Isabella Charrington?"

"I don't like her mother."

"Lady Blossom Tremaine?"

"I don't like her name."

"Oh, for heaven's sake, Leo, that's not her fault."

"I don't care. I can't have a wife named Blossom. Every night I would feel as if I were calling in one of the cows." Leo lifted his gaze heavenward. "I might as well marry the first woman off the street. Why, I'd be better off with Marks."

Everyone was silent.

Still tucked in the corner of the room, Catherine Marks looked up slowly as she realized that she was the focus of the Hathaways' collective gaze. Her eyes turned huge behind the spectacles, and a tide of pink rushed over her face. "That is *not* amusing," she said sharply.

"It's the perfect solution," Leo said, taking perverse satisfaction in annoying her. "We argue all the time. We can't stand each other. It's like we're already married."

41

Catherine sprang to her feet, staring at him in outrage. "I would *never* consent to marry you."

"Good, because I wasn't asking. I was only making a point."

"Do not use me to make a point!" She fled the room, while Leo stared after her.

"You know," Win said thoughtfully, "we should have a ball."

"A ball?" Merripen asked blankly.

"Yes, and invite all the eligible young women we can think of. It's possible one of them will strike Leo's fancy, and then he could court her."

"I'm not going to court anyone," Leo said.

They all ignored him.

"I like that idea," Amelia said. "A bride-hunting ball."

"It would be more accurate," Cam pointed out dryly, "to call it a groom-hunting ball. Since Leo will be the item of prey."

"It's just like Cinderella," Beatrix exclaimed. "Only without the charming prince."

Deciding to calm the brewing squabble, Cam lifted his hand in a staying gesture. "Easy, all of you. If it happens that we lose Ramsay House—God forbid—we can build another one on the freehold portion of the estate."

"That would take forever, and the cost would be enormous," Amelia protested. "And it wouldn't be the same. We've spent too much time restoring this place, and putting our hearts into it."

"Especially Merripen," Win added quietly.

Merripen gave her a slight shake of his head. "It's only a house."

But they all knew it was more than a structure of brick and mortar . . . it was their home. Cam and Amelia's son had been born there. Win and Merripen had been married there. With all its haphazard charm, Ramsay House was a perfect expression of the Hathaway family itself.

And no one understood that better than Leo. As an architect, he knew well that some buildings had an inherent character that was far more than the sum of their parts. Ramsay House had been damaged and restored . . . it had gone from a neglected shell to a thriving, happy home, all because one family had cared. It was a crime that the Hathaways would be displaced by a pair of women who had invested nothing in it, through what amounted to nothing more than a legal sleight of hand.

Swearing beneath his breath, Leo dragged his hand through his hair. "I want to have a look at the ruins of the old manor home," he said. "Merripen, what's the best way to reach it?"

"I'm not certain," Merripen admitted. "I rarely go out that far."

"I know," Beatrix volunteered. "Miss Marks and I have ridden there to sketch the ruins. They're very picturesque."

"Would you like to ride there with me?" Leo asked.

"I'd love to," she said.

Amelia frowned. "Why do you want to visit the ruins, Leo?"

He smiled in a way he knew would annoy her. "Why, to measure for curtains, of course."

Chapter Six

"Thunderbolts," Beatrix exclaimed, entering the library where Leo had been waiting, "I can't go with you to the ruins after all. I've just checked on Lucky, and she's about to have her babies. I can't leave her at such a time."

Leo smiled quizzically, replacing a book on a shelf. "Who's Lucky?"

"Oh, I forgot you hadn't met her. She's a three-legged cat who used to belong to the cheesemaker in the village. The poor thing got her paw caught in a rat trap, and it had to be amputated. And now that she's no longer a good mouser, the cheesemaker gave her to me. He never even named her, can you imagine?"

"Given what happened to her, the name 'Lucky' is something of a misnomer, isn't it?"

"I thought it might improve her fortunes."

"I'm sure it will," Leo said, amused. Beatrix's passion for helping vulnerable creatures had always worried and touched the other Hathaways in equal measure. They all recognized that Beatrix was the most unconventional person in the family.

Beatrix was always sought after at London social events. She was a pretty girl, if not classically beautiful, with her blue eyes, dark hair, and tall, slender figure. Gentlemen were attracted by her freshness and charm, unaware that she showed the same patient interest to hedgehogs, field mice, and misbehaving spaniels. And when it came time for active courtship, men reluctantly left Beatrix's engaging company and turned to more conventional misses. With each successive season, her chances at marriage diminished.

Beatrix didn't seem to care. At the age of nineteen—nearly twenty—she had yet to fall in love. It was universally agreed among the Hathaways that few men would be able to understand or handle her. She was a force of nature, unhampered by conventional rules.

"Go take care of Lucky," Leo said gently. "I don't expect to have any difficulty finding the ruins by myself."

"Oh, you're not going alone," she told him. "I arranged for Miss Marks to accompany you."

"You did? And she was willing?"

Before Beatrix could answer, Catherine entered the library, her slim figure dressed in riding clothes, her hair pulled back in a tight braided chignon. A sketchbook was clasped beneath her arm. She stopped short at the sight of Leo, who was wearing a gentleman's riding coat, close-fitting breeches, and well-worn boots.

Her wary gaze went to Beatrix. "Why haven't you changed into your riding habit, dear?"

Beatrix replied apologetically, "I'm sorry, Miss Marks, I can't go after all. Lucky needs me. But it's just as well—you can show Leo the way even better than I." Her sunny smile encompassed them both. "It's a fine day for riding, isn't it? Have a good outing!" And she left the library in her long, lithe stride.

Catherine's slender brows rushed downward as she looked at Leo. "Why do you want to visit the ruins?"

"I just want to look at them. Hang it all, do I have to explain myself to you? Just refuse if you're afraid to go somewhere alone with me."

"Afraid of *you*? Not in the least."

Leo gestured to the doorway in a parody of gentlemanly manners. "After you, then."

As a result of the strategic importance of the ports of Southampton and Portsmouth, Hampshire was filled with ancient castles and picturesque ruins of forts and Saxon dwellings. Although Leo had known that there were remains of an old manor on the Ramsay estate, he hadn't yet found the opportunity to visit them. Among the concerns of farming, the accounting of rents, rates, and labor, the timber cutting and the architectural commissions Leo took on occasion, there hadn't been much time left for idle touring.

Together he and Catherine rode past fields of flowering turnips and wheat, and clover pastures where fat white sheep grazed. They crossed through the timber forest to the northwest of the estate, where heavy streams cut through green hills and limestone crags. The ground was less arable here, more rock than loam, but its location was a solidly defensible position for an ancient fortified manor home.

As they ascended a hill, Leo took covert glances at Catherine. She was slim and graceful on horseback, guiding the horse with a smooth economy of motion. An accomplished woman, he mused. Poised, articulate, competent in nearly everything she did. And yet when another woman would have advertised such qualities, Catherine went to great lengths to keep from drawing attention to herself.

They reached the site of the original manor, where the remains of ancient walls protruded from the ground like the vertebrae of fossilized creatures. Inequalities in the scrub-covered ground marked the locations of the manor's outbuildings. A shallow circular ring, approximately twenty-five feet wide, revealed the dimensions of the moat that had surrounded a sixty-square-foot elevation of land.

After dismounting and tethering his horse, Leo went to assist Catherine. She disengaged her right leg from the pommel and took her foot from the stirrup, letting Leo control her descent. She alighted on the ground, facing him. Her face lifted, the brim of her riding hat partially shadowing her opalescent eyes.

They stood together with her hands on his shoulders. Her face was flushed with exertion, her lips parted . . . and all at once Leo knew how it would be to make love to her, her body light and supple beneath his, her breath rushing against his throat as he moved between her thighs. He would bring her to ecstasy, slowly and ruthlessly, and she would claw and moan and sigh his name . . .

"Here it is," Catherine said. "Your ancestral home."

Tearing his gaze from her, Leo regarded the crumbling ruins. "Charming," he said. "A little dusting and sweeping, and the place will be as good as new."

"Will you go along with the family's plan to find a bride for you?"

"Do you think I should?"

"No, I don't think you have the makings of a decent husband. You haven't the character for it."

Leo's sentiments exactly. Except that it rankled to hear her say it.

"What makes you a fit judge of my character?" he asked.

Her shoulders lifted in an uncomfortable shrug. "One can't

47

help hearing about your exploits when all the dowagers and matrons are together at the balls."

"I see. And you believe every rumor you hear?"

She was silent. Leo expected her to argue, or insult him. To his surprise, however, she stared at him with something like remorse. "You have a point. And whether the rumors are true or false, it was wrong of me to listen."

Leo waited for her to follow that with some stinging insult, but she appeared genuinely chastened. Which was a surprise. It made him realize there was much he didn't know about her, this solitary and serious young woman who had hovered at the edge of his family for so long.

"What do the gossips say about me?" he asked casually.

She gave him a wry glance. "Your prowess as a lover is much vaunted."

"Oh, well, those rumors are definitely true." He clucked his tongue as if shocked. "Do dowagers and chaperones really prattle about such things?"

Her slender brows arched. "What did you imagine they talked about?"

"Knitting. Jelly recipes."

She shook her head and bit back a smile.

"How tedious these affairs must be for you," Leo said. "Standing at the side of the room, listening to gossip and watching everyone else dance."

"I don't mind it. I don't like dancing."

"Have you ever danced with a man?"

"No," she admitted.

"Then how can you be sure you wouldn't like it?"

"I can have an opinion about something even if I haven't done it."

48

"Of course. It's so much easier to form opinions without being troubled by experience or facts."

She frowned but kept silent.

"You've given me an idea, Marks," Leo went on. "I'm going to allow my sisters to plan the ball they mentioned earlier. Only for this reason: I'm going to come to you in the middle of it and ask you to dance with me. In front of everyone."

She looked appalled. "I would refuse."

"I'm going to ask nevertheless."

"To make a mockery of me," she said. "To make fools of us both."

"No." His voice gentled. "Just to dance, Marks."

Their gazes locked in a long, fascinated stare.

And then to Leo's surprise, Catherine smiled at him. A sweet, natural, brilliant smile, the first she had ever given him. Leo felt his chest tighten, and he went hot all over, as if some euphoric drug had gone straight to his nervous system.

It felt like . . . happiness.

He remembered happiness from a long time ago. He didn't want to feel it. And yet the giddy warmth kept washing over him for no reason whatsoever.

"Thank you," Catherine said, the smile still hovering on her lips. "That is kind of you, my lord. But I will never dance with you."

Which, of course, made it the goal of Leo's life.

Catherine turned to retrieve a sketchbook and roll of pencils from the saddle pouch.

"I didn't know you sketched," Leo said.

"I'm not very good at it."

He gestured to the book in her hands. "May I see that?"

"And give you reason to mock me?"

49

"I won't. My solemn promise. Let me see." Slowly Leo extended his hand, palm up.

Catherine glanced at his open hand, and then his face. Hesitantly she gave the book to him.

Opening the book, he glanced through the sketches. There was a series of the ruins from different angles, perhaps too careful and disciplined in places where a bit of looseness would have given the sketch more vitality. But on the whole it was very well done. "Lovely," he said. "You have a nice feeling for line and form."

She colored, seeming uncomfortable with the praise. "I understand from your sisters that you are an accomplished artist."

"Competent, perhaps. My architectural training included a number of art classes." Leo gave her a casual grin. "I'm especially good at sketching things that stay still for long periods of time. Buildings. Lampposts." He leafed through the book. "Do you have any of Beatrix's drawings?"

"On the last page," Catherine said. "She began to sketch a protruding section of the wall, over there, but she became preoccupied with a squirrel that kept hopping into the foreground."

Leo found a perfectly rendered and detailed portrait of a squirrel. He shook his head. "Beatrix and her animals."

They exchanged a grin.

"Many people talk to their pets," Catherine said.

"Yes, but very few understand the replies." Closing the sketchbook, Leo gave it back to her and began to walk the perimeter of the manor enclosure.

Catherine followed, picking her way among the gorse studded with yellow flowers and shiny black pods. "How deep was the original moat, do you estimate?"

"I would guess no more than eight feet where it cuts into the

50

higher ground." Leo shielded his eyes as he surveyed their surroundings. "They must have diverted one of the streams to fill it. You see those mounds over there? They were probably farm buildings and serf quarters, made of clay and stud."

"What was the manor home like?"

"The central keep was almost certainly made of stone, with the rest a combination of materials. And it was likely crowded with sheep, goats, dogs, and serfs."

"Do you know the history of the original overlord?" Catherine sat on a portion of the exposed wall and arranged her skirts.

"You mean the first Viscount Ramsay?" Leo stopped at the edge of the circular depression that had once been the moat. His gaze traveled across the broken landscape. "He started as Thomas of Blackmere, known for his lack of mercy. Apparently he had a talent for pillaging and burning villages. He was regarded as the left arm of Edward the Black Prince. Between them, they virtually destroyed the practice of chivalry."

Glancing over his shoulder, he smiled at the sight of Catherine's wrinkled nose. She sat with schoolgirl straightness, the sketchbook in her lap. He would have liked to snatch her off the wall and do some pillaging of his own. Reflecting that it was a good thing she couldn't read his thoughts, he continued the story.

"After fighting in France and being held prisoner for four years, Thomas was released and returned to England. I suppose he thought it was time to settle down, because he subsequently rode on this keep, killed the baron who had built it, seized his lands and ravished his widow."

Her eyes were wide. "Poor lady."

Leo shrugged. "She must have had some influence on him. He married her afterward and sired six children by her."

"Did they live to a peaceful old age?"

51

Leo shook his head, approaching her leisurely. "Thomas went back to France, where they put an end to him at Castillon. But the French were quite civilized about it and raised a monument to him on the field."

"I don't think he deserved any kind of tribute."

"Don't be too hard on the fellow—he was only doing what the times demanded."

"He was a barbarian," she said indignantly. "Regardless of the times." The wind had teased a lock of light golden hair loose from her tight chignon, and sent it straying over her cheek.

Unable to resist, Leo reached out and stroked the tendril back behind her ear. Her skin was baby-fine and smooth. "Most men are," he said. "It's only that they have more rules now." He removed his hat, set it on the wall, and stared into her upturned face. "You may put a man in a cravat, teach him manners, and make him attend a soiree, but hardly any of us are truly civilized."

"From what I know of men," she said, "I agree."

He gave her a mocking glance. "What do you know of men?"

She looked solemn, the clear gray irises now tinged with ocean green. "I know not to trust them."

"I would say the same of women." He shed his coat, tossed it over the wall, and went to the hill at the center of the ruins. Surveying the surrounding land, Leo couldn't help wondering if Thomas of Blackmere had stood on this exact spot, looking over his property. And now, centuries later, the estate was Leo's to make of what he would, his to shape and order. Everyone and everything on it was his responsibility.

"How is the view from up there?" he heard Catherine's voice from below.

"Exceptional. Come see it, if you like."

She left the sketchbook on the fence and began up the slope of the mound, lifting her skirts as she climbed.

Turning to watch Catherine, Leo let his gaze linger on her slender, pretty figure. She was fortunate that medieval times were long past, he thought with a private smile, or she would have found herself snapped up and devoured by some marauding lord. But the touch of amusement faded quickly as he imagined the primitive satisfaction of claiming her, picking her up and carrying her to a soft patch of ground.

For just a moment he let himself dwell on the idea . . . lowering himself to her writhing body, tearing her dress, kissing her breasts—

Leo shook his head to clear it, troubled by the direction of his thoughts. Whatever else he was, he was not a man to force himself on a woman. And yet the fantasy was too potent to ignore. With an effort, he bludgeoned the barbaric impulses back into submission.

Catherine was halfway up the slope when she gave a low cry and seemed to stumble.

Concerned, Leo started for her immediately. "Did you trip? Are you—*bloody hell.*" He stopped in place as he saw that the ground had partially given way beneath her. "Stop, Cat. Don't move. *Wait.*"

"What's happening?" she asked, her face bleached of color. "Is it a sinkhole?"

"More like a bloody architectural miracle. We seem to be standing on a portion of a roof that should have caved in at least two centuries ago."

They were approximately five yards apart, with Leo on higher ground.

"Cat," he said with great care, "slowly lower yourself to the ground to redistribute your weight over a greater surface. Easy. Yes, like that. Now you're going to crawl back down the slope."

"Can you help me?" she asked, and the tremor in her voice wrenched his heart.

He answered in a thick voice that didn't sound like his own. "Sweetheart, I would love nothing more. But joining my weight to yours could collapse the roof entirely. Start moving. If it makes you feel better, with all the debris in there, it can't be too far to fall."

"Actually, that doesn't make me feel better at all." White-faced, she moved slowly on her hands and knees.

Leo stayed in place, not taking his gaze from Catherine. The ground that seemed so solid beneath his feet was possibly nothing more than a layer of earth and ancient rotted timber. "You'll be fine," he said in a soothing tone, while his heart pounded with anxiety for her. "You weigh no more than a butterfly. It's my weight that's put a strain on what's left of the beams and bridging joints."

"Is that why you're not moving?"

"Yes. If I cause a collapse when I try to get off, I'd like you to be out of harm's way first."

They both felt the ground shift beneath them.

"My lord," Catherine asked, her eyes wide, "do you think this has anything to do with the Ramsay curse?"

"Actually, that hadn't occurred to me yet," Leo said. "Thank you so much for bringing it to my attention."

The roof collapsed, and they simultaneously plunged amid a torrent of earth, rock, and timber into the dark space below.

Chapter Seven

Catherine stirred and coughed. There was grit in her mouth and eyes, and she was sprawled on a wretchedly uncomfortable surface.

"Marks." She heard Leo shove debris aside as he made his way to her. His voice was unsteady and urgent. "Are you hurt? Can you move?"

"Yes . . . I'm all in one piece . . ." She sat up and rubbed her face. Evaluating the collection of aches and pains in her body, she decided they were all insignificant. "Just a bit bruised. Oh, dear. My spectacles are gone."

She heard him swear. "I'll try to find them."

Disoriented, she tried to make out what she could of their surroundings. Leo's lean form was a dark blur nearby as he searched the rubble. Dust clouded the air, settling slowly. From what little she could see, they were in a pit, perhaps six feet deep, with sunlight drizzling in through the broken roof. "You were right, my lord. It wasn't far to fall. Is this the keep?"

Leo's breathing sounded strained as he replied, "I'm not sure. It could be an undercroft beneath the keep. I see the remains of a stone partition over there . . . and hollows in the side wall where transverse joints would support—"

In a burst of fresh terror, Catherine launched herself at his indistinct form, scrabbling to reach him in the dimness.

"What is it?" Leo's arms closed around her.

Gasping, she buried her face against the solid surface of his chest. They were half sitting, half lying amid heaps of rotted timber, stone, and earth.

One of his hands came to her head, curving over her skull protectively. "What happened?"

Her voice was muffled in his shirt. *"Undercroft."*

He smoothed her hair and pressed her even closer into the protection of his body. "Yes. Why does that frighten you?"

She could hardly speak between panting breaths. "Isn't that . . . where they keep the bodies?"

The tremulous question hung in the air as Leo puzzled over it. *"Oh.* No, it's not that kind of undercroft." A quiver of rueful amusement ran through his voice, and she felt his mouth touch the rim of her ear. "You're thinking of one of the rooms beneath modern churches, where the deceased are put away. But a medieval undercroft is different. It's only a storeroom beneath the keep."

Catherine didn't move. "There are no s-skeletons in here?"

"No. Nor skulls, nor coffins." His hand continued to stroke tenderly over her hair. "Poor darling. It's all right. Nothing fearsome down here. Take a deep breath. You're safe."

Catherine continued to lie in his arms as she caught her breath. She tried to take in the fact that Leo, her enemy and tormentor, was calling her "poor darling" and petting her. His lips brushed her temple and lingered gently. Holding still, she absorbed the sensation. She had never been attracted to men of his size, preferring those of less intimidating stature. But he was strong and comforting, and he seemed so genuinely concerned, and his voice was like dark velvet wrapping around her.

56

How perplexing.

Had anyone told her that she would one day be trapped alone in a filthy pit with Leo, Lord Ramsay, she would have said that was her worst nightmare. And yet it was turning out to be a rather agreeable experience. No wonder Ramsay was so sought after by the ladies of London . . . If this was how he set about seducing them, all this lovely soothing and stroking, Catherine could easily understand how he got his way with them.

To her regret, he gently eased her away from him. "Marks . . . I'm afraid I'm not going to be able to find your spectacles in this wreckage."

"I have another pair at home," she ventured.

"Thank God." Leo sat up with a quiet grunt of discomfort. "Now, if we stand on the highest pile of debris, it's only a short distance to the surface. I'm going to hoist you up, get you out of here, and then you're going to ride back to Ramsay House. Cam trained the horse, so you won't need to guide him. He'll find his way back home with no trouble."

"What are you going to do?" she asked, bewildered.

He sounded rather sheepish. "I'm afraid I'm going to have to wait here until you send someone for me."

"Why?"

"I have a—" He paused, searching for a word. "Splinter."

She felt indignant. "You're going to make me ride back alone and unescorted and virtually blind, to send someone to rescue you? All because you have a splinter?"

"A large one," he volunteered.

"Where is it? Your finger? Your hand? Maybe I can help to . . . Oh, *God.*" This last as he took her hand and brought it to his shoulder. His shirt was wet with blood, and a thick shard of timber protruded from his shoulder. "That's not a splinter," she said in horror. "You've been *impaled*. What can I do? Shall I pull it out?"

"No, it might be lodged against an artery. And I wouldn't care to bleed out down here."

She crawled closer to him, bringing her face close to his to examine him anxiously. Even in the shadows, he appeared pale and gray, and when she pressed her fingers to his forehead, she felt cool moisture.

"Don't worry," he murmured. "It looks worse than it is."

But Catherine didn't agree. If anything, it was worse than it looked. She was infused with panic as she wondered if he were going into shock, a condition in which the heart did not pump enough blood to maintain the body. It had been described as a "momentary pause in the act of death."

Stripping off her riding coat, she tried to lay it over his chest.

"What are you doing?" he asked.

"Trying to keep you warm."

Leo plucked the garment off his chest and made a scoffing sound. "Don't be ridiculous. First, the injury isn't that bad. Second, this tiny thing is not capable of keeping any part of me warm. Now, about my plan—"

"It is obviously a significant injury," she said, "and I do not agree to your plan. I have a better one."

"Of course you do," he replied sardonically. "Marks, *for once* would you do as I ask?"

"No, I'm not going to leave you here. I'm going to pile up enough debris for both of us to climb out."

"You can't even see, damn it. And you can't move these timbers and stones. You're too small."

"There is no need to make derogatory remarks about my stature," she said, lurching upward and squinting at her surroundings.

58

Identifying the highest pile of debris, she made her way to it and hunted for nearby rocks.

"I'm not being derogatory." He sounded exasperated. "Your stature is absolutely perfect for my favorite activity. But you're not built for hauling rocks. Blast it, Marks, you're going to hurt yourself—"

"Stay there," Catherine said sharply, hearing him push some heavy object aside. "You'll worsen your injury, and then it will be even more difficult to get you out. Let me do the work." Finding a heap of ashlar blocks, she picked one up and lugged it up the pile, trying not to trip over her own skirts.

"You're not strong enough," Leo said, sounding aggravated and out of breath.

"What I lack in physical strength," she replied, going for another block, "I make up for in determination."

"How inspiring. Could we set aside the heroic fortitude for one bloody moment and dredge up some common sense?"

"I'm not going to argue with you, my lord. I need to save my breath for"—she paused to heft another block—"stacking rocks."

Somewhere amid the ordeal, Leo decided hazily that he would never underestimate Catherine Marks again. Ounce for ounce, she was the most insanely obstinate person he had ever known, dragging rocks and debris while half blind and hampered by long skirts, diligently crossing back and forth across his vision like an industrious mole. She had decided to build a mound upon which they could climb out, and nothing would stop her.

Occasionally she stopped and put her hand on his forehead or throat, checking his temperature and pulse. And then she would be off again.

It was maddening not to be able to help her—humiliating to let a woman do such work without him—but every time he tried to stand, he became dizzy and disoriented. His shoulder was on fire, and he couldn't use his left arm properly. Cold sweat dripped from his face and stung his eyes.

He must have drifted off for a few minutes, because the next thing he was aware of was Catherine's urgent hands shaking him awake.

"Marks," he said groggily. "What are you doing here?" He had the confused impression that it was morning, and she wanted him to awaken before his usual hour.

"Don't sleep," she said with an anxious frown. "I've built the pile high enough that we can climb out now. Come with me."

His body felt as if it had been encased in lead. He was overwhelmed with weariness. "In a few minutes. Let me doze a bit longer."

"*Now,* my lord." Clearly she would bully and badger him until he obeyed. "Come with me. Up with you. *Move.*"

Leo complied with a groan, lurching until he had staggered to his feet. A cold burst of pain radiated from his shoulder and arm, and a few helpless curses slipped out before he could stop himself. Oddly, Catherine didn't rebuke him.

"Over there," she said. "And don't trip—you're too heavy for me to catch."

Profoundly irritated but aware that she was trying to help him, he concentrated on placing his feet and maintaining his balance.

"Is Leo short for Leonard?" she asked, confusing him.

"Confound it, Marks, I don't want to talk now."

"Answer me," she persisted.

He realized she was trying to keep him alert. "No," he said, breathing heavily. "It's just Leo. My father loved the constellations. Leo is the . . . constellation of high summer. The brightest star marks his heart. Regulus." He paused to stare blearily at the pile she had made. "Well. How efficient you are. The next time

I take an architectural commission—" He paused to catch his breath. "I'll recommend you as the contractor."

"Just think if I'd had my spectacles," she said. "I could have made proper stairs."

He let out a huff of laughter. "You go first, and I'll follow."

"Hold on to my skirts," she said.

"Why, Marks, that's the nicest thing you've ever said to me."

They climbed out together laboriously, while Leo's blood turned to ice and his wound ached and his brains went to mush. By the time he'd flopped to the ground in an awkward sideways sprawl, he was infuriated with Catherine for making him go to such effort when he'd wanted to stay in the pit and rest. The sun was blinding, and he felt hot and strange. A ferocious ache had settled behind his eyes.

"I'll fetch my horse," Catherine said. "We'll ride back together."

The prospect of mounting a horse and riding to Ramsay House was exhausting. But faced with her ruthless insistence, he had no choice but to comply. Very well. He would ride. He would bloody well ride until he expired, and Catherine would appear at the house with his corpse seated behind her.

Leo sat there fuming and boiling until Catherine brought the horse. The anger gave him the strength for one last massive effort. He swung up behind her, sat the horse, and put his good arm around her slim body. He held on to her, shivering with discomfort. She was small but strong, her spine a steady axis that centered them both. Now all he had to do was endure. His resentment evaporated, dispersed by thrills of pain.

He heard Catherine's voice. "Why have you decided never to marry?"

His head bobbed closer to her ear. "It isn't fair to ask personal questions when I'm nearly delirious. I might tell you the truth."

61

"Why?" she persisted.

Did she realize she was asking for a piece of him, of his past, that he never gave to anyone? Had he been feeling even a little less wretched, he would have cut her off at once. But his usual defenses were no more effective than the broken stone wall surrounding the manor-house remains.

"It's because of the girl who died, isn't it?" Catherine stunned him by asking. "You were betrothed. And she perished from the same scarlet fever that afflicted you and Win. What was her name . . . ?"

"Laura Dillard." It seemed impossible that he could share this with Catherine Marks, but she seemed to expect that he would. And somehow he was obliging her. "Beautiful girl. She loved to watercolor. Few people are good at that, they're too afraid of making mistakes. You can't lift the color or hide it, once it's put down. And water is unpredictable—an active partner in the painting—you have to let it behave as it will. Sometimes the color diffuses in ways you don't expect, or one shade backruns into another. That was fine with Laura. She liked the surprises of it. We had known each other all during childhood. I went away for two years to study architecture, and when I came back, we fell in love. So easily. We never argued—there was nothing to argue over. Nothing in our way. My parents had both died the previous year. My father had a heart ailment. He went to sleep one night and never woke up. And my mother followed him just a few months later. She couldn't stop mourning him. I hadn't known until then that some people could die of grief."

He was quiet then, following the memories as if they were leaves and twigs floating on a stream. "When Laura caught the fever, I never thought it would be fatal. I thought I loved her so much that the power of it would be greater than any illness. But I held her for three days and felt her dying a little more each hour.

62

Like water trickling through my fingers. I held her until her heart stopped beating, and her skin finally turned cool. The fever had done its work and left her."

"I'm sorry," she said softly, when he fell silent. She covered his good hand with her own. "Truly sorry. I . . . oh, what an inadequate thing to say."

"It's all right," Leo said. "There are some experiences in life they haven't invented the right words for."

"Yes." Her hand remained over his. "After Laura died," she said in a moment, "you fell ill with the same fever."

"It was a relief."

"Why?"

"Because I wanted to die. Except that Merripen, with his bloody Gypsy potions, wouldn't let me. It took a long time for me to forgive him for that. I hated him for keeping me alive. Hated the world for spinning without her. Hated myself for not having the bollocks to end it all. Every night I fell asleep begging Laura to haunt me. I think she did for a while."

"You mean . . . in your mind? Or literally, as a ghost?"

"Both, I suppose. I put myself and everyone around me through hell until I finally accepted that she was gone."

"And you still love her." Catherine's voice was bleak. "That's why you'll never marry."

"No. I have an extraordinary fondness for her memory. But it was a lifetime ago. And I can't ever go through that again. I love like a madman."

"It might not be like that again."

"No, it would be worse. Because I was only a boy then. And now who I am, what I need . . . it's too damned much for anyone to manage." A sardonic laugh rustled in his throat. "I overwhelm even myself, Marks."

63

Chapter Eight

By the time they reached the timber yard, set a short distance from Ramsay House, Catherine was desperately worried. Leo had become monosyllabic, and he was leaning on her heavily. He was shivering and sweating, his arm a cold weight across her front as he held on to her. A portion of her dress stuck to her shoulder where his blood had soaked it. She saw a blurry group of men preparing to unload a timber wagon. *Please, dear God, let Merripen be among them.*

"Is Mr. Merripen with you?" she called out.

To her vast relief, Merripen's dark, lean form emerged. "Yes, Miss Marks?"

"Lord Ramsay has been injured," she said desperately. "We took a fall—his shoulder was pierced—"

"Take him to the house. I'll meet you there."

Before she could reply, he had already begun to run to the house with smooth, ground-eating speed.

By the time Catherine had guided the horse to the front entrance, Merripen was there.

"There was an accident at the ruins," Catherine said. "A shard of timber has been lodged in his shoulder for at least an hour. He's very cold, and his speech is disoriented."

"That's my usual way of talking," Leo said behind her. "I'm perfectly lucid." He tried to descend from the horse in a kind of slow topple. Reaching up for him, Merripen caught him deftly. He wedged his shoulder beneath Leo's and guided his good arm around his neck. The pain jolted Leo and caused him to grunt. "Oh, you sodding filthy whoreson."

"You are lucid," Merripen said dryly, and he looked at Catherine. "Where is Lord Ramsay's horse?"

"Still at the ruins."

Merripen gave her an assessing glance. "Are you injured, Miss Marks?"

"No, sir."

"Good. Run into the house and find Cam."

Accustomed as the Hathaways were to emergencies, they managed the situation with brisk efficiency. Cam and Merripen helped Leo into the manor and up the stairs, one on either side of him. Although a bachelor's house had been built beside the estate for Leo's use, he had insisted that Merripen and Win live there instead, pointing out that as a fairly recently married couple, they needed the privacy far more than he. When he came to Hampshire, he stayed in one of the guest rooms in the main house.

They formed a fairly harmonious triad, Cam and Merripen and Leo, each with his own area of responsibility. Although Leo was the holder of the estate, he had no objection to sharing authority. Upon returning from France after a two-year absence, Leo had been grateful to see how Cam and Merripen had rebuilt the Ramsay estate in his absence. They had turned the ramshackle property into a thriving and prosperous enterprise, and neither of them had asked for anything in return. And Leo had recognized that he had much to learn from both of them.

Running an estate required far more than lounging in the

library with a glass of port, as the aristocrats in novels did. It took extensive knowledge of agriculture, business, animal husbandry, construction, timber production, and land improvement. All that added to the responsibilities of politics and Parliament was more than one man could undertake. Therefore, Merripen and Leo had agreed to share the timber and agricultural concerns, while Cam handled the estate business and investments.

In medical emergencies, although Merripen was competent in such matters, Cam usually took charge. Having learned the healing arts from his Romany grandmother, Cam was relatively experienced at treating illness and injury. It was better, safer even, to let him do what he could for Leo rather than send for a doctor.

The established practice in modern medicine was for doctors to bleed their patients for every imaginable ailment, despite controversies within the medical community. Statisticians had begun to track case history to prove that bloodletting did no good whatsoever, but the procedure persisted. Sometimes bloodletting was even used to treat hemorrhaging, in accordance with the belief that it was better to do something than nothing at all.

"Amelia," Cam said as he and Merripen settled Leo into his bed, "we'll need cans of hot water sent up from the kitchen, and all the toweling you can spare. And Win, perhaps you and Beatrix might take Miss Marks to her room and help her?"

"Oh, no," Catherine protested, "thank you, but I don't need assistance. I can wash by myself and—"

Her objections were overridden, however. Win and Beatrix would not relent until they had overseen her bath and helped to wash her hair and change her into a fresh gown. The extra pair of spectacles was found, and Catherine was relieved to have her vision restored. Win insisted on tending Catherine's hands and applying salve and bandages to her fingers.

Finally Catherine was allowed to go to Leo's room, while Win and Beatrix went to wait downstairs. She found Amelia, Cam, and Merripen all crowded around the bedside. Leo was shirtless, and heaped with blankets. It shouldn't have surprised her that he was arguing simultaneously with the three of them.

"We don't need his permission," Merripen said to Cam. "I'll pour it down his throat if necessary."

"The hell you will," Leo growled. "I'll kill you if you try—"

"No one is going to force you to take it," Cam interrupted, sounding exasperated. "But you have to explain your reasons, *phral,* because you're not making sense."

"I don't have to explain. You and Merripen can take that filthy stuff and shove it up your—"

"What is it?" Catherine asked from the doorway. "Is there a problem?"

Amelia came out into the hallway, her face taut with worry and vexation. "Yes, the problem is that my brother is a pig-headed idiot," she said, loudly enough for Leo to hear. She turned to Catherine and lowered her voice. "Cam and Merripen say the wound isn't serious, but it could become very bad indeed if they don't clean it properly. The piece of timber slipped in between the clavicle and the shoulder joint, and there's no way of knowing how deep it went. They have to irrigate the wound to remove splinters or clothing fibers, or it will fester. In other words, it's going to be a bloody mess. And Leo refuses to take any laudanum."

Catherine regarded her with bafflement. "But . . . he must have something to dull his senses."

"Yes. But he won't. He keeps telling Cam to go ahead and treat the wound. As if anyone could do such painstaking work when a man is screaming in agony."

"I told you I wouldn't scream," Leo retorted from the bedroom. "I only do that when Marks starts reciting her poetry."

Despite her consternation, Catherine almost smiled.

Peering around the doorjamb, she saw that Leo's coloring was terrible, his sun-browned complexion lightened to an ashy pallor. He was trembling like a wet dog. As his gaze met hers, he looked so defiant and exhausted and miserable that Catherine couldn't stop herself from asking, "A word with you, my lord, if I may?"

"By all means," came his sullen reply. "I would so love to have someone else to argue with."

She entered the room, while Cam and Merripen moved aside. With an apologetic expression, she asked, "If I might have a moment of privacy with Lord Ramsay . . . ?"

Cam gave her a quizzical glance, clearly wondering what influence she thought she could have with Leo. "Do what you can to persuade him to drink that medicine on the bedside table."

"And if that doesn't work," Merripen added, "try a hard knock on the skull with that fireplace poker."

The pair went out into the hallway.

Left alone with Leo, Catherine approached the bedside. She winced at the sight of the stake embedded in his shoulder, the lacerated flesh oozing blood. Since there was no bedside chair to sit on, she perched carefully on the edge of the mattress. She stared at him steadily, her voice soft with concern. "Why won't you take the laudanum?"

"Damn it, Marks . . ." He let out a harsh sigh. "I can't. Believe me, I know what it's going to be like without it, but I have no choice. It's . . ." He stopped and looked away from her, setting his jaw against a new spate of shivering.

"Why?" Catherine wanted so badly to reach him, to understand, that she found herself touching his hand. When no resistance was offered, she became emboldened and slid her bandaged fingers beneath his cold palm. "Tell me," she urged. "Please."

Leo's hand turned and enclosed hers in a careful grip that sent a response through her entire body. The sensation was one of relief, a feeling of something fitting exactly into place. They both stared at their joined hands, warmth collecting in the sphere of palms and fingers.

"After Laura died," she heard him say thickly, "I behaved very badly. Worse than I do now, if you can conceive it. But no matter what I did, nothing gave me the oblivion I needed. One night I went to the East End with a few of my more depraved companions, to an opium den." He paused as he felt Catherine's hand tighten in reaction. "You could smell the smoke all down the alley. The air was brown with it. They took me to a room filled with men and women all lying pell-mell on pallets and pillows, mumbling and dreaming. The way the opium pipes glowed . . . it was like dozens of little red eyes winking in the dark."

"It sounds like a vision of hell," Catherine whispered.

"Yes. And hell was exactly where I wanted to be. Someone brought me a pipe. With the first draw, I felt so much better, I almost wept."

"What does it feel like?" she asked, her hand clutched fast in his.

"In an instant, all is right with the world, and nothing, no matter how dark or painful, can change that. Imagine all the guilt and fear and fury you've ever felt, lifting away like a feather on a breeze."

Perhaps once Catherine would have judged him severely for indulging in such wickedness. But now she felt compassion. She understood the pain that had driven him to such depths.

69

"But the feeling doesn't last," she murmured.

He shook his head. "No. And when it goes, you're worse off than before. You can't take pleasure in anything. The people you love don't matter. All you can think of is the opium smoke and when you can have it again."

Catherine stared at his partially averted profile. It hardly seemed possible that this was the same man she had scorned and disdained for the past year. Nothing had ever seemed to matter to him—he had seemed utterly shallow and self-indulgent. When in truth, things had mattered far too much. "What made you stop?" she asked gently.

"I reached the point at which the thought of going on was too damned exhausting. I had a pistol in my hand. It was Cam who stopped me. He told me the Rom believe that if you grieve too much, you turn the spirit of the deceased into a ghost. I had to let Laura go, he said. For her sake." Leo looked at her then, his eyes a riveting blue. "And I did. I have. I swore to leave off the opium, and since then I've never touched the filthy stuff. Sweet Christ, Cat, you don't know how hard it was. It took everything I had to turn away. If I went back to it even once . . . I might find myself in the bottom of a pit I could never climb out of. I can't take that chance. I won't."

"Leo . . ." She saw him blink in surprise. It was the first time she had ever used his name. "Take the laudanum," she said. "I won't let you fall. I won't let you turn into a degenerate."

His mouth twisted. "You're offering to take me on as your responsibility."

"Yes."

"I'm too much for you to manage."

"No," Catherine said decisively, "you're not."

He let out a mirthless laugh, followed by a long, curious stare.

As if she were someone he ought to know but couldn't quite place.

Catherine could hardly believe that she was perched on the edge of his bed, holding the hand of a man she had battled so fiercely and for so long. She had never imagined that he would willingly make himself vulnerable to her.

"Trust me," she urged.

"Give me one good reason."

"Because you can."

Leo shook his head slightly, holding her gaze. At first she thought he was refusing her. But it turned out that he was shaking his head in rueful wonder at his own actions. He gestured for the small glass of liquid on the bedside table. "Give it to me," he muttered, "before I have a chance to think better of it." She handed the glass to him, and he downed it in a few efficient gulps. A shudder of revulsion swept through him as he gave the empty glass back to her.

They both waited for the medicine to take effect.

"Your hands . . ." Leo said, reaching for her bandaged fingers. The tip of his thumb brushed gently over the surface of her nails.

"It's nothing," she whispered. "Just a few scrapes."

The blue eyes turned hazy and unfocused, and he closed them. The pained grooves of his face began to relax. "Have I thanked you yet," he asked, "for hauling me out of the ruins?"

"No thanks are necessary."

"All the same . . . thank you." Lifting one of her hands, he cradled her palm against his cheek while his eyes remained closed. "My guardian angel," he said, the words beginning to slur. "I don't think I ever had one until now."

"If you did," she said, "you probably ran too fast for her to keep up with you."

He made a quiet sound of amusement.

The feel of his shaven cheek beneath her hand filled her with astonishing tenderness. She had to remind herself that the opium was exerting its influence on him. This feeling between them wasn't real. But it seemed as if something new were emerging from the wreckage of their former conflict. A thrill of intimacy went through her as she felt the ripple of his swallow in the space beneath his jaw.

They stayed like that until a noise from the doorway caused Catherine to start.

Cam entered the room, glanced at the empty glass, and gave Catherine an approving nod. "Well done," he said. "This will make it easer on Ramsay. And more importantly, on me."

"Bugger you," Leo replied mildly, slitting his eyes open as Cam and Merripen went to the bedside. Amelia followed with an armload of clean rags and toweling. Reluctantly, Catherine pulled away from Leo and retreated to the doorway.

Cam looked down at his brother-in-law with a mixture of concern and affection. The abundant sunlight from the window slid over the shiny black layers of his hair. "I can take care of this, *phral*. But we could send for a *gadjo* doctor if you prefer."

"God, no. Anything he did would be far worse than your blundering. And he'd start with his damned jar of leeches."

"No leeches here," Cam replied as he eased the pillows from behind Leo's back. "I'm terrified of them."

"Are you?" Amelia asked. "I didn't know that."

Cam helped Leo to lower to the mattress. "When I was a boy still living with the tribe, I went wading in a spring-fed pond with a few of the other children. We all came out with leeches attached to our legs. I would say I screamed like a girl, except the girls were much quieter."

"Poor Cam," Amelia said, smiling.

"Poor Cam?" Leo echoed, sounding indignant. "What about me?"

"I'm reluctant to give you too much sympathy," Amelia replied, "in light of my suspicion that you've only done this to get out of the turnip planting."

Leo replied with two choice words that made her grin.

Pulling the bed linens to her brother's waist, Amelia carefully tucked towels beneath his injured shoulder and side. The sight of his lean, smoothly muscled torso—and that intriguing dusting of hair on his chest—caused Catherine's stomach to dive in an odd little swoop. She retreated farther behind the door, not wanting to leave and yet knowing it was improper for her to stay.

Cam dropped a kiss atop his wife's head and nudged her away from the bed. "Wait over there, *monisha*—we need room to work." He turned to the nearby tray of supplies.

Catherine blanched as she heard the rattle of knives and metal implements.

"Aren't you going to sacrifice a goat or perform a tribal dance?" Leo asked woozily. "Or at least chant something?"

"We did all that downstairs," Cam said. He handed a piece of leather strap to Leo. "Put this between your teeth. And try not to make too much noise while we're working on you. My son is napping."

"Before I put this in my mouth," Leo said, "you might tell me the last place it's been." He paused. "On second thought . . . never mind. I don't want to know." He put the strap between his teeth, then removed it temporarily to add, "I'd rather you didn't amputate anything."

"If we do," Merripen said, swabbing carefully around the injured shoulder, "it won't be intentional."

73

"Ready, *phral*?" she heard Cam ask gently. "Hold him still, Merripen. All right. On the count of three."

Amelia joined Catherine in the hallway, her face tense. She wrapped her arms around her middle.

They heard Leo's low groan, followed by a voluble flow of Romany between Cam and Merripen. The foreign language was brisk but soothing.

It was clear that despite the effects of the opium, the procedure was difficult to endure. Every time Catherine heard a grunt or pained sound coming from Leo, she tensed all over and knotted her torn fingers together.

After two or three minutes had passed, Amelia looked around the doorway. "Did it splinter?" she asked.

"Only a little, *monisha*," came Cam's reply. "It could have been much worse, but—" He paused at a muffled sound from Leo. "Sorry, *phral*. Merripen, take the tweezers and—yes, that part right there."

Amelia's face was pale as she turned back to Catherine. And she astonished her by reaching out and drawing her close in the same way she might have hugged Win, Poppy, or Beatrix. Catherine stiffened a little, not in aversion but awkwardness. "I'm so glad you weren't harmed, Catherine," Amelia said. "Thank you for taking care of Lord Ramsay."

Catherine nodded slightly.

Drawing back, Amelia smiled at her. "He'll be fine, you know. He has more lives than a cat."

"I hope so," Catherine said soberly. "I hope this isn't a result of the Ramsay curse."

"I don't believe in curses, or spells, or anything of the sort. The only curse my brother faces is self-imposed."

"You . . . you mean because of his grief over Laura Dillard?"

Amelia's blue eyes turned round. "He talked to you about her?"

Catherine nodded.

Amelia seemed caught off guard. Taking Catherine's arm, she drew her further along the hallway, where there was less risk of being overheard. "What did he say?"

"That she liked to watercolor," Catherine replied hesitantly. "That they were betrothed, and then she caught the scarlet fever, and died in his arms. And that . . . she haunted him for a time. Literally. But that couldn't be true . . . could it?"

Amelia was silent for a good half minute. "I think it might be," she said with remarkable calmness. "I wouldn't admit that to many people—it makes me sound like a lunatic." A wry smile crossed her lips. "However, you've lived with the Hathaways long enough to know of a certainty that we are indeed a pack of lunatics." She paused. "Catherine."

"Yes?"

"My brother never discusses Laura Dillard with anyone. *Ever.*"

Catherine blinked. "He was in pain. He'd lost blood."

"I don't think that is why he confided in you."

"What other reason could there have been?" Catherine asked with difficulty.

It must have shown in her face, how much she dreaded the answer.

Amelia stared at her closely, and then shrugged with a rueful smile. "I've already said too much. Forgive me. It's only that I desire my brother's happiness so greatly." She paused before adding sincerely, "And yours."

"I assure you, ma'am, one has nothing to do with the other."

"Of course," Amelia murmured, and went back to the doorway to wait.

Chapter Nine

After the wound had been cleaned and bandaged, Leo was left gray-faced and exhausted. He slept for the rest of the day, waking occasionally to find broth or fever tea being poured down his throat. The family was merciless in their efforts to take care of him.

As he had expected, the opiate sent him into nightmares, filled with creatures rising from the earth to claw and pull at him, tugging him down below the surface where red glowing eyes blinked at him in the dark. Trapped in a narcotic daze, Leo couldn't fully awaken from the dreams, only struggled in the heat and misery, and subsided into more hallucinations. The only respite was when a cool cloth was applied to his forehead, and a gentle, comforting presence hovered beside him.

"Amelia? Win?" he mumbled in confusion.

"Shhhh . . ."

"Hot," he said with an aching sigh.

"Lie still."

He was vaguely aware of two or three other times when the cloth was changed . . . merciful coolness applied to his brow . . . a light hand curving against his cheek.

When he awoke in the morning, he was tired, feverish, and in the grip of a profound gloom. It was the usual aftermath of opium, of course, but the knowledge hardly helped to alleviate the overwhelming dreariness.

"You have a mild fever," Cam told him in the morning. "You'll need to drink more yarrow tea to bring it down. But there's no sign of festering. Rest today, and I expect you'll feel much better by tomorrow."

"That tea tastes like ditch water," Leo muttered. "And I'm not going to stay in bed all day."

Cam looked sympathetic. "I understand, *phral*. You don't feel ill enough to rest, but you're not well enough to do anything. All the same, you have to give yourself a chance to heal, or—"

"I'm going downstairs for a proper breakfast."

"Breakfast is done. They've already cleared the sideboard."

Leo scowled and rubbed his face, wincing at the fiery pull of his shoulder. "Have Merripen come up here. I want to talk to him."

"He is out with the tenants, drilling turnip seed."

"Where is Amelia?"

"Taking care of the baby. He's teething."

"What about Win?"

"She's with the housekeeper, taking inventory and ordering supplies. Beatrix is carrying baskets to elderly cottagers in town. And I have to visit a tenant who's two months lacking in his rent. I'm afraid there is no one available to entertain you."

Leo greeted this statement with surly silence. And then he brought himself to ask for the person he truly wanted. The person who hadn't bothered to look in on him or ask after his welfare even after she'd promised to safeguard him. "Where's Marks?"

"The last time I saw her, she was busy with needlework. It seems the mending has piled up, and—"

"She can do it here."

Cam's face was carefully blank. "You want Miss Marks to do the mending in your room?"

"Yes, send her up here."

"I'll ask if she's willing," Cam said, looking doubtful.

After Leo had washed and dragged on a dressing robe, he went back to bed. He was sore and infuriatingly unsteady. A housemaid brought a small tray with a solitary piece of toast and a cup of tea. Leo ate his breakfast while staring morosely at the empty doorway.

Where was Marks? Had Cam even bothered to tell her that she was wanted? If so, she had evidently decided to ignore the summons.

Callous, coldhearted harpy. And this after she had promised to be responsible for him. She had persuaded him to take the laudanum, and then she had deserted him.

Well, Leo didn't want her now. If she decided to appear after all, he would send her away. He would laugh scornfully and tell her that no company at all was better than having her there. He would—

"My lord?"

His heart gave a leap as he saw her at the doorway, dressed in a dark blue gown, her light golden hair caught up and pinned in its usual stern confinement.

She held a book in one hand and a glass of pale liquid in the other. "How are you this morning?"

"Bored out of my wits," Leo said with a scowl. "Why did you take so long to see me?"

"I thought you were still asleep." Entering the room, Catherine left the door wide open. The long, furry form of Dodger the ferret came loping in after her. After standing tall to view his surroundings, Dodger scurried beneath the dresser. Catherine

78

watched the ferret suspiciously. "Probably one of his new hiding places," she said, and sighed. She brought Leo a glass of cloudy liquid, and gave it to him. "Drink this, please."

"What is it?"

"Willowbark, for your fever. I stirred in some lemon and sugar to improve the flavor."

Leo drank the bitter brew, watching as Catherine moved about the room. She opened a second window to admit more of the outside breeze. Taking his breakfast tray out to the hallway, she gave it to a passing housemaid. When she returned to Leo, she laid her fingers on his forehead to test his temperature.

Leo caught her wrist, staying the motion. He stared at her in dawning recognition. "It was you," he said. "You came to me last night."

"I beg your pardon?"

"You changed the cloth on my forehead. More than once."

Catherine's fingers curled lightly around his. Her voice was very soft. "As if I would enter a man's bedroom in the middle of the night."

But they both knew she had. The weight of melancholy lifted considerably, especially as Leo saw the concern in her eyes.

"How are your hands?" he asked, turning her scraped fingers to inspect them.

"Healing nicely, thank you." She paused. "I am told you require companionship?"

"Yes," he said promptly. "I'll make do with you."

Her lips curved. "Very well."

Leo wanted to pull her against him and inhale her scent. She smelled light and clean, like tea and talcum and lavender.

"Shall I read to you?" she asked. "I brought a novel. Do you like Balzac?"

The day was improving rapidly. "Who doesn't?"

Catherine occupied the chair by the bedside. "He meanders a bit too much for my taste. I prefer novels with more plot."

"But with Balzac," Leo said, "you have to give yourself over fully. You have to wallow and roll in the language . . ." Pausing, he looked more closely at her small oval face. She was pale, and there were shadows beneath her eyes, no doubt as a result of having visited him so many times in the night. "You look tired," he said bluntly. "On my account. Forgive me."

"Oh, not at all, it wasn't you. I had nightmares."

"What about?"

Her expression turned guarded. Forbidden territory. And yet Leo couldn't help pressing. "Are the nightmares about your past? About whatever situation it was that Rutledge found you in?"

Drawing in a sharp breath, Catherine stood, looking stunned and slightly ill. "Perhaps I should go."

"No," Leo said quickly, making a staying gesture with his hand. "Don't leave. I need company—I'm still suffering the aftereffects of the laudanum that *you* convinced me to take." Seeing her continuing hesitation, he added, "And I have a fever."

"A mild one."

"Hang it, Marks, you're a companion," he said with a scowl. "Do your job, will you?"

She looked indignant for a moment, and then a laugh burst out despite her efforts to hold it in. "I'm Beatrix's companion," she said. "Not yours."

"Today you're mine. Sit and start reading."

To Leo's surprise, the masterful approach actually worked. Catherine resumed her seat and opened the book to the first page. She used the tip of a forefinger to push her spectacles into place—a meticulous little gesture that he adored. "*Un Homme d'Affaires*," she read. "*A Man of Business*. Chapter one."

"Wait."

Catherine glanced at him expectantly.

Leo chose his words with care. "Is there *any* part of your past that you would be willing to discuss?"

"For what purpose?"

"I'm curious about you."

"I don't like to talk about myself."

"You see, that's proof of how interesting you are. There's nothing more tedious than people who like to talk about themselves. I'm a perfect example."

She looked down at the book as if she were trying very hard to concentrate on the page. But after just a few seconds, she looked up with a grin that seemed to dissolve his spine. "You are many things, my lord. But tedious is not one of them."

As Leo gazed at her, he felt the same inexplicable flourish of warmth, of happiness, that he'd experienced yesterday, before their mishap at the ruins.

"What would you like to know?" Catherine asked.

"When did you first learn that you needed spectacles?"

"I was five or six. My parents and I lived in Holborn, in a tenement at Portpool Lane. Since girls couldn't go to school at the time, a local woman tried to teach a few of us. She told my mother that I was very good at memorization, but I was slow-witted when it came to reading and writing. One day my mother sent me on an errand to fetch a parcel from the butcher. It was only two streets away, but I got lost. Everything was a blur. I was found wandering and crying a few streets away, until finally someone led me to the butcher's shop." A smile curved her lips. "What a kind man he was. When I told him I didn't think I could

81

find my way home, he said he had an idea. And he had me try on his wife's spectacles. I couldn't believe how the world looked. Magical. I could see the pattern of bricks on walls, and birds in the air, and even the weave of the butcher's apron. That was my problem, he said. I just hadn't been able to see. And ever since then I've worn spectacles."

"Were your parents relieved to discover their daughter wasn't slow-witted after all?"

"Quite the opposite. They argued for days about which side of the family my weak eyes had come from. My mother was quite distressed, as she said spectacles would mar my appearance."

"What rot."

She looked rueful. "My mother did not possess what one would call a great depth of character."

"In light of her actions—abandoning a husband and son, running to England with her lover—I wouldn't have expected a surfeit of principles."

"I thought they were married, when I was a child," she said.

"Was there love between them?"

Considering that, she chewed her lower lip, drawing his attention to the enticing softness of her mouth. "They were attracted to each other in a physical sense," she admitted. "But that's not love, is it?"

"No," he said softly. "What happened to your father?"

"I'd rather not discuss that."

"After all I've confided in you?" He gave her a chiding glance. "Be fair, Marks. It can't be any more difficult for you than it was for me."

"All right." Catherine took a deep breath. "When my mother fell ill, my father felt it as a great burden. He paid a woman to look after her until the end, and sent me away to live with my

82

aunt and grandmother, and I never heard from him again. He may be dead, for all I know."

"I'm sorry," Leo said. And he was. Genuinely sorry, wishing he could somehow have gone back in time to comfort a small girl in spectacles, who had been abandoned by the man who should have protected her. "Not all men are like that," he felt the need to point out.

"I know. It would hardly be fair of me to blame the entire male population for my father's sins."

Leo became uncomfortably aware that his own behavior hadn't been any better than her father's, that he had indulged in his own bitter grief to the point of abandoning his sisters. "No wonder you've always hated me," he said. "I must remind you of him. I deserted my sisters when they needed me."

Catherine gave him a clear-eyed stare, not pitying, not censorious, just . . . appraising. "No," she said sincerely. "You're not at all like him. You came back to your family. You've worked for them, cared for them. And I've never hated you."

Leo stared at her closely, more than a little surprised by the revelation. "You haven't?"

"No. In fact—" She broke off abruptly.

"In fact?" Leo prompted. "What were you going to say?"

"Nothing."

"You were. Something along the lines of liking me against your will."

"Certainly not," Catherine said primly, but Leo saw the twitch of a smile at her lips.

"Irresistibly attracted by my dashing good looks?" he suggested. "My fascinating conversation?"

"No, and no."

"Seduced by my brooding glances?" He accompanied this

83

with a waggish swerving of his brows that finally reduced her to laughter.

"Yes, it must have been those."

Settling back against the pillows, Leo regarded her with satisfaction.

What a wonderful laugh she had, light and throaty, as if she had been drinking champagne.

And what a problem this could become, this madly inappropriate desire for her. She was becoming real to him, dimensional, vulnerable in ways he had never imagined.

As Catherine read aloud, the ferret emerged from beneath the dresser and climbed onto her lap. He fell asleep in an upside-down circle, his mouth open. Leo didn't blame Dodger in the slightest. Catherine's lap looked like a lovely place to rest one's head.

Leo feigned interest in the complex and detailed narrative, while his mind occupied itself with the question of what she would look like naked. It seemed tragic that he would never see her so. But even by Leo's dilapidated code of ethics, a man did not take a virgin unless he had serious intentions. He had tried it once, letting himself fall madly in love, nearly losing everything as a result.

And there were some risks a man couldn't take twice.

Chapter Ten

It was past midnight. Catherine woke to the sound of a baby's whimpering. Little Rye was teething, and the usually sweet-natured cherub had been fretful of late.

Catherine stared sightlessly in the darkness, kicked the bed linens away from her legs, and tried to find a more comfortable position in which to sleep. Her side. Her stomach. Nothing felt right.

After a few minutes, the baby's crying stopped. No doubt he was being soothed by his attentive mother.

But Catherine was left awake. Lonely, aching. The worst kind of awake.

She tried to occupy herself with old Celtic sheep-counting words, still used by rural farmers in place of modern numbers . . . *yan, tan, tethera, pethera* . . . One could hear the echo of centuries in the ancient syllables. *Sethera, methera, hovera, covera* . . .

Her mind summoned an image of singular blue eyes, striated light and dark, like strips of sky and ocean. Leo had watched her while she had read to him, and while she had done the mending. And underneath their banter, and his relaxed façade, she had known that he wanted her. *Yan, tan, tethera* . . .

Perhaps Leo was awake at this very moment. His fever had dissipated earlier in the evening, but it might have rekindled. He might need water. A cool cloth.

Catherine left the bed and snatched up her dressing robe before she could think twice. Finding her spectacles on the dressing table, she placed them precisely on her nose.

Her bare feet crossed the wood floors of the hallway as she went on her charitable mission.

The door to his room was partially open. She slipped in without a sound, like a thief, tiptoeing to the bed just as she had the previous night. The darkness of the room was penetrated by a few runnels of light from the open window, as if the shadows were a sieve. She could hear the soft and steady flow of Leo's breathing.

Making her way to his side, Catherine reached out tentatively, her heartbeat thickening as she laid her fingers on his forehead. No fever. Only smooth, healthy warmth.

Leo's breathing fractured as he awakened. "Cat?" His voice was sleep-thickened. "What are you doing?"

She shouldn't have gone to him. Any excuse she gave would sound false and ridiculous, because there was no rational reason to have bothered him.

Awkwardly she mumbled, "I . . . I came to see if . . ." Her voice died away.

She began to draw back but he caught her wrist with remarkable dexterity, considering that it was night and he was barely awake. They both went still as she was caught poised over him, her wrist imprisoned in his grip.

Leo exerted tension on her arm, forcing her to lean farther over him, farther, until her balance was compromised and she fell on him in a slow topple. Terrified of hurting him, she scrabbled to brace her hands on the mattress, and he used every move-ment to lever her more fully onto his body. She started as she encountered bare flesh tightly knit with muscle, his chest covered with a soft, crisp fleece.

"My lord," she whispered, "I didn't—"

His long hand curved around the back of her head, and he brought her mouth down to his.

It wasn't a kiss, it was a possession. He took her fully, the heat of his tongue thrusting inside her, draining her of volition and thought. The masculine incense of his skin filled her nostrils. Erotic. Delicious. Too many sensations to take in at once . . . the hot silk of his mouth, the assured grip of his hands, the hard masculine contours of his body.

The world revolved slowly as Leo turned with her in his arms, half pinning her to the bed. His kisses were rough and sweet, kisses involving lips and teeth and tongue. Gasping, she reached around his neck and bandaged shoulder. He moved over her, big and dark, kissing her as if he wanted to devour her.

The folds of her dressing gown listed open, the hem of her nightgown rising to her knees. Leo's mouth broke from hers to begin a luscious search of her throat, following tender nerve paths down to the place where her neck and shoulder met. His fingers worked at the front of her nightgown, unmooring tiny buttons, spreading the thin fabric.

His head lowered, his lips slowly ascending the trembling slope of her breast until he reached the tip. Taking her into his mouth, he warmed the cool bud with lambent strokes of his tongue. Ragged moans rose in her throat, mingling with the gusts of his breath. Leo settled more heavily between her thighs, giving her his weight until she felt the hard length of him press her intimately. He sought her other breast, closing his mouth over the peak and tugging wetly, creating waves of involuting pleasure.

With every movement, more sensation was uncovered, the soft edges of arousal wearing away to exquisite rawness. Leo took her mouth with long, drugging kisses, while lower down he had begun a subtle rhythm, nudging and sliding, using himself to arouse her. She twisted beneath him, desperately trying to follow that teasing hardness. Their bodies pressed together like the pages of a closed book, and it felt so right, so wildly pleasurable, that it frightened her.

"No," she gasped, pushing at him. "Wait. Please—"

One of her hands pressed heedlessly against his injured shoulder, and Leo rolled off her with a curse.

"My lord?" She scrambled from the bed and stood there, shaking in every limb. "I'm sorry. Did I hurt you? What can I—"

"Go."

"Yes, but—"

"*Now,* Marks." His voice was low and guttural. "Or else come back to bed, and let me finish."

She fled.

Chapter Eleven

After a wretched night, Catherine fumbled for her spectacles and realized she had lost them sometime during her visit to Leo's room. Groaning, she sat at her dressing table and buried her face in her hands.

A stupid impulse, she thought dully. A moment of madness. She should never have given in to it.

There was no one to blame but herself.

What remarkable ammunition she had given to Leo. He would torture her with this. He would take every opportunity to humiliate her. She knew him well enough not to doubt it.

Catherine's ill humor was not helped by the appearance of Dodger, who emerged from the slipper box by her bed. The ferret pushed the lid open with his head, clucked in cheerful greeting, and tugged her slipper out of the box. Heaven knew where he intended to take it.

"Stop that, Dodger," she said wearily, laying her head on her arms as she watched him.

Everything was blurry. She needed her spectacles. And it was awfully difficult to go looking for something when you couldn't see more than two feet in front of your face. Moreover, if one of the housemaids found the spectacles in Leo's room, or God help her, in his bed, everyone would find out.

Abandoning the slipper, Dodger trotted to her and stood tall, bracing his long, slender body against her knee. He was shivering, which Beatrix had told her was normal for ferrets. A ferret's temperature lowered when he was sleeping, and shivering was his way of warming himself upon awakening. Catherine reached down to stroke him. When he tried to climb into her lap, however, she nudged him away. "I don't feel well," she told the ferret woefully, although there was nothing wrong with her physically.

Chattering in annoyance at her rejection, Dodger turned and streaked out of the room.

Catherine continued to lie with her head on the table, feeling too dreary and ashamed to move.

She had slept late. She could hear the sounds of footsteps and muffled conversation coming from the lower floors. Had Leo gone down to breakfast?

She couldn't possibly face him.

Her mind returned to those blistering minutes of the previous night. A fresh swell of desire rolled through her as she thought of the way he had kissed her, the feel of his mouth on the intimate places of her body.

She heard the ferret come back into the room again, chuckling and hopping as he did whenever he was especially pleased about something. "Go away, Dodger," she said dully.

But he persisted, coming to her side and standing tall again, his body a long cylinder. Glancing at him, Catherine saw that something was clamped carefully in his front teeth. She blinked. Slowly she reached down and took the object from him.

Her spectacles.

Amazing, how much better a small gesture of kindness could make one feel.

"Thank you," she whispered, tears coming to her eyes as she stroked his tiny head. "I do love you, you disgusting weasel."

Climbing onto her lap, Dodger flipped upside down and sighed.

Catherine dressed with painstaking care, putting extra pins in her hair, tying the sash of her gray dress a bit tighter than usual, even double-knotting the laces of her sensible ankle boots. As if she could contain herself so thoroughly that nothing could stray loose. Not even her thoughts.

Entering the breakfast room, she saw Amelia at the table. She was feeding toast to baby Rye, who was gumming it and drooling copiously.

"Good morning," Catherine murmured, going to pour a cup of tea at the samovar. "Poor little Rye . . . I heard him cry in the night. The new tooth hasn't come yet?"

"Not yet," Amelia said ruefully. "I'm sorry he disturbed your sleep, Catherine."

"Oh, he didn't bother me. I was already awake. It was a restless night."

"It must have been for Lord Ramsay as well," Amelia remarked.

Catherine glanced at her quickly, but thankfully there seemed to be no arch meaning in the comment. She tried to keep her expression neutral. "Oh? I hope he is well this morning."

"He seems well enough, but he's unusually quiet. Preoccupied." Amelia made a face. "I suppose it didn't improve his disposition when I told him that we are planning to hold the ball in one month's time."

Stirring sugar into her tea with great care, Catherine asked, "Will you tell people that the event is for the purpose of finding a bride for Lord Ramsay?"

Amelia grinned. "No, even I am not that indelicate. However, it will be obvious that a great many eligible young women have been invited. And of course, my brother is a prime matrimonial target."

"I'm sure I don't know why," Catherine muttered, trying to sound offhand, when inside she was filled with despair.

She realized she would not be able to stay with the Hathaway family if or when Leo married. She literally wouldn't be able to bear the sight of him with another woman. Especially if she made him happy.

"Oh, it's simple," Amelia said impishly. "Lord Ramsay is a peer with a full head of hair and all his teeth, and he is still in his procreating years. And if he weren't my brother, I suppose I would consider him not bad-looking."

"He's very handsome," Catherine protested without thinking, and flushed as Amelia gave her an astute glance.

She applied herself to drinking her tea, nibbled at a breakfast roll, and left in search of Beatrix. It was time for their morning studies.

Catherine and Beatrix had settled on a pattern, beginning their lessons with a few minutes on etiquette and social graces, and then spending the rest of the morning on subjects such as history, philosophy, even science. Beatrix had long mastered the "fashionable" subjects that were taught to young ladies merely for the purpose of making them suitable wives and mothers. Now Catherine felt that she and Beatrix had become fellow students.

Although Catherine had never had the privilege of meeting the Hathaway parents, she thought that both of them, particularly Mr. Hathaway, would have been pleased by their children's accomplishments. The Hathaways were an intellectual family, all of them easily able to discuss a subject or issue on an abstract level. And there was something else they shared—an ability to make imaginative leaps and connections between disparate subjects.

One evening, for example, the discussion at dinner had centered on news of an aerial steam carriage that had been designed by a Somerset bobbin maker named John Stringfellow. It didn't work, of couse, but the idea was fascinating. During the debate about whether or not man might ever be able to fly in a mechanical invention, the Hathaways had brought up Greek mythology, physics, Chinese kites, the animal kingdom, French philosophy, and the inventions of Leonardo da Vinci. Trying to follow the discussion had very nearly been dizzying.

Privately Catherine had worried about whether such conversational pyrotechnics would put off potential suitors for Poppy and Beatrix. And in the case of Poppy, it had indeed turned out to be problematic. At least until she had met Harry.

However, when Catherine had tried to delicately raise the issue with Cam Rohan early on in her employment, he had been very decided in his reply.

"No, Miss Marks, don't try to change Poppy or Beatrix," Cam had told her. "It wouldn't work, and it would only make them unhappy. Just help them learn how to behave in society, and how to talk about nothing, as the *gadjos* do."

"In other words," Catherine had said wryly, "you want them to have the appearance of propriety, but you don't wish for them to actually *become* proper?"

Cam had been delighted by her understanding. "Exactly."

Catherine understood now how right Cam had been. None

of the Hathaways would ever be like the denizens of London society, nor would she want them to be.

She went to the library to procure some books for her studies with Beatrix. As she entered the room, however, she stopped with a gasp as she saw Leo leaning over the long library table, writing something on a set of spread-out drawings.

Leo turned his head to glance at her, his eyes piercing. She went hot and cold. Her skull throbbed in the places where she had pinned her hair too tightly.

"Good morning," she said breathlessly, falling back a step. "I didn't mean to intrude."

"You're not intruding."

"I came to fetch some books, if . . . if I may."

Leo gave her a single nod and returned his attention to the drawings.

Acutely self-conscious, Catherine went to the bookshelves and hunted for the titles she had wanted. It was so quiet that she thought the pounding of her heart must have been audible. Needing desperately to break the pressing silence, she asked, "Are you designing something for the estate? A tenant house?"

"Addition for the stables."

"Oh."

Catherine gazed sightlessly along the rows of books. Were they going to pretend that the events of the previous night had never happened? She certainly hoped so.

But then she heard Leo say, "If you want an apology, you're not going to get one."

Catherine turned to face him. "I beg your pardon?"

Leo was still contemplating the set of elevations. "When you visit a man in his bed at night, don't expect tea and conversation."

"I wasn't visiting you in your bed," she said defensively. "That

94

is, you were in your bed, but it was not my desire to find you there." Aware that she was making no sense at all, she resisted the urge to smack herself on the head.

"At two o'clock in the morning," Leo informed her, "I can nearly always be found on a mattress, engaged in either of two activities. One is sleeping. I don't believe I need to elaborate on the other."

"I only wanted to see if you were feverish," she said, turning crimson. "If you needed anything."

"Apparently I did."

Catherine had never felt so extraordinarily uncomfortable. All her skin had become too tight for her body. "Are you going to tell anyone?" she brought herself to ask.

One of his brows arched mockingly. "You fear I'm going to tattle about our nighttime rendezvous? No, Marks, I have nothing to gain from that. And much to my regret, we didn't do nearly enough to warrant decent gossip."

Blushing, Catherine went to a pile of sketches and scraps at the corner of the table. She straightened them into a neat stack. "Did I hurt you?" she managed to ask, recalling how she had inadvertently pushed on his wounded shoulder. "Does it ache this morning?"

Leo hesitated before replying. "No, it eventually eased after you left. But the devil knows it wouldn't take much to start up again."

Catherine was overcome with remorse. "I'm so sorry. Should we put a poultice on it?"

"A poultice?" he repeated blankly. "On my . . . *oh*. We're talking about my shoulder?"

She blinked in confusion. "Of course we're talking about your shoulder. What else would we be discussing?"

95

"Cat . . ." Leo looked away from her. To her surprise, there was a tremor of laughter in his voice. "When a man is aroused and left unsatisfied, he usually aches for a while afterward."

"Where?"

He gave her a speaking glance.

"You mean . . ." A wild blush raced over her as she finally understood. "Well, I don't care if you ache *there,* I was only concerned about your wound!"

"It's much better," Leo assured her, his eyes bright with amusement. "As for the other ache—"

"That has nothing to do with me," she said hastily.

"I beg to differ."

Catherine's dignity had been mowed down to nothing. Clearly there was no option but retreat. "I'm leaving now."

"What about the books you wanted?"

"I'll fetch them later."

As she turned to depart, however, the edge of her bell-shaped sleeve caught the stack of sketches she had just straightened, and they went spilling to the floor. "Oh, dear." Instantly she went to her hands and knees, gathering up papers.

"Leave them," she heard Leo say. "I'll do it."

"No, I'm the one who—"

Catherine broke off as she saw something among the drafts of structures and landscapes and the pages of notes. A pencil sketch of a woman . . . a naked woman reclining on her side, light hair flowing everywhere. One slender thigh rested coyly over the other, partially concealing the delicate shadow of a feminine triangle.

And there was an all-too-familiar pair of spectacles balanced on her nose.

Catherine picked up the sketch with a trembling hand, while

96

her heart lurched in hard strikes against her ribs. It took several attempts before she could speak, her voice high and airless.

"That's me."

Leo had lowered to the carpeted floor beside her. He nodded, looking rueful. His own color heightened until his eyes were startlingly blue in contrast.

"Why?" she whispered.

"It wasn't meant to be demeaning," he said. "It was for my own eyes, no one else's."

She forced herself to look at the sketch again, feeling horribly exposed. In fact, she couldn't have been more embarrassed had he actually been viewing her naked. And yet the rendering was far from crude or debasing. The woman had been drawn with long, graceful lines, the pose artistic. Sensuous.

"You . . . you've never seen me like this," she managed to say, before adding weakly, "Have you?"

A self-deprecating smile touched his lips. "No, I haven't yet descended to voyeurism." He paused. "Did I get it right? It's not easy, guessing what you look like beneath all those layers."

A nervous giggle struggled through her mortification. "If you did, I certainly wouldn't admit it." She put the sketch onto the pile, facedown. Her hand was shaking. "Do you draw other women this way?" she asked timidly.

Leo shook his head. "I started with you, and so far I haven't moved on."

Her flush deepened. "You've done other sketches like this? Of me unclothed?"

"One or two." He tried to look repentant.

"Oh, please, *please* destroy them."

"Certainly. But honesty compels me to tell you that I'll probably only do more. It's my favorite hobby, drawing you naked."

Catherine moaned and buried her face in her hands. Her voice slipped out between the tense filter of her fingers. "I wish you would take up collecting something instead."

She heard his husky laugh. "Cat. Darling. Can you bring yourself to look at me? No?" She stiffened but didn't move as she felt his arms draw around her. "I was only teasing. I won't sketch you like that again." Leo continued to hold her, carefully guiding her face to his good shoulder. "Are you angry?"

She shook her head.

"Afraid?"

"No." She drew a trembling breath. "Only surprised that you would see me that way."

"Why?"

"Because it's not like me."

He understood what she meant. "No one ever sees himself—or herself—with perfect accuracy."

"I'm certain that I never lounge about completely naked!"

"That," he said, "is a terrible shame." He took a ragged breath. "You should know that I've always wanted you, Cat. I've had fantasies so wicked, it would send us both straight to hell if I told them to you. And the way I want you has nothing to do with the color of your hair, or the appalling fashions you wear." His hand passed gently over her head. "Catherine Marks, or whoever you are . . . I have the most profane desire to be in bed with you for . . . oh, weeks, at least . . . committing every mortal sin known to man. I'd like to do more than sketch you naked. I want to draw directly on you with feather and ink . . . flowers around your breasts, trails of stars down your thighs." He let his warm lips brush the edge of her ear. "I want to map your body, chart the north, south, east, and west of you. I would—"

"Don't," she said, scarcely able to breathe.

A rueful laugh escaped him. "I told you. Straight to hell."

"This is my fault." She pressed her hot face against his shoulder. "I shouldn't have gone to you last night. I don't know why I did it."

"I think you do." His mouth grazed the top of her head. "Don't come back to my room at night, Marks. Because if it happens again, I won't be able to stop."

His arms loosened, and he released her to stand up from the floor. Reaching for her hand, he pulled her up with him. The sheaf of fallen papers was retrieved, and Leo took up the sketch of her. The parchment was neatly ripped, the pieces folded together, and ripped again. He gave her the shreds of paper and molded her fingers around them. "I'll destroy the others as well."

Catherine stood without moving as he left the room. And her fingers tightened over the strips of parchment, crushing them into a damp knot.

Chapter Twelve

In the month that followed, Leo deliberately kept himself too busy to see much of Catherine. Two new tenant farms required irrigation schemes. It was a subject on which Leo had developed a certain amount of expertise while Cam worked with the horses and Merripen supervised the timber harvesting. Leo had designed water meadows that would be irrigated with rills and ditches leading from the nearby rivers. In one place where the channel would run too low to be let out naturally, they would require a waterwheel. The wheel, provided with buckets, would lift out the necessary amount of water and send it along a manmade canal.

Shirtless and sweating under the soft blaze of the Hampshire sun, Leo and the tenants dug ditches and drainage canals, moved rock, and hauled soil. At the end of the day Leo ached in every muscle, nearly too tired to stay awake during dinner. His body toughened and became so lean that he was obliged to borrow trousers from Cam while the village tailor altered his clothes.

"At least work keeps you from your vices," Win quipped one

evening before supper, rubbing his hair affectionately as she joined him in the parlor.

"I happen to like my vices," Leo told her. "That's why I went to the trouble of acquiring them."

"What you need to acquire," Win said gently, "is a wife. And I'm not saying that out of self-interest, Leo."

He smiled at her, this gentlest of sisters, who had fought so many personal battles for the sake of love. "You don't possess a molecule of self-interest, Win. But as sound as your advice usually is, I'm not going to take it."

"You should. You need a family of your own."

"I have more than enough family to contend with. And there are things I would much rather do than marry."

"Such as?"

"Oh, cut out my tongue and join the Trappist Monks . . . roll naked in treacle and nap on an anthill . . . Shall I go on?"

"That won't be necessary," Win said, smiling. "However, you *will* marry someday, Leo. Both Cam and Merripen have said that you have a very distinct marriage line on your hand."

Bemused, Leo looked down at his palm. "That's a crease from the way I hold my pen."

"It's a marriage line. And it's so long, it practically wraps around both sides of your hand. Which means you will someday marry a fated love." Win raised her fair brows significantly, as if to say, *What do you think of that?*

"Romas don't really believe in palm reading," Leo informed her. "It's nonsense. They only do it to extract money from fools and drunkards."

Before Win could reply, Merripen entered the parlor. "*Gadjos* certainly know how to complicate matters," he said, handing a letter to Leo and lowering to the settee.

"What is this?" Leo asked, glancing at the signature at the bottom. "Another letter from the solicitor? I thought he was trying to *un*complicate matters for us."

"The more he explains," Merripen said, "the more confusing it is. As a Rom, I still have trouble understanding the concept of land ownership. But the Ramsay estate . . ." He shook his head in disgust. "It's a Gordian knot of agreements, grants, customs, exceptions, additions, and leases."

"That's because the estate is so old," Win said wisely. "The more ancient the manor, the more complications it's had time to acquire." She glanced at Leo. "By the way, I've just learned that Countess Ramsay and her daughter Miss Darvin wish to come for a visit. We received a letter from them earlier today."

"The devil you say!" Leo was outraged. "For what purpose? To gloat? Take inventory? I've still got a year left before they can lay claim to the place."

"Perhaps they wish to make peace and find an acceptable solution for all of us," Win suggested.

Win was always inclined to think the best of people and believe in the essential goodness of human nature.

Leo didn't have that problem.

"Make peace, my arse," he muttered. "By God, I'm tempted to get married just to spite that pair of witches."

"Do you have any candidates in mind?" Win asked.

"Not one. But if I ever did marry, it would be to a woman I was certain never to love."

A movement at the doorway caught his attention, and Leo watched covertly as Catherine entered the room. She gave the group a neutral smile, carefully avoiding Leo's gaze, and went to a chair near the corner. With annoyance, Leo noticed that she had lost weight. Her breasts were smaller, and her waist was reed slender, and her complexion was wan. Was she deliberately avoiding proper nourishment? What had caused her lack of appetite? She was going to make herself ill.

"For God's sake, Marks," he said irritably, "you're getting as scrawny as a birch branch."

"Leo," Win protested.

Catherine shot him a look of outrage. "*I'm* not the one whose trousers are being taken in."

"You look half dead from malnourishment," Leo went on with a scowl. "What's the matter with you? Why aren't you eating?"

"Ramsay," Merripen murmured, evidently deciding a boundary had been crossed.

Catherine shot up from her chair and glared at Leo. "You're a bully, and a hypocrite, and you have no right to criticize my appearance, so . . . so . . ." She cast about wildly for the right phrase. *"Bugger you!"* And she stormed from the parlor, her skirts rustling angrily.

Merripen and Win watched with open mouths.

"Where did you learn that word?" Leo demanded, hard on her heels.

"From you," she said vehemently over her shoulder.

"Do you even know what it means?"

"No, and I don't care. Stay away from me!"

As Catherine stormed through the house, and Leo went after her, it occurred to him that he had been craving an argument with her, any kind of interaction.

She went outside and partway around the house, and soon they found themselves in the kitchen garden. The air was pungent with the smell of sun-warmed herbs.

"Marks," he said in exasperation. "I'll chase you through the

103

parsley if you insist, but we may as well stop and have it out right here."

She whirled to face him, bright flags of color high on her cheeks. "There's nothing to discuss. You've hardly said a word to me in *days,* and then you make offensive personal remarks—"

"I didn't mean to be offensive. I merely said—"

"I am not scrawny, you despicable oaf! Am I less than a person to you, that you dare to treat me with such contempt? You are the most—"

"I'm sorry."

Catherine fell silent, her breath coming hard.

"I shouldn't have spoken to you that way," Leo said gruffly. "And you are not less than a person to me, you're a person whose well-being I care about. I would be angry with anyone who didn't treat you well—which in this case happens to be you. You're not taking care of yourself."

"Neither are you."

Leo parted his lips to reply, but he couldn't think of an effective rebuttal. He opened and closed his mouth again.

"Every day you work yourself into exhaustion," Catherine said. "You've dropped half a stone, at least."

"The new farms need irrigation systems. I'm the one best suited to design and implement them."

"You don't have to dig trenches and move rocks."

"Yes, I do."

"Why?"

Leo stared at her, considering whether or not to tell her the truth. He decided to be blunt. "Because working to the point of exhaustion is the only way I can keep from coming to you at night and seducing you."

104

Catherine gave him a round-eyed glance. Her mouth opened and closed in the same way his had just a moment earlier.

Leo stared back at her with a mixture of wary amusement and growing heat. He could no longer deny that he found nothing in the world more entertaining than talking to her. Or just being near her. Cantankerous, stubborn, fascinating creature . . . completely unlike his past lovers. And at times like this, she had all the cuddlesome appeal of a feral hedgehog.

But she challenged him, met him as an equal, in a way that no other woman ever had. He wanted her beyond reason.

"You couldn't seduce me," Catherine said testily.

They were both motionless, their gazes locked.

"You deny the attraction between us?" Leo's voice was pitched deeper than usual. He saw a shiver run through her before she set her jaw in determination.

"I deny that one's rational will can be undermined by physical sensation," she said. "One's brain is always in charge."

Leo couldn't prevent the mocking smile that rose to his lips. "Good God, Marks. Obviously you've never participated in the act, or you would know that the major organ in charge is *not* the brain. In fact, the brain ceases working altogether."

"I find it easy to believe that a man's would."

"A woman's brain is no less primitive than a man's, especially when it comes to physical distraction."

"I'm sure you'd like to think so."

"Shall I prove it to you?"

Catherine's delicate mouth twisted skeptically. But then, as if she couldn't resist, she asked, "How?"

Taking her arm, Leo drew her to a more secluded area of the kitchen garden, behind a pair of pergolas covered with scarlet runner beans. They stood next to a glass forcing house, which was used to compel plants into flower before they might have otherwise. A forcing house allowed a gardener to grow plants and flowers irrespective of the prevailing weather.

Leo glanced at their surroundings to make certain they were not being observed. "Here's a challenge for your higher brain function. First, I'll kiss you. Directly afterward, I'll ask you a simple question. If you answer correctly, I'll concede the argument."

Catherine frowned and looked away from him. "This is ridiculous," she said to no one in particular.

"You certainly have the right to refuse," Leo told her. "Of course, I'll take that as a forfeiture."

Folding her arms across her chest, Catherine gazed at him with narrowed eyes. "One kiss?"

Leo spread his hands palm up, as if to demonstrate that he had nothing to hide. His gaze never left her. "One kiss, one question."

Slowly her arms loosened and lowered. She stood before him uncertainly.

Leo hadn't actually expected her to agree to the challenge. He felt his heart begin to beat in concentrated thumps. As he stepped closer to her, anticipation tightened his insides into knots.

"May I?" he asked, reaching for her spectacles, easing them from her face.

She blinked but didn't resist.

Leo folded the spectacles and tucked them in his coat pocket. Very gently he tilted her face upward with both hands. He had made her nervous. *Good,* he thought darkly.

"Are you ready?" he asked.

She nodded within the careful bracket of his palms, her lips trembling.

Leo brought his mouth lightly to hers, kissing her with careful, undemanding pressure. Her lips were cool and sweet. Teasing them apart, he deepened the kiss. His arms slid around her, bringing her fully against him. She was slender but compact, her body as supple as a cat's. He felt her begin to mold against him, a slow and helpless relaxing. Concentrating on her mouth, he explored her with tender fire, searching with his tongue until he felt the vibration of her soft moan between their lips.

Lifting his head, Leo looked into her flushed face. He was so mesmerized by the drowsy green-gray of her eyes that it was a struggle to remember what he'd meant to ask her.

"The question," he reminded himself aloud, and shook his head to clear it. "Here it is. A farmer has twelve sheep. All but seven die. How many are left?"

"Five," she said promptly.

"Seven." A grin spread across his face as he watched her puzzle it out.

Catherine scowled. "That was a trick. Ask me another one."

"That wasn't the bargain," he said.

"Another one," she insisted.

A husky laugh escaped him. "God, you're stubborn. All right." He reached for her and lowered his head, and she stiffened.

"What are you doing?"

"One kiss, one question," he reminded her.

Catherine looked martyred. But she yielded to him, her head tilting back as he pulled her against him once more. This time he was not so tentative. His kiss was firm and urgent, his tongue sinking into the sweet, warm interior of her mouth. Her arms lifted around his neck, her fingers groping delicately in his hair.

Leo went dizzy with desire and pleasure. He couldn't pull her body close enough, he needed parts of her he couldn't reach. His hands shook with the need to find the sweet pale skin beneath the heavy fabric of her bodice. He kept trying to feel more of her, kiss her more deeply, and instinctively she tried to help him, sucking on his tongue with a little sound of pleasure. The hair on the back of his neck lifted as a chill of delight climbed up his spine to the base of his skull.

He broke the kiss, gasping.

"Ask me a question," she reminded him thickly.

Leo could barely remember his own name. All he wanted to concentrate on was the way she fit against him. But somehow he obliged her. "Some months have thirty-one days, some have thirty. How many months have twenty-eight days?"

A perplexed furrow appeared between her fine brows. "One."

"All of them," came his gentle reply. He tried to look sympathetic as he saw her incredulous outrage.

"Ask me another one," Catherine said, furious and determined.

Leo shook his head, breathless with laughter. "I can't think of any more. My brain is deprived of blood. Accept it, Marks, you lost the—"

She grabbed the lapels of his coat and dragged him back to her, and Leo's mouth fastened on hers before he knew what he was doing. The amusement vanished. Staggering forward with her in his arms, he put out one hand to brace himself against the glass forcing house. And he possessed her lips with rough, wholehearted ardor, reveling at the feel of her body arching against his. He was dying of lust, his flesh heavy and aching with the need to take her. He kissed her without restraint, sucking, almost gnawing, stroking the inside of her mouth in ways almost too delicious to bear.

Before he lost all semblance of self-control, Leo tore his lips from hers and held her tightly against his chest.

Another question, he thought dimly, and forced what was left of his mind to come up with something.

His voice was hoarse, as if he'd just tried to breathe in fire. "How many animals of each species did Moses take into the ark?"

Her answer was muffled in his coat. "Two."

"None," Leo managed to say. "It was Noah, not Moses."

But he no longer found the game amusing, and Catherine no longer seemed to care about winning. They stood together, gripped tight and close. Their bodies cast a single shadow that stretched along a garden path.

"We'll call it a draw," Leo muttered.

Catherine shook her head. "No, you were right," she said faintly. "I can't think at all."

They waited a little longer, while she leaned into the wild rhythm of his heart. They were both in a daze, mutually occupied with a question that couldn't be asked. An answer that couldn't be given.

Letting out an unsteady sigh, Leo eased her away. He winced as the fabric of his trousers chafed his aroused flesh. Thank God the cut of his coat was long enough to conceal the problem. Extracting her spectacles from his pocket, he replaced them carefully on her nose.

He offered his arm in wordless invitation—a truce—and Catherine took it.

"What *does* 'bugger' mean?" she asked unevenly, as he led her out of the kitchen garden.

"If I told you," he said, "it would lead to improper thoughts. And I know how you hate those."

Leo spent much of the next day at a stream on the west side of the estate, determining the best site for a waterwheel and marking the area. The wheel would be approximately sixteen feet in diameter, equipped with a row of buckets that would empty into a trough from which the water would course along a series of wooden flumes. Leo estimated that the system would irrigate approximately one hundred and fifty acres, or ten generously sized tenant farms.

After laying out plots with the tenants and laborers, hammering wooden stakes into the ground, and wading through a cold, muddy stream, Leo rode back to Ramsay House. It was late afternoon, the sun a condensed yellow, the meadows still and breezeless. Leo was tired, sweat-soaked, and annoyed from battling gadflies. Wryly he thought that all the romantic poets who waxed rhapsodic about being out in nature had certainly never been involved in an irrigation project.

His boots were so caked with mud that he went to the kitchen entrance, left them by the door, and went inside in his stocking feet. The cook and a maid were busy slicing apples and rolling dough, while Win and Beatrix sat at the worktable, polishing silver.

"Hello, Leo," Beatrix said cheerfully.

"Heavens, what a sight you are," Win exclaimed.

Leo smiled at both of them, then wrinkled his nose as he detected a bitter stench in the air. "I didn't think it was possible for any odor to eclipse mine at the moment. What is it? Metal polish?"

"No, actually it's . . ." Win looked guarded. "Well, it's a kind of dye."

"For cloth?"

"For hair," Beatrix said. "You see, Miss Marks wants to darken her hair before the ball, but she was afraid of using dye from the apothecary, since he got it so wrong last time. So Cook suggested a recipe that her own mother used. You boil walnut shells and cassia bark together with vinegar and—"

"Why is Marks dyeing her hair?" Leo asked, striving to keep his tone ordinary, even as his soul revolted against the idea. That beautiful hair, gleaming gold and pale amber, covered with a dull, dark stain.

Win replied cautiously. "I believe she wishes to be less . . . visible . . . at the ball, with so many guests in attendance. I didn't press her for answers, as I felt she was entitled to her privacy. Leo, please don't distress her by mentioning it."

"Does no one find it odd that we have a servant who insists on disguising herself?" Leo asked. "Is this family so bloody eccentric that we accept any manner of strangeness without even asking questions?"

"It's not all that strange," Beatrix said. "Many animals change their colors. Cuttlefish, for example, or certain species of frogs, and of course chameleons—"

"Excuse me," Leo said through clenched teeth. He left the kitchen with purposeful strides, while Win and Beatrix stared after him.

"I was leading to some very interesting facts about chameleons," Beatrix said.

"Bea, darling," Win murmured, "perhaps you'd better go out to the stables and find Cam."

Catherine sat at her dressing table, contemplating her own tense reflection in the looking glass. Several articles were neatly arranged in front of her: folded toweling, a comb, a pitcher and basin, and a pot filled with a strained dark sludge that looked like boot blacking. She had painted a single lock of hair with the stuff, and was waiting for it to take effect, to see what color had been imparted. After her last disaster with colorant, when her hair had turned green, she was taking no chances.

111

With the Hathaway ball only two days away, Catherine had no choice but to drab down her appearance as much as possible. Guests from surrounding counties would attend, as well as families from London. And as always, she was afraid of being recognized. However, as long as she obscured her appearance and kept to the corners, no one ever noticed her. Chaperones were most often spinsters or poor widows, undesirable women who had been assigned the task of watching over young girls who still had their best years ahead of them. Catherine was scarcely older than those girls, but she felt as if there were decades between herself and them.

Catherine knew that her past would catch up with her someday. And when it did, the time she had spent with the Hathaways would be over. It had been the only period of real happiness in her life. She would grieve to lose them.

All of them.

The door was flung open, shattering Catherine's quiet contemplation. She turned in her chair and saw Leo in remarkable disarray. He was sweaty and rumpled and filthy, standing there in his stocking feet.

She jumped up to face him, recalling too late that she wore nothing but a crumpled chemise.

His hard gaze raked over her, missing no detail, and Catherine turned red in outrage. "What are you doing?" she cried. "Have you gone mad? Leave my room this instant!"

Chapter Thirteen

Leo closed the door and reached Catherine in two strides. He hauled her forcibly to the pitcher and basin.

"Stop it," she screeched, flailing at him, while he pushed her head over the basin and poured water over the lock of hair she had saturated with dye. She spluttered furiously. "What is *wrong* with you? What are you doing?"

"Washing this slime from your hair." He dumped the rest of the water on her head.

Catherine yelped and struggled, managing to slosh water over him as well, until there were puddles on the floor and the carpet was soaked. They fought until Catherine found herself on the wet layer of wool covering the floor. Her spectacles had flown off, leaving the room a blur. But Leo's face was only inches above her own, his hot blue eyes staring into hers. He subdued her without effort, pinning her wrists, her torso, as if she had no more substance than a garment rippling on a clothesline. He was very heavy on her, muscle and weight and masculinity supported in the cradle of her thighs.

She twisted helplessly. She wanted him to let her go, and at the same time she wanted him to lie on her forever, his hips pressing hers harder, deeper. Her eyes turned wet.

"Please," she choked out. "Please don't hold my wrists."

As he heard the note of fear in her voice, his face changed. He released her arms at once. She was gathered up against him, her dripping head clasped to his shoulder.

"No," he muttered, "don't be afraid of me. I would never—" She felt him kiss the side of her face, the edge of her jaw, the frantic working of her throat. Waves of warmth slid over her, sensation rising in the places where they pressed. She let her arms remain limp and outstretched on the floor, but her knees tightened on his body, holding him instinctively.

"What does it matter to you?" she asked against his damp shirt. "What do you care what color my h-hair is?" She felt the hard wall of his chest beneath his shirt, and she wanted to delve beneath the garment, rub her mouth and cheeks through the dark fleece.

His voice was soft and fierce. "Because it's not you. It's not right. What are you hiding from?"

She shook her head weakly, her eyes swimming. "I can't explain. There's too much . . . I can't. If you knew, I would have to go. And I want to stay with you. Just a little longer." A sob slipped from her throat. "Not you, I meant your family."

"You can stay. Tell me, so I can protect you."

She swallowed back another sob. There was a hot, irritating trickle on the side of her face. A tear had slid into her hairline. She lifted a hand to brush at it, but he had already put his mouth there, his lips absorbing the trail of wet salt. Her trembling hand curved around his head. She hadn't meant to encourage him, but he took it as such, his mouth finding hers hungrily. And she moaned, lost in a flood of urgent feeling.

He slid an arm beneath her neck, supporting her as he kissed her. She felt the excitement in him, heard it in the rasp of his breathing as he searched and teased and licked deep. His weight lifted from her, his warm hand settling on the damp fabric covering her midriff. She might as well have been naked for all the concealment the chemise provided, her nipples rising tightly against the transparent chill of fabric. He kissed her over the wet muslin, his mouth fastening over the rosy veiled point. Impassioned, he tugged at the tie of her chemise and spread the garment to reveal the shapes of her breasts, high and small and round.

"Cat . . ." The rush of his breath against her damp skin made her shiver. "I could die of wanting you, you're so lovely . . . sweet . . . *God* . . ." He drew a flushed bud into his mouth, circling it with his tongue, tugging softly. At the same time his fingers went to her intimate flesh, tracing the delicate slit, stroking until she was open and wet. She felt the gentle pass of his thumb over a place of excruciating sensation, the caress sending fire up to the base of her throat. Her hips lifted into the soft stroking, and he teased her lightly, tenderly, until pleasure hummed through every part of her and an extraordinary promise of relief hovered just out of reach.

His touch deepened, a finger nudging the entrance of her body. The gentle invasion caused her to shrink backward in surprise. Except that she was on the floor on her back, and there was no place to retreat. She reached down reflexively, her hand going to his.

Leo nuzzled the side of her neck. "Innocent darling. Relax and let me touch you, let me . . ." She felt the intricate workings of bone and tendon in the back of his hand as his finger slid farther into the fluid softness. She caught her breath, her body grasping helplessly at the careful intrusion.

Leo's heavy lashes lowered over smoldering eyes, the color of the pale blue heart of a flame. A flush had crossed his cheeks and the bridge of his nose. "I want to be inside you," he said thickly, caressing her. "Here . . . and deeper . . ."

An incoherent sound climbed in her throat as the subtle inner teasing drew her knees up and caused her toes to curl. She was suffused with desperate heat, craving things she had no words for. Drawing his head down to hers, she kissed him frantically, needing the voluptuous pressure of his mouth, the thrust of his tongue—

A series of determined raps on the door broke through the lurid haze of sensation. Leo cursed and pulled his hand from between her thighs, and tucked her body beneath his. Cat whimpered, her heart pounding madly.

"Who is it?" Leo called out brusquely.

"Rohan."

"If you open that door, I will kill you." The statement was uttered with the vicious sincerity of a man who had been pushed to his limits. Apparently it was enough to give even Cam Rohan pause.

After a long moment, Cam said, "I want a word with you."

"Now?"

"Definitely now," came the inexorable reply.

Closing his eyes, Leo drew in a taut breath and expelled it slowly. "Downstairs in the library."

"Five minutes?" Cam persisted.

Leo stared at the closed door with an expression of incredulous wrath. *"Go,* Rohan."

As Cam's footsteps retreated, Leo looked down at Catherine. She couldn't seem to stop writhing and trembling, her nerves jangling with agitation. Murmuring quietly, he held her close and rubbed circles on her back and hips. "Easy, love. Let me hold you." Gradually the frantic need faded, and she lay still in his arms, her cheek pressed against his.

Leo stood and scooped her up easily, and carried her to the bed. He set her half-naked body on the mattress. While she perched on the edge of the bed and fumbled to draw the counterpane around herself, he hunted for her spectacles. Finding them in the corner of the room, he brought them back to her.

The spectacles were beginning to look rather the worse for wear, she thought ruefully, straightening the battered wire frames and polishing the lenses with a corner of the counterpane.

"What are you going to say to Mr. Rohan?" she asked hesitantly, putting the spectacles on.

"I don't know yet. But for the next two days, until the damned ball is over, I'm going to put some distance between us. Because our relationship seems to have become a bit too flammable for either of us to manage. Afterward, however, you and I are going to talk. No evasions, no lies."

"Why?" she asked through dry lips.

"We have to make some decisions."

What kind of decisions? Was he planning to dismiss her? Or was some kind of indecent proposition in the making? "Perhaps I should leave Hampshire," she said with difficulty.

Leo's eyes glinted dangerously. Taking her head in his hands, he bent down to whisper in her ear, in what could have been either a promise or a threat. "Anywhere you go, I'll find you."

He went to the door, and paused before leaving. "Incidentally," he said. "When I drew those sketches of you, I didn't begin to do you justice."

After Leo had washed and changed into decent attire, he went to the library. Cam was waiting there, looking no happier than Leo

117

felt. Even so, there was a calmness about him, a quality of relaxed tolerance that helped to blunt the edge of Leo's temper. There was no man on earth whom Leo trusted more.

When they had first met, Leo would never have chosen a man like Cam Rohan for Amelia. It just wasn't done. Cam was a Gypsy, and no one could claim that a Romany heritage was an advantage in English society. But the temperament of the man, his patience, humor, and inherent decency, was impossible to deny.

In a relatively short time, Cam had become a brother to Leo. He had seen Leo at his worst, and he had offered steady support as Leo had fought to reconcile himself to a life bereft of innocence or hope. And somehow, in the past few years, Leo had regained a little of both.

Standing at the window, Cam leveled a shrewd stare at him.

Wordlessly Leo went to the sideboard, poured a brandy, and let the snifter warm in his fingers. To his surprise, he saw that his hand wasn't quite steady.

"I was called in from the stables," Cam said, "to find your sisters worried and the housemaids in hysterics, because you decided to close yourself in a bedroom with Miss Marks. You can't take advantage of a woman in your employ. You know that."

"Before you tread the moral high ground," Leo said, "let's not forget that you seduced Amelia before you married her. Or is debauching an innocent acceptable as long as she's not working for you?"

There was a flash of annoyance in Cam's hazel eyes. "I knew I was going to marry her when I did it. Can you say the same?"

"I haven't slept with Marks. Yet." Leo scowled. "But at this rate I'll have bedded her by week's end. I can't seem to stop

118

myself." He raised his gaze heavenward. "Lord, please smite me." When it appeared there would be no response from the Almighty, he tossed back a swallow of brandy. It went down his throat in a rush of smooth fire.

"You think if you take her," Cam said, "it would be a mistake."

"Yes, that's what I think." Leo took another swallow of liquor.

"Sometimes you have to make a mistake to avoid making an even worse one." Cam smiled slightly as he saw Leo's baleful expression. "Did you think you could avoid this forever, *phral*?"

"That was the plan. And I've managed quite well until recently."

"You're a man in his prime. It's only natural to want your own woman. What's more, you have a title to pass on. And from what I understand of the peerage, your primary responsibility is to produce more of yourselves."

"Good God, are we back to that again?" Scowling, Leo finished his brandy and set the glass aside. "The last thing I want to do is sire brats."

Cam lifted a brow, looking amused. "What's wrong with children?"

"They're sticky. They interrupt. They cry when they don't have their way. If I want that kind of company, I have my friends."

Settling in a chair, Cam stretched out his long legs and regarded Leo with deceptive casualness. "You're going to have to do something about Miss Marks. Because this can't continue. Even for the Hathaways, it's . . ." He hesitated, searching for a word.

"Indecent," Leo finished for him. He paced across the room and back. Stopping at the cold, dark hearth, he braced his hands on the mantel and lowered his head. "Rohan," he said carefully. "You saw what I was like, after Laura."

"Yes." Cam paused. "The Rom would say you were a man who grieved too much. You trapped your beloved's soul in the in-between."

"Either that, or I went mad."

"Love is a form of madness, isn't it?" Cam asked prosaically.

Leo let out a humorless chuckle. "For me, undeniably."

They were both silent. And then Cam murmured, "Is Laura still with you, *phral*?"

"No." Leo stared into the empty fireplace. "I've accepted that she's gone. I don't dream about her anymore. But I remember what it was like, trying to live while I was dead inside. It would be even worse now. I can't go through it again."

"You seem to think you have a choice," Cam said. "But you have it backward. Love chooses you. The shadow moves as the sun commands."

"How I enjoy Romany sayings," Leo marveled. "And you know so many of them."

Rising from the chair, Cam went to the sideboard and poured himself a brandy. "I hope you're not entertaining any thought of making her your mistress," he said matter-of-factly. "Rutledge would have you drawn and quartered, no matter that you're his brother-in-law."

"No, I wouldn't, in any case. Taking her as a mistress would create more problems than it would solve."

"If you can't leave her alone, you can't keep her as a mistress, and you won't marry her, the only option is to send her away."

"The most sensible option," Leo agreed darkly. "Also my least favorite."

"Has Miss Marks indicated what she wants?"

Leo shook his head. "She's terrified to face that. Because, God help her, she may possibly want *me*."

Chapter Fourteen

For the next two days, the Hathaway household was a hive of activity. Vast quantities of food and flowers were brought in, furniture was temporarily stored, doors were taken off their hinges, rugs were rolled up, and the floors were waxed and polished.

Guests from Hampshire and surrounding counties would attend the ball, as well as families of distinction from London. To Leo's disgruntlement, the ball invitations had been eagerly accepted by a multitude of peers with daughters in marriageable circumstances. And as the lord of the manor, his duty was to act as host and dance with as many women as possible.

"This is the worst thing you've ever done to me," he told Amelia.

"Oh, not at all, I'm sure I've done worse things to you."

Leo considered that, running through a long list of remembered offenses in his mind. "Never mind, you're right. But to be clear . . . I'm only tolerating this to humor you."

"Yes, I know. I do hope you'll humor me further, and find someone to marry so you can produce an heir before Vanessa Darvin and her mother take possession of our home."

He gave his sister a narrow-eyed glance. "One could almost infer that the house means more to you than my future happiness."

"Not at all. Your future happiness means at least as much to me as the house."

"Thank you," he said dryly.

"But I also happen to believe that you'll be much happier when you fall in love and get married."

"If I ever fell in love with someone," he retorted, "I certainly wouldn't ruin it by marrying her."

The guests began to arrive early in the evening. Women dressed in silk or taffeta, jeweled brooches glittering at low rounded necklines, hands covered with wrist-length white gloves. Many feminine arms were adorned with matching bracelets in the new fashion.

Gentlemen, by contrast, were dressed with severe simplicity in black coats and matching creaseless trousers, and cravats in either white or black. The clothes were tailored with a touch of welcome looseness, making natural movement far easier than it had been in the constricting garments of the recent past.

Music floated through rooms abundantly dressed with flowers. Tables draped in gold satin nearly creaked beneath pyramids of fruit, cheese dishes, roast vegetables, sweetbreads, puddings, joints of meat, smoked fish, and roast fowl. Footmen moved through the circuit of public rooms, bringing cigars and liquor to men in the library, or wine and champagne to the card rooms.

The drawing room was crowded, with clusters of people all around the sides and couples dancing in the center. Leo had to admit, there was an uncommon number of attractive young women present. They all looked pleasant, normal, and fresh-faced. They all looked the same. But he proceeded to dance with as many of them as possible, taking care to include wallflowers, and he even persuaded a dowager or two to take a turn with him.

And all the while he hunted for glimpses of Catherine Marks.

She was wearing a lavender gown, the same one she'd worn at Poppy's wedding. Her hair was caught in a smooth, tight chignon at the back of her neck. She watched over Beatrix while remaining discreetly in the background.

Leo had seen Catherine do the same thing countless times before, stand quietly among the dowagers and chaperones as girls only a little younger than herself flirted and laughed and danced. It was absurd that Catherine should not be noticed. She was the equal of any woman there, background be damned.

Somehow Catherine must have felt his gaze on her. She turned and glanced at him, and she couldn't seem to look away any more than he could.

A dowager captured Catherine's attention, asking a question about something, and she turned to the dratted woman.

At the same time, Amelia came up to Leo's side and caught at his sleeve.

"My lord," she said tensely. "We have a situation. Not a good one."

Glancing at his sister with instant concern, Leo saw that she wore a false smile for the benefit of anyone who might be watching. "I had despaired of anything interesting happening this evening," he said. "What is it?"

"Miss Darvin and Countess Ramsay are here."

Leo's face went blank. "Here? Now?"

"Cam, Win, and Merripen are talking to them in the entrance hall."

"Who the devil invited them?"

"No one. They prevailed on mutual acquaintances—the

Ulsters—to bring them as guests. And we can't turn them away."

"Why not? They're not wanted."

"As improper as they've been in coming without invitations, it would be even worse for us to reject them. It would make us appear *exceedingly* ungracious, and to say the least, it wouldn't be good manners."

"Far too often," Leo reflected aloud, "good manners stand in direct opposition to what I want to do."

"I know that feeling well."

They shared a grim smile.

"What do you suppose they want?" Amelia asked.

"Let's find out," Leo said curtly. Offering her his arm, he escorted her out of the drawing room to the entrance hall.

More than a few curious gazes attended them as they joined the other Hathaways, who were speaking to a pair of women dressed in sumptuous ballgowns.

The older, presumably Countess Ramsay, was a woman of average appearance, a bit plump, neither attractive nor plain. The younger woman, Miss Vanessa Darvin, was a raving beauty, tall with an elegantly turned figure and a lavish bosom, all nicely displayed in a gown of blue-green trimmed with peacock feathers. Her midnight hair was arranged in a perfect mass of pinned-up curls. Her mouth was small and full, the color of a ripe plum, and her eyes were sultry, dark and heavily lashed.

Everything about Vanessa Darvin advertised sexual confidence, which Leo had certainly never held against a woman, except that in this girl it was a bit off-putting. Probably because she looked at him as if she expected him to fall at her feet and start panting like a pug dog with a respiratory ailment.

With Amelia on his arm, Leo approached the pair. Introductions were made, and he bowed with impeccable politeness.

"Welcome to Ramsay House, my lady. And Miss Darvin. What a pleasant surprise."

The countess beamed at him. "I hope our unexpected arrival does not inconvenience you, my lord. However, when Lord and Lady Ulster made it known that you were giving a ball—the first at Ramsay House since its restoration—we felt certain that you wouldn't mind the company of your nearest relations."

"Relations?" Amelia asked blankly. The kinship between the Hathaways and the Darvins was so distant as to hardly warrant the word.

Countess Ramsay continued to smile. "We are cousins, are we not? And when my poor husband passed on to his reward, may God rest his soul, we found consolation in the knowledge that the estate would pass into capable stewardship as yours. Although . . ." Her gaze flickered to Cam and Merripen. "We had not expected such a colorful variety of in-laws as you seem to have accumulated."

Fully comprehending the unsubtle reference to the fact that both Cam and Merripen were part Gypsy, Amelia scowled openly. "Now see here—"

"How refreshing it is," Leo interrupted, trying to stave off an explosion, "to finally be able to communicate without the interference of solicitors."

"I agree, my lord," Countess Ramsay replied. "The solicitors have made the situation regarding Ramsay House quite complex, have they not? But we are only women, and therefore much of what they relate goes right over our heads. Isn't that right, Vanessa?"

"Yes, Mama," came the demure reply.

Countess Ramsay's pillowy cheeks puffed out with another smile. Her gaze encompassed the entire group. "What matters most is the bond of familial affection."

"Does that mean you've decided not to take the house away from us?" Amelia asked bluntly.

Cam settled a hand at his wife's waist and gave her a warning squeeze.

Looking taken aback, Countess Ramsay regarded Amelia with wide eyes. "Goodness me. I'm not at all able to discuss legalities—my poor little brain fairly collapses when I try."

"However," Vanessa Darvin said in a silky voice, "as we understand, there is a chance we may not be entitled to Ramsay House, if Lord Ramsay marries and sires offspring within a year." Her gaze slid boldly over Leo, traveling from head to toe. "And he seems well equipped to do so."

Leo arched a brow, amused by the delicate emphasis she placed on the term "well equipped."

Cam intervened before Amelia could utter a scathing reply. "My lady, do you have need of lodging during your stay in Hampshire?"

"Thank you for your kind concern," Vanessa Darvin replied, "but we are staying at the residence of Lord and Lady Ulster."

"Some refreshments would be welcome, however," Countess Ramsay suggested brightly. "I think a glass of champagne would revive me nicely."

"By all means," Leo said. "May I escort you to the refreshment tables?"

"How delightful," the countess said, beaming. "Thank you, my lord." She came forward to take his proffered arm, and Vanessa went to his other side. Summoning a charming smile, Leo led the pair away.

"What dreadful people," Amelia said dourly. "They're probably here to inspect the house. And they'll monopolize Leo all evening, when he should be talking and dancing with eligible young women."

"Miss Darvin is an eligible young woman," Win said, looking troubled.

"Good heavens, Win. Do you think they came here so that Miss Darvin could meet Leo? Do you think she might set her cap for him?"

"There would be advantages to both sides if they married," Win said. "Miss Darvin would become Lady Ramsay and gain the entire estate instead of just the copyhold. And we could all continue living here, whether or not Leo fathers a child."

"The thought of having a sister-in-law like Miss Darvin is intolerable."

"One can't judge her on first acquaintance," Win said. "Perhaps she's a nice person on the inside."

"Doubtful," Amelia said. "Women who look like that never have to be nice on the inside." Noticing that Cam and Merripen were speaking to each other in Romany, she asked her husband, "What are you talking about?"

"There are peacock feathers on her gown," Cam remarked, in the same tone he might have said, *There are poisonous flesh-eating spiders on her gown.*

"It's a very dashing effect." Amelia looked at him quizzically. "You don't like peacock feathers?"

"To the Rom," Merripen said soberly, "a single peacock feather is an evil omen."

"And she was wearing *dozens* of them," Cam added.

They watched Leo walk away with Vanessa Darvin as if he were heading toward a pit filled with vipers.

Leo escorted Vanessa Darvin to the drawing room, while Countess Ramsay remained near the refreshment tables with Lord and Lady Ulster. After a few minutes of conversation with Vanessa, it was obvious that she was a young woman with adequate intelligence and a highly flirtatious nature. Leo had known and bedded women like Vanessa before. She inspired little interest in him. However, it might benefit the Hathaway family to become acquainted with Vanessa Darvin and her mother, if only to learn their plans.

Chattering lightly, Vanessa confided how dreadfully dull it had been to spend a year in mourning after her father had passed away, and how eager she had been to finally have a season in London the following year. "But how charming this estate is," she exclaimed. "I remember visiting it once when my father had the title. It was a pile of rubbish, and the gardens were barren. Now it's a gem."

"Thanks to Mr. Rohan and Merripen," Leo said. "The transformation was entirely due to their efforts."

Vanessa looked puzzled. "Well. One would never have guessed. Their people aren't usually so industrious."

"Romas are highly industrious, actually. It's only that they're nomadic, which limits their interest in farming."

"But your brothers-in-law are not nomadic, it seems."

"They have each found good reason to stay in Hampshire."

Vanessa shrugged. "They give the appearance of being gentlemen, which I suppose is all one could ask."

Leo was annoyed by her disdainful tone. "They're both related to nobility, as a matter of fact, being only half Romany. Merripen will inherit an Irish earldom someday."

"I had heard something to that effect. But . . . Irish nobility," she said with a little moue of distaste.

"You consider the Irish inferior?" Leo asked idly.

"Don't you?"

"Yes, I've always found it so crass when people refuse to be English."

Either Vanessa chose to ignore the comment, or it sailed over her head. She exclaimed with pleasure as they approached the drawing room, with its rows of glittering windows, cream-painted interior, and steep tray ceiling. "How lovely. I believe I will enjoy living here."

"As you remarked earlier," Leo pointed out, "you may not have the chance. I have a year left to marry and procreate."

"You have a reputation as an elusive bachelor, which leaves some doubt as to whether you will achieve the former." A provocative gleam appeared in her dark eyes. "The latter, I'm sure you're very good at."

"I would never make that claim," Leo said blandly.

"You don't have to, my lord. The claim has often been made on your behalf. Will you deny it?"

It was hardly a question one would have expected from a well-bred miss upon first acquaintance. Leo gathered that he was supposed to be impressed by her audacity. However, after participating in an infinite number of such conversations in London parlors, he no longer found such remarks intriguing.

In London, a little sincerity was far more shocking than audacity.

"I wouldn't claim to be accomplished in the bedroom," he said. "Merely competent. And women usually don't recognize the difference."

Vanessa giggled. "What makes one accomplished in the bedroom, my lord?"

Leo glanced at her without smiling. "Love, of course. Without it, the entire business is merely a matter of technicalities."

She looked disconcerted, but the flirtatious mask swiftly reappeared. "Oh, la, love is a passing thing. I may be young, but I'm hardly naïve."

"So I've gathered," he said. "Would you care to dance, Miss Darvin?"

"That depends, my lord."

"On what?"

"On whether you're competent or accomplished at it."

"Touché," Leo said, smiling despite himself.

Chapter Fifteen

Upon being told by Amelia of the unanticipated arrival of Countess Ramsay and Vanessa Darvin, Catherine was filled with curiosity.

Followed soon thereafter by gloom.

Standing at the side of the room, she and Beatrix watched as Leo waltzed with Miss Darvin.

They were a striking pair, Leo's dark handsomeness perfectly balanced by Miss Darvin's vibrant beauty. Leo was an excellent dancer, if a bit more athletic than graceful as he guided his partner around the room. And the skirts of Miss Darvin's blue-green gown swirled most becomingly, a fold of her skirts occasionally wrapping against his legs from the motion of the waltz.

Miss Darvin was quite beautiful, with glowing dark eyes and rich sable hair. She murmured something that elicited a grin from Leo. He looked charmed by her. Absolutely charmed.

Catherine had a peculiar feeling in her stomach as she watched them, as if she had just swallowed a handful of tenpenny nails. Beatrix stood beside her and touched her back briefly, as if to offer comfort. Catherine felt a reversal of their usual roles, that instead of being the wise older companion, she was the one in need of reassurance and guidance.

She tried to school her features into blankness. "How attractive Miss Darvin is," she commented.

"I suppose," Beatrix said noncommittally.

"In fact," Catherine added in a glum tone, "she's enchanting."

Beatrix watched Leo and Miss Darvin with thoughtful blue eyes as they executed a perfect turn. "I wouldn't say *enchanting* . . ."

"I can't see one flaw."

"I can. Her elbows are knobby."

Squinting through her spectacles, Catherine thought that perhaps Beatrix was right. They *were* a bit knobby. "That's true," she said, feeling a tiny bit better. "And doesn't her neck seem rather too long?"

"She's a giraffe," Beatrix said with an emphatic nod.

Catherine strained to see Leo's expression, wondering if he had noticed the abnormal length of Miss Darvin's neck. It didn't appear that he had. "Your brother seems taken with her," she muttered.

"I'm sure he's merely being polite."

"He's never polite."

"He is when he wants something," Beatrix said.

But that only sent Catherine plummeting into deeper gloom. Because the question of what Leo might want from the dark-haired beauty had no palatable answer.

A young gentleman came to ask Beatrix to dance, and Catherine gave her permission. Sighing, she leaned back against the wall and let her thoughts wander.

The ball was an unqualified success. Everyone was having a lovely time, the music was delightful, the food delicious, the evening neither too warm nor too cool.

And Catherine was miserable.

However, she was hardly going to let herself crumble like a dry teacake. Forcing a pleasant expression to her face, she turned to make conversation with a pair of elderly woman standing next to her. They were involved in an animated debate over the comparative merits of a chain stitch or a split stitch in outlining crewel embroidery. Trying to listen attentively, Catherine stood with her gloved fingers laced together.

"Miss Marks."

She turned to the familiar masculine voice.

Leo was there, breathtaking in the formal evening scheme of black and white, his blue eyes sparkling wickedly.

"Would you do me the honor?" he asked, gesturing to the whirl of waltzing couples. He was asking her to dance. As he had once promised.

Catherine blanched as she became aware of the multitude of gazes on them. It was one thing for the host of the evening to confer briefly with his sister's companion. It was something else entirely for him to dance with her. He knew it, and he didn't give a damn.

"Go away," she said in a sharp whisper, her heart beating wildly.

A faint smile touched his lips. "I can't. Everyone's watching. Are you going to give me a public setdown?"

She could not embarrass him that way. It was a violation of etiquette to refuse a man's invitation to dance if it could have been construed that she didn't wish to dance with him personally. And yet to be the focus of attention . . . to set tongues wagging . . . it was contrary to every instinct for self-preservation. "Oh, why are you doing this?" she whispered again, desperate and furious . . . and yet somewhere in the midst of her inner tumult, there was a tingle of delight.

"Because I want to," he said, his smile widening. "And so do you."

He was unforgivably arrogant.

He also happened to be right.

Which made her an *idiot*. If she said yes, she deserved whatever happened to her afterward.

"Yes." Biting her lip, she took his arm and let him lead her toward the center of the room.

"You could try smiling," Leo suggested. "You look like a prisoner being led to the gallows."

"It feels more like a beheading," she said.

"It's just one dance, Marks."

"You should waltz with Miss Darvin again," she said, wincing inwardly as she heard the sullen note in her own voice.

Leo laughed quietly. "Once was enough. I've no wish to repeat the experience."

Catherine tried, without success, to smother the ripple of pleasure that went through her. "You didn't get on?"

"Oh, we got on marvelously, as long as we didn't stray from the topic of utmost interest."

"The estate?"

"No, herself."

"I'm sure that with maturity, Miss Darvin will become less self-involved."

"Perhaps. It's of no importance to me."

Leo took her into his arms, his hold firm and supportive, and inexplicably right. And an evening that had seemed so dreadful only moments before became so wonderful that Catherine was light-headed.

He held her, his right hand precisely against her shoulder blade, his left hand securing hers. Even through the layers of their gloves, she felt the thrill of contact.

The dance began.

In the waltz, the man was thoroughly in control of the timing, the pace, the sequence of steps. And Leo left Catherine no opportunity to falter. It was easy to follow him, every movement nonnegotiable. There were moments in which they seemed almost to hover before sweeping into another series of turns. The music was an audible ache of yearning. Catherine was silent, afraid to break the spell, focusing only on the blue eyes above hers. And for the first time in her life, she was wholly happy.

The dance lasted three minutes, perhaps four. Catherine tried to collect every second and commit it to memory, so that in the future she could close her eyes and bring it all back. As the waltz ended on a sweet, high note, she found herself holding her breath, wishing it would go on just a little longer.

Leo bowed and offered her his arm.

"Thank you, my lord. It was lovely."

"Would you like to dance again?"

"I'm afraid not. It would be scandalous. I'm not a guest, after all."

"You're part of the family," Leo said.

"You are very kind, my lord, but you know that's not true. I am a paid companion, which means—"

She broke off as she became aware that someone, a man, was staring at her. Glancing in his direction, she saw a face that had haunted her in nightmares.

The sight of him, a figure from the past she had managed to evade for so long, extorted every bit of calm she possessed and sent her into full-scale panic. Only her grip on Leo's arm kept her from doubling over as if she'd been kicked in the stomach. She tried to take a breath, and could only wheeze.

"Marks?" Leo stopped and turned her to face him, looking down at her bleached face in concern. "What is it?"

"A touch of the vapors," she managed to say. "It must have been the exertion of the dance."

"Let me help you to a chair—"

"*No.*"

The man was still staring at her, recognition dawning on his features. She had to get away before he approached her. She swallowed hard against the biting pressure of tears welling in her eyes and throat.

What might have been the happiest night of Catherine's life had abruptly become the worst.

It's over, she thought with bitter grief. Her life with the Hathaways had come to an end. She wanted to die.

"What can I do?" Leo asked quietly.

"Please, will you see to Beatrix . . . tell her . . ."

She couldn't finish. Shaking her head blindly, she walked out of the drawing room as quickly as possible.

The exertions of the dance, my arse, Leo thought darkly. This was a woman who had moved a pile of rocks so that he could climb out of a pit. Whatever was bothering Catherine, it had nothing to do with the vapors. Glancing around the room with narrowed eyes, Leo saw a stillness amid the chattering crowd.

Guy, Lord Latimer, was watching Catherine Marks as intently as Leo was. And as she left the drawing room, Latimer began to make his way to the open doorway as well.

Leo scowled with the irritable awareness that the next time his family planned a ball or soirée, he was going to personally inspect the guest list. Had he known that Latimer would be invited, he would have drawn through the name with the darkest of ink.

136

Latimer, at the age of approximately forty, had reached the stage of life at which a man could no longer be called a rake, which implied a certain youthful immaturity, but instead a roué, which had the flavor of middle-aged unseemliness.

As next in line to an earldom, Latimer had little to occupy him, other than to wait for his father to die. In the meantime he had dedicated himself to the pursuit of vice and perversion. He expected others to clean up his messes, and he cared for no one's comfort but his own. The place in his chest where a heart should have been was as empty as a calabash gourd. He was wily, clever, and calculating, all in service of satisfying his own boundless needs.

And Leo, in the depths of his despair over Laura Dillard, had tried his best to emulate him.

Recalling the escapades he had been involved in with Latimer and his cadre of dissipated aristocrats, Leo felt distinctly unclean. Since his return from France, he had scrupulously avoided Latimer. However, Latimer's family was from the neighboring county of Wiltshire, and it would have been impossible to steer clear of him forever.

Seeing Beatrix approaching the side of the drawing room, Leo reached her in a few impatient strides and took her arm.

"No more dancing for now, Bea," he murmured close to her ear. "Marks isn't available to watch over you."

"Why not?"

"I intend to find out. In the meantime, don't get into trouble."

"What should I do?"

"I don't know. Go to the refreshment table and eat something."

"I'm not hungry." Beatrix heaved a sigh. "But I suppose one doesn't need to be hungry to eat."

"Good girl," he muttered, and left the room swiftly.

Chapter Sixteen

"Stop! Stop right there, I say!"

Catherine ignored the summons, keeping her head down as she hurried along a hallway toward the servants' stairwell. She was drowning in shame and fear. But she was also infuriated, thinking how monstrously unfair it was that this one man should keep ruining her life, over and over. She had known this would happen someday, that even though Latimer and the Hathaways moved in different circles, they would inevitably meet. But it had been worth the risk to be with the Hathaways, to feel that just for a little while, she had been part of a family.

Latimer grabbed her arm with bruising force. Catherine whirled to face him, her entire body shaking.

It surprised her to see the extent to which he had aged, his features blighted by coarse living. He was heavier, thick around the middle, and his ginger-colored hair was thinning. Most telling, his face had acquired the wizened look of habitual self-indulgence.

"I don't know you, sir," she said coolly. "You are importunate."

Latimer didn't let go of her arm. His devouring gaze made her feel polluted and ill. "I've never forgotten you. I looked for years. You went to another protector, didn't you?" His tongue emerged to swipe moistly over his lips, and his jaw worked as if he were preparing to unhook it and swallow her whole. "I wanted to be your first. I paid a bloody fortune for it."

Catherine took a shivering breath. "Release me at once, or I'll—"

"What are you doing here, dressed in a spinster's garb?"

She looked away from him, battling tears. "I am employed by the Hathaway family. By Lord Ramsay."

"*That* I can believe. Tell me what services you provide for Ramsay."

"Let go of me." Her voice was low and strained.

"Not on your life." Latimer drew her stiff body closer, his wine-soured breath wafting in her face. "Revenge," he said softly, "is the act of a despicable and petty character. Which is no doubt why I've always enjoyed it so much."

"What do you want revenge for?" Catherine asked, despising him to the bottom of her soul. "You lost nothing because of me. Except perhaps the merest fragment of pride, which you could easily afford."

Latimer smiled. "There's where you're mistaken. Pride is all I have. I'm quite sensitive about it, really. And I won't be satisfied until it's returned with interest. Eight years of compounded pride is a tidy sum, wouldn't you say?"

Catherine stared at him coldly. The last time she had seen him, she had been a fifteen-year-old girl with no resources, and no one to protect her. But Latimer had no idea that Harry Rutledge was her brother. Nor did it seem to have occurred to him that there might be other men who would dare to stand between him and what he wanted. "You disgusting lecher," she said. "I suppose the only way you can have a woman is to purchase one. Except that I'm not for sale."

"You were once, weren't you?" Latimer asked idly. "You were a costly piece, and I was assured that you were worth it. Obviously you're no virgin, being in service to Ramsay, but I'd still like a sample of what I paid for."

"I owe you nothing! Leave me alone."

Latimer stunned her by smiling, his face softening. "Come now, you do me a disservice. I'm not such a bad fellow. I can be generous. What does Ramsay pay you? I'll triple it. It would be no hardship, sharing my bed. I know a thing or two about pleasing a woman."

"I'm sure you know a great deal about pleasing yourself," she said, twisting in his grasp. "Let *go*."

"Don't struggle, you'll make me hurt you."

They were both so involved in their conflict that neither of them noticed the approach of a third party.

"Latimer." It was Leo's voice, severing the air like the quiet arc of a steel blade. "If anyone were going to molest my servants, Latimer, it would be me. And I certainly wouldn't require your assistance."

To Catherine's measureless relief, the brutal grip loosened and fell away. She backed up so hastily that she nearly stumbled. But Leo came to her swiftly, using a hand on her shoulder to arrest her momentum. The lightness of his grip, of a man mindful of fragility, was in stark contrast to Latimer's.

She had never seen Leo wear such an expression, a murderous glitter in his eyes. He wasn't at all the same man who had danced with her just minutes before.

"Are you all right?" he asked.

Catherine nodded, staring up at him in dazed misery. How closely acquainted was he with Lord Latimer? Dear God, was it possible they were friends? And if so . . . given the chance, might Leo have done the same thing to her that Latimer once had, all those years ago?

"Leave us," Leo murmured, removing his hand from her shoulder.

Glancing at Latimer, Catherine shivered in revulsion and fled from the pair, as her life came crashing down around her.

Leo stared after Catherine, resisting the urge to follow her. He would go to her later, and try to soothe or repair what damage had been done. And it was considerable damage—he had seen it in her eyes.

Turning to Latimer, Leo was powerfully tempted to slaughter the bastard where he stood. Instead he made his face implacable. "I had no idea you'd been invited," he said, "or I would have advised the housemaids to go into hiding. Really, Latimer, must you force yourself on unwilling females with all the available ones to be had?"

"How long have you had her?"

"If you're referring to Miss Marks's period of employ, she's been with the family not quite three years."

"There's no need to maintain the pretense that she's a servant," Latimer said. "Clever lad, installing your mistress in the family household for your own convenience. I want a go at her. Just for one night."

Leo found it increasingly difficult to restrain his temper. "What in God's name gave you the idea that she's my mistress?"

"*She's the girl,* Ramsay. The one I told you about! Don't you remember?"

"No," Leo said curtly.

"We were in our cups at the time," Latimer conceded. "But I thought you were paying attention."

"At your sober best, Latimer, you're irrelevant and annoying. Why would I have paid attention to anything you said when you were drunk? And what the devil do you mean, 'she's the girl'?"

"I purchased her from my old madam. I won her in a private auction of sorts. She was the most charming thing I'd ever seen, no more than fifteen, with those golden curls, and such remarkable eyes. The madam assured me the girl was absolutely untouched, and yet she had been told all the ways to pleasure a man. I paid a fortune to have the girl at my service for the period of a year, with an option to continue the arrangement if I desired."

"How convenient," Leo said, his eyes narrowed. "I suppose you never bothered to ask the girl if she desired the arrangement?"

"Irrelevant. The agreement was all to her benefit. It was her fortune to be born a beauty, and she would learn how to profit from it. Besides, they're all prostitutes, aren't they? It's only a question of circumstance and price." Latimer paused, smiling quizzically. "She told you none of this?"

Leo ignored the question. "What happened?"

"On the day Catherine was delivered to my house, before I'd sampled the goods, a man forced his way in and took her. Literally abducted her. One of my footmen tried to stop him and took a bullet in the leg for his pains. By the time I realized what was happening, the man had already taken Catherine past the front threshold. I can only assume that he had lost the private auction and decided to take what he wanted by force. Catherine disappeared after that. I've wanted her for eight years." Latimer gave a low laugh. "And now she's turned up in your possession. I don't know that I'm surprised, really. You've always been a devious bastard. How did you manage to acquire her?"

Leo was momentarily silent. His chest was filled with searing

142

anguish for Catherine's sake. Fifteen. Betrayed by those who should have protected her. Sold to a man without morals or mercy. The thought of what Latimer would have done to Catherine made Leo ill. Latimer's depravities wouldn't have stopped at mere physical violation—he would have destroyed her soul. No wonder Catherine found it impossible to trust anyone. It was the only rational response to impossible circumstances.

Leveling a cold stare at Latimer, Leo reflected that if he were just a bit less civilized, he would have killed the bastard on the spot. However, he would have to settle for keeping him away from Catherine, and doing whatever was necessary to keep her safe.

"She is owned by no one," Leo said with care.

"Good. Then I'll—"

"She is under my protection, however."

Latimer arched a brow, amused. "What am I to infer from that?"

Leo was deadly serious. "That you are to go nowhere near her. That she'll never have to endure the sound of your voice or the insult of your presence ever again."

"I'm afraid I can't oblige you."

"I'm afraid you'll have to."

A coarse laugh erupted. "Surely you're not threatening me."

Leo smiled coldly. "Much as I always tried to ignore your inebriated ravings, Latimer, a few things did stick in my memory. Some of your confessions of misconduct would make more than a few people unhappy. I know enough of your secrets to land you in Marshalsea prison without so much as a chum ticket. And if that's not enough, I would be more than willing to resort to bashing your skull in with a blunt object. In fact, I'm becoming quite enthused about the idea." Seeing the astonishment in the other man's eyes, Leo smiled without humor. "I see you grasp

143

my sincerity. That's good. It might save us both some inconvenience." He paused to give his next statement greater impact. "And now I'm going to instruct my servants to escort you off my estate. You're not welcome."

The older man's face went livid. "You'll regret having made an enemy of me, Ramsay."

"Not nearly as much as I've regretted having once made a friend of you."

"What happened to Catherine?" Amelia asked Leo when he returned to the drawing room. "Why did she leave so suddenly?"

"Lord Latimer accosted her," he said shortly.

Amelia shook her head in bewildered outrage. "That repulsive goat—why would he dare?"

"Because that's what he does. He's an affront to polite company and every standard of moral decency. A better question would be why the devil we invited him."

"We didn't invite him, we invited his parents. Obviously he came in their stead." She threw him an accusing glance. "And he's an old acquaintance of yours."

"From now on, let's assume that every old acquaintance of mine is either a lecher or a criminal and should be kept far away from the estate and the family."

"Did Lord Latimer harm Catherine?" Amelia asked anxiously.

"Not physically. But I want someone to see to her. I expect she's in her room. Will you go to her, or send Win?"

"Yes, of course."

"Don't ask questions. Just make certain she's all right."

A half hour later, Win came to Leo with the information that Catherine had declined to say anything other than she wished to retire undisturbed.

It was probably for the best, Leo thought. Although he wanted to go up to her and offer comfort, he would let her sleep.

On the morrow, they would sort everything out.

Leo awakened at the hour of nine and went to Catherine's door. It was still closed, and there was no sound from within. It took all his self-control to keep from opening the door and waking her. However, she needed to rest . . . especially in light of what he intended to discuss with her later.

It seemed to Leo as he went downstairs that the entire household, including servants, was practically sleepwalking. The ball hadn't ended until four in the morning, and even then some of the guests had been reluctant to leave. Sitting in the breakfast room, Leo drank a mug of strong tea and watched as Amelia, Win, and Merripen came in. Cam, always a late riser, was still absent.

"What happened to Catherine last night?" Amelia asked quietly. "And what of Lord Latimer's precipitate departure? More than a few tongues were wagging."

Leo had considered whether or not to discuss Catherine's secrets with the rest of the family. They would have to be told something. And although he would not go into detail, he felt it would be easier for Catherine if someone else gave the explanation. "As it turns out," he said carefully, "when Cat was a girl of fifteen, her so-called family made an arrangement with Latimer."

"What kind of arrangement?" Amelia asked. Her eyes widened as Leo sent her a speaking glance. "Dear Lord."

"Thankfully Rutledge intervened before she was forced to—" Leo broke off, surprised by the note of fury in his own voice. He struggled to moderate it before continuing. "I needn't elaborate. However, it's obviously not a part of Cat's past that she's fond

145

of dwelling on. She's been in hiding for the past eight years. Latimer recognized her last evening, and upset her badly. I'm sure she'll awaken this morning with some notion of leaving Hampshire."

Merripen's features were stern, but his dark eyes were warm with compassion. "There's no need for her to go anywhere. She's safe with us."

Leo nodded, rubbing the edge of the teacup with the pad of his thumb. "I'll make that clear when I talk with her."

"Leo," Amelia said carefully, "are you certain that you're the best one to manage this? With your history of quarreling . . ."

He gave her a hard look. "I'm certain."

"Amelia?" A hesitant voice came from the doorway.

It was Beatrix, wearing a ruffled blue dressing gown, her dark hair trailing in wild locks. Worry had creased her forehead.

"Good morning, dear," Amelia said warmly. "There's no need to rise early, if you don't wish to."

Beatrix replied in a tumble of words. "I wanted to see how the injured owl I'm keeping in the barn is faring. And I was also looking for Dodger, because I haven't seen him since yesterday afternoon. So I opened Miss Marks's door just a sliver, to see if he was in there. You know how he likes to sleep in her slipper box—"

"But he wasn't there?" Amelia asked.

Beatrix shook her head. "And neither was Miss Marks. Her bed is made, and her carpetbag is gone. And I found this on the dressing table."

She handed a piece of folded paper to Amelia, who opened it and scanned the written lines.

"What does it say?" Leo asked, already on his feet.

Amelia handed it to him without a word.

*Please forgive me for leaving without saying good-bye.
There is no other choice. I can never express the gratitude
I feel for your generosity and kindness. Hopefully you will
not think it presumptuous of me to say that although you
are not my family in truth, you are the family of my heart.
I will miss all of you.
Ever your
Catherine Marks*

"Good God," Leo growled, tossing the folded paper to the table, "the drama in this household is more than a man can tolerate. I would have assumed that we could have had a reasonable discussion in the comfort of Ramsay House, but instead she flees in the dark of night and leaves a letter filled with sentimental twaddle."

"It's not twaddle," Amelia said defensively.

Win's eyes filled with compassionate tears as she read the note. "Kev, we must find her."

Merripen slid a hand over hers.

"She's gone to London," Leo muttered. To his knowledge, Harry Rutledge was the only person Cat could turn to. Although Harry and Poppy had been invited to the ball, hotel business had kept them in London.

Anger, urgency, exploded inside Leo from nowhere. He tried not to show it, but the discovery that Cat had left . . . left *him* . . . had filled him with a possessive fury unlike anything he had ever felt before.

"The mail coach usually leaves Stony Cross at five-thirty," Merripen said. "Which means you have a fair chance of overtaking her before she reaches Guildford. I'll go with you, if you like."

147

"So will I," Win said.

"We should all go," Amelia declared.

"No," Leo said grimly. "I'm going alone. When I catch up with Marks, you won't want to be there."

"Leo," Amelia asked suspiciously, "what are you planning to do to her?"

"Why do you always insist on asking questions when you know you won't like the answers?"

"Because, being an optimist," she said tartly, "I always hope I'm wrong."

Chapter Seventeen

The coach schedule was limited, now that the mails were most often loaded onto locomotive trains. Catherine had been fortunate to obtain a seat inside a coach bound for London.

She didn't feel all that fortunate, however.

She was miserable and chilled, even in the stuffy interior of the coach. The vehicle was filled with passengers outside and in, with parcels and luggage tied precariously up top. The whole thing felt dangerously top-heavy as it rumbled over rough patches of road. Ten miles per hour, one of the gentleman passengers had estimated, admiring the strength and endurance of the team of massive drays.

Morosely Catherine stared out the window as the meadows of Hampshire rolled into the heavy woodland and bustling market towns of Surrey.

There was only one other woman inside the coach, a plump and well-dressed matron who was traveling with her husband. She dozed in the opposite corner from Catherine's, emitting delicate snores. Whenever the coach jolted, it caused the objects on her hat to rattle and quiver. And quite a hat it was, adorned with clusters of artificial cherries, a plume, and a small stuffed bird.

At midday the coach stopped at an inn where a new team would be put to, in preparation for the next stretch of road. Groaning in relief at the prospect of a brief respite, the passengers poured out of the vehicle and into the tavern.

Catherine carried her tapestry carpetbag, afraid to leave it in the coach. The bag was a weighty affair containing a nightgown, undergarments and stockings, an assortment of combs and pins and a hairbrush, a shawl, and a voluminous novel with a mischievous inscription from Beatrix . . . "This story is guaranteed to entertain Miss Marks without improving her in the least! With love from the incorrigible B.H."

The inn appeared moderately well appointed but hardly luxurious, the kind of place that stablemen and workingmen frequented. Catherine glanced disconsolately at a wooden yard wall covered with posting bills, and turned to watch a pair of ostlers change the team.

She nearly dropped the carpetbag at the side of the carriage yard as she felt a rustle of independent movement within. Not as if something had shifted around . . . it was more like . . . something was alive in there.

Her heartbeat became rapid and disorganized, like the bobbing of small potatoes in boiling water. "Oh no," she whispered. Turning to face the wall, trying desperately to keep the bag out of view, she unlooped the fastener and opened the bag a mere two inches.

A sleek little head popped out. Catherine was aghast to behold a familiar pair of bright eyes and a set of twitching whiskers.

"Dodger," she whispered. The ferret chattered happily, the corners of his mouth curling in his perpetual ferret smile. "Oh, you *naughty* boy!" He must have slipped into the bag while she had been packing. "What am I to do with you?" she asked in

despair. Pushing his head back down into the bag, she stroked him to keep him quiet. There was no choice but to take the dratted creature all the way to London, and give him into Poppy's keeping until he could be returned to Beatrix.

As soon as one of the ostlers shouted, "All ready!" Catherine went back into the coach and settled the carpetbag at her feet. Opening the top once more, she peeked at Dodger, who was coiled in the folds of her nightgown. "Be quiet," she said sternly. "And don't cause trouble."

"I beg your pardon?" came the matron's voice as she entered the carriage, her hat plume trembling with indignation.

"Oh, ma'am, I wasn't speaking to you," Catherine said hastily. "I was . . . lecturing myself."

"Indeed." The woman's eyes narrowed as she plopped into the opposite seat.

Catherine sat stiffly. She waited for a telltale rustling of the carpetbag or a betraying noise. However, Dodger remained quiet.

The matron closed her eyes and lowered her chin to the high, mounded shelf of her bosom. In a matter of two minutes, she appeared to be dozing again.

Perhaps this wouldn't be difficult after all, Catherine thought. If the woman remained asleep, and the gentlemen resumed their newspaper reading, she might be able to smuggle Dodger to London unnoticed.

But just as Catherine allowed herself to teeter on the brink of hope, the entire situation went tumbling out of her control.

Without warning Dodger poked his head out, surveyed his interesting new surroundings, and slithered from the bag. Catherine's lips parted in a silent cry, and she froze with her hands arrested in midair. The ferret ran up the upholstered seat to the matron's beckoning hat. A nibble or two, and his

151

sharp teeth had severed a cluster of artificial cherries from the hat. Triumphantly he scrambled down the seat and leaped into Catherine's lap with his prize. He did a happy ferret war dance, a series of hops and wriggles.

"No," Catherine whispered, grabbing the cherries from him and trying to shove him back into the carpetbag.

Dodger protested, squeaking and chattering.

The woman spluttered and blinked, waking irritably at the noise. "Wha . . . what . . ."

Cat went still, her pulse thundering in her ears.

Dodger streaked up around Cat's neck and hung limply, playing dead.

Like a scarf, Cat thought, struggling to repress a burst of demented giggles.

The matron's indignant gaze arrowed to the bunch of cherries in her lap. "Why . . . why, those are from *my hat*, aren't they? Were you attempting to *steal* those while I was napping?"

Catherine sobered immediately. "No, oh no, it was an accident. I'm so—"

"You *ruined* it, and this was my best hat, it cost two pounds and six! Give it back to me at—" But she broke off with a strangled sound, her mouth rounding into a calcified O as Dodger leaped to Catherine's lap, seized the cherries, and disappeared into the safety of the carpetbag.

The woman screamed with earsplitting force, exiting the coach in a full-rigged tumult of skirts.

Five minutes later, Catherine and the carpetbag had been unceremoniously ejected from the coach. She stood at the verge of the carriage yard, assaulted by a concurrence of strong smells: dung, horses, urine, combining queasily with scents of cooked meat and hot bread coming from the tavern.

The coachman mounted to the box, ignoring Catherine's outraged protests.

"But I paid to go all the way to London!" she cried.

"You paid for one passenger, not two. Two passengers get half the journey."

Incredulously Catherine looked from his stony expression to the carpetbag in her hand. "*This* is not a passenger!"

"We're a quarter hour behind time because of you and your rat," the coachman said, squaring his elbows and cracking the whip.

"He's not my rat, he's . . . wait, how am I to get to London?"

One of the ostlers replied implacably as the coach set out. "Next mails come tomorrow morning, miss. Maybe they'll let you and your pet ride up top."

Catherine glared at him. "I don't want to ride up top, I paid to ride *inside,* all the way to London, and I consider this a form of larceny! What am I to do until tomorrow morning?"

The ostler, a young man with a long-handled mustache, shrugged. "You might ask if there's a room available," he suggested. "Although they probably won't take kindly to guests with rats." He looked beyond her as another vehicle came into the yard. "Out of the way, miss, or you'll get thrown down by the carriage."

Infuriated, Catherine stomped to the entrance of the inn. She looked into her carpetbag, where Dodger was playing with the cherries. Was it not enough, she thought in frustration, that she'd just had to leave a life she had loved, that she'd been through an entire night of nearly ceaseless crying and was now exhausted? Why had an unkind fate also seen fit to deposit Dodger in her care? "*You,*" she fumed aloud, "are the last feather that broke the horse's back. You have plagued me for *years,* and stolen all my garters, and—"

"Pardon," came a polite voice.

153

Catherine looked up with a scowl. In the next moment she swayed, her balance momentarily off.

Her thunderstruck eyes beheld Leo, Lord Ramsay, who looked amused. He kept his hands tucked in his pockets as he approached her in a relaxed stride. "I'm sure I shouldn't ask. But why are you shouting at your luggage?"

Despite the negligence of his manner, his gaze went over her thoroughly, taking careful inventory.

The sight of him had knocked the breath from her. He was so handsome, so beloved and familiar, that Catherine was nearly overcome by the impulse to fling herself at him. She couldn't fathom why he had come after her.

How she wished he hadn't.

Fumbling to close the carpetbag, she decided that it probably wouldn't do to advertise Dodger's presence before she managed to secure a room for herself. "Why are you here, my lord?" she asked unsteadily.

A leisurely shrug. "When I awakened this morning after a mere four and a half hours of sleep, I thought it would be just the thing to hop in the carriage and go for a picturesque drive to Haslemere and visit the"—Leo paused to glance at the sign above the door—"Spread Eagle Inn. What a fortuitous name." His lips twitched at her bewildered expression, but his eyes were warm. His hand came up to her face, gently lifting her unwilling chin. "Your eyes are swollen."

"Travel dust," Catherine said with difficulty, swallowing hard at the sweetness of his touch. She wanted to push her chin harder against his hand, like a cat hungry to be stroked. Her eyes stung with the portent of tears.

This would not do. Her reaction to him was nothing short of appalling. And if they stood out in the carriage yard even a moment longer, she would lose her composure altogether.

"Did you have difficulty with the coach?" he asked.

"Yes, and there won't be another till morning. I need to arrange for a room."

He wouldn't release her from his gaze. "You could come back to Hampshire with me."

The suggestion was more devastating than Leo could have known.

"No, I can't. I'm going to London, to see my brother."

"And after that?"

"After that, I'll probably travel."

"Travel?"

"Yes, I'll . . . I'll tour the Continent. And settle in France or Italy."

"By yourself?" Leo didn't bother to hide his skepticism.

"I'll hire a companion."

"You can't hire a companion, you *are* a companion."

"I've just left the position," she shot back.

For just a moment, there was an alarming intensity in his gaze. Something predatory. Something dangerous. "I have a new position for you," he said, and a little chill went down her spine.

"No, thank you."

"You haven't heard it yet."

"I don't need to." Blindly she turned and walked into the building.

Finding the innkeeper's table, she waited resolutely until a short, stocky man came to greet her. Although his head was shiny and bald, he had a thick gray beard and muttonchop sideburns. "May I help you?" he asked, looking from Catherine to the man just behind her.

Leo spoke before she could say a word. "I'd like to arrange a room for my wife and myself."

His *wife*? Catherine twisted to give him an offended glance. "I want my own room. And I'm not—"

155

"She doesn't, really." Leo smiled at the innkeeper, the rueful, commiserating smile of one put-upon man to another. "A marital squabble. She's cross because I won't let her mother visit us."

"Ahhh . . ." The innkeeper made an ominous sound and bent to write in the registry book. "Don't give in, sir. They *never* leave when they say they will. When my mother-in-law visits, the mice throw themselves at the cat, begging to be eaten. Your name?"

"Mr. and Mrs. Hathaway."

"But—" Catherine began, nettled. She broke off as she felt the carpetbag quiver in her grasp. Dodger wanted to get out. She had to keep him hidden until they were safely upstairs. "All right," she said shortly. "Let's hurry."

Leo smiled. "Eager to make up after our quarrel, darling?"

She gave him a look that should have slayed him on the spot.

To Catherine's fidgety impatience, it took another ten minutes for the arrangements to be made, including securing lodging for Leo's driver and footman. Moreover, Leo's luggage—*two* sizable traveling bags—had to be brought in. "I thought I might not reach you until London," Leo said, having the grace to look slightly sheepish.

"Why did you arrange for only one room?" she whispered sharply.

"Because you're not safe by yourself. You need me for protection."

She glared at him. "You're the one I need protection from!"

They were shown to a tidy but sparsely furnished room, with a brass bed in need of polishing, and a faded, much-laundered quilt. Two chairs were poised by the tiny hearth, one upholstered, the other small and bare. A battered washstand occupied one corner, a small table in another. The floor was swept and the white-painted walls were vacant except for a framed work consisting of a motto embroidered on heavy perforated paper: "Time and tide wait for no man."

Mercifully there was a lack of strong odor in the room, only a slight whiff of roasted meat from the tavern below, and an ashy tang from the cold hearth.

After Leo had closed the door, Catherine set her carpetbag on the floor and opened it.

Dodger's head emerged and did a complete swivel as he surveyed the room. He leaped out and scurried beneath the bed.

"You brought Dodger with you?" Leo asked blankly.

"Not voluntarily."

"I see. Is that why you were forced off the coach?"

Glancing at him, Catherine felt her insides rearrange themselves, a warm lifting and resettling as she saw him remove his coat and cravat. Everything about the situation was improper, and yet propriety no longer seemed to matter.

She told him the story then, about the rustling in the bag, and how the ferret had stolen the cherries off the matron's hat, and by the time she got to the part about Dodger pretending to be a scarf around her neck, Leo was gasping with laughter. He looked so thoroughly tickled, so boyish in his amusement, that Catherine didn't care if it was at her expense or not. She even laughed with him, breaking into helpless giggles.

But somehow her giggling dissolved into sobs, and she felt her eyes welling even as she laughed, and she put her hands over her face to hold the giddy emotions back. Impossible. She knew she looked like a madwoman, laughing and crying all at once. This kind of emotional unhinging was her worst nightmare.

"I'm sorry," she choked, shaking her head, covering her eyes with a sleeved forearm. "Please leave. Please."

But Leo's arms went around her. He collected the quivering

bundle of her against his hard chest, and he held her firmly. She felt him kiss the hot, exposed curve of her ear. The scent of his shaving soap drifted to her nostrils, the masculine fragrance comforting and familiar. She didn't realize that she had continued to gasp out the word "sorry" until he answered, his voice low and infinitely tender. "Yes, you should be sorry . . . but not for crying. Only for leaving me without a word."

"I l-left a letter," she protested.

"That maudlin note? Surely you didn't think that would be enough to keep me from coming after you. Hush, now. I'm here, and you're safe, and I'm not letting go. I'm here." She realized that she was struggling to press closer to him, trying to fight her way deeper into his embrace.

When her crying broke into watery hiccups, she felt Leo tug the jacket of her traveling habit from her shoulders. In her exhaustion she found herself complying like an obedient child, pulling her arms from the sleeves. She didn't even protest as he took the combs and pins from her hair. Her scalp throbbed sharply as the tight coiffure was undone. Leo removed her spectacles and set them aside, and went to fetch a handkerchief from his discarded coat.

"Thank you," Catherine mumbled, mopping her sore eyes with the square of pressed cotton, wiping her nose. She stood with childlike indecision, the handkerchief balled in her fingers.

"Come here." Leo sat in the large hearthside chair and drew her down with him.

"Oh, I can't—" she began, but he hushed her and gathered her on his lap. The mounds of her skirts spilled heavily over them both. She rested her head on his shoulder, the agitated workings of her lungs gradually matching the measured rhythm of his. His hand played slowly in her hair. Once she would have shrunk away from a man's touch, no matter how innocuous. But in this room, removed from the rest of the world, it seemed neither of them were quite themselves.

"You shouldn't have followed me," she finally brought herself to say.

"The entire family wanted to come," Leo said. "It seems the Hathaways can't do without your civilizing influence. So I've been charged with bringing you back."

That nearly started her crying again. "I can't go back."

"Why not?"

"You already know. Lord Latimer must have told you about me."

"He told me a little." The backs of his fingers stroked the side of her neck. "Your grandmother was the madam, wasn't she?" His tone was quiet and matter-of-fact, as if having a grandmother who owned a house of prostitution was a perfectly ordinary circumstance.

Catherine nodded, swallowing miserably. "I went to live with my grandmother and Aunt Althea when Mother took ill. At first I didn't understand what the family business was, but after a while I realized what working for my grandmother meant. Althea had finally reached the age when she was no longer as popular among the customers. And then I turned fifteen, and it was supposed to be my turn. Althea said that I was lucky, because she'd had to start when she was twelve. I asked if I could be a teacher or a seamstress, something like that. But she and my grandmother said I'd never make enough money to repay what had been spent on me. Working for them was the only profitable thing I could do. I tried to think of somewhere to go, some way to survive by myself. But there was no position I could get without recommendations. Except for a factory job, which would have been

159

dangerous and the wages would have been too low to pay for a room anywhere. I begged my grandmother to let me go to my father, because I knew he would never have left me there, had he known of their plans. But she said—" Catherine stopped, her hands fisting in his shirt.

Leo disentangled her fingers and meshed his own with them, until their hands were caught together like the clasp of a brace-let. "What did she say, love?"

"That he already knew, and approved, and he would receive a percentage of the money I earned. I didn't want to believe it." She let out a broken sigh. "But he had to have known, didn't he?"

Leo was silent, his thumb softly rubbing into the cup of her palm. The question needed no answer.

Catherine set her jaw against a quiver of grief, and resumed. "Althea brought gentlemen to meet me one at a time, and she told me to be charming. She said that of all of them, Lord Latimer had made the highest offer." She made a face against his shirt. "He was the one I liked least of all. He kept winking and telling me there were naughty surprises in store for me."

Leo uttered a few choice words beneath his breath. At her uncertain pause, he ran his hand along her spine. "Go on."

"But Althea told me what to expect, because she thought I would fare much better if I knew. And the acts she described, the things I was supposed to . . ."

His hand went still on her back. "Were you required to put any of it in practice?"

She shook her head. "No, but it all sounded *dreadful*."

A note of sympathetic amusement warmed his voice. "Of course it did, to a fifteen-year-old girl."

Lifting her head, Catherine looked into his face. He was too handsome for his own good, and for hers as well. Although she

160

wasn't wearing her spectacles, she could see every breathtaking detail of him . . . the dark grain of shaved whiskers, the laugh lines at the outer corners of his eyes, little pale whisks against the rosewood color of his skin. And most of all the variegated blue of his eyes, light and dark, sunlight and shadow.

Leo waited patiently, holding her as if there were nothing else in the world he would have preferred doing. "How did you get away?"

"I went to my grandmother's desk one morning," Catherine said, "when the household was still asleep. I was trying to find money. I planned to run away and find lodging and a decent position somewhere. There wasn't a single shilling. But in one of the nooks in the desk, I found a letter, addressed to me. I'd never seen it before."

"From Rutledge," Leo said rather than asked.

Catherine nodded. "A brother I'd never known existed. Harry had written that if I were ever in need, I should send word to his address. I dashed off a letter to let him know the trouble I was in, and I gave it to William to deliver—"

"Who is William?"

"A little boy who worked there . . . he carried things up and down the stairs, cleaned shoes, went on errands, whatever he was told to do. I think he was the child of one of the prostitutes. A very sweet boy. He delivered the note to Harry. I hope Althea never found out. If she did, I fear for what happened to him." She shook her head and sighed. "The next day I was sent to Lord Latimer's house. But Harry came just in time." She paused reflectively. "He frightened me only a little less than Lord Latimer. Harry was extremely angry. At the time I thought it was directed at me, but now I think it was the situation."

"Guilt often takes the form of anger."

"But I never blamed Harry for what happened to me. I wasn't his responsibility."

Leo's face hardened. "Apparently you were no one's responsibility."

Catherine shrugged uneasily. "Harry didn't know what to do with me. He asked where I wanted to live, since I couldn't stay with him, and I asked if he could send me somewhere far from London. We settled on a school in Aberdeen, called Blue Maid's."

He nodded. "Some of the peerage send their more unruly daughters or by-blows there."

"How did you know about it?"

"I'm acquainted with a woman who attended Blue Maid's. A severe place, she said. Plain food and discipline."

"I loved it."

His lips twitched. "You would."

"I lived there for six years, teaching for the last two."

"Did Rutledge come to visit?"

"Only once. But we corresponded occasionally. I never went home on holiday, because the hotel wasn't really a home, and Harry didn't want to see me." She grimaced a little. "He wasn't very nice until he met Poppy."

"I'm not convinced that he's nice now," Leo said. "But as long as he treats my sister well, I'll have no quarrel with him."

"Oh, but Harry *loves* her," Catherine said earnestly. "Truly he does."

Leo's expression softened. "What makes you so certain?"

"I can see it. The way he is with her, the look in his eyes and . . . why are you smiling like that?"

"Women. You'll interpret anything as love. You see a man wearing an idiotic expression, and you assume he's been struck by Cupid's arrow when in reality he's digesting a bad turnip."

She looked at him indignantly. "Are you mocking me?"

Laughing, Leo tightened his arms around her as she tried to struggle from his lap. "I'm merely making an observation about your gender."

"I suppose you think men are superior."

"Not at all. Only simpler. A woman is a collection of diverse needs, whereas a man has only one. No, don't get up. Tell me why you left Blue Maid's."

"The headmistress asked me to."

"Really? Why? I hope you did something reprehensible and shocking."

"No, I was very well behaved."

"I'm sorry to hear that."

"But Headmistress Marks sent for me to come to her office one afternoon, and—"

"Marks?" Leo glanced at her alertly. "You took her name?"

"Yes, I admired her very much. I wanted to be like her. She was stern but kind, and nothing ever seemed to disrupt her composure. I went to her office, and she poured tea, and we talked for a long time. She said I'd done an excellent job, and I was welcome to return and continue teaching in the future. But first she wanted me to leave Aberdeen and see something of the world. And I told her that leaving Blue Maid's was the last thing I wanted to do, and she said that was why I needed to do it. She had received word from a friend at a placement agency in London that a family of . . . 'uncommon circumstances,' as she put it, was searching for a woman who could act as both governess and companion to a pair of sisters, one of whom had recently been expelled from finishing school."

"That would be Beatrix."

Catherine nodded. "The headmistress thought that I might

163

suit the Hathaways. What I never expected was how much they suited *me*. I went for an interview, and I thought the entire family was a bit mad—but in the loveliest possible way. And I've worked for them for almost three years, and I've been so happy and now—" She broke off, her face contorting.

"No, no," Leo said hastily, taking her head in his hands, "don't start that again."

Catherine was so shocked to feel his lips brush her cheeks and closed eyes that the tears instantly evaporated. When she finally brought herself to look at him again, she saw that he was wearing a faint smile. He smoothed her hair, and stared into her grief-ravaged face with a depth of concern she had never seen from him before.

It frightened her to realize how much of herself she had just given away. Now he knew everything she had tried to keep secret for so long. Her hands worked against his chest like the wings of a bird that had found itself trapped indoors.

"My lord," she said with difficulty, "why did you come after me? What do you want from me?"

"I'm surprised you have to ask," he murmured, still caressing her hair. "I want to offer for you, Cat."

Of course, she thought, bitterness welling. "To be your mistress."

His voice matched hers exactly for calmness, in a way that conveyed gentle sarcasm. "No, that would never work. First, your brother would arrange to have me murdered, or, at the very least, maimed. Second, you're far too prickly tempered to be a mistress. You're far better suited as a wife."

"Whose?" she asked with a scowl.

Leo stared directly into her narrowed eyes. "Mine, of course."

164

Chapter Eighteen

Hurt and outraged, Catherine struggled so violently that he was forced to release her.

"I've had enough of you and your tasteless, insensitive humor," she cried, leaping to her feet. "You cad, you—"

"I'm not joking, damn it!" Leo stood and reached for her, and she hopped backward, and he grabbed, and she flailed. They grappled until Catherine found herself tumbling backward onto the bed.

Leo fell over her in a controlled descent—a pounce, really. She felt him sinking into the mass of skirts, his superior weight urging her legs apart, the muscular mass of his torso pinning her down. She writhed in distress as excitement went skimming and tickling all through her. The more she wriggled, the worse it became. She subsided beneath him, while her hands kept opening and closing on nothing.

Leo stared down at her, eyes dancing with mischief . . . but there was something else in his expression, a purposefulness, that unsettled her profoundly.

"Consider it, Marks. Marrying me would solve both our problems. You would have the protection of my name. You wouldn't have to leave the family. And they couldn't nag me to get married any longer."

"I am illegitimate," she said distinctly, as if he were a foreigner trying to learn English. "You are a viscount. You can't marry a bastard."

"What about the Duke of Clarence? He had ten bastard children by that actress . . . what was her name . . ."

"Mrs. Jordan."

"Yes, that one. Their children were all illegitimate, but some of them married peers."

"You're not the Duke of Clarence."

"That's right. I'm not a blueblood any more than you are. I inherited the title purely by happenstance."

"That doesn't matter. If you married me, it would be scandalous and inappropriate, and doors would be closed to you."

"Good God, woman, I let two of my sisters marry Gypsies. Those doors have already been closed, bolted, and nailed shut."

Catherine couldn't think clearly, could scarcely hear him through the pounding in her ears, the wild clamor of her blood. Will and desire pulled at her with equal force. Turning her face away as his mouth descended, she said desperately, "The only way you could be certain of keeping Ramsay House for your family is to marry Miss Darvin."

He gave a derisive snort. "It's also the only way I could be certain of committing sororicide."

"Of what?" she asked in bewilderment.

"Sororicide. Killing one's wife."

"No, you mean to say 'uxoricide.'"

"Are you certain?"

"Yes, *uxor* is the Latin word for 'wife.'"

"Then what's 'sororicide'?"

"Killing one's sister."

"Oh, well, if I had to marry Miss Darvin, I'd probably end up doing that too." Leo grinned down at her. "The point is, I could never have this kind of conversation with her."

He was probably right. Catherine had lived with the Hathaways long enough to fall into their style of banter, slipping into the verbal detours that could start one talking about the increasing problem of the Thames River pollution, and end up debating the question of whether or not the Earl of Sandwich had actually invented sandwiches. Catherine restrained a miserable laugh as she realized that although she might have had a slight civilizing influence on the Hathaways, their influence on her had been much greater.

Leo's head lowered, and he kissed the side of her neck with a slow deliberation that made her squirm. Clearly he had lost interest in the subject of Miss Darvin. "Give in, Cat. Say you'll marry me."

"What if I couldn't give you a son?"

"There are never guarantees." Leo lifted his head and grinned. "But think of how much fun we'll have trying."

"I don't want to be responsible for the Hathaways losing Ramsay House."

A new seriousness infused his expression. "No one would hold you responsible for that. It's a house. No more and no less. There isn't a structure on earth that could last forever. But a family goes on."

The front of her bodice had gone loose. She realized that he had been unbuttoning her as they had been talking. She moved to stop him, but he had already managed to spread the front of her bodice open, revealing her corset and chemise.

"Therefore the only thing you'll be responsible for," Leo said

167

huskily, "is going to bed with me as often as I wish, and participating in all my heir-inducing efforts." As Catherine turned her face away, gasping, he bent to whisper in her ear. "I'm going to pleasure you. Fill you. Seduce you from head to toe. And you're going to love it."

"You are the most arrogant and absurd—oh, please don't do that." He was investigating her ear with the tip of his tongue, a silky-wet tickle. Paying no attention to her protests, he kissed and licked his way along the taut arch of her neck. "Don't," she moaned, but he took her panting mouth with his, and let his tongue play there as well, and the sensation and taste and smell of him made her feel drunk. Her arms groped around his neck, and she surrendered with a weak moan.

After her mouth had been teased, searched, and thoroughly ravished, Leo lifted his head and stared into her dazed eyes. "Do you want to hear the best part of my plan?" he asked thickly. "In order to make an honest woman of you, I'll have to debauch you first."

Catherine was dismayed to hear herself giggle in witless amusement. "No doubt you're good at that."

"Gifted," he assured her. "The trick is for me to find out what you like best, and then let you have only a little of it. I'll torment you until you're absolutely miserable."

"That doesn't sound at all pleasant."

"You think not? Then you'll be surprised when you beg me to do it again."

Catherine couldn't hold back another helpless giggle.

Then they were both motionless, flushed, staring at each other intently.

She heard herself whisper, "I'm afraid."

"I know, darling," Leo said gently. "But you'll have to trust me."

168

"Why?"

"Because you can."

Their gazes held. Catherine was paralyzed. What he asked was impossible. To give herself over entirely to a man, to anyone, was anathema to her very nature. Therefore, it should have been easy to refuse him.

Except that when she tried to form the word "no," she couldn't produce a sound.

Leo began to undress her, pulling the gown away in rustling armfuls. And Catherine let him. She actually helped him, loosening laces with shaking hands, lifting her hips, tugging her arms free. He unhooked her corset deftly, betraying easy familiarity with women's unmentionables. He was in no hurry, however. He was slow and deliberate as he removed the protective layers one by one.

Finally Catherine was covered in nothing more than a blush, her pale skin scored with temporary marks left by the edges of the corset and the seams of her clothes. Leo's hand descended to her midriff, fingertips moving sensitively along the faint lines like a traveler mapping unexplored territory. His expression was absorbed, tender, as his palm skimmed over her stomach . . . lower . . . softly grazing the fluff of intimate hair.

"Blond everywhere," he whispered.

"Is that . . . does that please you?" she asked bashfully, gasping as his hand ascended to her breast.

There was a hint of a smile in his voice. "Cat, everything about you is so lovely, I can hardly breathe." His fingers caressed the cool rise of her breast, toying with the tip until it was taut and rose-colored. He bent and took it in his mouth.

Her heart missed a beat as she heard a noise from downstairs, a clatter that sounded like dishes being dropped in the

169

tavern, the pitch of a raised voice. It was unimaginable that other people were going about the perfectly ordinary business of their day while she was naked in bed with Leo.

One of his hands slid beneath her hips, aligning her exactly with the hard ridge behind his trousers. She whimpered against his lips, shaken by intense pleasure, wanting to stay against him like that forever. He kissed her deeply, and down below his hand pressed her against him in a corresponding rhythm, the voluptuous nudges driving her into some new dimension of feeling. Closer, closer, lapping waves urging her forward . . . but then he was easing her away. She made an agitated sound, her body aching with unspent sensation.

Leo sat up and stripped his clothes off, revealing a powerful masculine body, efficiently lean and paved with muscle. There was hair on his chest, an intriguing dark fleece, and more of it lower down. His body was ready to couple with hers, she saw. Her stomach clenched in nervous anticipation. He returned to her, gathering her against him, length to length.

She explored him hesitantly, her fingers moving over his chest to the sleek skin of his side. Finding the small scar on his shoulder from their mishap at the ruins, Catherine pressed her lips to it. She heard his rough intake of breath. Encouraged, she inched lower on the bed and rubbed her nose and mouth through the soft mat on his chest. Everywhere their bodies touched, she felt his muscles tighten in response.

Trying to remember Althea's long-ago instructions, she reached down to the upthrust shape of his arousal. The skin was like nothing she had ever felt, thin and silky, moving easily over astonishing hardness. Timidly she leaned down to kiss the side of the shaft, her lips brushing against a strong pulse. She looked up to gauge his reaction, her gaze questioning.

170

Leo wasn't breathing at all well. A tremor shook his hand as he passed it over her hair. "You are the most adorable woman, the sweetest—" He gasped as she kissed him again, and laughed unsteadily. "No, love—it's all right. No more of that for now." Reaching down to her, he pulled her up beside him.

He was more insistent now, more authoritative, in a way that allowed her to relax completely. How strange that she could so easily relinquish all control to him, when they had been such fierce adversaries. He parted her thighs with his hand, and she felt herself turn wet even before he touched her there. He teased through the protective curls, spreading her intimately. Her head tilted back against his supportive arm, and she closed her eyes, breathing deeply as his finger slipped inside her.

Leo seemed to luxuriate in her response. His head bent to her breast, and he used his teeth gently, licking and gnawing in time to the slow thrust of his finger. It seemed her entire body aligned with that coaxing rhythm, every quiver, pulse, muscle, thought, surging together, and again, until sensation amassed into one exquisite rush of pleasure. She sobbed, riding the swell, letting it take her, letting the heat pump and swirl and ripple all through her . . . then finally she subsided into trembling weakness.

He loomed over her, panting, staring into her dazed face. Reaching up, she pulled him closer, her limbs moving easily to accommodate him. As he pressed against the entrance to her body, a sharp pain burned through her. He went deeper. Too much of him, the intrusion slow and hard and relentless. When he had gone as far as her resisting flesh could take him, he held still and tried to soothe her. His mouth slid gently over her cheeks and throat.

The intimacy of the moment, the sensation of holding him within her body, was stunning. She found herself trying to soothe

171

him as well, her hands stroking his sleek back. Murmuring his name, she slid her palms to his flanks and urged him to continue. He began to thrust cautiously. It hurt, and yet there was something assuaging in the deep, low pressure. She opened to him instinctively, pulling him closer.

She loved the sounds he made, the quiet groans and fragmented words, his roughcast breathing. It became easier to take him, her hips lifting naturally with each forward motion, slippery flesh plunging and grasping. Her knees bent, angling to cradle him. His body trembled roughly, a grunt of something that sounded like pain coming from his throat.

"Cat . . . Cat . . ." Leo withdrew from her abruptly and thrust against her stomach, and she felt heat spill in wet pulses over her skin. He held her tightly, groaning into the joint of her shoulder and neck.

They lay together, trying to catch their breath. Catherine was limp with exhaustion, her limbs heavy. Contentment had saturated and softened her, like water seeping into a dry sponge. For the moment, at least, it was impossible to worry about anything.

"It's true," she said drowsily. "You are gifted."

Leo eased to his side heavily, as if the movement had required great effort. He pressed his lips to her shoulder, and she felt the shape of his smile on her skin. "How delicious you are," he whispered. "It was like making love to an angel."

"Sans halo," she murmured, and was rewarded by his low chuckle. She touched the film of moisture on her stomach. "Why did you do it that way?"

"Withdrawing, you mean? I don't want to get you with child, if you're not ready."

"Do you want children? I mean . . . not because of the copyhold clause, but for their own sake?"

Leo considered that. "In abstraction, not especially. With you, however . . . I wouldn't mind."

"Why with me?"

Taking a handful of her hair, Leo let the pale runners sift through his fingers, playing with it. "I'm not sure. Perhaps because I can see you as a mother."

"Can you?" Catherine had never seen herself that way.

"Oh, yes. The practical kind who makes you eat your turnips, and scolds you for running with sharp objects."

"Is that how your mother was?"

He stretched, his feet reaching far past hers. "Yes. And thank God for it. My father, bless him, was a brilliant scholar one step removed from lunacy. Someone had to be sensible." Rising up on one elbow, he studied her. He used the pad of his thumb to smooth the arc of her eyebrow. "Don't move, love, I'll get a cloth for you."

Catherine waited with her knees drawn up, watching as he left the bed and went to the washstand. He took up a cloth, dampened it with water from a jug, and cleaned himself efficiently. Taking up another cloth, he moistened it liberally and brought it to her. She sensed that he intended to perform the service for her, but she reached for the cloth and said bashfully, "I'll do it."

Leo found his discarded clothing, pulled on his linens and trousers, and returned to Catherine bare-chested. "Your spectacles," he murmured, setting them carefully on her nose. His hands were strong and warm against the humid coolness of her cheeks. Seeing the shiver that went through her, he pulled the quilt up to her shoulders, and half sat on the edge of the mattress.

"Marks," he said soberly. "What just happened . . . am I to take that as a 'yes' to my proposal?"

She hesitated, and shook her head. And then she gave him a

wary but resolute glance, as if to indicate that there was nothing he could do or say to change her mind.

His hand found the shape of her hip, squeezing her through the quilt. "I promise it will get better for you, once you heal and have time to—"

"No, it's not that. I enjoyed it." She paused, blushing fiercely. "Very much. But we don't suit in any way other than in the bedroom. We argue so dreadfully."

"It won't be like that now. I'll be nice. I'll let you win every argument, even when I'm right." His lips twitched with amusement. "You're not convinced, I see. What are you afraid we'll argue about?"

Catherine looked down at the quilt, smoothing out a frayed seam. "It is fashionable among the peerage for the husband to take mistresses and the wife to take lovers. I could never accept that." As he opened his mouth to argue, she continued in a rush. "And you've never concealed your aversion to marriage. For you to change your mind so quickly . . . it's impossible to believe."

"I understand." Leo's hand covered hers in a vital grip. "You're right—I've been against the idea of marriage ever since I lost Laura. And I've invented all kinds of excuses to keep from taking such a risk again. But I can't deny any longer that you are entirely worth it. I wouldn't propose to you unless I knew without a doubt that you could satisfy all my needs, and I could satisfy yours." He slid his fingers beneath her chin and urged her to look at him. "As for fidelity—I'll have no difficulty with that." His smile turned wry. "My conscience is burdened enough with past sins—I doubt it could stand any more."

"You would become bored with me," she said anxiously.

That brought a slight smile to his lips. "Obviously you have no idea of the prodigious variety of ways a man and woman can entertain each other. I won't be bored. Neither will you." He stroked her pink cheek with a gentle finger. His gaze was steady. "If I went to another woman's bed, it would be a betrayal of two people—my wife and myself. I wouldn't do that to either of us." He paused. "Do you believe me?"

"Yes," she admitted. "I've always known you to be truthful. Annoying, but truthful."

There was a glint of amusement in his eyes. "Then give me your answer."

"Before I make any decisions, I would like to talk with Harry."

"Of course." A smile played on his lips. "He married my sister, now I want to marry his. If he objects, I'll tell him that it's a fair trade."

As he sat leaning over her, his dark brown hair falling over his brow, Cat could hardly believe that Leo Hathaway was trying to convince her to marry him. Although she was certain that he meant what he said, some promises were broken despite people's best intentions to keep them.

Reading her expression, Leo reached out and pulled her against his warm, hard chest. "I'd tell you not to be afraid," he murmured, "but that's not always possible. On the other hand . . . you've already started to trust me, Marks. There's no point in stopping now."

Chapter Nineteen

Upon learning that the private dining rooms in the tavern would be occupied for some time, Leo requested a tray to be sent up to their room, as well as a hot bath.

Catherine fell asleep beneath the quilt while waiting. She stirred and blinked as she heard the door opening, chairs being moved, the clinking of plates and flatware, the thump of a large tin washtub.

There was a warm, furry weight next to her. Dodger had crawled beneath the quilt and was snoozing beside her shoulder. As Catherine looked at him, she saw the gleam of his bright eyes and heard a tiny yawn before he resettled.

Recalling that she was wearing only Leo's discarded shirt, Catherine hid beneath the quilt and peeked over the edge as a pair of chambermaids set out the bath. Would they suspect what had occurred between her and Leo earlier? She braced herself for a sly or accusing glance, perhaps a contemptuous giggle, but it seemed the chambermaids were too busy to care. They were nothing but businesslike as they tipped two steaming pails into the washtub, and returned with another two pails full. One of the girls set out a three-legged stool piled with folded toweling.

176

The chambermaids would have left the room without incident, except that Dodger, attracted by the scent of food, emerged from beneath the quilt. He stood tall on the bed and regarded the dinner tray on the small table, his whiskers twitching. *Oh, lovely, I was getting hungry!* his expression seemed to say.

As one of the maids saw Dodger, her face contorted in terror. *"Eeeek!"* She pointed a plump, trembling finger at the ferret. "It's a rat, or a mouse, or—"

"No, it's a ferret," Leo explained, his tone reasonable and soothing. "A harmless and highly civilized creature—the favored pet of royalty, actually. Queen Elizabeth had a pet ferret, and—really, there's no need for violence—"

The chambermaid had picked up a fireplace poker and was raising it in anticipation of an attack.

"Dodger," Catherine said shortly. "Come here."

Dodger slithered up to her. Before she could push him away, he licked her on the cheek in a nuzzling ferret kiss.

One of the chambermaids looked horror-struck, while the other appeared ill.

Fighting to keep a straight face, Leo gave a half-crown to each chambermaid and ushered them from the room. When the door was closed and locked, Catherine lifted the affectionate ferret from her chest and regarded him with a scowl. "You are the most troublesome creature in the world, and not at all civilized."

"Here, Dodger." Leo set out a saucer of beef and parsnips, and the ferret streaked over to it.

While the ferret was busy devouring his meal, Leo came to Catherine and took her face in gentle hands. He lowered his mouth to hers in a brief, warm kiss. "Dinner or bath first?"

She was mortified to hear her stomach tighten with an audible *kworr*.

Leo grinned. "Dinner, it seems."

The meal consisted of beef rounds and mashed parsnips, and a bottle of strong red wine. Catherine ate ravenously, even swabbing the plate with a crust of bread.

Leo was an entertaining companion, telling amusing stories, gently winnowing out confidences, refilling her wine glass. In the light of the single candle that had been set on the table, his face was severely handsome, with thick lashes shadowing incandescent blue eyes.

It occurred to Catherine that this was the first meal she'd ever shared alone with him. Once she would have dreaded the prospect, knowing she would have to be on her guard every second. But there was no conflict in this easy conversation. How remarkable. She almost wished that one of the Hathaway sisters were somewhere nearby, so that she could share this discovery . . . *Your brother and I just spent an entire meal together without arguing!*

It had begun to rain outside, the sky darkening steadily, sprinkles thickening into a steady rush that obliterated the sounds of people and horses and the activity in the carriage yard. Even dressed in the heavy robe that Leo had given her to wear, Catherine shivered and felt gooseflesh rise all over.

"Time for your bath," Leo said, coming to pull her chair back.

Wondering if he intended to stay in the room, Catherine ventured, "Perhaps you might allow me some privacy."

"I wouldn't dream of it," he said. "You may need assistance."

"I can bathe myself. And I would prefer not to be watched."

"My interest is purely aesthetic. I'll imagine you as Rembrandt's *Hendrickje Bathina*, wading in the waters of innocence."

"Purely?" she asked doubtfully.

"Oh, I have a very pure soul. It's only my private parts that have gotten me into trouble."

Catherine couldn't help laughing. "You may stay in the room, as long as you turn your back."

"Agreed." He went to stand by the window.

Catherine glanced at the tub with keen anticipation. She didn't think she had ever looked forward to a bath so much. After securing her hair to the top of her head, she shed the robe, the shirt, and her spectacles, placed them on the bed, and glanced cautiously at Leo, who seemed to have taken a great interest in the view of the carriage yard. He had opened the window a few inches, letting rain-scented air into the room.

"Don't look," she said anxiously.

"I won't. Although you really should discard your inhibitions," he said. "They could get in the way of yielding to temptation."

She sank gingerly into the battered tub. "I would say that I've yielded quite thoroughly today." She sighed in relief as the water soothed all her intimate stings and aches.

"And I was delighted to be of assistance."

"You didn't assist," she said. "You are the temptation." She heard him chuckle.

Leo kept his distance as Catherine bathed, looking out at the rain. After she had washed and rinsed herself, she was so tired that she doubted her own ability to climb out of the bath. Rising on shaking legs, she fumbled to retrieve the folded toweling from the stool next to the tub.

As Catherine stepped out of the water, Leo came to her quickly and held up the toweling, wrapping it around her. Swathing her in a temporary cocoon, he held her for a moment. "Let me sleep with you tonight," he said against her hair, a question in his voice.

Catherine looked up at him quizzically. "What would you do if I refused? Arrange for another room?"

He shook his head. "I would worry about your safety if I were in a different room. I'll sleep on the floor."

"No, we'll share the bed." She pressed her cheek to his chest, relaxing fully in his hold. How comfortable this was, she thought in wonder. How calm and safe she felt with him. "Why wasn't it like this before?" she asked dreamily. "If you'd been the way you are now, I would never have argued with you about anything."

"I tried being nice to you, once or twice. It didn't go well."

"Did you? I never noticed." Her skin, already pink from the bath, turned a deeper shade. "I was suspicious. Mistrustful. And you . . . were everything I feared."

Leo's arms tightened at the admission. He looked down at her with a pensive gaze, as if he were untangling something in his mind, approaching a new realization. The blue eyes were warmer than she had ever seen them. "Let's make a bargain, Marks. From now on, instead of assuming the worst of each other, we'll try to assume the best. Agreed?"

Catherine nodded, transfixed by his gentleness. Somehow those few simple sentences seemed to have wrought a greater change between them than everything that had gone before.

Leo released her carefully. She went to bed while he washed awkwardly in a tub that couldn't begin to accommodate a man his size. She lay and watched him drowsily, the warmth of her body gathering between the sheets of the clean, dry bed. And in spite of all the problems that awaited her, she sank into a deep sleep.

In her dreams, she went back to the day she had turned fifteen. She had been parentless for five years, living with her grandmother and Aunt Althea. Her mother had died during that time. She had never known exactly when this event occurred, having been informed well after the fact. She had asked Althea if she might visit her ailing mother, and Althea had replied that she had already died.

Even knowing that her mother had suffered a fatal wasting disease, knowing there was no hope, the news had come as a shock. Catherine had started to weep, but Althea had grown impatient and snapped, "There's no use crying. It happened long before now, and she's been in the ground since high summer." Which had left Catherine with a bewildering sense of lateness, of off-timing, like a theatergoer who had applauded at the wrong moment. She couldn't grieve properly because she had missed the appropriate opportunity for grieving.

They had lived in a small house in Marylebone, a shabby but respectable dwelling lodged between a dental surgeon's office with a replica of a set of teeth hanging from its sign, and a sub-scription library supported by private funds. The library was owned and run by her grandmother, who had gone there every day to work.

It had been the most tantalizing place in the world, this heavily frequented building with its vast and hidden collection of books. Catherine had stared at the place from her window, imagining how lovely it would be to browse among rooms of old volumes. Undoubtedly the air had smelled like vellum and leather and book dust, a literary perfume that filled the quiet rooms. She had told Althea that she wanted to work there one day, a declaration that had earned an odd smile from her aunt, and a promise that she undoubtedly would.

However, despite the sign that clearly proclaimed its purpose as a library for the use of distinguished gentlemen, Catherine had gradually realized there was something wrong about the place. No one ever left with any books.

Whenever Catherine mentioned this incongruity, Althea and her grandmother became cross, the same reaction they had displayed when she asked if her father would ever return for her.

On Catherine's fifteenth birthday, she had been given two new dresses. One was blue and one white, with long skirts that had reached all the way to the floor, and waists that had fitted at her own natural waist, instead of childishly high. From now on, Aunt Althea had told her, she would put her hair up and behave as a woman. She was no longer a child. Catherine had absorbed this promotion with pride and anxiety, wondering what would be expected of her now that she had become a woman.

Althea had proceeded to explain, her long, lean face looking harder than usual, her gaze not quite able to meet Catherine's. The establishment next door, as suspected, was not a lending library. It was a house of prostitution, for which she had worked since the age of twelve. It was an easy enough occupation, she assured Catherine . . . let the man do as he pleased, turn your mind elsewhere, and take his money. No matter what his desires or how he used your body, there was relatively little discomfort as long as you didn't resist.

"I don't want to do that," Catherine had said, turning ashen as she realized why the advice was being given.

Althea had raised her plucked, arched brows. "What else do you think you're fit for?"

"Anything but that."

"Mutton-headed girl, do you know how much we've spent on your upkeep? Do you have any idea what a sacrifice it was to take you on? Of course not—you think it was owed to you. But

182

now it's time to repay. You're not being asked to do anything that I haven't done. Do you think you're better than me?"

"No," Catherine said, shamed tears slipping from her eyes. "But I'm not a prostitute."

"Each one of us is born for a purpose, my dear." Althea's voice was calm, even kind. "Some people are born into privilege, some are blessed with artistic talent or natural intelligence. You, unfortunately, are average in every regard . . . average intellect, average wit, and no distinguishable talent. You have inherited beauty, however, and a whore's nature. Therefore, we know what your purpose is, don't we?"

Catherine flinched. She tried to sound composed, but her voice shook. "Being average in most regards doesn't mean I have the makings of a prostitute."

"You're deceiving yourself, child. You are the product of two families of faithless women. Your mother was incapable of being constant to anyone. Men found her irresistible, and she could never resist being wanted. And as for our side . . . your great-grandmother was a procuress, and she trained her daughter in the business. Then it was my turn, and now it is yours. Of all the girls who work for us, you will be the most fortunate. You won't be hired out to any man who comes off the street. You'll be the luminary of our little business. One man at a time, for a negotiated period. You'll last much longer that way."

No matter how Catherine resisted, she had soon found herself being sold to Guy, Lord Latimer. He had been as alien to her as all men were, with his sour breath and scratchy face and crawling hands. Trying to kiss her, forcing his hands into the openings of her clothes, tearing at her like a gamekeeper plucking a dead grouse. He had been amused by her struggles, grunting in her ear about what he was going to do to her, and she had loathed him, loathed all men.

"I won't hurt you . . . if you don't fight me . . ." Latimer had said, grabbing her hands, forcing them down to his groin. "You'll like it. Your little quim knows what's what, I'll show you . . ."

"No, don't touch me, don't—"

She woke up sobbing, straining pitifully against a hard chest. "No—"

"Cat. It's me. Hush, it's me." A warm hand moved over her back.

She went still, her wet cheek pressed to a soft mat of hair. The sound of his voice was deep and familiar. "My lord?"

"Yes. It was just a nightmare. It's over. Let me hold you."

Her head was pounding. She felt shaky and ill, and ice-cold with shame. Leo cuddled her against his chest. As he felt the way she trembled, he smoothed her hair repeatedly. "What were you dreaming of?"

She shook her head with a shuddery sound.

"It had to do with Latimer, didn't it?"

After a long hesitation, she cleared her throat and replied, "Partly."

He caressed her shrinking back in soothing circles, and his lips moved to her damp cheeks. "You're afraid he'll come after you?"

She shook her head. "Something worse."

Very gently he asked, "Can't you tell me?"

Pulling away from him, Catherine curled into a ball, facing the opposite direction. "It's nothing. I'm sorry for waking you."

Leo fit himself against her spoon fashion. She quivered at the sensation of warmth applied all along her back, long hairy legs tucked up beneath hers, a muscular arm thrown across her. All

184

the textures and scents and pulses of him were wrapped around her, his breath falling on her neck. What an extraordinary creature a man was.

It was wrong to take such pleasure in this. Everything Althea had said about her was probably true. She had a whore's nature, a craving for masculine attention . . . she was indeed her mother's daughter. She had repressed and ignored that side of herself for years. But now it was being shown to her, as surely as a reflection in a looking glass. "I don't want to be like her," she whispered without thinking.

"Like who?"

"My mother."

His hand settled on her hip. "Your brother gave me the strong impression that you were definitely not like her." He paused. "In what way are you afraid of being similar?"

Catherine was silent, her breath wavering as she tried not to choke on a new surge of tears. He was undoing her with this newfound tenderness. She would have much preferred the old mocking Leo. It seemed she had no defenses against this one.

He pressed a kiss into the hollow behind her ear. "My dear girl," he whispered, "don't tell me you feel guilty for having enjoyed sexual relations?"

It unnerved her further that he had reached an accurate conclusion so quickly. "Perhaps a little," she said, her voice catching.

"Good God, I'm in bed with a puritan." Leo uncoiled her stiff body and spread her out beneath him, ignoring her protest. "Why is it wrong for a woman to enjoy it?"

"I don't think it's wrong for other women."

"Just you, then?" His voice was gently sardonic. "Why?"

"Because I'm the fourth generation of a family of prostitutes. And my aunt said I had a natural proclivity for it."

185

"Everyone does, love. It's how the world is populated."

"No, not for that. For prostitution."

He snorted derisively. "There is no such thing as a natural proclivity for selling oneself. Prostitution is forced on women by a society that allows them damned few options to support themselves. And as for you . . . I've never met a woman less equipped for it." He played with the tangled runners of her hair. "I'm afraid I don't follow your logic. It's no sin to enjoy a man's touch, nor does that have anything to do with prostitution. Anything your aunt told you was pure manipulation—for obvious reasons." His mouth lowered to her neck, pressing kisses along the taut surface. "We can't have you feeling guilty," he said. "Especially when it's so misguided."

She sniffled. "Morality isn't misguided."

"Ah. There's the problem. You have morality, guilt, and pleasure all mixed together." His hand went to her breast, cupping tenderly. The sensation shot to the pit of her stomach. "There's nothing moral about denying pleasure, and nothing wrong about wanting it." She felt him smile against her skin. "What you need is to indulge in several long nights of uncivilized lust with me. It would drive all the guilt out of you. And if that didn't work, at least I would be happy." His hand swept down her body, his thumb brushing the top edge of intimate curls. Her belly tightened beneath his palm. His fingers trailed deeper.

"What are you doing?" she asked.

"Helping you with your problem. No, don't thank me, it's no trouble at all." His smiling mouth brushed against hers, and he moved over her in the darkness. "What word do you use for this, love?"

"For what?"

"For this sweet place . . . here."

186

Her body jerked at his gentle caress. She could hardly speak. "I don't have a word for that."

"Then how do you refer to it?"

"I don't!"

He laughed quietly. "I know several words. But the French, not surprisingly, have the nicest one. *Le chat*."

"The cat?" she asked, bewildered.

"Yes, a double meaning for a feline and a woman's softest part. Puss. Pussy. The sweetest fur . . . no, don't be shy. Ask me to pet you."

The words stole her breath away. "My lord," she protested faintly.

"Ask and I'll do it," he prompted, his fingers withdrawing to play in the sensitive hollow behind her knee.

She swallowed back a moan.

"Ask," came his coaxing whisper.

"Please."

Leo kissed her thigh, his mouth soft and hot, his bristle an exciting scrape against the tender skin. "Please what?"

Wicked man. She squirmed and covered her face with her hands, even though they were in complete darkness. Her voice was muffled by the screen of her fingers. "Please pet me there."

His touch came so lightly she could scarcely feel it at first, fingertips stirring, teasing. "Like this?"

"Yes, oh yes . . ." Her hips lifted, inviting more. He fingered the folds of her sex, massaging delicately, tracing the softness within. The skillful caresses brought her body to trembling readiness.

"What else should I do?" Leo whispered, moving lower in the darkness. She felt his breath on her, heat against moisture, a soft intermittent blowing. Her hips arched and strained without volition.

"Make love to me."

He sounded gently regretful. "No, you're too sore."

"*Leo,*" she whimpered.

"Shall I kiss you instead? Here?" His fingertip swirled.

Catherine's eyes widened in the darkness. Stunned and acutely aroused by the suggestion, she licked her dry lips. "No. I don't know." She writhed as she felt him breathe against her, his fingers gently holding her apart. "Yes."

"Ask me nicely."

"Ask you to . . . Oh, I can't."

The teasing fingers left her. "Shall we go to sleep, then?"

She caught his head in her hands. "No."

He was inexorable. "You know how to ask."

She couldn't. The shamed syllables stuck in her throat, and she could only moan in frustration.

And Leo, the monstrous cad, smothered a chuckle against her thigh.

"I'm so glad you find this amusing," she said furiously.

"I do," he assured her, his voice thick with laughter. "Oh, Marks, we have so far to go with you."

"Don't bother," she snapped, trying to move away, but he pinned her legs in place, holding her easily.

"There's no need to be stubborn," he coaxed. "Go on, say it. For me."

A long silence passed. She swallowed and made herself say, "Kiss me."

"Where?"

"Down there," she managed, her voice shaking. "On my pussy. Please."

Leo fairly purred in approval. "What a naughty girl you are." His head lowered, and he nuzzled into the damp softness, and

188

she felt his mouth cover the most sensitive part of her in a wet, open kiss, and the world caught fire.

"Is that what you wanted?" she heard him ask.

"More, more," she cried, gasping.

His tongue traced her in fluid, savoring strokes. Her body drew taut as he began to tug and flick, and the voluptuous expanding pleasure went all through her. She was suffused in wet sensation, each slide of his tongue opening her to greater pleasure. His hands cupped beneath her, making a vessel of her hips, tilting her to meet his mouth. She convulsed in raw shudders, crying out, her nerves dancing with exquisite heat. His mouth lingered softly, as if he were reluctant to stop. For a scalding moment she felt his tongue enter her, teasing out a last few quivers.

She was soon chilled as rain-scented air from the partially open window swept over her skin. She thought Leo would satisfy his own needs then, and she moved toward him in exhausted confusion. But he settled her in the crook of his arm and pulled the quilts over them both. She was replete and enervated, unable to stay awake.

"Sleep," she heard him whisper. "And if you have any more nightmares . . . I'll kiss them all away."

Chapter Twenty

The rainy night had yielded to a damp green morning. Leo
awakened to the sounds of the carriage yard coming alive with
the whicker and jangling and stomping of horses. A muffled
clatter of footsteps advanced along the hallways as people left
their rooms and went to the tavern for food.

Leo's favorite part of a romantic rendezvous had always been
the moments of anticipation right before lovemaking. His least
favorite part had been the morning after, when his first waking
thought was how quickly he could leave without causing offense.

This morning, however, was different from any other. He had
opened his eyes to discover that he was in bed with Catherine
Marks, and there was nowhere else in the world he wanted to
be. She was still sleeping deeply, on her side with her hand palm
up. Her fingers were curled like the edges of an orchid. She was
beautiful in the morning, tumbled and relaxed and sleep-flushed.

His fascinated gaze traveled over her. He had never confided so
much in any woman, but he knew that his secrets were safe with
her. And hers with him. They were well matched. No matter what
happened now, their days of battling were over. They knew too
much about each other.

Unfortunately, the question of their betrothal was not at all settled. Leo knew that Cat was not nearly as convinced of the rightness of their match as he was. Furthermore, Harry Rutledge was going to have an opinion about it, and so far Leo had rarely liked his opinions. It was even possible that Harry might encourage Cat in her idea of traveling the Continent.

A frown tugged at Leo's brow as he pondered how she had gone through life virtually unprotected until now. How could a woman so deserving of affection have received so little? He wanted to make up for everything she had missed. He wanted to give her whatever she had been deprived of. The trick would be convincing her to let him.

Catherine's face was peaceful, her lips slightly parted. Curled among the white bed linens, a glimpse of her pink shoulder visible, that golden hair streaming everywhere, she looked like a confection placed amid swirls of whipped cream.

There was a disturbance at the foot of the bed as Dodger hoisted himself up to the corner of the mattress and crept along Catherine's side. She stirred and yawned, and fumbled to pet him. The ferret curled by her hip and closed his eyes.

Catherine awakened slowly, her body lengthening in a trembling stretch. Her lashes lifted. She looked at Leo in bewilderment, clearly wondering why he should be there with her. It was a stare of disarming innocence, those lovely sea-gray eyes contemplating him while her mind collected itself. Hesitantly she reached a cool hand to his cheek, investigating the bristle that had grown during the night. Her voice was low and wondering. "You're as scratchy as Beatrix's hedgehog."

Leo kissed her palm.

Catherine nestled against him cautiously. Her breath stirred the hair on his chest as she asked, "Are we going to London today?"

"Yes."

She was quiet for a moment. "Do you still want to marry me?" she asked abruptly.

He kept her hand in his. "I'm going to insist on it."

Her face was angled so that he couldn't see it. "But . . . I'm not like Laura."

Leo was somewhat startled by the comment. "No," he said frankly. Laura had been the product of a loving family, an idyllic life in a small village. She had known nothing like the fear and pain that had shaped Catherine's childhood. "You resemble Laura no more than I resemble the boy I was then," he continued. "How is that relevant?"

"Perhaps you would be better off with someone like her. Someone you—" She stopped herself.

Leo turned and braced himself on an elbow, looking down into myopic blue-gray eyes. "Someone I love?" he finished for her, and watched her frown and chew her lower lip uncertainly. He wanted to gently bite and suck that perfect little mouth as if it were a fresh plum. Instead he traced the edge of her lower lip with a gentle fingertip. "I've told you before, I love like a madman," he said. "Immoderate, jealous, possessive . . . I'm absolutely intolerable."

He let the backs of his fingers glide over her chin and along the front of her throat, where he felt the swift tattoo of her heartbeat and the flutter of her swallow. No stranger to the signs of feminine arousal, he slid his palm over the front of her body, skimming the hard bud of her nipple, the curve of her side. "If I loved you, Cat, I would have you for breakfast, lunch, and dinner. You'd never have any peace."

"I would set limits. And make you heed them." She drew a sharp breath as he pulled the sheet away from her. "You want a firm hand, that's all."

192

Annoyed by the disturbance, Dodger slid off the bed indignantly and went to hop into Catherine's carpetbag.

Leo nuzzled the warm curve of her breast and stroked the tip with his tongue. "Perhaps you're right," he said, catching her hand, drawing it down to his hard flesh.

"I . . . I didn't mean . . ."

"Yes, I know. But I'm a terribly literal-minded person." He showed her how to grip and stroke him, guiding her in the ways he liked to be touched. They lay together in the warm bed, both of them breathing fast as she explored him with delicate pale fingers. How many times Leo had fantasized about this moment, the prim and prudish Marks naked in bed with him. It was glorious.

Her hand tightened on his stiff length, and the delicious pressure nearly sent him over the edge.

"*God* . . . no, no, wait . . ." He pried her hand away with a gasping laugh.

"Did I do something wrong?" Catherine asked anxiously.

"Not at all, love. But one rather hopes to last more than five minutes, especially before the lady is satisfied." He reached for her breasts, kneading gently. "How beautiful you are. Bring yourself higher and let me kiss your breast." As she hesitated, he closed his thumb and forefinger over her nipple in a playful pinch.

She jerked in surprise.

"Too hard?" Leo asked contritely, his gaze intent on her face. "Then do as I asked, and I'll soothe it." He didn't miss her quick double-blink, or the altered rhythm of her breathing. Reaching out, he drew his hands slowly over the slender curves of her body, learning more about her by the second.

"You *are* intolerable," she told him unevenly. But she obeyed the encouraging pressure of his palms, and climbed slowly over him. She was light and supple, her skin like silk, the blond thatch of curls brushing crisply against his stomach.

The peak of her breast was already tightly contracted as Leo took it into his mouth. He played with her, dragging the flat of his tongue across the gathered point, relishing the helpless sounds that climbed in her throat.

"Kiss me," he said, slipping a hand behind her neck, pulling her mouth to his. "And rest your hips on mine."

"Stop giving orders," she protested breathlessly.

On impulse, Leo decided to provoke her. He let an arrogant smile touch his lips. "Here in bed, I'm the master. I'll give orders, and you'll follow them without question." He paused deliberately, lifting his brows. "Understood?"

Catherine stiffened. Leo had never enjoyed anything so much as the sight of her struggling between outrage and arousal. He felt the heat rise in her, the excited thrum of her pulse. She took an agitated breath, while gooseflesh rose on her arms. And then her body seemed to lose all its tension, her limbs loosening. "Yes," she finally whispered, not quite able to meet his gaze.

Leo's own heartbeat escalated. "Good girl," he said thickly. "Now spread your thighs so I can feel you against me."

Gradually the angle of her legs widened.

She looked dazed, a little lost, her gaze turning inward as if to contemplate the puzzle of her own reactions to him. Her eyes glittered, an involuntary welling of pleasure and confusion, and the sight sent a tide of lust through him. He wanted to fulfill her beyond imagining, discover and satisfy every need.

"Put your hand beneath your breast," he said, "and bring it to my mouth."

She leaned over him to obey, trembling. And then he was the one who was lost, fiercely absorbed in the sweet softness of her.

194

He lost awareness of everything but instinct, the primitive intent to claim, conquer, possess.

He made her kneel over him, and he followed the intoxicating salt-scented moisture to the tender entrance of her body. Delving with his tongue, he traced and licked until he felt the long, fine muscles of her thighs tightening rhythmically.

With a hoarse murmur, Leo eased her away and helped her to straddle his hips. He fit himself against the soft slit and clasped her waist to steady her. She quivered as she understood what he wanted.

"Slowly," he murmured as she eased onto him. "All the way down." He barely managed to stifle an agonized groan as he felt her clenching around him, her swollen flesh working to pull him inside. Nothing had ever felt so good. "Oh, sweet Jesus . . . take it all."

"I can't." She writhed and went still, looking disgruntled.

It was inconceivable that Leo should have found any amusement in the moment, when his body was tortured with desire. But she was so adorably awkward astride him. Somehow managing to repress a laugh, Leo put his shaking hands on her, arranging and stroking. "You can," he said huskily. "Put your hands on my shoulders, and lean your sweet little body forward."

"It's too much."

"It's not."

"It *is*."

"I'm the experienced one. You're the novice, remember?"

"That doesn't change the fact that you're too . . . *oh*."

Somewhere in the midst of their debate, he had pressed upward the last crucial distance, and their bodies slid together fully.

"Oh," she said again, her eyes half closing, new color sweeping over her.

Leo felt an explosive climax rolling up to him, requiring only a hint of stimulation to reach irresistible momentum. Catherine's body tightened around him, a voluptuously contained rhythm that threatened to drive him mad. She moved tentatively, the tender friction causing them both to shudder.

"Cat, wait," he whispered through dry lips.

"I can't, I can't . . ." She moved again, and he arched as if on a torture rack.

"Be still."

"I'm trying." But she had begun to rock against him instinctively, and he groaned and took up the rhythm, watching her lips parting with delighted gasps, and as he felt the spasms overtake her, the sensations rushed too powerfully for him to withstand.

With a herculean effort, Leo withdrew and spilled his pleasure on the sheets, while his breath hissed through his clenched teeth. Every muscle screamed in protest at being deprived of the lush warmth that had enclosed him. Panting, blinking against a shower of sparks, Leo felt Catherine curl up against him.

One of her hands came to the center of his chest, pressing over his pounding heart. She pressed her lips to his shoulder. "I didn't want you to stop," she whispered.

"Neither did I." He wrapped his arms around her, and smiled ruefully against her hair. "But that's the problem with coitus interruptus. One always has to exit at the station before one's final destination."

Chapter Twenty-one

Leo proposed twice more to Catherine on the way to London. She refused both times, determined to proceed in a sensible manner and discuss the situation with her brother first. When Leo pointed out that running harum-scarum from Ramsay House in the middle of the night could hardly be characterized as sensible behavior, she allowed that perhaps she shouldn't have acted so impetuously.

"As much as I dislike to admit it," she told Leo as their carriage rolled along the post road, "I haven't been in my right mind since the ball. It was a shock to see Lord Latimer so unexpectedly. And when he put his hands on me, I felt myself shrink down to a frightened child again, and all I could think of was getting away." She paused reflectively. "But I found comfort in knowing I had Harry to run to."

"You also had me," Leo said quietly.

She stared at him in wonder. "I didn't know that."

His gaze held hers. "You know it now."

Let me be your big brother, Harry had told Catherine at their last meeting in Hampshire, making it clear that he wanted to attempt the kind of familial relationship they had never been capable of before. With no small amount of unease, Catherine reflected that she was about to test his claim far sooner than either of them could have expected. And they were still practically strangers.

But Harry had altered greatly during the short time of his marriage to Poppy. He was far kinder and warmer now, and certainly willing to think of Catherine as something more than an inconvenient half sister who didn't belong anywhere.

Upon arriving at the Rutledge Hotel, Leo and Catherine were shown immediately to the sumptuous private apartments that Harry and Poppy shared.

Of all the Hathaways, Poppy was the one Catherine had always felt the most comfortable with. Poppy was a warm and talkative young woman who loved order and routine. Hers was an essentially sunny and accepting nature, providing a necessary balance to Harry's driven intensity.

"Catherine," she exclaimed, embracing her, then standing back to view her with concern. "Why are you here? Is something wrong? Is everyone well?"

"Your family is quite well," Catherine said hastily. "But there was . . . a situation. I had to leave." Her throat became very tight.

Poppy looked at Leo with a frown. "Did you do something?"

"Why do you ask that?"

"Because if there is trouble of any kind, you're usually involved."

"True. But this time I'm not the problem, I'm the solution."

Harry approached them, his green eyes narrowed. "If you're the solution, Ramsay, I'm terrified to hear the problem." He gave Cat an alert glance, and astonished her by bringing her against him in a protective embrace. "What is it, Cat?" he asked near her ear. "What's happened?"

198

"Oh, Harry," she faltered, "Lord Latimer came to the ball at Ramsay House."

He understood everything from that one sentence. "I'll take care of it," he said without hesitation. "I'll take care of you."

Catherine closed her eyes and let out a slow sigh. "Harry, I don't know what to do."

"You were right to come to me. We'll manage it together." Harry raised his head and glanced at Leo. "Presumably Cat has told you about Latimer."

Leo looked grim. "Believe me, had I known anything about the situation before, he wouldn't have gotten anywhere near her."

Harry kept Catherine in the crook of his arm as he turned to face Leo fully. "Why was the bastard invited to Ramsay House in the first place?"

"His family was invited as a courtesy befitting their social position in Hampshire. He came in their stead. After he tried to force himself on Marks, I booted him from the premises. He won't be returning."

Harry's eyes gleamed dangerously. "I'll put a word in the right ear. By tomorrow evening he'll wish he were dead."

Catherine felt a nervous pang in her stomach. Harry was a man of extensive influence. As well as his hotel dealings, he had access to a great quantity of highly confidential and valuable information. What Harry kept in his head could probably have been used to start wars, fell kingdoms, destroy families, and dismantle the British financial system.

"No, Harry," Poppy said. "If you're planning to have Lord Latimer butchered or maimed, you're going to have to think of something else."

"I like Harry's plan," Leo said.

"It's not up for debate," Poppy informed him. "Come, let's sit and discuss reasonable alternatives." She looked at Catherine. "You must be famished after traveling so far. I'll ring for tea and sandwiches."

"None for me, thank you," Catherine said. "I'm not—"

"Yes, she wants sandwiches," Leo interrupted. "She had only bread and tea for breakfast."

"I'm not hungry," Catherine protested. He answered her annoyed glance with an implacable one.

It was a new experience, having someone care about the mundane details of her welfare, having him notice what she'd eaten for breakfast. She examined the feeling, tested it, and found it strangely alluring, even as she resisted the idea of being told what to do. The small interaction was similar to a thousand instances she had seen between Cam and Amelia, or Merripen and Win, the way they occasionally fussed over each other. Cared for each other.

After tea was sent for, Poppy returned to the private parlor. Sitting beside Catherine on the velvet-covered settee, Poppy said, "Tell us what happened, dear. Did Lord Latimer approach you early in the evening?"

"No, the ball had been under way for some time . . ."

Catherine relayed the events of the evening in a matter-of-fact manner, her hands clenched in her lap. "The problem is," she said, "that no matter how we try to keep Lord Latimer quiet about the past, he will make it public. A scandal is coming, and nothing will stop it. The best way to throw water on the flames is for me to disappear again."

"A new name, a new identity?" Harry asked, and shook his head. "You can't run forever, Cat. We'll stand and confront it this time—together—as we should have done years ago." He pinched the bridge of his nose, turning various options over in his mind. "I'll start by acknowledging you publicly as my sister."

Catherine felt herself turn ashen. People would be ravenously curious when they learned that the mysterious Harry Rutledge had a long-lost sister. She was fairly certain she wouldn't be able to bear the scrutiny and the questions.

"People would recognize me as the Hathaways' governess," she said in a suffocated voice. "They would ask why the sister of a wealthy hotelier would have accepted such a position."

"They'll make of it what they will," Harry said.

"It won't reflect well on you."

Leo spoke dryly. "With your brother's associations, Marks, he's accustomed to unflattering rumors."

The familiar way he had addressed her caused Harry's eyes to narrow. "I find it interesting," he said to Catherine, "that you came to London with Ramsay as your traveling companion. When was it decided that the two of you would depart together? And what hour did you leave last night, to reach London by noon?"

All the color that had left Catherine's face earlier now came rushing back at a surplus. "I . . . he . . ." She glanced at Leo, who had adopted an expression of innocent interest, as if he too wanted to hear her explanation. "I left by myself yesterday morning," she managed to say, dragging her gaze back to Harry.

Harry leaned forward, a scowl gathering on his face. "*Yesterday* morning? Where did you spend the night?"

She lifted her chin and tried to sound matter-of-fact. "A coaching inn."

"Do you have any idea how dangerous those places are for a woman alone? Have you taken leave of your senses? When I think of what could have happened to you—"

"She wasn't alone," Leo said.

Harry stared at him incredulously.

It was one of those silences that was far more eloquent than words. One could almost see Harry's brain working like the elaborate mechanisms he liked to construct in his spare time. One could also see the moment at which he reached an accurate and highly unwelcome conclusion.

Harry spoke to Leo in a tone that chilled Catherine to the bone. "Even you wouldn't take advantage of a frightened and vulnerable woman who had just suffered an upheaval."

"You've never given a damn about her," Leo replied. "Why should you start now?"

Harry rose to his feet, his fists clenched.

"Oh, dear," Poppy murmured. "Harry—"

"Did you share a room with her?" Harry demanded of Leo. "A bed?"

"That's none of your bloody business, is it?"

"It is when it's my sister and you were supposed to be protecting her, not molesting her!"

"Harry," Catherine broke in, "he didn't—"

"I'm rarely disposed to listen to a lecture on morality," Leo said to Harry, "when it's given by someone who knows even less about it than I do."

"Poppy," Harry said, his gaze fastened on Leo as if he were contemplating murder. "You and Cat need to leave the room."

"Why must I leave when I'm the subject of discussion?" Catherine demanded. "I'm not a child."

"Come, Catherine," Poppy said quietly, heading to the door. "Let them bluster and brawl in their manly fashion. You and I will go somewhere to discuss your future sensibly."

This struck Catherine as an excellent idea. She followed Poppy from the room, while Harry and Leo continued to glare at each other.

"I'm going to marry her," Leo said.

Harry's face went blank. "You despise each other."

"We've come to an understanding."

"Has she accepted you?"

"Not yet. She wants to discuss it with you first."

"Thank God. Because I'll tell her that it's the worst idea I've ever heard."

Leo arched a brow. "You doubt I could protect her?"

"I doubt you could keep from murdering each other! I doubt she could ever be happy in such volatile circumstances. I doubt . . . no, I won't bother listing all my concerns, it would take too bloody long." Harry's eyes were ice-cold. "The answer is no, Ramsay. I'll do what is necessary to take care of Cat. You can return to Hampshire."

"I'm afraid it won't be that easy to get rid of me," Leo said. "Perhaps you didn't notice that I haven't asked for your permission. There is no choice. Certain things have happened that can't be undone. Do you understand?"

He saw from Harry's expression that only a few fragile constraints stood between him and certain death.

"You seduced her deliberately," Harry managed to say.

"Would you be happier if I claimed it was an accident?"

"The only thing that would make me happy is to weight you with rocks and toss you into the Thames."

"I understand. I even sympathize. I can't imagine what it would be like to face a man who's compromised your sister, how difficult it would be to keep from murdering him on the spot. Oh, but wait . . ." Leo tapped a forefinger thoughtfully on

203

his chin. "I *can* imagine. Because I went through it *two bloody months ago*."

Harry's eyes narrowed. "That wasn't the same. Your sister was still a virgin when I married her."

Leo gave him an unrepentant glance. "When I compromise a woman, I do it properly."

"That does it," Harry muttered, leaping for his throat.

They crashed to the floor, rolling and grappling. Although Harry managed to slam Leo's head on the floor, the thick carpet absorbed most of the impact. Harry sought a chokehold, but Leo ducked his chin and wrenched free. They rolled twice, exchanging blows, aiming for the throat, the kidneys, the solar plexus, in the kind of fight that usually took place in East End slum alleys.

"You won't win this one, Rutledge," Leo panted as they broke apart and lurched to their feet. "I'm not one of your prick-me-dainty fencing partners." He dodged a hard right and took a jab of his own. "I've fought my way in and out of every gaming hell and tavern in London—" He faked a jab with his left and followed with a swift right hook, making a satisfying impact with Harry's jaw. "And aside from all that, I live with Merripen, who has a left uppercut like a kick from a mule—"

"Do you *ever* stop talking?" Harry threw a counterpunch and stepped back before Leo could retaliate.

"It's called communication. You ought to try it sometime." Exasperated, Leo dropped his guard and stood there undefended. "Especially with your sister. Have you ever bothered to listen to her? Damn it, man, she came to London hoping for some kind of brotherly counsel or consolation, and the first thing you do is send her from the room."

Harry's fists lowered. He pinned Leo with a damning glare, but when he spoke, his voice was heavy with self-condemnation.

"I've failed her for years. Do you think I'm unaware of all that I could have done for her but didn't? I'll do anything possible to atone. But damn you, Ramsay . . . the last thing she needed in this situation was for her innocence to be taken when she couldn't defend herself."

"It's exactly what she needed."

Harry shook his head in disbelief. "Damn you." He scrubbed a hand through his black hair, and gave a peculiar strangled laugh. "I *hate* arguing with a Hathaway. You all say something lunatic as if it's perfectly logical. Is it too early for brandy?"

"Not at all. I'm feeling far too sober for this conversation."

Harry went to a sideboard and pulled out two glasses. "While I pour," he said, "you can explain why being deflowered by you was so bloody beneficial to my sister."

Shrugging out of his coat, Leo draped it over the back of his chair and sat. "Marks has been isolated and alone for much too long—"

"She hasn't been alone, she's been living with the Hathaways."

"Even so, she's stayed at the edges of the family with her nose pressed against the window, like some Dickensian orphan. A false name, drab clothes, dyed hair . . . she's concealed her identity for so long that she hardly knows who she is. But the real Catherine emerges when she's with me. We've gotten beneath each other's guards. We speak the same language, if you take my meaning." Leo paused, staring into the glowing swirl of his brandy. "Marks is a contradictory woman, and yet the more I know her, the more the contradictions make sense. She's spent too long in the shadows. No matter how she tries to convince herself otherwise, she wants to belong somewhere, with someone. And yes, she wants a man in her bed. Me in particular." Taking the brandy that Harry handed to him, Leo tossed back a swallow. "She'll thrive with me.

205

Not because I'm a stellar example of virtuous manhood, nor have I ever claimed to be. But I'm right for her. I'm not cowed by her sharp tongue, and she can't outmaneuver me. And she knows it."

Harry sat nearby and drank his own brandy. He watched Leo pensively, on one level trying to assess his sincerity, on another judging his veracity. "What would you get from this arrangement?" he asked quietly. "As I understand, you need to marry and sire a child rather soon. If Cat doesn't succeeded in bearing a son, the Hathaways will lose Ramsay House."

"We've survived many things far worse than losing a bloody house. I'll marry Marks and take the risk."

"Perhaps you're testing the waters," Harry said, his face expressionless. "Trying to determine if she's fertile before you marry her."

Instantly offended, Leo forced himself to remember that he was dealing with the legitimate concern of a brother for a sister. "I don't give a damn if she's fertile or not," he said evenly. "If it will settle your concerns, we'll wait however long it will take to make the copyhold clause irrelevant. I want her regardless."

"And what about what Cat wants?"

"That's up to her. As for dealing with Latimer—I've already made him aware that I have leverage against him. I'll use it if he starts to make trouble. But the best protection I can offer her is my name." Finishing his brandy, Leo set the empty snifter aside. "What do you know of this grandmother and aunt?"

"The old crone died not long ago. The aunt, Althea Hutchins, runs the place now. I sent my assistant Valentine to take inventory of the situation, and he returned looking somewhat sickened. Apparently in a bid to revive business, Mrs. Hutchins turned it into a whipping brothel, where any number of depravities are catered to. The unfortunate women who work there are usually too well worn to be employed at other brothels." Harry finished his brandy. "It seems the aunt is ailing, most likely from some untreated bawdy-house disease."

Leo looked at him alertly. "Have you told Marks?"

"No, she's never asked. I don't believe she wants to know."

"She's afraid," Leo said quietly.

"Of what?"

"Of what nearly became of her. Of things Althea said to her."

"Such as?"

Leo shook his head. "She told me in confidence." He smiled faintly at Harry's obvious annoyance. "You've known her for years, Rutledge—what in God's name did you talk about when you were together? Taxes? The weather?" He stood and picked up his coat. "If you'll excuse me, I'm going to arrange for a room."

Harry frowned. "Here?"

"Yes, where else?"

"What about the terrace you usually lease?"

"Closed away for the summer. But even if it weren't, I'd still stay here." Leo smiled slightly. "Consider it yet another chance to experience the joys of a close family."

"It was a far greater joy when the family stayed in bloody Hampshire," Harry said as Leo left the apartment.

Chapter Twenty-two

"Harry was right about something," Poppy told Catherine as they walked through the gardens at the back of the hotel.

In contrast to the modern preference for the romantic appearance in gardening—unstructured, with beds of blossoms that appeared to have sprung up spontaneously, and paths laid out in meandering curves—the Rutledge gardens were orderly and grand. Disciplined hedges formed walls that guided one through a careful arrangement of fountains, statuary, parterres, and elaborate flower beds.

"It is definitely time," Poppy continued, "for Harry to introduce you to people as his sister. And for you to be known by your real name. What is it, by the way?"

"Catherine Wigens."

Poppy considered that. "I'm sure it's only because I've always known you as Miss Marks . . . but I like Marks better."

"So do I. Catherine Wigens was a frightened girl in difficult circumstances. I've been much happier as Catherine Marks."

"Happier?" Poppy asked gently. "Or merely less frightened?"

Catherine smiled. "I've learned quite a lot about happiness over the past few years. I found peace at school, although I was

208

too quiet and private to make friends there. It wasn't until I came to work for the Hathaways that I saw the day-to-day interactions of people who love each other. And then in the past year, I've finally experienced moments of true joy. The feeling that at least for the moment, everything is as it should be, and there's nothing else one could ask for."

Poppy sent her a smiling glance. "Moments such as . . . ?"

They entered the rose garden, filled with a profusion of blossoms, the air heavy with sun-warmed perfume.

"Evenings in the parlor, when the family was together and Win was reading. Going on walks with Beatrix. Or that rainy day in Hampshire when we all had a picnic on the veranda. Or—" She broke off, shaken by the realization of what she had been about to say.

"Or?" Poppy prompted, pausing to examine a large and resplendent rose, inhaling its scent. Her astute gaze darted to Catherine's face.

It was difficult to express her most personal thoughts, but Catherine forced herself to admit the uncomfortable truth. "After Lord Ramsay hurt his shoulder at the old manor ruins . . . he was in bed with fever the next day . . . and I sat with him for hours. We talked while I did the mending, and I read Balzac to him."

Poppy smiled. "Leo must have loved that. He adores French literature."

"He told me about the time he spent in France. He said the French have a marvelous way of uncomplicating things."

"Yes, he needed that very much. When Leo went to France with Win, he was a wreck of a man. You wouldn't have known him. We didn't know whom to fear for more, Win with her weak lungs, or Leo, who was bent on destroying himself."

"But they came back well," Catherine said.

"Yes, both of them were finally well. But different."

"Because of France?"

"That, and also the struggles they'd been through. Win told me that one isn't improved by being at the top of the mountain, one is improved by the climb."

Catherine smiled as she thought of Win, whose patient fortitude had carried her through years of illness. "That sounds exactly like her," she said. "Perceptive. And strong."

"Leo is like that too," Poppy said. "It's only that he's far more irreverent."

"And cynical," Catherine said.

"Yes, cynical . . . but also playful. Perhaps it's an odd combination of qualities, but there's my brother."

Catherine's smile lingered. There were so many images of Leo in her mind . . . patiently rescuing a hedgehog that had fallen into a fencepost hole . . . working on a set of plans for a new tenant house, his face severe with concentration . . . lying wounded on his bed, his eyes glazed with pain as he murmured, *I'm too much for you to manage.*

No, she had replied, *you're not.*

"Catherine," Poppy said hesitantly, "the fact that Leo came to London with you . . . I wonder if . . . that is, I hope . . . is there a betrothal in the making?"

"He has offered for me," Catherine admitted, "but I—"

"Has he?" Poppy astonished her with an enthusiastic embrace. "Oh, it's too good to be true! Please say you'll accept him."

"I'm afraid the situation isn't that simple," Catherine said ruefully, drawing back. "There is much to consider, Poppy."

Poppy's exuberance faded quickly, an anxious pucker appearing between her brows. "You don't love him? But in time you will, I'm sure of it. There is so much about him worth—"

"It's not a question of love," Catherine said with a slight grimace.

"Marriage isn't a question of love?"

"No, it is, of course, but I meant to say that love cannot overcome certain difficulties."

"Then you do love him?" Poppy asked hopefully.

Catherine turned deep red. "There are many qualities I esteem in Lord Ramsay."

"And he makes you happy, you said so."

"Well, on that one day, I'll admit—"

" 'A moment of true joy,' was how you put it."

"Heavens, Poppy, I feel as if I'm being interrogated."

Poppy grinned. "I'm sorry, it's just that I want this match so very much. For Leo's sake, and yours, and for the family."

Harry's dry voice came from behind them. "It appears we're at cross-purposes, my love." The women turned as he approached them. Harry regarded his wife warmly, but there was an air of preoccupation about him. "The tea and sandwiches are waiting," he said. "And the brawl is over. Shall we go back to the apartments?"

"Who won the brawl?" Poppy asked impishly.

That earned one of Harry's rare grins. "A conversation broke out in the middle of the fight. Which was undoubtedly a good thing, as it turned out that neither of us knows how to fight like a gentleman."

"You fence," Poppy pointed out. "That's a very gentlemanly way to fight."

"Fencing isn't really fighting. It's more like chess with the risk of puncture wounds."

"Well, I'm glad you didn't hurt each other," Poppy said cheerfully, "since there's a distinct possibility that you may soon be brothers-in-law."

"We're already brothers-in-law."

"Brothers-in-law squared, then." Poppy slipped her arm through his.

Harry glanced at Catherine as they began to walk. "You haven't decided yet, have you? About marrying Ramsay?"

"Certainly not," she said quietly, keeping pace with them. "My head's in a whirl. I need time to think."

"Harry," Poppy said, "when you say that we're at cross-purposes, I hope you don't mean that you're against the idea of Leo and Catherine marrying."

"For the time being," he said, seeming to choose his words carefully, "I believe caution is in order."

"But don't you want Catherine to become part of my family?" Poppy asked, bewildered. "She would have the protection of the Hathaways, and she would be close to your influence."

"Yes, I would like that very much. Except that it would necessitate Cat's marrying Ramsay, and I'm not at all convinced that would be best for her."

"I thought you liked Leo," Poppy protested.

"I do. If there's a man in London with more charm or wit, I have yet to meet him."

"Then how could you have any objections?"

"Because his past doesn't recommend itself as that of a reliable husband. Cat has been betrayed many times in her life." His tone was sober and grim. He looked at Catherine. "And I'm one of the people who failed you. I don't want you to suffer that way again."

"Harry," Catherine said earnestly, "you're far too severe on yourself."

"Now isn't the time to pour sweetener on unpleasant truths," he returned. "If I could change the past, I would go back and do so without hesitation. But all I can do is try to make amends, and do better in the future. And I would say the same of Ramsay."

"Everyone deserves a second chance," Catherine said.

"Agreed. And I'd like to believe that he's turned over a new leaf. But it remains to be seen."

"You're afraid he'll fall back into bad habits," Catherine said.

"He wouldn't be the first. However, Ramsay is nearing the age at which a man's character is more or less fixed. If he continues to avoid his former libertine practices, I think he'll make a fine husband. But until he manages to prove himself, I'm not willing to risk your future as the wife of a man who may prove incapable of keeping his vows."

"He would keep his vows," Poppy insisted.

"How do you know that?"

"Because he's a Hathaway."

Harry smiled down at her. "He is fortunate to have you defend him, sweet. And I hope you're right." His gaze flickered to Catherine's troubled face. "Am I wrong in suspecting that you have the same doubts, Cat?"

"I find it difficult to trust any man," she admitted.

The three of them were quiet as they continued along a neatly edged path.

"Catherine," Poppy ventured, "may I ask something exceptionally personal?"

Cat sent her a mock-worried look, and smiled. "I can't imagine anything more personal than what we've been discussing. Yes, of course."

"Has my brother told you that he loves you?"

Catherine hesitated for a long moment. "No," she said, her gaze fixed on the path before them. "In fact, I recently overheard him telling Win that he would only marry a woman if he were

213

certain *not* to love her." She darted a glance at Harry, who thankfully forbore comment.

Poppy frowned. "He may not have meant it. Leo often jokes about things and says the opposite of how he really feels. One never knows with him."

"Precisely my point," Harry said in a neutral tone. "One never knows with Ramsay."

After Catherine had eaten a plate of sandwiches with an impetus born of a renewed appetite, she went to a private suite that Harry had obtained for her.

"Later, after you've rested," Poppy told her, "I'll send a housemaid down with some of my clothes. They'll be a bit loose for you, but they can be altered easily."

"Oh, there's no need for that," Catherine protested. "I'll send for the things I left in Hampshire."

"You'll need something to wear in the meantime. And I have *scores* of gowns that have never been worn. Harry is ridiculously excessive when it comes to buying things for me. Besides, there's no need for all your stodgy spinster dresses now. I've always longed to see you in beautiful colors . . . pink, or jade green . . ." She smiled at Catherine's expression. "You'll be like the proverbial butterfly emerging from the cocoon."

Catherine tried to respond with humor, although her nerves were strung tight with anxiety. "I was really quite comfortable as a caterpillar."

Poppy went to find Harry in his curiosities room, where he often went to mull over a problem or work on something in a place where he was certain not to be interrupted. Only Poppy was allowed to come and go as she pleased.

The room was lined with shelves of exotic and interesting objects, gifts from foreign visitors, clocks and figurines and odd things he had collected in his travels.

Harry sat at his desk in his shirtsleeves, fiddling with gears and springs and bits of wire, as he did whenever he was deep in thought. Poppy approached him, feeling a little pang of pleasure as she watched the movements of those hands, thinking of how they played on her body.

Harry looked up as she closed the door, his gaze attentive and thoughtful. He discarded the handful of metallic objects. Turning in his chair, he took her by the waist and pulled her between his spread thighs.

Poppy let her hands slide into his shiny dark hair, brown-black silk that curled slightly over her fingers. "Am I distracting you?" she asked as she leaned down to kiss him.

"Yes," he said against her mouth. "Don't stop."

Her chuckle dissolved between their lips, like sugar melting in hot tea. Lifting her head, Poppy tried to remember what she had come there for. "Mmmn, don't," she said as his mouth went to her throat. "I can't think when you do that. I was going to ask you something . . ."

"The answer is yes."

Drawing back, she grinned and looked down at him, her arms still linked around his neck. "What do you really think about this situation with Catherine and Leo?"

"I'm not sure." He toyed with the front of her bodice, running his fingers along the row of decorative buttons.

"Harry, do not pull at those," she warned, "they're decorative."

"What good are buttons that don't do anything?" he asked, looking puzzled.

"It's the fashion."

"How am I to get this dress off you?" Intrigued, Harry began to search for hidden fastenings.

Poppy touched her nose to his. "It's a mystery," she whispered. "I'll let you find out after you tell me what you intend to do about Catherine."

"Scandal burns itself out far sooner when ignored. Any attempt to smother it only fans the flames. I'm going to introduce Cat as my sister, explain that she went to school at Blue Maid's, and subsequently took a position with the Hathaways as a kindness to you and your sister."

"And what about all the uncomfortable questions?" Poppy asked. "How shall we answer?"

"In the manner of politicians. Willfully misinterpret and evade."

She considered that with thoughtfully pursed lips. "I suppose that's the only choice," she said. "But what of Leo's proposal?"

"You think she should accept him?"

Poppy nodded decisively. "I don't see what is to be gained by waiting. One never knows what kind of husband a man will be until one marries him. And then it's too late."

"Poor little wife," Harry murmured, patting her rump over the gathered folds of her skirts. "It's far too late for you, isn't it?"

"Well, yes, I've resigned myself to a lifetime of having to endure your passionate lovemaking and witty conversation." She heaved a sigh. "It's better than being a spinster, I tell myself."

Harry stood and pulled her up against him, kissing her until she was dizzy and pink-cheeked.

"Harry," she persisted, as he nuzzled beneath her ear, "when will you give your blessing to the match between Catherine and my brother?"

"When she tells me that it doesn't matter what I say, she's

216

going to marry him come hell or high water." Lifting his head, he stared deeply into her eyes. "Let's go to the apartment and take a nap."

"I'm not sleepy," she whispered, and he grinned.

"Neither am I." Taking her hand, he drew her out of the room. "Now about those buttons . . ."

Chapter Twenty-three

In the morning, Catherine was awakened by a maid who lit a fire in the grate and brought breakfast. One of the joys of staying at the Rutledge was the delicious food prepared by the talented Chef Broussard. Catherine sighed in enjoyment as she saw the contents of the tray: tea, fresh eggs coddled in cream and sided with pistolettes, small oval-shaped rolls, and a dish of ripe berries.

"There was a note under the door, miss," the maid said. "I put it on the side of the tray."

"Thank you." Picking up the small sealed card, Catherine felt a twinge of pleasure when she saw her name written in Leo's unmistakable style, the neat, semi-joined italic of a trained architect.

"Ring when you're finished with the tray, miss, and I'll run up to get it. And if you need help dressing or arranging your hair, I'm a fair hand at that too."

Catherine waited until the maid had left before opening the note.

Mysterious outing planned for this morning. Be ready at ten o'clock sharp. Wear walking shoes.
  —R

A smile broke out on Catherine's face. "Mysterious outing," she said, watching as Dodger hoisted himself up on the bed, his tiny nose working appreciatively as he detected food nearby. "What could he be planning? No, Dodger, don't even think of disturbing my breakfast. You'll have to wait till I'm done. I draw the line at sharing a plate with you."

Seeming to understand her stern tone, Dodger stretched and rolled slowly, completing three revolutions across the mattress.

"And don't expect this to be a permanent arrangement," Catherine added, stirring sugar in her tea. "I'm only taking care of you until you go back to Beatrix."

She was so hungry that she ate every morsel on her plate, except for the small portion she reserved for the ferret. The eggs were perfect, the steaming yellow centers perfect for dipping the crisp pistolette crusts. When she was done, she spooned a coddled egg into a saucer for Dodge, placed a few berries on the side, and went to set it on the floor for him. Happily Dodger circled her, paused for a petting, and went to devour his food.

Catherine had just finished washing and brushing out her hair when there came a knock at the door. It was Poppy, accompanied by the housemaid she had seen earlier. Poppy was carrying at least three dresses draped across her arms, while the maid held a large basket filled with what appeared to ladies' linens, stockings, gloves, and other fripperies.

"Good morning," Poppy said cheerfully, coming in to lay the gown across the bed. Glancing at the ferret eating in the corner, she shook her head and grinned. "Hello, Dodger."

"Are all those things for me?" Catherine asked. "I don't need so much, truly—"

"I'm forcing it on you," Poppy informed her, "so don't dare try to give anything back. I've included a few new underthings from the dressmaker, and a 'reform' corset—do you remember when we saw them displayed at the ladies' outfitter stand at the Great Exhibition?"

"Of course." Catherine smiled. "Impossible to forget a collection of women's private garments being hung out for all the world to view."

"Well, there was a good reason why Madame Caplin won the prize medal at the exhibition. The Caplin corsets are much lighter than the usual ones, and they don't have nearly as many poky, pointy stays, and the whole thing adjusts to the body rather than molding you into an uncomfortable shape. Harry told the hotel housekeeper, Mrs. Pennywhistle, that any of the maids who wished to wear one could charge it to the Rutledge."

Catherine's brows lifted. "Truly?"

"Yes, because it allows them so much more freedom of movement. And you can breathe." Poppy lifted a pale seafoam-green dress from the bed and showed it to her. "You must wear this today. I'm sure it will fit you—we're the same height, only you're slimmer, and I have to tight-lace to fit into it."

"You are too generous, Poppy."

"Nonsense, we're sisters." She sent Catherine an affectionate glance. "Whether or not you marry Leo, we'll always be sisters. Leo told me about your outing at ten o'clock. Did he tell you where you're going?"

"No, did he tell you?"

"Yes." Poppy grinned.

"Where is it?"

"I'll let him surprise you. However, I will say that the expedition has my—and Harry's—full approval."

After the combined efforts of Poppy and the maid, Catherine was dressed in a pale seafoam gown, neither blue nor green but

220

some perfect shade between the two. The bodice was close-fitting, stylishly cut without a waist seam, the skirts plain until the knee, where they draped in rows of flounces. The matching jacket, tailored to the waist, was trimmed with silk fringe in interwoven shades of blue, green, and silver-gray. A small, flirtatious hat was set on the upsweep of her hair, which had been done in a waterfall chignon with the ends tucked up and pinned beneath.

To Catherine, who had gone so long without wearing anything pretty or modish, the effect was disconcerting. She saw a stylishly turned-out woman in the looking glass, decidedly feminine and dashing.

"Oh, miss, you're as pretty as the girls they paint on tins of sweets," the housemaid exclaimed.

"She's right, Catherine," Poppy said, beaming. "Wait until my brother sees you! He'll rue every awful word he's ever said to you."

"I've said awful things to him too," Catherine replied soberly.

"We all knew there was a reason behind the animosity between you," Poppy said. "But we could never agree on what it was. Beatrix was right, of course."

"About what?"

"That you and Leo were like a pair of ferrets, a bit rough-and-tumble in courtship."

Catherine smiled sheepishly. "Beatrix is very intuitive."

Poppy directed a wry glance at Dodger, who was carefully licking the last residue of egg off the saucer. "I used to think Beatrix would outgrow her obsession with animals. Now I realize it's the way her brain works. She sees hardly any difference between the animal world and the human one. I only hope she can find a man who will tolerate her individuality."

221

"What a tactful way to put it," Catherine said, laughing. "You mean a man who won't complain about finding rabbits in his shoes or a lizard in his cigar box?"

"Exactly."

"She will," Catherine assured her. "Beatrix is far too loving, and worthy of being loved, to go unmarried."

"As are you," Poppy said meaningfully. She went to scoop up the ferret as he proceeded to investigate the contents of the basket. "I'll take Dodger for the day. I'm doing correspondence all morning, and he can sleep on my desk while I work."

The ferret hung limp in Poppy's hold, grinning at Catherine as he was carried away.

Leo hadn't wanted to leave Catherine alone last night. He had wanted to stay beside her, watch over her, like a griffin guarding an exotic treasure. Although Leo had never possessed a jealous nature before, it seemed he was quickly making up for lost time. It was particularly annoying that Catherine was so reliant upon Harry. But it was natural that she should want to depend on her brother, especially when Harry had once rescued her from a dire situation and had been her only constant in the years afterward. Even though Harry had shown little love or interest in her until recently, he was all she'd ever had.

The problem was that Leo had a consuming desire to be *everything* to Catherine. He wanted to be her exclusive confidant, her lover and closest friend, to tend to her most intimate needs. To warm her with his body when she was cold, hold a cup to her lips when she was thirsty, rub her feet when she was tired. To join his life with hers in every significant and mundane way.

However, he would not win her with one gesture, one conversation, one passion-filled night. He would have to chip away at her, removing strategic slivers here and there until her objections finally collapsed. That would require patience, attention, time. So be it. She was worth all of that and more.

Arriving at the door of Catherine's suite, Leo knocked discreetly and waited. She appeared promptly, opening the door and smiling at him. "Good morning," she said with an expectant glance.

Any words of greeting Leo had intended to say vanished instantly. His gaze traveled slowly over her. She was like one of the exquisite feminine images painted on bandboxes or displayed in print shops. The pristine perfection of her made him long to unwrap her, like a bonbon done up in a neat paper twist.

Leo's silence went on so long that Catherine was forced to speak again. "I'm ready for the outing. Where are we going?"

"I can't remember," Leo said, still staring. He moved forward as if to crowd her back into the room.

Holding her ground, Catherine placed a gloved hand on his chest. "I'm afraid I can't allow you inside, my lord. It wouldn't be proper. And I do hope that for this outing you have hired an open carriage instead of a closed one?"

"We can take a carriage if you prefer. But our destination is a short distance, and the walk is pleasant, through St. James's Park. Would you like to go on foot?"

She nodded immediately.

As they left the hotel, Leo took the side nearest the curb. Walking with her hand tucked into the crook of Leo's arm, Catherine told him what she and Beatrix had read concerning the park, that King James had kept a collection of animals there, including camels, crocodiles, and an elephant, as well as a row of aviaries along what became Birdcage Walk. That led to Leo telling her about the architect John Nash, who had designed the central mall through the park. The avenue had become the royal ceremonial route from Buckingham Palace.

"Nash was what they called a coxcomb back then," Leo said. "Arrogant and self-important, which are requirements for an architect of that caliber."

"Are they?" Catherine seemed amused. "Why, my lord?"

"The staggering amount of money expended on an important work, and the public nature of it . . . it's effrontery, really, to believe that a design in one's head has enough merit to be built on a large scale. A painting hangs in a museum where people have to seek it out, or avoid it if they prefer. But there's not much one can do to avoid a building, and God help us all if it's an eyesore."

She glanced at him astutely, paying close attention. "Do you ever dream of designing a grand public palace or monument, as Mr. Nash did?"

"No, I have no ambitions to be a great architect. Only a useful one. I like designing smaller projects, such as the tenant houses on the estate. They're no less important than a palace, in my opinion." He shortened his stride to match hers, and steered her carefully over a rough patch in the pavement. "When I went back to France the second time, I happened to encounter one of my professors from the Académie des Beaux-Arts, while I was on a walk in Provence. Lovely old man."

"What a fortunate coincidence."

"Fate."

"You believe in fate?"

Leo gave her a crooked grin. "Impossible not to, living with Rohan and Merripen, don't you think?"

Catherine smiled back, and shook her head. "I'm a skeptic. I believe fate is who we are and what we make of our chances. Go on . . . tell me about the professor."

"I visited Professor Joseph often after that chance meeting, drawing and drafting and studying in his *atelier*." He pronounced the surname the French way, with the stress on the second syllable. Pausing, he smiled in rueful reminiscence. "We often talked over glasses of *chartreuse*. I couldn't abide the stuff."

"What did you talk about?" came the soft question.

"Usually architecture. Professor Joseph had a pure view of it . . . that a small, perfectly designed cottage has as much value as a grand public edifice. And he spoke of things he'd never mentioned at the Académie; his sense of the connections between the physical and spiritual . . . that a perfect man-made creation, such as a painting, sculpture, or a building, could provide you with a moment of transcendence. Clarity. A key to unlock a glimpse of heaven."

Leo paused as he glimpsed her troubled expression. "I've bored you. Forgive me."

"No, it's not that at all." They walked in silence for nearly a half minute before Catherine burst out, "I've never really known you. You are overturning so much of what I assumed about you. It's very disconcerting."

"Does that mean you're softening toward the idea of marrying me?"

"Not at all," she said, and he grinned.

"You will," he said. "You can't resist my charms forever." He guided her away from the park and onto a prosperous street of shops and businesses.

"Are you taking me to a haberdashery?" Catherine asked, viewing the windows and signs. "A flower shop? A book shop?"

"Here," Leo said, stopping in front of a window. "What do you think of this place?"

She squinted at the printed sign hung inside the window.

"Telescopes?" she asked in bewilderment. "You want me to take up astronomy?"

Leo turned her back to the window. "Continue reading."

"'Purveyors of camp, racecourse, opera, and perspective glasses,'" she read aloud, "'by Her Majesty's royal letters patent. Illuminated ocular examinations performed by Dr. Henry Schaeffer with modern devices for the purpose of scientific correction of vision acuity.'"

"Dr. Schaeffer is the finest oculist in London," Leo said. "Some say in the world. He was a professor of astronomy at Trinity, when his work with lenses led him to an interest in the human eye. He was habilitated as an ophthamologist, and has made remarkable strides in the field. I made an appointment for you to see him."

"But I don't need the finest oculist in London," she protested, puzzled that Leo would have gone to such lengths.

"Come, Marks," he said, drawing her to the door. "It's time for you to have proper spectacles."

The interior of the shop was intriguing, lined with shelves of telescopes, magnifying glasses, binoculars, stereoscope instruments, and all manner of eyeglasses. A pleasant young clerk greeted them and went to fetch Dr. Schaeffer. The doctor came out very soon, displaying an expansive and jovial temperament. A handsome set of white whiskers framed his pink cheeks, and a thick snowy mustache curved upward when he smiled.

Schaeffer showed them around his shop, pausing to demonstrate a stereoscope and explain how the illusion of depth was created. "This instrument serves two purposes," the doctor said, his eyes twinkling behind his own spectacle lenses. "First, the stereogram cards are sometimes of use in treating focusing dis-

226

orders in certain patients. And second, they are helpful in entertaining high-spirited children."

Catherine was cautious but willing as she and Leo followed Dr. Schaeffer to the rooms at the back of his shop. Whenever she had purchased spectacles in the past, the optician had simply brought out a tray of lenses, handed her various ones to hold up to her eyes, and when she felt she had obtained sufficient vision, he had proceeded to make spectacles for her.

Dr. Schaeffer, however, insisted on examining her eyes with a lens he called a "corneal loupe," after putting drops into her eyes to dilate the pupils. After pronouncing that there were no signs of disease or degeneration, he asked her to read letters and numbers from a series of three charts on the wall. She was obliged to reread the charts with various strengths of lenses, until finally they achieved a near-miraculous clarity.

When it came time to discuss the frames for the lenses, Leo surprised both Catherine and Dr. Schaeffer by taking an active part. "The spectacles that Miss Marks wears at present," Leo said, "leave a mark at the bridge of her nose."

"The contour of the support arch must be adjusted," the doctor said.

"Undoubtedly." Leo withdrew a slip of paper from the pocket of his coat and placed it on the table. "However, I have a few more ideas. What if the bridge is built up to hold the lenses a bit farther away from her face?"

"You're thinking of a design similar to the clips of a pince-nez?" Schaeffer asked thoughtfully.

"Yes, they would fit more comfortably and also stay in place."

Schaeffer stared closely at the sketch Leo had given him. "You've drawn curved earpieces, I see. An unusual feature."

"The intention is to hold the spectacles more firmly onto her face."

"This is a problem, keeping them on?"

"Without question," Leo replied. "This is a very active woman. Chasing animals, falling through rooftops, stacking rock—all an average day for her."

"My lord," Catherine said in reproof.

Schaeffer smiled as he examined the contorted shapes of her spectacles. "From the condition of these frames, Miss Marks, one could almost believe Lord Ramsay's claims." His mustache curved upward. "With your permission, I will instruct the jeweler I work with to build the frames you've drawn."

"Make them in silver," Leo said. He paused, regarding Catherine with a faint smile. "And have him put a touch of filigree on the earpieces. Nothing vulgar . . . keep it delicate."

Catherine shook her head immediately. "Such adornment is expensive and unnecessary."

"Do it nevertheless," Leo said to the doctor, his gaze still holding Catherine's. "Your face deserves adornment. I would hardly put a masterpiece in a ordinary frame, would I?"

She sent him a reproving glance. She neither liked nor trusted such outrageous flattery, nor did she intend to melt at his charm. But Leo gave her an unrepentant grin. And as he sat there and surveyed her with wicked blue eyes, she felt a painfully sweet contraction of her heart, followed by the sensation of being knocked off balance. Such a long distance to fall . . . and yet she couldn't seem to back away from the danger.

She could only stay there with her precarious equilibrium, suspended in longing and peril . . . unable to save herself.

Chapter Twenty-four

It has been confirmed by Mr. Harry Rutledge, the London hotelier, that a woman identified as Miss Catherine Marks is in fact a half sister who has heretofore lived in relative obscurity as a companion to the family of Viscount Ramsay of Hampshire. Upon inquiry as to why the young woman was not previously brought out into society, Mr. Rutledge explained the discretion as appropriate to the circumstances of her birth, as the natural child of Mr. Rutledge's mother and an unnamed gentleman. Mr. Rutledge proceeded to emphasize the decorous and refined nature of his sister, and his own pride in acknowledging kinship with a woman he describes as "estimable in every regard."

"How very flattering," Catherine said lightly, setting down the copy of *The Times*. She sent Harry a rueful glance across the breakfast table. "And now the questions will begin."

"I'll deal with the questions," Harry said. "All you have to do is behave in the aforementioned decorous and refined manner when Poppy and I take you to the theater."

"When are we going to the theater?" Poppy asked, popping a last bite of honey-soaked crumpet into her mouth.

"Tomorrow evening, if that pleases you."

Catherine nodded, trying not to look troubled by the prospect. People would stare, and whisper. Part of her shrank at the idea of being on display. On the other hand, it was a play, which meant the audience's attention would focus mainly on the activity within the proscenium.

"Shall we invite Leo?" Poppy asked. She and Harry both looked at Catherine.

She hitched her shoulders in an unconcerned shrug, although she suspected it didn't deceive either of them.

"Would you have any objection?" Harry asked her.

"No, of course not. He is Poppy's brother, and my former employer."

"And possibly your fiancé," Harry murmured.

Catherine looked at him quickly. "I haven't accepted his proposal."

"You are considering it, however . . . aren't you?"

Her heart gave a few thick beats in her chest. "I'm not sure."

"Cat, I don't mean to harass you about this, but how long do you intend to wait before giving Ramsay an answer?"

"Not long." Cat frowned into her tea. "If there's any hope of retaining Ramsay House, Lord Ramsay will have to marry someone soon."

A tap at the door heralded the entrance of Harry's right-hand man, Jake Valentine. He brought Harry a stack of daily manager's reports, as well as a handful of letters. One of these was addressed to Poppy, who received it with a warm smile.

"Thank you, Mr. Valentine."

"Mrs. Rutledge," he said with an answering smile, bowing

before he left. He looked the tiniest bit smitten with Poppy, which Catherine couldn't blame him for in the least.

Poppy broke the seal and read the letter, her fine brows inching higher and higher as she neared the conclusion. "My goodness, this is odd."

Harry and Catherine both looked at her questioningly.

"It's from Lady Fitzwalter, with whom I am acquainted through some charity work. She asks me in this letter, very earnestly, if I will prevail on my brother to call upon Miss Darvin and Countess Ramsay, who are in town. And she provides the address of the house they have let."

"Not so very odd," Catherine said pragmatically, although the news caused a stir of anxiety. "After all, a lady may never call on a man for any reason, and therefore it is certainly not unheard-of for one to prevail upon a mutual acquaintance to arrange the meeting."

"Yes, but why does Miss Darvin wish to speak to Leo?"

"It might be about the copyhold clause," Harry said, looking interested. "Perhaps she wishes to offer some manner of concession."

"I'm sure she means to offer him *something*," Catherine said sullenly. She couldn't help remembering how beautiful the dark-haired Miss Darvin was, and what a striking couple she and Leo had made as they had waltzed. "However, I doubt she intends to discuss legalities. It's something personal. Otherwise she would allow the solicitors to deal with it."

"Cam and Merripen were terrified by Miss Darvin," Poppy told Harry with a grin. "Amelia wrote that her ballgown was trimmed with peacock feathers, which the Rom view as an omen of danger."

"In some Hindu sects," Harry said, "the peacock's cries are associated with the rainy season, and therefore, fertility."

231

"Danger or fertility?" Poppy asked dryly. "Well, it should be interesting to see which one Miss Darvin will evince."

"I don't want to," Leo said immediately upon being informed of the necessity of calling on Miss Darvin.

"That doesn't matter, you have no choice," Poppy said, taking his coat as he entered the apartment.

Seeing Catherine seated in the parlor with Dodger in her lap, Leo came to her. "Good afternoon," he said, reaching for Catherine's hand and brushing a kiss on the backs of her fingers. The feel of his lips, so warm and soft against her skin, caused a quick indrawn breath.

"May I?" he asked, glancing at the place on the settee beside her.

"Yes, of course."

After Poppy was seated in a chair by the hearth, Leo sat beside Catherine.

She smoothed Dodger's fur repeatedly, but he didn't move. A sleeping ferret was so limp and impossible to awaken that one might have reasonably assumed he was dead. One could pick him up, even shake him, and he would slumber on undisturbed.

Leo reached over to toy with the ferret's tiny arms and legs, lifting them gently and letting them drop back into her lap. They both chuckled as Dodger remained unconscious.

Catherine detected an unusual fragrance about Leo, a scent of feed and hay and some pungent animal scent. She sniffed curiously. "You smell a bit like . . . horses . . . Did you go for a ride this morning?"

"It's *eau de zoo*," Leo informed her, his eyes twinkling. "I went for a meeting with the secretary of the zoological society of London, and we toured the newest pavilion."

"Whatever for?" Catherine asked.

"An old acquaintance of mine, with whom I apprenticed for Rowland Temple, has been commissioned at the Queen's behest to design a gorilla enclosure at the zoo. They keep them in small cages, which is nothing short of cruelty. When my friend complained to me about the difficulty of designing a sufficiently large and safe enclosure without costing a fortune, I suggested that he dig a moat."

"A moat?" Poppy echoed.

Leo smiled. "Gorillas won't cross deep water."

"How did you know that, my lord?" Catherine asked in amusement. "Beatrix?"

"Naturally." He looked rueful. "And now after my suggestion, it seems I've been recruited as a consultant."

"At least if your new clients complain," Catherine told him, "you won't understand what they're saying."

Leo smothered a laugh. "Obviously you haven't seen what gorillas fling when they're displeased." His mouth twisted. "All the same, I'd rather spend my time with primates than pay a call to Miss Darvin and her mother."

The play that evening was mawkish but highly entertaining. The story was about a handsome Russian peasant who was striving for an education, but on his wedding day to his true love, the poor girl was assaulted by the prince of the domain, and while she swooned, was fatally stung by an asp. Before death overtook her, she reached her home and told her fiancé what had happened, whereupon the handsome peasant swore revenge against the prince. These efforts led him to impersonate another nobleman in the royal court, where he happened to meet a woman who looked exactly like his dead love. As it turned out, the woman

233

was an identical twin of the murdered peasant girl, and to further complicate matters, she was in love with the evil prince's honorable young son.

Then it was intermission.

Unfortunately Catherine's and Poppy's enjoyment of the drama was hampered by low-voiced comments from both Harry and Leo, who insisted on pointing out that in her death throes, the asp-stung woman was clutching the wrong side of her body, and furthermore, a person dying of poison probably wouldn't cross the state back and forth while uttering poetic declarations of love.

"You have no romance in your soul," Poppy told Harry at intermission.

"Not in my soul, no," he replied gravely. "However, I have a great deal of it in other locations."

She laughed, reaching up to smooth an imaginary crease in his crisp white cravat. "Darling, would you please have someone bring champagne to our box? Catherine and I are thirsty."

"I'll send for it," Leo said, standing and buttoning his coat. "I need to stretch my legs after an hour and a half in that absurdly small chair." He looked down at Catherine. "Would you care for a promenade?"

She shook her head, feeling much safer in the confines of the theater box than out walking in the crowd. "Thank you, but I am comfortable here."

As Leo pushed aside the curtains at the back of their box, it was evident that the hallways were exceedingly crowded. A pair of gentlemen and a lady came through the curtains and greeted the Rutledges warmly. Catherine tensed as Harry introduced her to Lord and Lady Despencer and Lady Despencer's sister, Mrs. Lisle. She anticipated a cool reception from them, perhaps a dismissive remark, but instead they were polite and affable. Perhaps, she thought wryly, she should stop expecting the worst of people.

Poppy asked Lady Despencer about one of her children, who had been ill recently, and the woman listed all the medications and precautions it had taken for their ailing son to get well. Another cluster of people entered the box, waiting for a turn to speak to Harry, and Catherine moved to make room for them. She stood at the back of the box beside the curtain panels, waiting with forced patience as conversation flowed in currents in the hallway, in the box, large swells of noise rising from the audience below. The relentless clamor and movement irritated her. It was stuffy in the theater, the air warm from the mass of human bodies crowding everywhere. She hoped that intermission would conclude soon.

As she stood with her hands behind her back, she felt a hand reach through the box curtains and close around her wrist. A masculine body pressed behind hers. A smile touched her lips as she wondered what game Leo was playing.

But the voice that slithered into her ear wasn't Leo's. It was a voice from her nightmares.

"How pretty you look in your fine feathers, my pigeon."

Chapter Twenty-five

Catherine stiffened, her hand clenching into a fist, but she couldn't jerk her arm away from Lord Latimer's grasp. He twisted her gloved wrist, forced it an inch or two higher, and continued to speak in a soft undertone.

Stunned and frozen, Catherine could hear nothing at first but the frantic velocity of her heartbeat. Time seemed to flicker, falter, and resume at a crawl. ". . . so many questions about you . . ." he was saying, his voice saturated with contempt. "Everyone wants to know more about Rutledge's enigmatic sister . . . is she fair or ill-favored? Accomplished or vulgar? Endowed or destitute? Perhaps I should supply the answers. 'She's a beauty,' I'll tell my curious friends, 'trained by an infamous procuress. She's a fraud. And most of all she's a whore.'"

Catherine was quiet, breathing through flared nostrils. She couldn't make a scene during her first public outing as Harry's sister. Any conflict with Lord Latimer would expose their past connection, and bring about her social ruin that much faster.

"Why don't you further explain," she whispered, "that you're a filthy lecher who tried to rape a fifteen-year-old girl?"

"Tsk, tsk . . . You should know better, Catherine. People never blame a man for his passions, no matter how perverse. People blame the woman for arousing them. You won't get far, asking for sympathy. The public despises victimized women, especially attractive ones."

"Lord Ramsay will—"

"Ramsay will use you and discard you, which is what he does with all women. Surely you're not so vain or stupid as to think you're different from the others."

"What do you want?" she asked through gritted teeth.

"I want what I paid for," he whispered, "all those years ago. And I'll have it. There's no other future for you, my dear. You were never meant for a respectable life. By the time you've been run through the rumor mills, you'll never have a chance of being received anywhere."

The manacling fingers fell away, and her tormentor disappeared.

Stricken, Catherine stumbled forward to her chair and sat heavily, trying to compose herself. She stared straight ahead, seeing nothing, while the clamor of the theater pressed around her from all sides. She tried to examine her fear objectively, to put a barrier around it. It wasn't that she actually feared Latimer. She loathed him, but he was certainly not the threat to her now that he once had been. She now had sufficient wealth to live as she pleased. She had Harry and Poppy, and the Hathaways.

But Latimer had identified her legitimate worries with cruel accuracy. One could fight a man, but not a rumor. One could lie about the past, but the truth would eventually surface. One could promise fidelity and commitment, but such promises were often broken.

She felt overwhelmed with melancholy. She felt . . . stained.

Poppy sat next to her, smiling. "Nearly time for the second

act," she said. "Do you think the peasant will gain revenge against the prince?"

"Oh, undoubtedly," Catherine replied, trying to sound light, but her voice was forced.

Poppy's smile faded, and she looked at her closely. "Do you feel well, dear? You look pale. Did something happen?"

Before Catherine replied, Leo shouldered his way back into the box, accompanied by a steward bearing a tray of champagne. A little bell rang from the orchestra box, signaling that the intermission would soon conclude. To Catherine's relief, the visitors began to drift out of the box, and the throng in the hallway receded.

"Here we are," Leo said, handing champagne to Poppy and Catherine. "You may want to drink it quickly."

"Why?" Catherine asked, forcing a smile.

"The champagne goes flat much faster in these coupe glasses."

Catherine drained her champagne with unladylike haste, closing her eyes and swallowing against the sparkling burn in her throat.

"I didn't mean that quickly," Leo said, viewing her with a faint, concerned smile.

The lights began to dim, and the audience settled.

Catherine glanced at the silver stand where the bottle of chilled champagne had been placed, a white napkin tied neatly at its neck. "May I have another?" she whispered.

"No, you'll get tipsy if you have it so soon." Leo took the empty glass from her, set it aside, and took her gloved hand in his. "Tell me," he said gently. "What are you thinking about?"

"Later," she whispered back, easing her hand from his. "Please." She didn't want the evening to be ruined for everyone, nor did she want to take the chance that Leo might seek out

Latimer in the theater and confront him. There was nothing to be gained by saying anything at the moment.

The theater darkened and the play resumed, although the story's melodramatic charms couldn't pull Catherine out of her frozen misery. She watched the stage with a fixed gaze, hearing the actors' dialogue as if it were a foreign language. And all the while her mind kept trying to find a solution to her internal dilemma.

It didn't seem to matter that she already knew the answers. It had never been her fault, the situation she had once been put in. The blame was Latimer's, and Althea's, and her grandmother's. Catherine could reassure herself of that for the rest of her life, and yet the feelings of guilt, pain, confusion, were still there. How could she rid herself of them? What could possibly free her?

For the next ten minutes, Leo glanced at Catherine repeatedly, perceiving that something was deeply wrong. She was trying very hard to concentrate on the play, but it was clear that her mind was consumed with some overpowering problem. She was distant, unreachable, as if she had been encased in ice. Trying to comfort her, he took her hand once more, and ran his thumb above the edge of her wrist-length glove. The iciness of her skin was startling.

Frowning deeply, Leo leaned toward Poppy. "What the devil happened to Marks?" he whispered.

"I don't know," she returned helplessly. "Harry and I were talking to Lord and Lady Despencer, and Catherine was off to the side. Then we both sat, and I noticed that she looked ill."

"I'm taking her back to the hotel," Leo said.

Harry, who had caught the last of the exchange, frowned and murmured, "We'll all go."

"There's no need for any of us to leave," Catherine protested.

Ignoring her, Leo stared at Harry. "It would be better if you stayed and watched the rest of the play. And if anyone asks about Marks, say something about the vapours."

"Don't tell anyone I had vapours," Catherine whispered sharply.

"Then say I had them," Leo told Harry.

That seemed to rouse Catherine from her numbness. Leo was relieved to see a flicker of her usual spirit as she said, "Men can't have vapours. It's a female condition."

"Nevertheless, I do," Leo said. "I may even swoon." He helped her from her seat.

Harry rose as well, looking down at his sister with concern. "Is this what you want, Cat?" he asked.

"Yes," she said, looking annoyed. "If I don't, he'll be asking for smelling salts."

Leo escorted Catherine outside and summoned a hackney carriage. It was a two-wheeled, partially open vehicle, with an elevated driver's seat at the rear. One could speak to the driver through a trapdoor at the top.

As Catherine approached the vehicle with Leo, she had a crawling sensation of being watched. Afraid that Latimer had followed her, she glanced to her left, where a man stood beside one of the theater's massive portico columns. To her relief, it was not Latimer, but a much younger man. He was tall, rawboned, and dressed in shabby dark clothing and a tattered hat, with the overall effect of a scarecrow. He had the distinctive London pallor common to those who spent most of their time indoors, whose skin was never touched by sun without the filter of polluted city air. His brows were strong black stripes across his gaunt face, his skin creased with lines that he was too young to have.

He was staring at her fixedly.

Catherine paused uncertainly, aware of a vague sense of recognition. Had she seen him somewhere before? She couldn't fathom where they might have met.

"Come," Leo said, intending to hand her into the carriage.

But Catherine resisted, caught by the riveted stare of the stranger's raven-dark eyes.

Leo followed the direction of her gaze. "Who is that?"

The young man came forward, removing his hat to reveal a mop of shaggy black hair. "Miss Catherine?" he said awkwardly.

"William," she breathed in wonder.

"Yes, miss." His mouth curled upward in the beginnings of a smile. He took another hesitant step, and bobbed in a sort of clumsy bow.

Leo intruded between them protectively and looked down at Catherine. "Who is he?"

"I think he's the boy I once told you about . . . who worked at my grandmother's house."

"The errand boy?"

Catherine nodded. "He was the reason I was able to send for Harry . . . he took my letter to him. My lord, do let me speak to him."

Leo's face was implacable. "You would be the first one to tell me that a lady never stands and converses with a man on the street."

"*Now* you want to pay heed to etiquette?" she asked in annoyance. "I'm going to speak to him." Seeing the refusal in his face, she softened her voice, and surreptitiously touched his hand. "Please."

Leo relented. "Two minutes," he muttered, looking none too happy. He remained right beside her, his eyes ice-blue as he stared at William.

241

Looking cowed, William obeyed Catherine's motion to come to them. "You turned into a lady, Miss Catherine," he said in his thick South London accent. "But I knew it was you—that face, and those same little spectacles. I always hoped you was all right."

"You've changed more than I, William," she said, trying to summon a smile. "How tall you've grown. Are you still . . . working for my grandmother?"

He shook his head and smiled ruefully. "She passed on two years ago, miss. Doctor said 'er heart gave out, but the girls at the 'ouse said it couldn't be, she didn't 'ave one."

"Oh," Catherine whispered, her face turning bleached and stiff. It was only to be expected, of course. Her grandmother had suffered from a heart ailment for years. She thought she should feel relieved by the news, but instead she only felt chilled. "And . . . my aunt? Is Althea still there?"

William cast a guarded glance around them. "She's the madam now," he said, his voice low. "I work for her, odd jobs, same as I did for your grandmother. But it's a different place now, miss. Much worse."

Compassion stirred inside her. How unfair it was for him to be trapped in such a life, with no training or education to afford him any other choice. Privately she resolved to ask Harry if there might be some kind of employment for William at the hotel, something that would lead him to a decent future. "How is my aunt?" she asked.

"Ailing, miss." His thin face was sober. "Doctor said she must of got a bawdy-'ouse disease some years back . . . got in 'er joints and went up to 'er brain. Not well in the 'ead, your aunt. And she can't see none too good, neither."

"I'm sorry," Catherine murmured, trying to feel pity, but

instead a mass of fear rose in her throat. She tried to swallow it back, to ask more questions, but Leo interrupted brusquely.

"That's enough," he said. "The hackney's waiting."

Catherine gave her childhood friend a troubled glance. "Is there something I can do to help you, William? Do you need money?" She instantly regretted the question as she saw the shame and offended pride on his face. Had there been more time, had the circumstances allowed, she would have found a better way to ask.

William gave a stiff shake of his head. "Don't need noffing, miss."

"I'm at the Rutledge Hotel. If you wish to see me, if there is something I can—"

"I wouldn't nivver trouble you, Miss Cathy. You was always kind to me. You brought me medicine once when I was sick, 'member? Came to the kitchen pallet where I slept, and covered me wiv one of the blankets from your bed. You sat on the floor and watched over me—"

"We're leaving," Leo said, flipping a coin to William.

William caught it in midair. His fist lowered, and he looked at Leo with a mixture of greed and resentment, his face turning hard. When he spoke, his accent was exaggerated. "Fank you, guvnah."

Leo guided Catherine away with an uncompromising grasp on her elbow, and helped her into the carriage. By the time she had settled in the narrow seat and looked out again, William was gone.

The passenger seat was so small that the mass of Catherine's skirts, layers of pink silk arranged like rose petals, spilled over one of Leo's thighs.

Staring at her profile, Leo thought she looked stern and nettled, like the Marks of old.

"You needn't have dragged me away like that," she said. "You were rude to William."

He gave her an unrepentant glance. "No doubt later, upon reflection, I'll feel terrible about that."

"There were some things I still wanted to ask him."

"Yes, I'm sure there was quite a lot more to be learned about bawdy-house diseases. Forgive me for depriving you of such an enlightening conversation. I should have let the two of you reminisce about the good old times at the brothel while you were standing on a public street."

"William was the dearest boy," Catherine said quietly. "He deserved a better lot in life. He had to work from the time he could toddle, cleaning shoes and carrying heavy buckets of water up and down the stairs . . . he had no family, no education. Have you no sympathy at all for those in unfortunate circumstances?"

"The streets are filled with such children. I do what I can for them in Parliament, and I give to charity. Yes, I have sympathy for them. But at the moment I'm more interested in your unfortunate circumstances than anyone else's. And I have a few questions for you, starting with this: What happened at intermission?"

When Catherine didn't reply, he took her jaw in a gentle but secure grasp, and forced her to look at him. "Let's have it."

She gave him a strained glance. "Lord Latimer approached me."

Leo's eyes narrowed, his hand lowering from her chin. "While you were in the theater box?"

"Yes. Harry and Poppy didn't see. Latimer spoke to me through the curtain at the back of the box seating."

Leo was filled with explosive rage. For a moment he didn't

244

trust himself to speak. He wanted to go back and slaughter the bastard. "What did he say?" he asked roughly.

"That I was a prostitute. And a fraud."

Leo wasn't aware that his grip had tightened until she winced. His hand loosened instantly. "I'm sorry you were subjected to that," he managed to say. "I shouldn't have left you. I didn't think he would dare approach you after the warning I gave him."

"I think he wanted to make it clear that he's not intimidated by you." She drew an unsteady breath. "And I think it hurt his pride all those years ago, to have paid for something he didn't receive. Perhaps I could give him some of the money Harry settled on me, and that might be enough to make him leave me alone. To keep quiet about me."

"No, that would only start us on a course of prolonged blackmail. And Latimer would never keep quiet. Listen to me, Cat . . . Harry and I have discussed how to manage the problem. Suffice it to say that in a few days, Latimer will find himself in a position in which he'll either end up in prison or be forced to flee England."

"For what crime?" she asked, her eyes widening.

"There's a long list to choose from," Leo said. "He's tried nearly everything. And I'd rather not tell you the specific offense, because it's not appropriate for a lady's ears."

"You can make him leave England? Truly?"

"Truly."

He felt her relax a little, her shoulders slumping. "That would be a relief," she said. "However . . ."

"Yes?"

Catherine angled her face away from his searching gaze. "It doesn't really matter. Because what he said was no less than the truth. I am a fraud."

"What self-pitying tripe. You were a fraud as an aspiring prostitute. As a proper and well-mannered lady who holds an irresistible attraction for ferrets, you're completely authentic."

"Not all ferrets. Just Dodger."

"Proof of his excellent taste."

"Don't try to be charming," she muttered. "There's nothing more annoying than someone trying to make one feel better when one wants to wallow."

Leo bit back a grin. "I'm sorry," he said contritely. "Go on and wallow. You were doing so well at it until I interrupted."

"Thank you." She heaved a sigh and waited a moment. "Blast," she finally said, "I can't do it now." Her fingers crept further into his, and he smoothed his thumb over the backs of her knuckles. "I want to correct something," Catherine said. "I was never an aspiring prostitute."

"What did you aspire to?"

"To live somewhere peaceful, and be safe."

"That's all?"

"Yes, that's all. And I haven't managed to do it yet. Although . . . the past few years have been the closest I've ever gotten."

"Marry me," Leo told her, "and you can have both. You'll be safe, and you'll live in Hampshire. And you'll have me, which is obviously icing on the cake."

A reluctant laugh escaped her. "Rather more icing than the cake needs."

"There is no such thing as too much icing, Marks."

"My lord, I don't believe that you sincerely want to marry me as much as you want to have your way."

"I want you to marry me so that I don't have my way all the time," he said, which was the truth. "It's not good for me to be indulged. And you tell me no quite frequently."

She gave a huff of wry amusement. "I haven't said it to you nearly enough lately."

"Then let's practice in your hotel suite. I'll try to have my way with you, and you can try to refuse me."

"No."

"There, you see? You're sharpening your skills already."

Leo directed the driver to take them to the alley that bordered the mews behind the hotel. It was a far more discreet way to enter than parading through the lobby. They went up the back stairs and along the hallway that led to Catherine's suite. The hotel was extraordinarily quiet at that hour, everyone either out for their evening pursuits, or sleeping soundly.

When they reached Catherine's door, Leo waited as Catherine searched for the key in the little knitted silk bag she had looped around one wrist.

"Allow me," Leo said when she had found the key. Taking it from her, he unlocked the door.

"Thank you." Catherine took back the key and turned to face him at the threshold.

Leo stared down into her fine-boned face, reading the emotions that flickered in her eyes: despair, refusal, yearning. "Invite me in," he said softly.

She shook her head. "You must go. It's not seemly for you to stand here."

"The night's still young. What will you do in there, alone?"

"Sleep."

"No, you won't. You'll stay awake as long as possible, worrying about nightmares." Seeing that he had scored a point, Leo pressed his advantage. "Let me in."

Chapter Twenty-six

Leo stood in the doorway, tugging off his gloves casually, as if he had all the time in the world. Catherine went dry-mouthed as she watched him. She needed him. She needed to be held and comforted, and he knew it. If she allowed him into her hotel suite, there was no question as to what would happen next.

She started as the sound of voices came from the end of the long hallway. Reaching out hastily, she grabbed the lapels of Leo's coat, pulled him across the threshold, and closed them both safely inside the room. *"Hush,"* she whispered.

Leo braced his hands on either side of her, caging her against the door. "You know how to keep me quiet."

The voices became louder as people advanced further along the hallway.

Smiling into her tense face, Leo began in a perfectly audible tone, "Marks, I wonder if—"

She drew in an exasperated breath and crammed her mouth against his, anything to shut him up. Leo fell obligingly silent, kissing her with bold and avid pleasure. Even through the elegant layers of his clothes, she could feel the heat and hardness of him. Desperately she fumbled with his clothes, pushing her hands beneath his coat where his body heat had collected.

She moaned, the sound catching between their lips. His tongue went deep, and she felt corresponding twinges of pleasure low in her stomach. Her legs lost their strength, her balance eroding. Her spectacles became dislodged, catching between their faces. Leo reached up to remove them carefully. He slipped them into his pocket. With deliberate slowness, he put the key in the door and locked it from the inside. Catherine stood mutely, torn between desire and caution.

In the silence, Leo went to light a lamp. A rasp, as a match was struck . . . a glow, as the wick kindled. Catherine blinked owlishly at the shadow-crossed room, at the large dark shape of him before her. She ached for him, her body clenching on intimate emptiness. A tremor went through her as she thought of how he had filled her, the sweet heaviness of him inside her.

Blindly she turned to face away from him, offering access to the row of hooks that fastened the back of her dress. The fabric tightened across her breasts as he grasped the dress at the back. There was a series of deft tugs, the garment loosening, slipping lower. She felt his mouth brush the tender nape of her neck, a whisk of exciting warmth. He pushed the gown to her waist and over her hips. She moved to help him, stepping out of the heap of layered pink silk, kicking off her slippers. Turning her around again, Leo unhooked her corset, pausing to kiss each of her shoulders in turn.

"Take down your hair." The touch of his breath on her skin made her shiver.

Catherine obeyed, pulling the pins from her chignon, collecting them in a little bundle. After setting them on the dressing table, she went to the bed and climbed onto the mattress, waiting tensely as he undressed. She couldn't help wishing she had her spectacles back as she stared at the intriguing, hazy shape of him, the play of light and shadow on his skin.

"Don't squint so hard, love. You'll strain your eyes."

"I can't see you."

He approached her, every line of his body replete with masculine grace. "Can you see me at this distance?"

She contemplated him thoroughly. "Certain parts."

Leo gave a husky laugh, crawling onto the bed, over her, bracing his weight on his arms. The tips of her breasts hardened beneath the light veil of her chemise. Their stomachs pressed together, the erect shape of him caught exquisitely against the corresponding notch of her body.

"What about now?" Leo whispered. "Am I close enough?"

"Almost," she managed to say, staring into his face, taking in every breathtaking detail. She had to force out words between uneven breaths. "But not quite . . ."

Leo bent to take her lips, locking his mouth over hers in a blaze of sensation. She lost herself in it, a kiss that was at once giving and demanding. He searched her gently, meeting the shy advances of her own tongue. She tasted inside his mouth for the first time, and felt the jolt of his response.

With a ragged sound, Leo reached for the hem of her chemise. Pulling the garment upward, he helped Catherine to lift it over her head. He untied the tapes of her drawers with torturous slowness, running his fingers along the loosening waist, easing the thin muslin fabric down her hips. Her garters and stockings soon followed, leaving her completely exposed.

Murmuring his name, Catherine twined her arms around his neck and tried to draw him over her again. She arched into him, gasping with delight at the varied textures of him, roughness and silk, smoothness and steel.

He brought his mouth to her ear, his lips toying with the soft lobe before he whispered, "Cat. I'm going to kiss all the way down your body and up again. And I want you to lie perfectly still and let me do as I please. You can do that, can't you?"

"No," she said earnestly, "I really don't think so."

Leo averted his face for a moment. When he looked back at her, his eyes were sparkling with amusement. "That was actually a rhetorical question."

"A rhetorical question has an obvious answer," she argued, "and what you're asking is not—" She broke off, unable to speak or think as she felt him nibble and lick at a sensitive part of her neck. His mouth was hot and silken, the flat of his tongue like velvet. He worked his way along her arm, pausing at the hollows of her inner arm and wrist, caressing the pulse that beat visibly in the fragile skin. Every inch of her body prickled with awareness of him and what he was doing.

His mouth wandered back along her arm to the side of her breast, the trail of his mouth leaving her skin flushed and damp. He kissed all around the rosy peak without touching it, until she felt a whimper climb in her throat. "My lord, *please*," she gasped, sliding her hands into his hair, trying to guide him.

He resisted, grasping her wrists and pulling them to her sides. "Don't move," he reminded her gently. "Or do you want me to start over?"

She closed her eyes and lay with aggrieved stillness, her chest heaving. Leo had the gall to laugh softly, his mouth returning to nuzzle the undercurve of her breast. A cry escaped her when she felt his lips brush against the gathered crest. Slowly his mouth opened and sealed over her, and he began to suckle. Heat writhed in her stomach, and her hips lifted from the mattress. His hand settled on her taut abdomen, rubbing in a soothing circle, pressing her back down.

It was impossible to lie motionless as Leo tormented her, arousing her skillfully but providing no relief. Impossible to endure . . . but he wouldn't allow otherwise. He made his way down to her stomach, licking and blowing lightly into the hollow of her navel. She was weak and perspiring, wet at the roots of her hair, her body racked with delight that verged on pain.

His mouth glided across the vulnerable softness of her groin to her inner thighs, his tongue playing gently on either side . . . everywhere except the wet pulsing center.

"Leo," she panted. "This . . . is not very nice of you."

"I know," he said. "Move your legs apart."

She obeyed with a shudder, letting him guide her, opening her body in ever more revealing positions. He used his mouth in ways that infuriated and aroused her . . . nibbling along her thigh, investigating the ticklish hollows behind her knees, stringing kisses around her ankles, sucking lazily on her toes. She swallowed back a supplicating moan, and another, impatience thumping through her body.

After an eternity, Leo had finally progressed all the way back to her neck. Catherine parted her thighs, dying for him to take her, but instead he rolled her to her stomach. She whimpered in frustration.

"Impatient wench." Leo's hand smoothed over her bottom and slipped between her thighs. "There, will this satisfy you for now?" She felt him parting her swollen flesh. Her body stiffened in bliss as his fingers entered her, slipping into the wetness. He held them there, deep and flexing, while he kissed along her spine. She found herself grinding against his hand, gasping in pleasure. Closer . . . closer . . . and yet the climax shimmered just out of reach.

Finally Leo turned her to her back again, his features hard and sweat-misted, and it was only then that she realized he had been torturing himself as well as her. He pinned her arms over her head and spread her legs. For an instant she knew a flare of panic at her own helplessness, seeing his powerful body above hers. But then he entered her in a hard, slick plunge, and the fear vanished in a flood of pleasure. He slipped his free arm beneath her neck. Her eyes closed, and her head lolled as he bent to kiss her throat.

She was nothing but feeling, heat coming through her in waves, stronger and stronger as he took her with slow, luscious drives. He rolled his hips with each forward pitch, repeating the movement until she went crimson and whimpered in a last burst of release. And he stayed with her, riding every drawn-out spasm until she was limp and quiet. Murmuring to her, he coaxed her to wrap one leg around his waist, and he lifted her other leg until it hooked over his shoulder. The position opened her, changed the angle between them, so that when he thrust again, it caressed a new place inside her. Another rush of pleasure started, surging so high and fast that she could hardly breathe. She lay still beneath him, her legs trembling as she took him more deeply than she had thought possible. She was propelled into another climax, strong and dizzying, but before the last tremors had faded, he withdrew abruptly to take his own release, his sex throbbing viciously against her stomach.

"Oh, Cat," he said after a while, still over her, his hands gripped in the bedclothes.

She turned her face until her lips brushed the rim of his ear. The erotic perfume of sex and damp skin filled her nostrils. Her palm went to his back, smoothing over the taut surface, and she felt him shiver in pleasure at the gentle scratch of her nails. How remarkable it was to lie with a man, feeling him soften inside her as their pulses slowed. What an astonishing assimilation of flesh and moisture and sensation, the lingering twinges and pulses in the places they pressed together.

Leo lifted his head and looked down at her. "Marks," he said, his voice uneven, "you are not a perfect woman."

"I'm aware of that," she said.

"You have an evil temper, you're as blind as a mole, you're a deplorable poet, and frankly, your French accent could use some work." Supporting himself on his elbows, Leo took her face in his hands. "But when I put those things together with the rest of you, it makes you into the most perfectly imperfect woman I've ever known."

Absurdly pleased, she smiled up into his face.

"You are beautiful beyond words," Leo went on. "You are kind, amusing, and passionate. You also have a keen intellect, but I'm willing to overlook that."

Her smile faded. "Are you leading to another marriage proposal?"

His gaze was intent. "I have a special license from the Archbishop's Court of Faculties. We could wed at any church, whenever we please. We could be married by morning, if you say yes."

Catherine turned her face away from his, pressing a frown into the mattress. She owed him an answer—she owed him honesty. "I'm not certain I'll ever be able to say yes to that."

Leo was very still. "Do you mean only when I propose, or if any man did?"

"Any man," she admitted. "It's only that with you, it's very difficult to refuse."

"Well, that's encouraging," he said, although his tone conveyed the opposite.

Leo left the bed and went to get a damp cloth for her. Returning, he stood beside the bed and watched her. "Think of it this way," he said. "Marriage would change hardly anything between us, except that we would end our arguments in a much more satisfying way. And of course I would have extensive legal rights over your body, your property, and all your individual freedoms, but I don't see what's so alarming about that."

His quip almost made Catherine smile again, despite her encroaching despair. Finishing her ablutions, she set the cloth on the bedside table and pulled the bed linens up to her breasts. "I wish people were like the clocks and mechanisms that Harry is so clever at constructing. Then I could have whatever is wrong with me repaired. As it is, though, I have some parts that aren't working properly."

Leo sat on the side of the bed, his gaze holding hers. He extended a muscular arm and caught the back of her neck in his hand, and held her steady. His mouth possessed hers roughly, until her head swam and her heart pounded. Lifting his head, he said, "I adore all of your parts exactly as they are." He drew back and touched her taut jawline, his fingers gentle. "Can you at least admit that you're fond of me?"

Catherine swallowed against the soft caress. "I . . . it's obvious that I am."

"Then say it," he urged, stroking the side of her throat.

"Why must I say something if it's obvious?"

But he persisted, damn him, seeming to understand how difficult it was for her. "It's only a few words." His thumb brushed the hard, anxious pulse at the base of her neck. "Don't be afraid."

"Please, I can't—"

"Say it."

Catherine couldn't look at him. She went hot and cold. Taking

255

a deep breath, she managed a shaking whisper. "I'm f-fond of you."

"There," Leo murmured, beginning to draw her close. "Was that so bad?"

Her body was wrenched with the longing to huddle against his inviting chest. But instead she put her arms between them, preserving a crucial distance. "It makes no difference," she forced herself to say. "In fact, it makes it worse."

His arms loosened. He gave her a quizzical glance. "Worse?"

"Yes, because I can never give you anything more than that. And regardless of what you claim to the contrary, you'll want the kind of marriage your sisters have. The way Amelia is with Cam, the devotion and intimacy . . . you'll want that too."

"I don't want intimacy with Cam."

"Don't joke about it," she said wretchedly. "This is serious."

"I'm sorry," came his quiet reply. "Sometimes serious conversations make me uncomfortable, and I tend to resort to humor as a result." He paused. "I understand what you're trying to tell me. But what if I say that attraction and fondness would be enough?"

"I wouldn't believe you. Because I know how unhappy you would become, seeing your sisters' marriages, remembering how devoted your parents were to each other, and knowing that ours was a counterfeit by comparison. A parody."

"What makes you so certain that we won't come to care for each other?"

"I just am. I've looked inside my heart, and it's not there. That's what I meant before. I don't think I'll ever be able to trust anyone enough to love them. Even you."

Leo's face was expressionless, but she sensed something dark lurking beneath his self-control, something that hinted of anger, or exasperation. "It's not that you're unable," he said. "It's

256

that you don't want to." He released her carefully and went to retrieve his discarded clothes. As he dressed, he spoke in a voice that chilled her with its pleasant blandness. "I have to leave."

"You're angry."

"No. But if I stay, I'll end up making love to you and proposing to you repeatedly, until morning. And even my tolerance for rejection has its limits."

Words of regret and self-reproach hovered on her lips. But she held them back, sensing that it would only infuriate him. Leo was hardly a man to fear a challenge. But he was beginning to comprehend that he could do nothing with the challenge she presented, some inexplicable quandary that couldn't be solved.

After dressing and shrugging into his coat, Leo returned to the bedside. "Don't try to predict what you're capable of," he murmured, sliding his fingers beneath her chin. He bent to press his lips to her forehead, and added, "You may surprise yourself." Going to the door, he opened it and glanced up and down the hallway. He glanced at Catherine over his shoulder. "Lock the door when I leave."

"Good night," she said with difficulty. "And . . . I'm sorry, my lord. I wish I were different. I wish I could—" She stopped and shook her head miserably.

Pausing a bit longer, Leo gave her a look of amusement edged with warning. "You're going to lose this battle, Cat. And despite yourself, you're going to be very happy in defeat."

Chapter Twenty-seven

Paying a call on Vanessa Darvin the following day was the last thing Leo wanted to do. However, he was curious about why she wanted to see him. The address that Poppy had given to him was of a Mayfair residence in South Audley Street, not far from the terrace he leased. It was a Georgian town house, neat red brick with white trim, fronted by a white pediment with four slender pilaster columns.

Leo liked Mayfair immensely, not so much for its fashionable reputation as the fact that it had once been deemed a "lewd and disorderly" place in the early eighteenth century by the Grand Jury of Westminster. It had been condemned for its practices of gaming, bawdy stage plays, prizefighting and animal baiting, and all the attendant vices of crime and prostitution. Over the next hundred years it had gradually gentrified until John Nash had sealed its hard-won respectability with Regent Street and Regent's Park. To Leo, however, Mayfair would always be a respectable lady with a notorious past.

Upon arriving at the residence, Leo was shown to a reception room overlooking a two-tiered garden. Vanessa Darvin and Countess Ramsay were both present, welcoming him warmly. As they all sat and made the obligatory small talk, inquiring after the health of their family, and his, and the weather, and other safe and polite subjects of an opening acquaintance, Leo found that his impressions of the two women from the ball in Hampshire were unchanged. The countess was a garrulous biddy, and Vanessa Darvin was a self-involved beauty.

A quarter hour passed, and then a half hour. Leo began to wonder if he would ever discover why they had prevailed on him to call.

"Dear me," the countess eventually exclaimed, "I quite forgot that I had intended to consult with Cook about the evening meal. Pardon, I must go at once." She stood, and Leo automatically rose to his feet.

"Perhaps I should leave, as well," he said, grateful for the opportunity to escape.

"Do stay, my lord," Vanessa said quietly. A look passed between Vanessa and the countess before the latter left the room.

Recognizing the obvious pretext to leave them alone, Leo lowered back into the chair. He raised a brow as he regarded Vanessa. "So there is a point to this."

"There is a point," Vanessa confirmed. She was beautiful, her shining dark hair arranged in pinned-up curls, her eyes exotic and striking in her porcelain complexion. "I wish to discuss a highly personal matter with you. I hope I may rely on your discretion."

"You may." Leo studied her with a flicker of interest. There was a hint of uncertainty, urgency, beneath her provocative façade.

"I'm not certain how best to begin," she said.

"Be blunt," Leo suggested. "Subtleties are usually wasted on me."

259

"I would like to put forth a proposition, my lord, that will satisfy our mutual needs."

"How intriguing. I wasn't aware that we had mutual needs."

"Obviously yours is to marry and have a son quickly, before you die."

Leo was mildly startled. "I hadn't planned to expire any time soon."

"What about the Ramsay curse?"

"I don't believe in the Ramsay curse."

"Neither did my father," she said pointedly.

"Well, then," Leo said, both annoyed and amused, "in light of my rapidly approaching demise, we shouldn't waste a moment. Tell me what you want, Miss Darvin."

"I need to find a husband as quickly as possible, or I will soon find myself in a very unpleasant position."

Leo watched her alertly, making no response.

"Although we are not well acquainted," she continued, "I know a great deal about you. Your past exploits are hardly a secret. And I believe all the qualities that would make you an unsuitable husband for anyone else would make you ideal for me. We are very much alike, you see. From all accounts, you are cynical, amoral, and selfish." A deliberate pause. "So am I. Which is why I would never try to change any of those things about you."

Fascinating. For a girl no more than twenty, she possessed preternatural self-confidence.

"Whenever you chose to stray," Vanessa continued, "I wouldn't complain. I probably wouldn't even notice, because I would be similarly occupied. It would be a sophisticated marriage. I can give you children to ensure that the Ramsay title and estate will stay in your line of descent. Furthermore, I can—"

"Miss Darvin," Leo said carefully, "pray don't continue." The irony of the situation was hardly lost on him—she was proposing a true marriage of convenience, free from messy desires and feelings. The diametric opposite of the marriage he wanted with Catherine.

Not long ago, that might have appealed to him.

Settling back in his chair, Leo regarded her with detached patience. "I don't deny the stories of my past sins. But despite all that . . . or perhaps because of it . . . the idea of a sophisticated marriage doesn't appeal to me in the least."

He saw by the frozen stillness of Vanessa's face that he had surprised her. She took her time about replying. "Perhaps it should, my lord. A better woman would be disappointed and shamed by you, and come to hate you. Whereas *I*'—she touched her chest in a practiced gesture, drawing his attention to her round, perfect bosom—"would never expect anything from you."

The arrangement Vanessa Darvin proposed was a perfect recipe for aristocratic domesticity. How fantastically bloodless and civilized.

"But I need someone to expect something from me," he heard himself say.

The truth of that bolted through him like lightning. Had he really just said it? And did he truly mean it?

Yes. Dear God.

When and how had he changed? It had been a mortal struggle to leave behind the excesses of grief and self-loathing. Somewhere along the way he had stopped wanting to die, which was not quite the same thing as wanting to live. But that had been enough for a while.

Until Catherine. She had reawakened him like a cold dash of water in his face. She made him want to be a better man, not just for her, but for himself, as well. He should have known that Catherine would push him over the edge. Good God, how she pushed him. And he loved it. Loved *her*. His small, bespectacled warrior.

I won't let you fall, she had said to him, the day he'd been injured at the ruins. *I won't let you turn into a degenerate.* She had meant it, and he had believed her, and that had been the turning point.

How deeply he had resisted loving someone like this . . . and yet it was exhilarating. He felt as if his soul had been set on fire, every part of him burning with impatient joy.

Aware that his color had heightened, Leo took a deep breath and let it out slowly. A smile twitched his lips as he reflected on the peculiar inconvenience of realizing that he was in love with one woman, when he had just been proposed to by another.

"Miss Darvin," he said gently, "I am honored by your suggestion. But you want the man I was. Not the man I am now."

The dark eyes flashed with malice. "You're claiming to be reformed? You think to disown your past?"

"Not at all. But I have hopes for a better future." He paused deliberately. "Ramsay curse notwithstanding."

"You're making a mistake." Vanessa's pretty features hardened. "I knew you were no gentleman, but I didn't take you for a fool. You should leave now. It seems you'll be of no use to me."

Leo rose obligingly. He paused before taking his leave, giving her an astute glance. "I can't help but ask, Miss Darvin . . . why don't you simply marry the baby's father?"

It turned out to be a very good guess.

Vanessa's eyes flared before she managed to school her expression. "He is too far beneath me," she said in a tight little voice. "I'm rather more discriminating than your sisters, my lord."

"A pity," Leo murmured. "They seem to be very happy in their lack of discrimination." He bowed politely. "Farewell, Miss Darvin. I wish you luck in your search for a husband who's not beneath you."

"I don't need luck, my lord. I will marry, and soon. And I've no doubt my future husband and I will be happy indeed when we come to take possession of Ramsay House."

Returning to the hotel from a morning dressmaker's appointment with Poppy, Catherine shivered in pleasure as they entered the Rutledge apartments. It was raining steadily, in fat chilling drops that heralded the approach of autumn. Despite the precautions of cloaks and umbrellas, she and Poppy had not escaped entirely from the damp. They both went to the parlor hearth, standing before the snapping fire.

"Harry ought to be coming back from Bow Street soon," Poppy said, pushing back a wet tendril of hair that had stuck to her cheek. He had gone for a meeting with a special constable and a Bow Street magistrate to discuss Lord Latimer. So far Harry had been maddeningly close-mouthed as to the specifics of the situation, promising that after he'd gone to the magistrate's office, he would explain in detail. "And so should my brother, after seeing Miss Darvin."

Catherine removed her spectacles and used a fold of her sleeve to clear the steam from the lenses. She heard a welcoming sound from Dodger, a sort of ferrety chuckling noise, and he came loping toward her out of seemingly nowhere. Replacing her spectacles, she bent to pick him up, and he wriggled into her arms. "You odious rat," she murmured, cradling his long, sleek body.

"He loves you, Catherine," Poppy said, shaking her head and smiling.

"Nevertheless, I'm returning him to Beatrix at the first opportunity." But she furtively lowered her cheek and let Dodger kiss her.

There was a knock at the door, followed by the bustle of someone entering, a masculine murmur, a maid taking his coat and hat. Leo entered the parlor, bringing in the scents of damp wool and rain. His hair was wet at the ends, curling slightly against his neck.

"Leo," Poppy exclaimed with a laugh, "how wet you are! Didn't you take an umbrella?"

"Umbrellas are of little use when it's raining sideways," he informed her.

"I'll fetch a towel." Poppy darted out of the room.

Left alone with Leo, Catherine met his gaze. His smile faded, and he stared at her with alarming intensity. Why did he look at her that way? It seemed as if something had been cut loose in him, his eyes demon-blue and dangerous.

"How was your conversation with Miss Darvin?" she asked, tensing as he approached her.

"Illuminating."

She frowned at the brief reply, taking refuge in a show of exasperation. "What did she ask of you?"

"She proposed a marriage of convenience."

Catherine blinked. It was what she had expected, and yet to hear it caused a stab of jealousy.

Leo stopped beside her, the firelight flickering over his features. Tiny droplets of rain glittered like jewels on his sun-browned face. She wanted to touch that light mist, put her mouth on it, taste his skin.

"What was your response?" she forced herself to ask.

"I was flattered, of course," he said smoothly. "One always appreciates being wanted."

264

He knew she was jealous. He was toying with her. Catherine struggled to keep her temper from igniting.

"Perhaps you should accept her," she said coolly.

His gaze didn't move from hers. "Perhaps I did."

Catherine drew in a sharp breath.

"Here you are," Poppy said cheerfully, oblivious to the tension between them as she entered the room with a neat stack of toweling. She brought a cloth to Leo, who took it and blotted his face.

Catherine sat on the settee, letting Dodger coil in her lap.

"What did Miss Darvin want?" she heard Poppy ask.

Leo's voice was muffled in the towel. "She proposed to me."

"Good heavens," Poppy said. "She clearly hasn't any idea of what it's like to tolerate you on a daily basis."

"In her situation," he returned, "a woman can't afford to be particular."

"What situation is that?" Catherine asked tersely.

Leo handed the towel back to Poppy. "She's expecting a child. And she doesn't care to marry the father. That's not to go any further than this room, of course."

The two women were silent. Catherine wrestled with a curious mixture of feelings . . . sympathy, hostility, jealousy, fear. With this bit of news, the advantages of a match between Leo and Miss Darvin were abundantly clear.

Poppy regarded her brother gravely. "Her circumstances must be quite desperate, for her to confide in you like that."

Leo's reply was forestalled as Harry entered the apartments, his coat and hat streaming with water. "Good afternoon," Harry said, flashing a smile. The maid took the sodden hat and coat, and Poppy approached him with a fresh towel.

"You walked?" she asked, her gaze sweeping from the sodden

hems of his trouser legs to his rain-dappled features. She reached up to dry his face with wifely solicitude.

"I very nearly swam," Harry told her, seeming to enjoy her ministrations.

"Why didn't you take a hackney or send for a carriage?"

"All the hackneys were taken as soon as the rain started," Harry replied. "And it's a short distance. Only a milksop would send for a carriage."

"Better a milksop than to catch your death of cold," Poppy fussed, following as he drew near the hearth.

Harry smiled and leaned down to steal a kiss from her as he worked at the wet knot of his cravat. "I never catch cold." Drawing off the damp length of linen, he tossed it aside and stood by the fire. He glanced at Leo expectantly. "What of your meeting with Miss Darvin?"

Leo sat and leaned forward with his elbows braced on his knees. "Never mind that, tell us about the visit to Bow Street."

"Special Constable Hembrey has considered the information you provided, and he's willing to take up an investigation."

"What kind of investigation?" Catherine asked, looking from Harry to Leo.

Leo's face was impassive as he explained. "A few years ago, Lord Latimer invited me to join an exclusive club. A kind of rakehell society, with secret meetings held in a former abbey."

Catherine's eyes widened. "What is the purpose of the society?"

Harry and Leo were both silent. Eventually Leo replied in a flat tone, his gaze fixed on a distant point outside the rain-streaked windows. "Unmitigated depravity. Mock religious rituals, assaults, unnatural crimes. I'll spare you the details, except to say they were so distasteful that even at the height of my debauchery, I turned down Latimer's invitation."

Catherine watched him carefully. His face was set, a small muscle in his jaw flexing. The firelight gilded the taut lines of his face.

"Latimer was so certain I would want to participate," Leo continued, "that he went into some detail regarding some of the crimes he was involved in. And by some fluke I happened to be sober enough to remember most of what he said."

"Is the information enough to support prosecution?" Catherine asked. "And as a peer, doesn't Lord Latimer have the right of freedom from arrest?"

"Only in civil cases," Harry told her. "Not in criminal ones."

"Then you think he'll be brought to trial?"

"No, it won't come to that," Leo said quietly. "The society can't allow their activities to be exposed. When they realize that Latimer is the focus of an investigation, they'll probably force him to leave England before he can be prosecuted. Or better yet, they'll see to it that he ends up as a floater in the Thames."

"Will Constable Hembrey want to depose me?" Catherine brought herself to ask.

"Absolutely not," Leo said with reassuring firmness. "There's more than enough evidence against him without your involvement."

"However it plays out," Harry added, "Latimer will be far too busy to trouble you further, Cat."

"Thank you," Catherine told Harry. Her gaze flickered back to Leo as she added, "That is a great relief." After an awkward pause, she repeated herself lamely. "A great relief, indeed."

"You don't seem all that relieved," Leo observed lazily. "Why is that, Marks?"

This lack of sympathy, along with his earlier taunts about Miss Darvin, were too much for Catherine's shredded nerves.

"If you were in my position," she said stiffly, "you wouldn't exactly be dancing a jig, either."

"You're in a fine position." Leo's eyes were like blue ice. "Latimer will soon be gone, Rutledge has acknowledged you publicly, you're a woman of means, and you have no obligations or commitments to anyone. What could you possibly want that you don't have?"

"Nothing at all," she snapped.

"I think you're sorry to stop running and hiding. Because now you have to face the unfortunate fact that you have nothing . . . and no one . . . to run to."

"It's enough for me to stay still," she said coldly.

Leo smiled with provoking insouciance. "That brings to mind the old paradox."

"What paradox?"

"About what happens when an unstoppable force meets an immovable object."

Harry and Poppy were both silent, looking back and forth between them.

"I suppose I'm the immovable object?" Catherine asked sarcastically.

"If you like."

"Well, I *don't* like," she said, scowling, "because I've always thought that was an absurd question."

"Why?" Leo asked.

"There is no possible answer."

Their gazes clashed and held.

"Yes, there is," Leo said, seeming to enjoy her rising fury.

Harry joined in the debate. "Not from a scientific standpoint. An immovable object would require infinite mass, and the unstoppable force would require infinite energy, neither of which is possible."

"If you argue in terms of semantics, however," Leo countered with maddening calmness, "there is an answer."

"Naturally," Harry said dryly. "A Hathaway can always find a way to argue. Enlighten us—what is the answer?"

Leo replied with his gaze fixed on Catherine's tense face. "The unstoppable force takes the path of least resistance and goes right around the object . . . leaving it far behind."

He was challenging her, Catherine realized. Arrogant, manipulative cad, using poor Vanessa Darvin's plight to provoke her *and* implying what might happen if Catherine didn't give in to him. *Go right around the object . . . leave it far behind . . .* Indeed!

She jumped to her feet, glaring at him. "Why don't you go on and marry her, then?" Snatching up her reticule, and Dodger's limp body, she stormed out of the apartments.

Leo was instantly at her heels.

"Ramsay—" Harry began.

"Not now, Rutledge," Leo muttered, striding after Catherine. The door was closed with a force that caused it to tremble in its frame.

In the ensuing stillness, Harry looked at Poppy in bewilderment. "I'm not usually slow-witted," he said. "But what the devil were they bickering about?"

"Miss Darvin, I think." Going to him, Poppy sat in his lap and linked her arms around his neck. "She's with child and wants to marry Leo."

"Oh." Harry leaned his head against the back of the chair. His mouth twisted. "I see. He's using it to try and push Catherine into making a decision."

"You don't approve," Poppy said rather than asked, stroking a damp lock of hair off his forehead.

Harry gave her a wry glance. "It's exactly what I would do in his position. Of course I don't approve."

"Stop following me!"

"I want to talk to you." Leo kept pace with Catherine as she hurried along the hallway, his ground-eating strides accounting for every two of her short ones.

"I have no interest in anything you have to say."

"You're jealous." He sounded more than a little pleased by the fact.

"Of you and Miss Darvin?" She forced a scornful laugh. "I pity the both of you. I can't conceive of a more ill-destined match."

"You can't deny that she's a very attractive woman."

"Except for her neck," Catherine couldn't resist saying.

"What the devil is the matter with her neck?"

"It's abnormally long."

Leo tried, unsuccessfully, to smother a laugh. "I can overlook that. Because if I marry her, I'll get to keep Ramsay House, and we'll have a baby already on the way. Convenient, isn't it? Moreover, Miss Darvin promised that I could philander to my heart's content, and she would look the other way."

"What about fidelity?" Catherine asked in outrage.

"Fidelity is so passé. It's laziness, really, not bothering to go out and seduce new people."

"You told me that you would have no difficulty with fidelity!"

"Yes, but that was when we were talking about *our* marriage. Marriage with Miss Darvin will be another thing entirely."

Leo stopped with her as they reached the door of her suite. While Catherine held the sleeping ferret, Leo reached inside her reticule and extracted the key. Catherine didn't spare him a glance as he opened the door for her.

"May I come in?" he asked.

"No."

Leo pushed his way in regardless, and closed the door behind them.

"Pray don't let me keep you," Catherine said grimly, going to set Dodger in his little basket. "I'm sure you have much to do. Starting with changing the name on the special license."

"No, the license is only good for you. If I marry Miss Darvin, I'd have to pay for a new one."

"I hope it's expensive," she said vehemently.

"It is." Leo approached her from behind and put his arms around her, hauling her back securely against him. "And there's another problem."

"What is it?" she asked, struggling in his grasp.

His mouth touched the edge of her ear. "I want you," he whispered. "Only you. Always you."

Catherine went still. Her eyes closed against a sudden wet sting. "Did you accept her proposal?"

Leo nuzzled tenderly into the hollow beneath her ear. "Of course not, pea-goose."

She couldn't prevent a little sob of angry relief. "Then why did you imply that you had?"

"Because you need to be pushed. Otherwise you'll drag this affair out until I'm too decrepit to be of any use to you." Steering Catherine toward the bed, he scooped her up and tossed her to the mattress. Her spectacles went flying to the side.

"What are you doing?" Catherine struggled indignantly, propping herself up on her elbows. She was buried in the masses of her skirts, with their sodden hems and heavy damp flounces. "My dress is wet."

271

"I'll help you remove it." His solicitous tone was belied by the wicked gleam in his eyes.

She floundered amid the layers and flounces, while Leo unhooked and unfastened her with astonishing efficiency. One would have thought he had more than two arms, as he turned her this way and that, his hands reaching everywhere. Ignoring her protests, he pulled the heavy skirt, with its stiffened muslin lining, away from the detachable bodice, and tossed it to the floor. Her shoes were removed and dropped over the side of the bed. Flipping Catherine to her stomach, he began on the fastenings of the heavily ruched bodice.

"I beg your pardon, I did not ask to be husked like an ear of corn!" She twisted in an effort to push away his busy hands. A squeak escaped her as he found the tapes of her drawers and pulled them loose.

With a low chuckle, Leo anchored her squirming body with his legs, and kissed the exposed nape of her neck. She felt warm all over, her nerves sparked by the touch of his sensuous mouth.

"Did you kiss her?" she heard herself blurt out, her voice muffled in the bedclothes.

"No, love. I wasn't tempted by her in the least." Leo bit lightly into the soft muscle of her neck, stroked the fine skin with his tongue, and she gasped. His hand slipped inside her drawers and circled over her bottom. "No other woman in the world could excite me as you do. But you're too damn stubborn, and far too good at protecting yourself. There are things I want to say to you . . . do to you . . . and the fact that you're not ready for any of it is going to drive us both mad."

He touched further between her thighs, finding wetness, stroking in soft circles. She moaned and writhed beneath him. Her corset was still snugly laced, the compression of her waist seeming to divert sensation down between her thighs. Although part of her rebelled at the feeling of being held down and caressed, her body reacted with helpless pleasure.

"I want to make love to you." Leo traced the inner structure of her ear with the tip of his tongue. "I want to go as deep as you can take me, and feel you tighten around me, and I want to come inside you." A finger slid inside her, and another, and she whimpered softly. "You know how good it would feel," he whispered, stroking her slowly. "Yield to me, and I'll love you without stopping. I'll stay in you all night."

Catherine gasped for breath, while her heart thumped madly. "You would have me in the same position as Miss Darvin," she said. "Pregnant and pleading for you to marry me."

"God, yes, I would love that."

She nearly choked with indignation, while his long fingers teased her inside and out. Her body began to clench in a slow, steady pulse of desire. There were great swaths of fabric caught between their bodies, layers of remaining clothing, and all she could feel was his mouth at the back of her neck, and that devilishly persuasive hand.

"I have never said this to anyone before." Leo's voice was like ragged velvet. "But the idea of you with child is the most insanely arousing thing I've ever imagined. Your belly all swollen, your breasts heavy, the funny little way you would walk . . . I would worship you. I would take care of your every need. And everyone would know that I'd made you that way, that you belonged to me."

"You . . . you are so . . ." She couldn't even think of a suitable word.

"I know. Woefully primitive." Laughter threaded through his voice. "But I must be tolerated, because I'm a man and I really can't help it."

He caressed her with gentle, explicit manipulation, his fingers slick and tireless. She felt a new flush of arousal, the liquid heat spreading out to her fingers and toes. Moving behind her, he tugged her drawers to her knees, and fumbled with the fastenings of his trousers. He let his weight settle on her deliciously. A blunt, moist pressure slipped between her thighs, not quite entering. White fire raced through her senses, and her body trembled at the verge of release . . . so close . . .

"You have a decision to make, Cat." Leo kissed the side of her throat hungrily, his mouth strong and wet. "Either tell me to stop right now, or let me take you all the way. Because I can't withdraw at the last moment any longer. I want you too much. And I probably will make you pregnant, love, because I'm feeling rather potent at the moment. So it's all or nothing. Tell me yes or no."

"I *can't*." Catherine thrashed in frustration as his hips lifted from hers. As he rolled her over to face him, she glared up at him. Unable to stop himself, he lowered his head and kissed her voraciously, savoring the sound of need that came from her throat.

"A pity," he said, breathing heavily. "I was working up to something really lascivious." Rolling off her, he reached for the fall of his trousers, muttering something about the risk of doing himself permanent injury as he tried to fasten them again.

Catherine watched him incredulously. "You're not going to finish?"

He let out an unsteady sigh. "As I said, all or nothing."

She wrapped her arms around herself, trembling with desire until her teeth chattered. "Why are you trying to torture me?"

"It's becoming clear that a lifetime of patience wouldn't be enough to break through your guard. So I'll have to try some-

274

thing else." Leo kissed her gently and left the bed. After he raked both hands through his disheveled hair and straightened his clothes, he gave her a smoldering glance, followed by a grin that seemed to mock both of them simultaneously. "I'm waging war, love. And the only way to win this kind of war is to make you want to lose."

Chapter Twenty-eight

Only a woman made of stone could have lasted against the campaign Leo launched over the next week. It was courtship, he claimed, but there should have been another word for it, the way he kept Catherine constantly off balance with his sweetly subversive charm.

One moment he provoked her into some nonsensical and highly entertaining argument, and the next he was soothing and kind. He whispered whimsical compliments and lines of poetry in her ear, and taught her naughty French words, and made her laugh at inappropriate moments. What Leo did not do, however, was try to kiss or seduce her. At first Catherine was amused by this obvious tactic, and then secretly miffed, and then intrigued. She frequently found herself staring at his mouth, so flawless and firm . . . she couldn't help remembering their past kisses, daydreaming about them.

When they attended a private musical evening at a mansion on Upper Brook Street, Leo stole Catherine away as the hostess led a group of guests on a tour of the house. Following Leo to a private corner behind an arrangement of tall potted ferns, Catherine went eagerly into his arms. Instead of kissing her, however, he pulled her into the warm strength of his body . . . and held her. Simply held her, keeping her warm and close, letting his hands course slowly over her back. He whispered something secretive amid the pinned-up swirls of her hair, the words too soft for her to hear.

What Catherine enjoyed above all was walking with Leo through the Rutledge gardens, where sunlight stuttered through trees and hedges, and the breezes carried the crisp hint of approaching autumn. They had long conversations, sometimes touching on sensitive subjects. Careful questions, difficult answers. And yet it seemed they were both struggling toward the same goal, a kind of connection that neither of them had ever known before.

Sometimes Leo drew back and looked at her for wordless moments as one might stare at a work of art in a museum, trying to discover its truth. It was compelling, the interest he showed in her. Seductive. And he was a wonderful conversationalist, telling her stories about his childhood misadventures, about what it had been like to grow up in the Hathaway family, about the time he had spent in Paris and Provence. Catherine listened carefully to the details, gathering them like quilting scraps, piecing them together to form a better understanding of one of the more complex men she had ever met.

Leo was an unsentimental rogue who was capable of great sensitivity and compassion. He was an articulate man who could use words either to soothe like a balm of honey, or dissect like a surgeon's knife. When it suited him, Leo played the part of a jaded aristocrat, adeptly concealing the quicksilver workings of his brain. But sometimes in unguarded moments, Catherine caught glimpses of the gallant boy he had once been, before experience had weathered and hardened him.

"In some ways he's very much like our father was," Poppy told her in private. "Father *loved* conversation. He was a serious man, an intellectual, but he possessed a streak of whimsy." She grinned, remembering. "My mother always said she might have married a more handsome man, or a wealthier one, but never one who talked as he did. And she knew herself to be the kind of woman who would never have been happy with a dullard."

Catherine could well understand that. "Did Lord Ramsay favor your mother in any regard?"

"Oh, yes. She had an artistic eye, and she encouraged Leo in his architectural pursuits." Poppy paused. "I don't think she would have been pleased to learn that Leo would inherit a title— she didn't have a high opinion of the aristocracy. And she certainly wouldn't have approved of Leo's behavior in the past few years, although she would be very glad that he had decided to mend his ways."

"Where did his wicked wit come from?" Catherine asked. "Your mother or your father?"

"That," Poppy said wryly, "is entirely Leo's own."

Nearly every day, Leo brought Catherine a small gift: a book, a box of sweets, a collar made of Brussels bobbin lace in a delicate pattern of openwork flowers. "This is the loveliest lacework I've ever seen," she told him regretfully, setting the exquisite gift on a nearby table with great care. "But my lord, I'm afraid—"

"I know," Leo said. "A gentleman shouldn't give personal items to a lady he's courting." He lowered his voice, mindful of being overheard by Poppy and the housekeeper, who were talking by the threshold of the Rutledge apartments. "But I can't take it back—no other woman could do it justice. And Marks, you have no idea of the self-restraint I exercised. I wanted to buy

278

you a pair of embroidered stockings with little flowers that run all the way up the insides of your—"

"My lord," Catherine whispered, a light blush covering her face. "You forget yourself."

"I haven't forgotten a thing, actually. Not one detail of your beautiful body. Soon I may start sketching you naked again. Every time I put a pencil to paper, the temptation nearly overwhelms me."

She tried to look severe. "You promised not to do that again."

"But my pencil has a will of its own," he said gravely.

Catherine's color deepened, even as a smile tugged at her lips. "You're incorrigible."

His lashes lowered fractionally. "Kiss me, and I'll behave."

She made an exasperated little sound. "*Now* you want to kiss me, when Poppy and the housekeeper are standing only a few yards away?"

"They won't notice. They're involved in a riveting conversation about hotel toweling." Leo's voice lowered to a whisper. "Kiss me. One little kiss. Right here." He pointed to his cheek.

Perhaps it was the fact that Leo looked rather boyish as he teased her, his blue eyes alight with mischief. But as Catherine looked at him, she was nearly overwhelmed with a strange new feeling, a warm giddiness that invaded every part of her body. She leaned forward, and instead of kissing his cheek, she put her mouth directly on his.

Leo drew in a surprised breath, letting her take the lead. And, giving in to temptation, she lingered longer than she had intended, her mouth softly teasing, her tongue shyly touching his lips. He responded with a low sound, his arms going around her. She sensed the rising heat in him, the carefully banked urges threatening to flare out of control.

Ending the kiss, Catherine half expected to see Poppy and the housekeeper, Mrs. Pennywhistle, both staring at them with scandalized expressions. But as she peeked over Leo's shoulder, she saw that the housekeeper's back was still turned toward them.

Poppy had taken in the situation with an astute glance. "Mrs. Pennywhistle," she said glibly, ushering the housekeeper away from the threshold, "do come out into the hallway with me, I thought I saw a dreadful stain on the carpeting the other day, and I wanted to show you . . . is it here? . . . No, perhaps over there . . . Oh, drat, where is it?"

Left in temporary privacy, Catherine looked into Leo's heavy-lidded blue eyes.

"Why did you do that?" he asked, his voice husky.

She tried to think of an answer that would amuse him. "I wanted you to test my higher brain function."

A smile tugged at the corners of his lips. Taking a deep breath, he let it out slowly. "If you have a match when you enter a dark room," he finally said, "which would you light first—the oil lamp on the table, or the kindling in the hearth?"

Catherine squinted as she considered the question. "The lamp."

"The match," he said, shaking his head. His tone was soft and chiding. "Marks, you're not even trying."

"Another one," she prompted, and he complied without hesitation, his head bending over hers. He gave her a long, smoldering kiss, and she relaxed against him, her fingers sinking into his hair. He finished the kiss with a voluptuous nudge.

"Is it legal or illegal for a man to marry his widow's sister?" he asked.

"Illegal," she said languidly, trying to pull his head back to hers.

"Impossible, because he's dead." Leo resisted her efforts and looked down at her with a crooked grin. "It's time to stop."

"No," she protested, straining toward him.

"Easy, Marks," he whispered. "One of us has to have some self-control, and it really should be you." He brushed his lips against her forehead. "I have another present for you."

"What is it?"

"Look in my pockets." He jumped a little and laughed unsteadily as she began to search him. "No, you little ravisher, not my trouser pockets." Grabbing her wrists in his hands, he held them suspended in the air, as if he were trying to subdue a playful kitten. Seeming unable to resist, he leaned forward and took her mouth again. Being kissed while he held her wrists might have frightened her once, but now it awakened something deep and ticklish inside.

Leo tore his mouth away and released her with a gasping laugh. "Coat pocket. My God, I want to—no, I won't say it. Yes, there's your present."

Catherine drew out an object wrapped in soft cloth. Gently she unwrapped a new pair of spectacles made of silver . . . gleaming and perfect, the oval lenses sparkling. Marveling at the workmanship, she drew a finger along one of the intricate filigreed earpieces, all the way to the curved tip. "They're so beautiful," she said in wonder.

"If they please you, we'll have another pair made in gold. Here, let me help you . . ." Leo gently drew the old spectacles off her face, seeming to savor the gesture.

She put the new ones on. They felt light and secure on the bridge of her nose. As she looked around the room, everything was wonderfully detailed and in focus. In her excitement, she jumped up and hurried to the looking glass that hung over the entryway table. She inspected her own glowing reflection.

"How pretty you are." Leo's tall, elegant form appeared behind hers. "I do love spectacles on a woman."

Catherine's smiling gaze met his in the silvered glass. "Do you? What an odd preference."

"Not at all." His hands came to her shoulders, lightly fondling up to her throat and back again. "They emphasize your beautiful eyes. And they make you look capable of secrets and surprises—which, as we know, you are." His voice lowered. "Most of all I love the act of removing them—getting you ready for a tumble in bed."

She shivered at his bluntness, her eyes half closing as she felt him pull her back against him. His mouth went to the side of her neck.

"You like them?" Leo murmured, kissing her soft skin.

"Yes." Her head listed to the side as his tongue traced a subtle path along her throat. "I . . . I don't know why you went to such trouble. It was very kind."

Leo's dark head lifted, and he met her drowsy gaze in the looking glass. His fingers went to the side of her throat, stroking as if to rub the feel of his mouth into her skin. "I wasn't being kind," he murmured, a smile touching his lips. "I merely wanted you to see clearly."

I'm beginning to, she was tempted to tell him, but Poppy returned to the apartment before she was able.

That night Catherine slept badly, stumbling into the nightmare world that seemed as real, if not more real, than the infinitely kinder world she inhabited in her waking moments.

It was part dream, part memory, the recollection of running through her grandmother's house until she had found the old woman sitting at her desk, writing in a ledger.

282

Heedlessly Catherine threw herself at her grandmother's feet and buried her face in the voluminous black skirts. She felt the old woman's skeletal fingers slide under her wet chin and lift it.

Her grandmother's face was masked with a sediment of powder, the ashy whiteness contrasting with her artificially darkened brows and hair. Unlike Althea, she wore no lip rouge, only colorless salve.

"Althea talked to you," Grandmother said, in a voice like dried leaves rubbing together.

Catherine struggled to force out words between sobs. "Yes . . . and I don't underst . . . *understand* . . ."

Grandmother responded with a scratchy croon, pressing Catherine's head on her lap. She stroked her hair, narrow fingers combing lightly through the loose locks. "Did Althea fail to explain adequately? Come, you're not a clever girl, but neither are you stupid. What don't you understand? Stop crying, you know I detest it."

Catherine squeezed her eyes tightly, trying to stop the tears from slipping out. Her throat was tight with misery. "I want something else, anything else. I want a choice."

"You don't want to be like Althea?" The question was spoken with unnerving gentleness.

"No."

"And you don't want to be like me?"

Catherine hesitated and shook her head slightly, afraid to say "no" again. She had learned in the past that the word should be used sparingly with her grandmother. It was an unfailing irritant regardless of the circumstances.

"But you already are," Grandmother told her. "You're a woman. All women have a whore's life, child."

Catherine froze, afraid to move. Her grandmother's fingers

283

became talons, the stroking changing into a sort of slow, rhythmic clawing on her head.

"All women sell themselves to men," her grandmother continued. "Marriage itself is a transaction, in which a woman's value is tied to purposes of copulation and breeding. At least we, in our time-honored profession, are honest about it." Her tone turned reflective. "Men are foul, brutish creatures. But they own the world and always will. And to get the most from them, you must practice submission. You'll be very good at it, Catherine. I've seen the instinct in you. You like being told what to do. You'll like it even more when you're paid for it." Her hand lifted from Catherine's head. "Now, don't trouble me again. You may ask Althea all the questions you like. Mind you, when she began on her career, she was no happier about it than you. But she quickly saw the advantages of her situation. And we all have to earn our keep, don't we? Even you, dear. Being my granddaughter affords you no entitlement. And fifteen minutes on your back will earn you as much as other women earn in two or three days. Willing submission, Catherine."

Feeling stunned, as if she had just fallen from a great height, Catherine had left her grandmother's study. She knew a momentary, mad urge to bolt for the front door. But without a place to go to, without money, an unprotected girl would last only a matter of hours in London. The trapped sobs in her chest had dissolved into shivers.

She went upstairs to her room. But then the dream changed, the memories transforming into dark vagaries of imagination . . . becoming a nightmare. The stairs seemed to multiply, and the climb became difficult and she went upward into deeper and deeper shadows. Alone and shivering with cold, she reached her room, illuminated only by the glaze of moonlight.

284

There was a man sitting at the window. He was straddling the frame, actually, one long leg placed firmly on the floor, the other swinging negligently outside. She knew him from the shape of his head, from the powerful lines of his silhouette. And from the dark, a velvety voice that lifted the hairs on the back of her neck.

"There you are. Come here, Marks."

Catherine was suffused with relief and yearning. "My lord, what are you doing here?" she cried, running to him.

"Waiting for you." His arms went around her. "I'll take you far away from here—would you like that?"

"Oh, yes, yes . . . but how?"

"We'll go right out this window. I have a ladder."

"But is it safe? Are you certain—"

He put his hand gently to her mouth, silencing her. "Trust me." His hand pressed harder. "I won't let you fall."

She tried to tell him that she would go anywhere with him, do anything he said, but he was covering her mouth too tightly for her to speak. His grip became hurtful, clamping on her jaw. She couldn't breathe.

Catherine's eyes opened. The nightmare fell away, revealing a far worse reality. She struggled beneath a crushing weight, and tried to cry out against the callused hand that covered her mouth.

"Your aunt wants to see you," came a voice in the darkness. "I 'as to do this, miss. I 'as no choice."

In the space of just a few minutes, it was done.

William gagged her with a tight cloth that bit into her mouth, a large knot pressing hard against her tongue. After binding her hands and feet, he went to light a lamp. Even without the aid of her spectacles, Catherine perceived that he wore the dark blue coat of a Rutledge Hotel employee.

If only she could get a few words out, plead or bargain with him, but the knotted lump of cloth made coherent sound impossible. Her saliva spiked unpleasantly at the intensely acrid flavor of the gag. There was something on it, she realized, and at that same moment she felt her consciousness breaking into pieces, scattered like an unfinished puzzle. Her heart turned sluggish, pumping poisoned blood through her collapsing limbs, and there was a ballooning, thumping sensation in her head as if her brain had suddenly become too large for her skull.

William came to her with a hotel laundry bag. He began to pull it over her, starting at her feet. He didn't look at her face, only kept his gaze on his task. She watched passively, seeing that he took care to keep the hem of her nightgown primly down at her ankles. Some distant part of her brain wondered at the small kindness of preserving her modesty.

The bedclothes rustled near her feet, and Dodger streaked out with a furious chatter. With quicksilver speed he attacked William's arm and hand, inflicting a series of deep, gouging bites. Catherine had never seen the little animal behave in such a manner. William grunted in surprise and flung out his arm with a low curse. The ferret went flying, slamming hard against the wall and falling limply to the floor.

Catherine moaned behind the gag, her eyes burning with acid tears.

Breathing heavily, William examined his bleeding hand, found a cloth at the washstand to wrap around it, and returned to Catherine. The laundry bag was pulled higher and higher until it went over her head.

She understood that Althea didn't really want to see her. Althea wanted to destroy her. Perhaps William didn't know. Or perhaps he thought it was kinder to lie. It didn't matter. She felt nothing, no fear, no anguish, although tears leaked steadily from the outward corners of her eyes. What a terrible fate to leave the world feeling nothing at all. She was nothing more than a tangle of limbs in a sack, a headless doll, all memories receding, all sensation falling away.

A few thoughts needled through the blanket of nothingness, pinpricks of light in the dark.

Leo would never know that she had loved him.

She thought of his eyes, all those colors of blue. Her mind was filled with a constellation of high summer, stars in a lion's shape. *The brightest star marks his heart.*

He would grieve. If only she could spare him that.

Oh, what they could have had. A life together, such a simple thing. To watch that handsome face weather with age. She had to admit now that she had never been happier than in the moments with him.

Her heart beat faintly beneath her ribs. It was heavy, aching with contained feeling, a hard knot within the numbness.

I didn't want to need you, Leo, I fought so hard to stay standing at the edge of my own life . . . when I should have had the courage to walk into yours.

Chapter Twenty-nine

Late in the morning Leo returned from a visit with his old mentor, Rowland Temple. The architect, now a professor at University College, had recently been awarded the Royal Gold Medal for his work in advancing the academic study of architecture. Leo had been amused but hardly surprised to discover that Temple was as imperious and irascible as ever. The old man viewed the aristocracy as a source of patronage to keep him financially solvent, but he had contempt for their traditional and unimaginative sense of style.

"You're not one of those parasitical dunderheads," Temple had told him emphatically, which Leo gathered had been a compliment. And later, "My influence on you cannot be eradicated, can it?" And of course Leo had assured him that it could not, that he remembered and valued everything he had learned from Temple. He hadn't dared to mention the far greater influence of the elderly professor in Provence.

"Architecture is how we reconcile to the difficulties of life," Joseph had once told Leo at his *atelier*. The old professor had been repotting some herbs at a long wooden table, while Leo tried to help. "*Non,* don't touch these, *mon fils,* you pack the roots too tightly, they need more air than you allow them." He took a pot away from Leo and resumed the lecture. "To be an architect, you have to accept the environment around you, no matter what its conditions. Then, in full awareness, you take your ideals and form them into structure."

"Can I do it without ideals?" Leo had asked, only half joking. "I've learned I can't live up to them."

Professor Joseph had smiled at him. "Neither can you reach the stars. But you still need their light. You need them to navigate, *n'est-ce pas?*"

Take your ideals and form them into structure. Only in that way could a good house, a good building, be designed.

Or a good life.

And Leo had finally found the cornerstone, the essential piece to build the rest on.

A very stubborn cornerstone.

His lips curved as he considered what to do with Catherine that day, how to woo her, or annoy her, since she seemed to enjoy both equally. Perhaps he would start a small argument and kiss her into capitulation. Perhaps he would propose to her again, if he could catch her in a moment of weakness.

Heading to the Rutledge apartments, Leo entered after a careless knock, and found Poppy rushing to the entrance foyer.

"Have you—" she started, then broke off as she saw him. "Leo. I wondered when you'd get back. I didn't know where you were, or I would have sent for you—"

"What is it, sis?" he asked gently, understanding at once that something was very wrong.

Poppy looked wretched, her eyes large in her white face. "Catherine didn't come up for breakfast this morning. I assumed that she wanted to sleep late. Sometimes her nightmares—"

"Yes, I know." Leo gripped her cold hands, staring at her alertly. "Out with it, Poppy."

"An hour ago I send a housemaid to Catherine's room, to see if she needed something. She wasn't there, and these were on the table by the bed." Reaching out with a trembling hand, she gave him the new silver spectacles. "And . . . there was blood on the bed."

It took Leo a moment to contain the rush of panic. He felt it as instant stinging from head to toe, and a heart-thundering blast of energy. A dizzying urge to kill.

"The hotel is being searched," he heard Poppy say over the roar in his ears, "and Harry and Mr. Valentine are talking to the floor stewards."

"Latimer has her," Leo said thickly. "He sent someone for her. I'll rip the filthy whoreson's guts out and hang him with them—"

"Leo," she whispered, her hand fluttering to his mouth. What she saw in his face frightened her. "Please."

Relief partially smoothed Poppy's brow as her husband entered the apartment. "Harry, is there any sign?"

Harry's face was grim and hard. "One of the night stewards said that last night he saw a man dressed as an employee—he assumed he was newly hired—carrying a laundry sack down the back stairs. He noticed it because the housemaids usually take care of laundry, and never at that time of night." He put a restraining hand on Leo's shoulder, and Leo shook him off. "Ramsay, keep your head. I know what you assume, and you're probably right. But you can't go dashing off like a madman. We need to—"

"Try and stop me," Leo said in a guttural tone. There was no controlling what had been unleashed in him. He was gone before Harry could draw another breath.

"Christ," Harry muttered, dragging his hands through his black hair. He gave Poppy a distracted glance. "Find Valentine," he said. "He's still talking with the floor managers. Tell him to go to Special Constable Hembrey—or whoever he can find at Bow Street, and let them know what's happening. Hembrey can start by sending a man to Lord Latimer's house. Tell Valentine to say there's a murder in progress."

"Leo won't kill Lord Latimer," Poppy said, her face blanched.

"If he doesn't," Harry replied with cold certainty, "I will."

Catherine awakened in a strange euphoria, light-headed and list-less, and very glad to awaken from her nightmares. Except that when she opened her eyes, she was still in a nightmare, in a room hazed with sickening-sweet smoke, the windows shrouded with heavy curtains.

She took a long time to collect herself, straining to see with-out spectacles. Her jaw was sore, her mouth unbearably dry. She was desperate for a sip of cold water, a breath of clean air. Her wrists were fastened behind her back. She half reclined, half sat on a settee, dressed in her nightgown. Awkwardly she used her shoulder to try to push back some of the loose tangles of her hair that had fallen over her face.

Catherine knew this room, blurry as it was. And she knew the old woman sitting near her, stick thin and dressed in black. The woman's hands moved with the delicacy of an insect's pincers as she lifted a thin leather hose attached to a hookah vase. Putting the hose to her lips, she sucked in a breath, held it, and expelled a puff of white smoke.

"Grandmother?" Catherine asked, her voice rough, her tongue thick in her mouth.

The woman moved closer, until her face came into Catherine's limited view. A powdered white face, vermillon lips. Hard, familiar eyes rimmed with kohl. "She's dead. It's my house now. My business."

Althea, Catherine realized in dull horror. A cadaverous version of Althea, the once attractive features shrunken and calcified. The face powder covered the top stratum of skin but hadn't settled into the web of wrinkles, giving her complexion the appearance of crackled glaze on porcelain. She was far more fearsome than even Grandmother had been. And she looked more than a little mad, her eyes bulging and blue-glazed like those of a baby bird.

"William told me he'd seen you," Althea said. "And I said, 'We must fetch her for a long overdue visit, mustn't we?' It took a bit of planning on his part, but he executed it nicely." She glanced into a shadowed corner. "You're a good boy, William."

He replied in an unintelligible murmur. Or at least it was unintelligible to Catherine, through the irregular pulse that thumped in her ears. It seemed the inner systems of her body had been rearranged, a new order of channels and nerves that she couldn't quite integrate.

"May I have some water?" she asked hoarsely.

"William, give our guest some water."

He complied clumsily, going to fill a glass, standing over Catherine. Holding the cup to her lips, he watched as she sipped carefully. The water was instantly absorbed into the parched tissue of her lips, inner cheeks, throat. It carried a dusty, brackish taint, or perhaps that was just the taste of her mouth.

William retreated, and Catherine waited while her aunt puffed thoughtfully on the hookah.

"Mother never forgave you," Althea said, "for running away as you did. Lord Latimer hounded us for years, demanding the return of his money . . . or you. But you don't care about what trouble you caused. You never gave a thought to what you owed."

Catherine fought to keep her head steady, when it kept lolling to the side. "I didn't owe you my body."

"You thought you were too good for that. You wanted to avoid *my* downfall. You wanted a choice." Althea paused, as if waiting for confirmation. When none was forthcoming, she continued with soft vehemence. "But why should you have one when I didn't? My own mother came to my bedroom one night. She said she'd brought a nice gentleman to help tuck me in. But first he was going to show me some new games. After that night, there was no innocent part of me left. I was twelve."

Another long inhalation through the hookah, another dizzying puff of smoke. There was no way for Catherine to avoid breathing in more. The room seemed to sway gently, as Catherine had imagined the deck of a ship would rock at sea. She floated on the waves, buoyant, listening to Althea's seething. And she felt a stirring of sympathy, but like the rest of her emotions, it remained deep under the surface, drowning.

"I thought of running away," Althea said. "I asked my brother—your father—to help me. He lived with us then, coming and going as he pleased. Using the whores for free any time he wanted, and they didn't dare complain to Mother. 'I need just a little money,' I told him. 'I'll go far away to the country.' But he went to Mother and told her what I'd asked. I wasn't let out of the house for months afterward."

From what little Catherine remembered of her father, a brusque and pitiless individual, this story was easy to believe. But she found herself asking distantly, "Why didn't he help you?"

"My brother liked the situation as it was—he had the best of everything without lifting a finger. Mother gave him whatever he wanted. And the selfish pig didn't mind sacrificing me to keep himself comfortable. He was a man, you see." She paused. "So I became a whore. And for years I prayed for rescue. But God doesn't hear the prayers of women. He cares only for those He made in His own image."

Befuddled and squinting, Catherine labored to keep her thoughts in order. "Aunt," she said carefully, "why did you bring me here? If that was done to you . . . why must it be done to me?"

"Why should you escape when I couldn't? I want you to become me. Just as I became Mother."

Yes . . . this was one of Catherine's fears, the worst one. That if she were put in the wrong situation, the wickedness in her own nature would take over all the rest.

Except . . . it wouldn't.

Catherine's foggy brain seized on the idea and turned it over, examining it. The past was not the future. "I'm not like you," she said slowly. "Won't ever be. I grieve for what was done to you, Aunt. But I didn't make the same choice."

"I have a choice for you now."

Despite Catherine's opiated detachment, Althea's caressing tone made her flesh creep.

"You will either make good on that long-ago arrangement with Lord Latimer," Althea continued, "or you will service customers in the brothel, as I did. Which shall it be?"

Catherine refused to choose. "Doesn't matter what you do," she said, drugged but intractable. "Nothing will change who I am."

"And who are you?" Althea's voice dripped with contempt. "A decent woman? Too good for the likes of this place?"

Catherine's head became too heavy for her to hold up any longer. She lowered herself to the settee, resting her head on the arm. "A woman who is loved."

294

It was the worst, most hurtful answer she could have given Althea. And it was the truth.

Unable to open her eyes, Catherine was aware of a bustling movement nearby, of Althea's tentaclelike grip on her face, of the leather hose from the hookah shoved between her lips. Her nose was pinched shut, and she breathed in helplessly. A flood of cool, pungent smoke entered her lungs. She coughed, and was forced to draw it in again, and then she wilted into a placid and near-insensible heap.

"Take her upstairs, William," Althea said. "To her old bedroom. Later we'll move her to the brothel."

"Yes, ma'am." William gathered Catherine up carefully. "Ma'am . . . may I undo her wrists?"

Althea shrugged. "She certainly won't go anywhere under her own power."

William carried Catherine upstairs, settled her on the small, musty bed of her old room, and untied her hands. He arranged her arms with her hands touching at her middle, in the position of a body in a casket. "Sorry, miss," he murmured, looking into her half-open, unseeing eyes. "She's all I 'ave. I 'as to do what she says."

Chapter Thirty

Guy, Lord Latimer, lived in a newer section of London on the west side, with a picturesque and peaceful common, and a row of stucco-fronted houses built in a deeply wooded hollow. Leo had visited the house on more than one occasion, several years earlier. Although the street and the house were neatly kept, the place was littered with distasteful memories that would have made an East End slum look like a rectory by comparison.

Dismounting from his horse before it had even halted, Leo raced up to the front door and pounded on it with his fists. All his thoughts had diverted into parallel currents, one occupied with the anguished desperation to find Catherine before harm could come to her. Or, if something already had befallen her—please, God, *no*—how to make her well again.

The other current was directed toward the one goal of turning Latimer into butcher's refuse.

There was no sign of Harry yet—Leo was certain that he was not far behind, but Leo had no inclination to wait for him.

A perturbed-looking butler opened the door, and Leo shouldered his way in. "Sir—"

"Where is your master?" Leo asked brusquely.

"I beg your pardon, sir, but he is not—" The butler broke off with an astonished yelp as Leo grabbed him by the coat and shoved him against the nearest wall. "Good God. Sir, I beg you—"

"Tell me where he is."

"The . . . the library . . . but he's not well . . ."

Leo's lips curled in an evil smile. "I have just the cure for him."

A footman came into the hall, and the butler began to sputter for help, but Leo had already released him. In a matter of seconds he had reached the library. It was dark and overheated, an unseasonably large fire blazing in the hearth. Latimer was slumped in a chair, his chin on his chest, a half-empty bottle in one hand. With his bloated face lit by tongues of yellow and red flame, he looked like a damned soul. His incurious gaze lifted to the harsh contours of Leo's face, and Leo saw from his difficulty in focusing that he was sow-drunk. Too bloody drunk to see a hole in a ladder. It would have taken hours of steady imbibing to arrive at this state.

The realization filled Leo with furious despair. Because the one thing worse than finding Catherine with Latimer was *not* finding her there. He leaped on the bastard, clenched his hands around Latimer's thick, clammy throat, and hauled him to a standing position. The bottle dropped to the floor. Latimer's eyes bulged, and he choked and spat as he tried to pry Leo's hands free.

"Where is she?" Leo demanded, giving him a hard shake. "What have you done with Catherine Marks?" He loosened his bruising grip just enough to allow Latimer to speak.

The bastard coughed and wheezed, and stared at him incredulously. "Sodding lunatic! What the bloody hell are you talking about?"

"She's disappeared."

"And you think I have her?" Latimer let out a disbelieving bark of laughter.

"Convince me that you don't," Leo said, clenching his neck more tightly, "and I may let you live."

Latimer's bloated face turned dark. "I have no use for that woman, or any other harlot, because of the . . . the stew you've put me in! You are tearing my life apart! Investigations, questions from Bow Street . . . allies threatening to turn on me. D' you know how many enemies you're making?"

"Not nearly as many as you."

Latimer writhed in his merciless grasp. "They want me dead, damn you."

"What a coincidence," Leo said through clenched teeth. "So do I."

"What has become of you?" Latimer demanded. "She's *only a woman.*"

"If anything happens to her, I'll have nothing left to lose. And if I don't find her within the next hour, you'll pay with your life."

Something in his tone caused Latimer's eyes to widen in panic. "I have nothing to do with it."

"Tell me, or I'll garrot you until you swell up like a toad."

"Ramsay." Harry Rutledge's voice sliced through the air like a sword.

"He says she's not here," Leo muttered, not taking his gaze from Latimer.

A few metallic clicks, and then Harry placed the muzzle of a flintlock in the center of Latimer's forehead. "Let go of him, Ramsay."

Leo complied.

Latimer made an incoherent sound in the sepulchral quiet of the room. His gaze locked with Harry's.

"Remember me?" Harry asked softly. "I should have done this eight years ago."

It appeared that Harry's ice-cold eyes frightened Latimer even more than Leo's murderous ones. "Please," Latimer whispered, his mouth shaking.

"Give me information about my sister's whereabouts in the next five seconds, or I'll put a hole in your head. Five."

"I don't know anything," Latimer pleaded.

"Four."

"I swear it on my life!" Tears sprang from his eyes.

"Three. Two."

"Please, I'll do anything!"

Harry hesitated, giving him an assessing stare. He read the truth in his eyes. "Damn it," he said softly, and lowered the pistol. He looked at Leo, while Latimer collapsed in a sobbing drunken heap on the floor. "He doesn't have her."

They exchanged a quick, bleak glance. It was the first time Leo had ever felt a kinship with Harry, sharing this moment of despair over the same woman.

"Who else would want her?" Leo muttered. "There's no one with a connection to her past . . . except the aunt." He paused. "The night of the play, Cat happened to see a man who worked at the brothel. William. She knew him as a child."

"The brothel is in Marylebone," Harry said abruptly, heading for the door. He motioned for Leo to follow.

"Why would the aunt have taken Cat?"

"I don't know. Perhaps she's finally gone mad."

The brothel was sagging and flat-breasted, with trim that had chipped and been painted a thousand times until someone had finally decided the effort was no longer worth it. The windows were soot-darkened, the front door askew like a lascivious half-smile. The house next door was far smaller, stoop-shouldered, a maltreated child standing next to its promiscuous older sister.

It was often the arrangement that when a brothel was a family business, the owners lived in a separate dwelling. Leo recognized the house from Catherine's description. This was where she had lived as a naïve young girl, unaware that her future had already been stolen from her.

They rode through a cross-street to a fetid alley behind the brothel, a crumbling mews with tilting sides, one of many in the labyrinth of nooks and tiny streets concealed behind the main thoroughfare.

Two men lounged in the doorway of the larger building, the brothel, one of them possessing a massive physical stature that distinguished him as the Bully of the house. In the world of prostitution, the office of Bully was to keep order at a brothel and settle disputes between whores and clients. The other man was small and slight, a hawker of some manner, with a pocketed apron knotted around his waist and a small covered handchaise at the side of the alley.

Noting the attention the visitors paid to the back entrance of the brothel, the Bully spoke in an affable tone. "Sporting ladies aren't working yet, guvnahs, you 'as to come back at nightfall."

Leo summoned all his will to keep his tone pleasant as he spoke to the strongman. "I have business with the mistress of the house."

"She won't see you, I 'spect . . . but you can ask Willy." The Bully gestured toward the dilapidated house with a meaty hand, his manner relaxed, his eyes sharp.

Leo and Harry went to the dilapidated entrance of the smaller house. A cluster of nail holes was all that remained of a long-gone door knocker. Leo struck the door with his knuckles in a controlled hammer, when he longed to kick it down with the full force of his impatience.

In a moment, the door creaked open, and Leo was faced with the pale and undernourished countenance of William. The young man's eyes dilated in alarm as he recognized Leo. Had there been any color to his complexion, it would have leached out at once. He tried to close the door again, but Leo shouldered his way forward.

Grabbing William's wrist, Leo forced it upward and surveyed the bloodstained bandage on his hand. Blood on the bed . . . the thought of what this man might have done to Cat ignited a rage so violent that it obliterated every other awareness. He stopped thinking altogether. A minute later, he found himself on the floor, straddling William's body and battering him mercilessly. He was dimly aware of Harry shouting his name and endeavoring to pull him off.

Alerted by the fracas, the Bully stormed through the doorway and launched at him. Leo flipped the heavier, larger man over his head, causing his body to slam to the floor with an impetus that shook the house to its frame. The Bully lurched to his feet, and his fists, the size of Sunday roasts, whipped through the air with bone-crushing force. Leo leaped back, raising his guard, then jabbed forward with his right. The Bully blocked him easily. Leo, however, did not fight according to the London Prize Ring rules. He followed with a side kick to the kneecap. As the Bully bent over with a grunt of pain, Leo delivered a fouetté, or whip kick, to the head. The Bully toppled to the floor, right at Harry's feet.

Reflecting that his brother-in-law was one of the dirtier fighters he'd ever seen, Harry gave him a short nod and headed into the empty receiving room.

The house was eerily vacant, quiet except for Leo's and Harry's shouts as they searched for Catherine. The place reeked of opium smoke, the windows filmed with such thick grime that curtains were entirely unnecessary. Every room was shrouded in filth. Dust upon dust. Corners clotted with webs, carpets blossomed with stains, wood floors scarred and buckled.

Harry saw a room upstairs where lamplight oozed into the hallway shadows, filtering through a miasma of smoke. He took the steps two and three at a time, his heart hammering.

The form of an old woman was curled on the settee. The loose folds of her black dress couldn't conceal the stick-thin lines of her body, gnarled like the trunk of a crab apple tree. She appeared only half conscious, her bony fingers caressing the length of a leather hookah hose as if it were a pet serpent.

Harry approached her, put his hand on her head, and pushed it back to view her face.

"Who are you?" she croaked. The whites of her eyes were stained, as if they had been soaked in tea. Harry struggled not to recoil at the smell of her breath.

"I've come for Catherine," he said. "Tell me where she is."

She stared at him fixedly. "The brother . . ."

"Yes, where is she? Where are you keeping her? The brothel?"

Althea let go of the leather hose and hugged herself.

"My brother never came for me," she said plaintively, perspiration and tears seeping through the powder on her face, turning it into a creamy paste. "You can't have her." But her gaze chased off to the side, in the direction of the stairs leading to the third floor.

Galvanized, Harry rushed from the room and up the stairs. A blessed waft of cool air and a ray of natural light came from one of the two rooms at the top. He went inside, his gaze sweeping across the stagnant room. The bed was in disarray and the window had been thrown open.

Harry froze, sharp pain lancing through his chest. His heart had stopped with fear. *"Cat!"* he heard himself shout, running to the window. Gulping for air, he looked down at the street three stories below.

But there was no broken body, no blood, nothing on the street below except rubbish and manure.

At the periphery of his vision, a white flutter caught his attention, like the flapping of a bird's wings. Turning his head to the left, Harry drew in a quick breath as he saw his sister.

Catherine was in a white nightgown, perched on the edge of a winged gable. She was only about three yards away, having crept along an incredibly narrow sill that was cantilevered over the second story below. Her arms were locked around her slender knees, and she was shivering violently. The breeze played with the loose locks of her hair, glittering banners dancing against the gray sky. One puff of wind, one momentary loss of balance, would knock her off the gable.

Even more alarming than Catherine's precarious perch was the vacancy of her expression.

"Cat," Harry said carefully, and her face turned in his direction.

She didn't seem to recognize him.

"Don't move," Harry said hoarsely. "Stay still, Cat." He ducked his head inside the house long enough to shout, *"Ramsay!"* and then his head emerged from the window again. "Cat, don't move a muscle. Don't even blink."

She didn't say a word, only sat and continued to shiver, her gaze unfocused.

Leo came up behind Harry and stuck his own head out the window. Harry heard Leo's breath catch. "Sweet mother of God." Taking stock of the situation, Leo became very, very calm. "She's as high as a piper," he said. "This is going to be a pretty trick."

Chapter Thirty-one

"I'll walk along the sill," Harry said. "I'm not afraid of heights."

Leo's expression was grim. "Neither am I. But it won't hold either of us—too much stress on the trusses. The ones above us are rotting, which means they probably all are."

"Is there another way to reach her? From the third-story roof?"

"That would take too long. Keep talking to her while I find some rope."

Leo disappeared, while Harry hung farther out the window. "Cat, it's me," he said. "It's Harry. You know me, don't you?"

"'Course I do." Her head dropped to her bent knees, and she wobbled. "I'm so tired."

"Cat, wait. This isn't the time for a nap. Lift your head and look at me." Harry continued to talk to her, encouraging her to stay still, stay awake, but she barely responded. More than once she altered her position, and Harry's heart plummeted as he expected her to roll right off the winged gable.

To his relief, Leo returned in no time at all with a substantial length of rope. His face was misted with sweat, and he was drawing in deep lungfuls of air.

"That was fast," Harry said, taking the rope from him.

"We're next door to a notorious whipping den," Leo said. "There was a lot of rope."

Harry measured two spans of rope with his arms and began to tie a knot. "If you're planning to coax her to come back to the window," he said, "it won't work. She won't respond to anything I say."

"You tie the knot. I'll do the talking."

Leo had never experienced fear like this before, not even when Laura had died. That had been a slow process of loss, watching her life slip away like sand from an hourglass. This was even worse. This was the deepest level of hell.

Leaning out of the window, Leo stared at Catherine's huddled, exhausted form. He understood the effects of the opium, the confusion and dizziness, the sense that one's limbs were too heavy to move, and at the same time a feeling of buoyant lightness as if one could fly. And added to that, Catherine couldn't even see.

If he managed to get her to safety, he was never going to let her out of his arms again.

"Well, Marks," he said in as normal a voice as he could manage. "Of all the ridiculous situations you and I have found ourselves in, this one takes the biscuit."

Her head lifted from her knees, and she squinted blindly in his direction. "My lord?"

"Yes, I'm going to help you. Stay still. Naturally you would make my heroic rescue effort as difficult as possible."

"I didn't plan on this." Her voice was slurred, but there was a familiar—and welcome—touch of indignation in it. "Was trying to get away."

"I know. And in just a minute, I'm going to bring you inside so that we can argue properly. For the time being—"

"Don't want to."

"Don't want to come in?" Leo asked, puzzled.

"No, don't want to argue." She lowered her head to her knees again, and gave a muffled sob.

"Christ," Leo said, his emotions nearly getting the better of him. "Darling love, *please,* we won't argue. I promise. Don't cry." He took a shuddering breath as Harry handed him the rope, looped with a perfect bowline knot. "Cat, listen to me . . . lift your head and put your knees down just a little. I'm going to throw a rope to you, but it's very important that you not reach for it, do you understand? Just sit still and let it fall into your lap."

She held obediently still, squinting and blinking.

Leo let the loop swing a few times, testing its weight, estimating how much line to allow. He tossed it in a slow, careful motion, but the loop fell short of its mark, bouncing off the shingles near Catherine's feet.

"You need to throw it harder," she said.

Despite Leo's desperation and bone-deep anxiety, he had to bite back a grin. "Will you ever stop telling me what to do, Marks?"

"I don't think so," she said after a moment's reflection.

He gathered up the rope and tossed the loop again, and this time it caught neatly on her knees.

"I've got it."

"Good girl," Leo said. He fought to keep his voice calm. "Now, put your arms through the circle, and lift it over your head. I want it to go around your chest. Not too fast, keep your balance—" His breath quickened as she fumbled with the loop. "Yes, just so. *Yes.* God, I love you." He let out breath of relief as he saw that the rope was in place, fitting just above her breasts and beneath her arms. He gave the other end of the rope to Harry. "Don't let go."

"Not a chance." Harry quickly tied it around his own waist.

Leo's attention returned to Catherine, who was saying something to him, her face drawn with a frown. "What is it, Marks?"

"You didn't have to say that."

"I didn't have to say what?"

"That you love me."

"But I do."

"No, you don't. I heard you say to Win that . . ." Catherine paused, struggling to recollect. "That you would only marry a woman you were certain never to love."

"I often say idiotic things," Leo protested. "It never crossed my mind that anyone actually listens to me."

A window opened in the brothel next door, and an annoyed prostitute leaned out. "There's girls what's tryin' to sleep in 'ere, and you're shoutin' fit to wake the dead!"

"We'll be finished soon," Leo called back to her, scowling. "Go back to bed."

The prostitute continued to lean out. "What are you doin' wiv a girl on the bleedin' roof?"

"None of your business," Leo said curtly.

A few more windows opened, and more heads stuck out, with incredulous exclamations.

"'Oo is he?"

"Is she goin' to jump?"

"Gor, what a filfy mess that would be."

Catherine didn't seem to notice the audience they had attracted, her squinting gaze fastened on Leo. "Did you mean it?" she asked. "What you said?"

"We'll talk about it later," Leo said, straddling the windowsill, holding on to the frame. "For now, I want you to put your hand against the side of the house and step onto the sill. Carefully."

"Did you mean it?" Catherine repeated, unmoving.

Leo gave her an incredulous glance. "Good God, Marks, do you have to be stubborn now, of all times? You want me to declare myself in front of a chorus of prostitutes?"

She nodded emphatically.

One of the whores called out, "Go on an' tell 'er, dearie!"

The others joined in enthusiastically. "Go on, luv!"

"Let's 'ear it, 'andsome!"

Harry, who was standing just behind Leo, was shaking his head slowly. "If it will get her to come in off the blasted roof, just say it, damn it."

Leo leaned farther out the window. "I love you," he said shortly. As he stared at Catherine's small, shivering figure, he felt his color run high, and his soul open with an emotion deeper than he had ever imagined could reside in him. "I love you, Marks. My heart is completely and utterly yours. And unfortunately for you, the rest of me comes with it." Leo paused, struggling for words, when they had always come so easily to him. But these had to be the right words. They meant too much. "I know I'm a bad bargain. But I'm begging you to have me anyway. Because I want the chance to make you as happy as you make me. I want to build a life with you." He fought to steady his voice. "Please come to me, Cat, because there's no surviving you. You don't have to love me back. You don't have to be mine. Just let me be yours."

"Ohhh . . ." one of the prostitutes sighed.

Another blotted her eyes. "If she won't 'ave 'im," she sniffled, "I'll take 'im."

Before Leo had even finished, Catherine had gotten to her feet and was creeping to the sill. "I'm coming," she said.

"Slowly," Leo cautioned, tightening his grip on the rope as he watched the movements of her small, bare feet. "Do it exactly the way you did before."

She inched toward him, her back to the wall. "I don't remember doing it before," she said breathlessly.

"Don't look down."

"I can't see anyway."

"That's just as well. Keep moving." Gradually Leo gathered the excess rope, as if he were reeling her in. Closer and closer she came, until she was finally within arm's reach. Leo stretched his hand as far as possible, his fingers trembling with effort. Another step, another, and then he finally had his arm around her, and he dragged her inside.

Cheers erupted from the brothel, and the multitude of windows began to close.

Leo sank to the floor with his knees splayed, his face buried in Catherine's hair. Tremors of relief ran through his body, and he let out a shuddering sigh. "I have you. I have you. Oh, Marks. You've just put me through the worst two minutes of my entire life. And for that you're going to spend *years* atoning."

"It was only two minutes," she protested, and he choked on a laugh.

Fumbling at his pocket, he pulled out her spectacles, and placed them carefully on her nose. The world became clear again.

Harry knelt beside them and touched Catherine's shoulder. She turned and put her arms around him, hugging him tightly. "My big brother," she whispered. "You came for me again."

She felt Harry smile against her hair. "Always. Whenever you need me." Lifting his head, he glanced ruefully at Leo as he continued, "You'd better marry him, Cat. Any man willing to put himself through *that* is probably worth keeping."

It was with the greatest reluctance that Leo surrendered Catherine to Poppy and Mrs. Pennywhistle when they arrived back at the hotel. The two women brought her to her room and helped her to bathe and wash her hair. She was exhausted and disoriented, and infinitely grateful for the soothing attention. Clad in a fresh nightgown and dressing robe, she sat before the fire while Poppy combed out her hair.

The room had been cleaned and tidied, the bed changed and freshly made. The housekeeper left with an armload of damp toweling, allowing Catherine and Poppy some privacy.

There was no sign of Dodger anywhere. Remembering what had happened to him, Catherine felt her throat clench in grief. Tomorrow she would ask about the gallant little creature, but for now she couldn't quite bring herself to face it.

Hearing her sniffle, Poppy reached around to give her a handkerchief. The comb moved gently through her hair. "Harry told me not to bother you with this tonight, dear, but if it were me, I would want to know. After you left with Leo, Harry stayed behind until the police came to your aunt's house. They went upstairs to find your aunt, but she was dead. They found raw opium paste in her mouth."

"Poor Althea," Catherine whispered, pressing the handkerchief against her welling eyes.

"You're very kind, to have any sympathy at all for her. I'm sure I wouldn't."

"What about William?"

"He ran off before they could arrest him. I heard Harry and

310

Leo discussing it—they're going to commission a runner to find him."

"I don't want that," Catherine protested. "I want them to let him go."

"I have no doubt Leo will agree to whatever you ask," Poppy said. "But why? After what that dreadful man did to you—"

"William was a victim, as surely as I," Catherine said earnestly. "He was only trying to survive. Life was brutally unfair to him."

"And to you, dear. But you made something far better of it than he did."

"But I had Harry. And I had you and your family."

"And Leo," Poppy said, a smile in her voice. "I would say you have him without question. For a man who was so determined to go through life as an observer, he's certainly been pulled back into the stream. Because of you."

"Would you mind if I marry him, Poppy?" she asked almost timidly.

Poppy hugged her from behind, and rested her head briefly against Catherine's. "I'm sure I speak for all the Hathaways in saying that we would be eternally grateful if you would marry him. I can't imagine who else would dare to take him on."

After a light supper of toast and broth, Catherine went to bed and dozed for a while, waking every now and then with a fearful start. Each time she was reassured to see Poppy reading in a chair by the bed, her hair gleaming like mahogany in the glow of lamplight.

"You should go back to the apartment," Catherine finally mumbled, not wishing to seem like a child afraid of the dark.

"I'll stay a little longer," came the soft answer.

The next time Catherine awoke, Leo was sitting in the chair.

Her drowsy gaze moved over him, taking in the contours of his handsome face, his serious blue eyes. His shirt was partly unbuttoned, revealing a shadow of chest hair. Suddenly desperate to be held against that hard, strong chest, she reached for him wordlessly.

Leo came to her at once. Wrapping his arms around her, he reclined back against the pillows with her. Catherine luxuriated in the feel and scent of him. "Only I," she whispered, "would feel so safe in the arms of the wickedest man in London."

He made a sound of amusement. "You like them wicked, Marks. An ordinary man would be tame sport for a woman like you."

She snuggled closer, her legs tense beneath the bed linens. "I'm so weary," she said, "but I can't sleep."

"You'll be better tomorrow morning. I promise." His hand settled on her hip, over the covers. "Close your eyes, love, and let me take care of you."

She tried to obey. But as the minutes ticked by, she was plagued by increasing restlessness and irritated nerves, a sense of dryness that permeated to her bones. Her skin clamored to be touched, scratched, rubbed, but even the delicate chafing of the sheets was enough to make her raw.

Leo left the bed and returned with a glass of water, and she drank thirstily. Her mouth tingled agreeably from the cool wetness.

Taking away the empty glass, Leo extinguished the lamp and returned to her. She flinched at the feel of his weight depressing the mattress, the disparate information of her senses distilling into one compelling need. In the darkness, Leo's mouth found hers, tender and gentle, and she couldn't prevent her own exaggerated response. His hand came to her breast, finding the tip already hard beneath the veil of muslin.

312

"It sometimes happens with opium smoke," Leo said quietly. "Later with habit, it decreases. But when you first try it, it can act upon you this way. As the effects leave your body, your nerves start screaming for more of it, and the result is . . . frustration."

As he spoke, his hand cupped her breast, his thumb gently circling the tight bud. She felt the sensation everywhere, streamers of fire unraveling to the pit of her belly, and along her legs and arms. She panted and squirmed, too desperate to feel embarrassed by her own muffled cries as his hand slipped beneath the covers.

"Easy, love," Leo whispered, caressing the taut plane of her stomach. "Let me help you."

His fingers were gentle on her swollen flesh, stroking and parting and entering, sliding easily into the moisture. She hitched upward, her body craving and willful, every movement enticing him to stroke deeper, harder.

Leo bent his head and kissed her throat. The tip of his thumb rested just above the little spot that burned with white fire, manipulating delicately as his invading fingers stretched her. It sent her into spasms of near-painful release, tearing an unwilling groan from her, and she clutched the back of his shirt in her fists until she felt the fine linen begin to rip. Breathing hard, she let go of the shirt and stammered out an apology. He stripped off the ruined shirt and hushed her with his mouth.

He spread his hand over her intimately, teasing her with exquisite care, while she whimpered and stiffened. Another burst of fire, a series of deep shudders, and she opened her thighs as he slid his fingers in. When the last vibrations had faded, she lay heavily in his arms and let exhaustion overtake her.

In the middle of the night, Catherine pressed against him furtively, needing him again. He rose above her, murmuring that she

313

must relax, he would help her, he would take care of her, and she sobbed openly as she felt him kiss his way down her body. He lifted her legs over his shoulders and cupped her bottom in his hands. His mouth searched gently, his tongue stroking deep into the tender chalice. He did not find a rhythm but instead played with her, pulling softly, licking and nuzzling. The pleasure broke over her in waves, making her gasp in relief.

"Take me," she whispered as he lay beside her again.

"No," Leo said gently, turning to pin her to the mattress. "No chance of that tonight. We'll have to wait until your judgment isn't clouded. By morning, most of the opium will have worn off. If you still want me then, I'll be ready and willing."

"I want you now," she said, but he held her down and pleasured her with his mouth once more.

Catherine woke a few hours later, glimpsing the plum-colored sky as it began to lighten with the premonition of dawn. Leo's long body was tucked comfortably behind hers, one arm beneath her neck, the other draped across her middle. She loved the feel of him, vibrant heat and muscle, his skin like satin in some places, hair-roughened in others. Although she was careful not to move, Leo stirred and murmured.

Slowly she reached for his hand and drew it to her breast. Leo began to fondle her before he was even awake. His lips touched the back of her neck. Feeling him harden against her bottom, she pressed against him. One of his legs intruded between hers, as his hand slid down to the light fleece of curls.

She felt the taut pressure of him, nudging against her entrance, circling into the moisture. He pushed partway inside her and stopped, while her flesh, swollen from the night's excesses, had difficulty accommodating him.

His soft, amused voice tickled her ear. "Mmmn . . . you'll

314

have to try harder, Marks. We both know you can take more than this."

"Help me," she gasped.

With a sympathetic murmur, he lifted her top leg and adjusted her position. Her eyes closed as she felt him slide inside her.

"There," he whispered. "Is this what you want?"

"Harder . . . harder . . ."

"No, love . . . let me be gentle with you. Just for now."

He moved inside her with slow, deliberate drives, his caressing hand sliding back between her thighs. He took his time, and she had no choice but to let him. She was suffused with warmth, sensation building as he courted her, stroked her. Pressing love words and kisses against her neck, he sank more deeply inside her. She cried out his name, cresting, and he gently urged her even higher. Her shaking hand went to his hip and gripped the flexing surface.

"Don't leave me. Please, Leo."

He understood. As her wet flesh clenched around him once more, delicately wringing and pulling at the hardness, he pumped forcefully, letting himself go. And at last she knew the feel of his release, the way his belly tightened, the trembling of a powerful man rendered helpless in that ultimate moment.

They stayed joined as long as possible, resting together and watching as the dawn seeped through the parted curtains.

"I love you," she whispered, "so dearly, my lord. My Leo."

He smiled and kissed her. Rising, he went to drag on his trousers.

While Leo sluiced his face at the washstand, Catherine reached for her spectacles. Her gaze happened to fall on Dodger's empty basket by the door, and her smile dimmed. "Poor weasel," she murmured.

Leo returned to her, instantly concerned as he saw her watering eyes. "What is it?"

"Dodger," she said with a sniffle. "I miss him already."

Leo sat and drew her up against him. "Would you like to see him?"

"Yes, but I can't."

"Why not?"

Before she could answer, she saw an odd movement beneath the door . . . a furry, skinny body wiggling industriously beneath the ridiculously narrow space. Catherine blinked, afraid to move. *"Dodger?"*

The ferret came loping toward the bed, chuckling and chirping, his eyes bright as he hurried to her.

"Dodger, you're alive!"

"Of course he's alive," Leo said. "We put him in Poppy's apartment last night to allow you some rest." He smiled as the ferret bounded onto the mattress. "Mischievous little beggar. How did you get all the way down here?"

"He came to find me." Catherine held out her arms, and Dodger climbed up to her and snuggled against her chest. She stroked him over and over, murmuring endearments. "He tried to protect me, you know. He bit William's hand quite terribly." She nuzzled her chin against Dodger and crooned, "Good little watch ferret."

"Well done, Dodger," Leo said. Leaving the bed for a moment, he went to his discarded coat and rummaged through the pockets. "I suppose that leads to the question . . . in marrying you, am I going to be gaining a ferret, as well?"

"Do you think Beatrix would let me keep him?"

"There's no doubt of it." Leo returned to sit beside her. "She's always said that he belongs to you."

316

"Has she?"

"Well, it's rather obvious, in light of his fascination for your garters. And one certainly can't blame him for that." Leo reached for her hand. "I have something to ask you, Marks."

She sat up eagerly, letting Dodger drape around her neck.

"I can't remember if this is the fifth or sixth proposal," he said.

"It's only the fourth."

"I asked you yesterday. Are you counting that one?"

"No, that wasn't really 'will you marry me,' that was more 'will you come down off the roof.'"

One of Leo's brows arched. "By all means, let's be technical." He slid a ring onto the fourth finger of her left hand. It was the most breathtaking ring she had ever seen, a flawless silver opal with flashes of blue and green fire hidden deep inside. With every movement of her hand, the opal glimmered with unearthly color. It was encircled by a rim of glittering small diamonds. "This reminded me of your eyes," he said. "Only not nearly as beautiful." He paused, looking at her intently. "Catherine Marks, love of my life . . . will you marry me?"

"I want to answer another question first," she told him. "Something you asked me before."

He smiled and put his forehead against hers. "The one about the farmer and the sheep?"

"No . . . the one about what happens when an unstoppable force meets an immovable object."

A laugh rustled in his throat. "Tell me your answer, love."

"The unstoppable force stops. And the immovable object moves."

"Mmmn. I like that." His lips brushed hers tenderly.

"My lord, I'd rather not wake up as Catherine Marks ever again. I want to be your wife as soon as possible."

317

"Tomorrow morning?"

Catherine nodded. "Although . . . I will miss you calling me Marks. I've gotten rather fond of it."

"I'll still call you Marks from time to time. During moments of lurid passion. Let's try it." His voice lowered to a seductive whisper. "Kiss me, Marks . . ."

And she lifted her smiling mouth to his.

Epilogue

One year later

The cry of an infant broke through the silence.

Leo flinched at the sound, lifting his head. Having been banished from the bedroom where Catherine was giving birth, he had waited with the rest of the family in the parlor. Amelia had stayed with Catherine and the doctor, occasionally emerging to give a brief report to Win or Beatrix. Cam and Merripen were maddeningly sanguine about the process, both having seen their own wives safely through childbirth.

The Hathaway family was proving remarkably fertile. In March, Win had given birth to a robust boy, Jason Cole, nicknamed Jàdo. Two months later, Poppy had produced a petite red-haired daughter, Elizabeth Grace, upon whom Harry and the entire Rutledge Hotel staff doted.

Now it was Catherine's turn. And while childbirth was a perfectly ordinary event for other people, it was the most nerve-racking experience Leo had ever gone through. The sight of his wife in pain was intolerable, and yet there was nothing he could do. It didn't matter how often he was reassured that the birth was going splendidly . . . endless hours of labor pains did not seem all that splendid to Leo.

For eight hours Leo had waited in the parlor with his head in his hands, brooding and quiet and inconsolable. He was afraid for Catherine, and he could hardly bear to be separated from her. As he had predicted, he loved Catherine like a madman. And as she had once claimed, she was entirely able to manage him. They were different in so many ways, and yet somehow it made them exactly right for each other.

The result had been a remarkably harmonious marriage. They entertained each other with furious, funny bickering and long, thoughtful conversations. When they were alone, they often spoke in a kind of shorthand that no one else would have been able to interpret. They were a physical pair, passionate and affectionate. Playful. But the real surprise of the marriage was the kindness they showed each other . . . they, who had once fought so bitterly.

Leo had never expected that the woman who had formerly brought out the worst in him would now bring out the best in him. And he had never dreamed that his love for her would deepen to such proportions that there was no hope of controlling or restraining it. In the face of a love this vast, a man could only surrender.

If anything happened to Catherine . . . if something went wrong during the childbirth . . .

Leo stood slowly, his fists clenched, as Amelia entered the parlor with a bundled-up newborn. She paused near the doorway as the family gathered around her with soft exclamations. "A perfect little girl," she said, beaming. "The doctor said her color is excellent and her lungs are strong." She brought the baby to Leo.

He was too afraid to move. He didn't take the baby, only stared at Amelia and asked hoarsely, "How is Marks?"

She understood at once. Her tone gentled as she replied. "Absolutely fine. She's quite well, dear, and you can go up to see her now. But first say hello to your daughter."

An unsteady sigh escaped Leo, and he took the baby from her gingerly. He looked down in wonder at the miniature pink face, the rosebud mouth. How light the baby was . . . it was difficult to believe he was holding an entire human being in his arms.

"There's a great deal of Hathaway in her," Amelia said with a smile.

"Well, we'll do what we can to correct that." Leo bent to kiss his daughter's tiny forehead, the wisps of dark hair tickling his lips.

"Have you chosen a name?" Amelia asked.

"Emmaline."

"French. Very pretty." For some reason, Amelia laughed quietly before asking, "What would you have named a boy?"

"Edward."

"After Father? How lovely. And I think it suits him."

"Suits who?" Leo asked, still engrossed in his daughter.

Reaching up to his face, Amelia guided him to look at the doorway, where Win stood with another bundle, displaying it to Merripen, Cam, and Beatrix.

Leo's eyes widened. "My God. *Twins*?"

Cam approached him with a broad grin. "He's a fine-looking boy. You've come into fatherhood with a vengeance, *phral*."

"And Leo," Beatrix added. "You've had an heir just in time . . . with one day to spare!"

"In time for what?" Leo asked dazedly. Handing his daughter back to Amelia, he took his son from Win. Looking down at the infant's face, he fell in love for the second time in the same day. It was almost too much for his overwhelmed heart to endure.

"The copyhold clause, of course," he heard Beatrix say. "The Hathaways will keep Ramsay House now."

"I can't believe you would even think about that at a time like this," Leo said.

"Why not?" Merripen asked, his dark eyes twinkling. "Personally speaking, I find it a relief to know that we'll all be able to stay at Ramsay House."

"You're all concerned about a bloody house, when I've just endured eight hours of sheer hell."

"I'm sorry, Leo," Beatrix said, trying to sound contrite. "I wasn't thinking about what you'd just been through."

Leo kissed his son and handed him carefully to Win. "I'm going to see Marks now. It's probably been difficult for her, too."

"Give her our congratulations," Cam said, a tremor of laughter in his voice.

Taking the stairs two at a time, Leo went to the bedroom where Catherine rested. She looked very small beneath the covers, her face exhausted and pale. A weary grin curved her lips as she saw him.

He went to her and pressed his mouth to hers. "What can I do for you, love?"

"Nothing at all. The doctor gave me some laudanum for the pain. He's coming back in just a moment."

Continuing to lean over her, Leo smoothed her hair. "Damn you for not letting me stay," he whispered against her cheek.

He felt her smile.

"You were frightening the doctor," she said.

"I merely asked if he knew what he was doing."

"Forcefully," she pointed out.

Leo turned to rummage through the articles on the bedside table. "That was only because he'd pulled out a case of instruments that looked more suited to a medieval inquisition than childbirth." He found a little pot of salve and applied a dab of the unguent to Catherine's dry lips.

"Sit with me," she said against his fingertips.

"I don't want to hurt you."

"You won't." She patted the mattress invitingly.

Leo sat beside her with extreme caution, trying not to jostle her. "I'm not at all surprised that you produced two children at once," he said, taking her hand and kissing her fingers. "You're terrifyingly efficient, as usual."

"What do they look like?" she asked. "I didn't see them after they were washed."

"Bowlegged, with large heads."

Catherine chuckled and winced. "Please, please don't make me laugh."

"They're beautiful, actually. My dearest love . . ." Leo pressed a kiss into her palm. "I never fully realized what a woman went through during childbirth. You are the bravest, strongest person who's ever lived. A warrior."

"Not really."

"Oh, yes. Attila the Hun, Genghis Khan, Saladin . . . all milksops, compared to you." Leo paused, a grin spreading across his face. "It was well done of you to make certain one of the babies was a boy. The family is rejoicing, of course."

"Because we can keep Ramsay House?"

"Partly. But I suspect what they're truly ecstatic about is that now I'll have to contend with twins." He paused. "You know they'll be hellions."

"I should hope so. They wouldn't be ours otherwise."

Catherine snuggled closer, and he settled her carefully against his shoulder. "Guess what happens at midnight?" she whispered.

"Two hungry infants will wake up screaming simultaneously?"

"Besides that."

"I have no idea."

"The Ramsay curse will be broken."

"You shouldn't have told me. Now I'll be terrified for the next . . ."—Leo paused to glance at the mantel clock—"seven hours and twenty-eight minutes."

"Stay with me. I'll keep you safe." She yawned and let her head drop more heavily against him.

Leo smiled and stroked her hair. "We'll both be fine, Marks. We've just begun our journey . . . and there's so much we have yet to do." He spoke more softly as he heard her breathing turn even and steady. "Rest against my heart. Let me watch over your dreams. And know that tomorrow morning, and every morning after that, you'll awaken next to someone who loves you."

"Dodger?" she mumbled against his chest, and he grinned.

"No, your confounded ferret will have to stay in his basket. I was referring to myself."

"Yes, I know." Catherine slid her hand up to his cheek. "Only you," she said. "Always you."

Don't miss the next wonderful novel by Lisa Kleypas

Love in the Afternoon

Coming soon from Piatkus

Prologue

Captain Christopher Phelan
1st Battalion Rifle Brigade
Camp near Cape Mapan
Crimea

June 1855

Dearest Christopher,
I can't write to you again.
I'm not who you think I am.
I didn't mean to send love letters, but that is what they be-
came. On their way to you, my words turned into heart-
beats on the page.
Come back, please come home, and find me.

—unsigned

Chapter One

Hampshire, England
Eight months earlier

It all began with a letter.

To be precise, it was the mention of the dog.

"What about the dog?" Beatrix Hathaway asked. "Whose dog?"

Her friend Prudence, the reigning beauty of Hampshire County, looked up from the letter that had been sent by her suitor, Captain Christopher Phelan.

Although it wasn't proper for a gentleman to correspond with an unmarried girl, they had arranged to discreetly send letters back and forth with Phelan's sister-in-law as a go-between.

Prudence sent her a mock-frown. "Really, Bea, you're displaying far more concern over a dog than you ever have for Captain Phelan."

"Captain Phelan has no need of my concern," Beatrix said pragmatically. "He has the concern of every marriageable miss in Hampshire. Besides, he chose to go to war, and I'm sure he's having a lovely time strutting about in his smart uniform."

"It's not at all smart," came Prudence's glum reply. "In fact, his new regiment has *dreadful* uniforms—very plain, dark green with black facings, and no gold braiding or lace at all. And when I asked why, Captain Phelan said it was to help the Rifles stay concealed, which makes no sense, as everyone knows that a British soldier is far too brave and proud to conceal himself during battle. But Christopher—that is, Captain Phelan—said it had something to do with . . . oh, he used some French word . . ."

"Camouflage?" Beatrix asked, intrigued.

"Yes, how did you know?"

"Many animals have ways of camouflaging themselves to keep from being seen. Chameleons, for example. Or the way an owl's feathering is mottled to help it blend with the bark of its tree. That way—"

"Heavens, Beatrix, do *not* start another lecture on animals."

"I'll stop if you tell me about the dog," Beatrix coaxed.

Prudence handed her the letter. "Read it for yourself."

"But, Pru," Beatrix protested as the small, neat pages were pushed into her hands. "Captain Phelan may have written something personal."

"I should be so fortunate! It's utterly gloomy. Nothing but battles and bad news."

Although Christopher Phelan was the last man Beatrix would ever want to defend, she couldn't help pointing out, "He is away fighting in the Crimea, Pru. I'm not sure there are many pleasant things to write about in wartime."

"Well, I have no interest in foreign countries, and I've never pretended to."

A reluctant grin spread across Beatrix's face. "Pru, are you certain you want to be an officer's wife?"

"Well, *of course* . . . most commissioned soldiers never go to war. They're very fashionable men about town, and if they agree to go on half-pay, they have hardly any duties and they don't have to spend any time at all with the regiment. And that was the case with Captain Phelan, until he was alerted for foreign service." Prudence shrugged. "I suppose wars are always inconveniently timed. Thank heavens Captain Phelan will return to Hampshire soon."

"Will he? How do you know?"

"My parents say the war will be over by Christmas."

"I've heard that as well. However, one wonders if we aren't severely underestimating the Russians' abilities, and overestimating our own."

"How unpatriotic," Prudence exclaimed, a teasing light in her eyes.

"Patriotism has nothing to do with the fact that the War Office, in its enthusiasm, didn't do nearly enough planning before it launched thirty thousand men to the Crimea. We don't have adequate knowledge of the place, nor any sound strategy for its capture."

"How do you know so much about it?"

"From *The Times*. It's reported on every day. Don't you read the papers?"

"Not the political section. My parents say it's ill-bred for a young lady to take an interest in such things."

"My family discusses politics every night at dinner, and my sisters and I all take part." Beatrix paused deliberately before adding with an impish grin, "We even have *opinions*."

Prudence's eyes widened. "My goodness. Well, I shouldn't be surprised. Everyone knows your family is . . . different."

"Different" was a far kinder adjective than was often used to describe the Hathaway family. The Hathaways were comprised of five siblings, the oldest of which was Leo, followed by Amelia, Winnifred, Poppy, and Beatrix. After the death of their parents, the Hathaways had gone through an astonishing change of fortune. Although they were common-born, they were distantly related to an aristocratic branch of the family. Through a series of unexpected events, Leo had inherited a viscouncy for which he and his sisters hadn't been remotely prepared. They had moved from their small village of Primrose Place to the Ramsay estate in the southern county of Hampshire.

After six years, the Hathaways had managed to learn just enough to accommodate themselves to good society. However, none of them had learned to think like the nobility, nor had they acquired aristocratic values or mannerisms. And whereas a family in similar circumstances might have endeavored to improve their situations by marrying their social betters, the Hathaways had so far chosen to marry for love.

As for Beatrix, there was doubt as to whether she would marry at all. She was only half-civilized, spending most of her time out of doors, riding or rambling through the woodlands, marsh, and meadows of Hampshire. Beatrix preferred the company of animals to people, collecting injured and orphaned creatures and rehabilitating them. The creatures that couldn't survive on their own in the wild were kept as pets, and Beatrix occupied herself with caring for them. That had always been enough for her . . . until lately.

More and more frequently, Beatrix had become aware of a chafing sense of dissatisfaction. Of yearning. The problem was that Beatrix had never met a man who was right for her. Certainly none of the pale, overbred specimens of the London drawing rooms she had frequented. And although the more robust men in the country were appealing, none of them had the unnameable *something* Beatrix longed for. She dreamed of a man whose force of will matched her own. She wanted to be passionately loved . . . challenged . . . overtaken.

Beatrix glanced at the folded letter in her hands.

It wasn't that she disliked Christopher Phelan as much as she recognized that he was inimical to everything she was. He was sophisticated, born to privilege, able to move with ease in the civilized environment that was so alien to her. He was the second son of a well-to-do local family, his maternal grandfather an earl, his father's family distinguished by a significant shipping fortune.

Although the Phelans were not in line for a title, the oldest son, John, would inherit an estate in Warwickshire upon the earl's death. John was a sober and thoughtful man, devoted to his young wife, Audrey.

But the younger brother, Christopher, was another sort of man entirely. As so often happened with second sons, Christopher had purchased an army commission at the age of twenty-two. He had gone in as a cornet, a perfect occupation for such a splendid-looking fellow, since his chief responsibility was to carry the cavalry colors during parades and drills. He was also a great favorite among the ladies of London, where he constantly went without proper leave, spending his time dancing, drinking, gaming, purchasing fine clothes, and indulging in scandalous love affairs.

Beatrix had met Christopher Phelan on two occasions, the first at a local dance, where she had judged him to be the most arrogant man in Hampshire. The next time she had met him was a picnic, where she had revised her opinion: He was the most arrogant man in the entire world.

"That Hathaway girl is a peculiar creature," Beatrix had overheard him say to a companion. "With none of her sisters' beauty, unfortunately."

"I find her charming and original," his companion had protested. "And she can talk horses better than any woman I've ever met."

"Naturally," came Phelan's dry rejoinder. "With her appearance and manners, she's better suited to the stables than the drawing room."

From then on, Beatrix had avoided him whenever possible. Not that she minded being compared to a horse, since horses were lovely animals with generous and noble spirits. And she knew that although she wasn't a great beauty, she had her own charms. More than one man had commented favorably on her dark brown hair and blue eyes.

These moderate attractions, however, were nothing compared to Christopher Phelan's golden splendor. He was as fair as Lancelot. Gabriel. Perhaps Lucifer, if one believed that he had once been the most beautiful angel in heaven. Phelan was tall and silver-eyed, his hair the color of dark winter wheat touched by the sun. His form was strong and soldierly, the shoulders straight and strong, the hips slim. Even as he moved with indolent grace, there was something undeniably potent about him, something selfishly predatory.

Recently Phelan had been one of the select few to be culled from various regiments to become part of the Rifle Brigade. The "Rifles," as they were called, were an unusual brand of soldier, trained to use their own initiative. They were encouraged to take up positions forward of their own front lines and pick off officers and horses that were usually beyond target range. Because of his singular marksmanship skills, Phelan had been promoted to a captaincy in the Rifle Brigade.

It had amused Beatrix to reflect that the honor probably hadn't pleased Phelan at all. Especially since he'd been obliged to trade his beautiful Hussars uniform, with its black coat and abundant gold braiding, for a plain dark green one.

"Go on and read it," Prudence said as she sat at her dressing table. "I must repair my coiffure before we go on our walk."

"Your hair looks lovely," Beatrix protested, unable to see any flaw in the elaborately pinned twist of blond braids. "And we're only going to Stony Cross. None of the townspeople will know or care if your hair isn't perfect."

"*I'll* know. Besides, there is never any telling whom one might run across."

Accustomed as she was to her friend's ceaseless primping, Beatrix grinned and shook her head. "All right. If you're certain you don't mind me looking at Captain Phelan's letter, I'll just read the part about the dog."

"You'll fall asleep long before you get to the dog," Prudence said, expertly inserting a hairpin into a twisted braid.

Beatrix looked down at the scrawled lines. The words looked cramped, tight coils of letters ready to spring from the page.

Dear Prudence,

As I sit in this dusty tent and try to think of something eloquent to write to you, I find I'm at wit's end. You deserve beautiful words, but all I have left are these: I think of you constantly. I think of this letter in your hand and the scent of perfume on your wrist. I want you. I want silence and clear air, and a bed with a soft white pillow . . .

Beatrix felt her eyebrows lifting, and a quick rise of heat beneath the high collar of her dress. She paused and glanced at

335

Prudence. "You find this boring?" she asked mildly, while her blush spread like spilled wine on a linen tablecloth.

"The beginning is the only good part," Prudence said. "Go on."

. . . Two days ago in our march down the coast to Sebastopol, we fought the Russians at the Alma River. I'm told it was a victory for our side. It doesn't feel like one. We've lost at least two-thirds of our regiment's officers, and a quarter of the non-commissioned men. Yesterday we dug graves. They call the final tally of dead and wounded the "butcher's bill." Three hundred and sixty British dead so far, and more as soldiers succumb to their wounds.

One of the fallen, Captain Brighton, brought a rough terrier named Albert, who is undoubtedly the most badly behaved canine in existence. After Brighton was lowered into the ground, the dog sat by his grave and whined for hours, and tried to bite anyone who came near. I made the mistake of offering him a portion of a biscuit, and now the benighted creature follows me everywhere. At this moment he is sitting in my tent, staring at me with half-crazed eyes. The whining rarely stops. Whenever I get near, he tries to sink his teeth into my arm. I want to shoot him, but I'm too tired of killing.

Families are grieving for the lives I've taken. Sons, brothers, fathers. I've earned a place in hell for the things I've done, and the war's barely started. I'm changing, and not for the better. The man you knew is gone for good, and I fear you may not like his replacement nearly so well.

The smell of death, Pru . . . it's everywhere.

The battlefield is strewn with pieces of bodies, clothes,

soles of boots. Imagine an explosion that could tear the soles from your shoes. They say that after a battle, wildflowers are more abundant the next season—the ground is so churned and torn, it gives the new seeds room to take root. I want to grieve, but there is no place for it. No time. I have to put the feelings away somewhere.

Is there still some peaceful place in the world? Please write to me. Tell me about some bit of needlework you're working on, or your favorite song. Is it raining in Stony Cross? Have the leaves have begun to change color?
Yours,
Christopher Phelan

By the time Beatrix had finished the letter, she was aware of a peculiar feeling, a sense of surprised compassion pressing against the walls of her heart.

It didn't seem possible that such a letter could have come from the arrogant, all-knowing Christopher Phelan. It wasn't at all what she had expected. There was a vulnerability, a quiet need, that had touched her.

"You must write to him, Pru," she said, closing the letter with far more care than she had previously handled it.

"I'll do no such thing. That would only encourage more complaining. I'll be silent, and perhaps that will spur him to write something more cheerful next time."

Beatrix frowned. "As you know, I have no great liking for Captain Phelan, but this letter . . . he deserves your sympathy, Pru. Just write him a few lines. A few words of comfort. It would take no time at all. And about the dog, I have a little advice that might help—"

"I am not writing anything about the dratted dog." Prudence gave an impatient sigh. "You write to him."

337

"*Me?* He doesn't want to hear from me. He thinks I'm peculiar."

"I can't imagine why. Just because you brought Medusa to the picnic . . ."

"She's a very well-behaved hedgehog," Beatrix said defensively.

"The gentleman whose hand was pierced didn't seem to think so."

"That was only because he tried to handle her incorrectly. When you pick up a hedgehog, you have to slide your palms beneath—"

"No, there's no use telling me, since I'm never going to handle one. As for Captain Phelan . . . if you feel all that strongly about it, write a response and sign my name."

"Won't he recognize that the handwriting is different?"

"No, because I haven't written him yet."

"But he's not my suitor," Beatrix protested. "I don't know anything about him."

"You know as much as I do, actually. You're acquainted with his family, and you're very close with his sister-in-law. And I wouldn't say that Captain Phelan is my suitor, either. At least not my only one. I certainly won't promise to marry him until he comes back from the war with all his limbs intact. I don't want a husband I would have to push around in an invalid's chair for the rest of my life."

"Pru, you have the depth of a puddle."

Prudence grinned. "At least I'm honest."

Beatrix gave her a dubious glance. "You're actually delegating the writing of a love letter to one of your friends?"

Prudence waved her hand in a dismissive gesture. "Not a love letter. There was nothing of love in his letter to me. Just write something cheerful and encouraging."

Beatrix fumbled for the pocket of her walking dress, and tucked the letter inside. Inwardly she argued with herself, reflecting that it never ended well when one did something morally questionable for the right reasons. On the other hand . . . she couldn't rid herself of the image her mind had conjured, of an exhausted soldier scribbling a hasty letter in the privacy of his tent, his hands blistered from digging the graves of his comrades. And a ragged dog whining in the corner.

She felt entirely inadequate to the task of writing to him. And she suspected that Prudence did as well.

She tried to imagine what it was like for Christopher, leaving his elegant life behind, finding himself in a world where his survival was threatened day by day. Minute by minute. It was impossible to picture a spoiled, beautiful man like Christopher Phelan contending with danger and hardship. Hunger. Loneliness.

Beatrix stared at her friend pensively, their gazes meeting in the looking glass. "What *is* your favorite song, Pru?"

"I don't have one, actually. Tell him yours."

"Should we discuss this with Audrey?" Beatrix asked, referring to Phelan's sister-in-law.

"Certainly not. Audrey has a problem with honesty. She wouldn't send the letter if she knew I hadn't written it."

Beatrix made a sound that could have either been a laugh or a groan. "I wouldn't call that a *problem* with honesty. Oh, Pru, please change your mind and write to him. It would be so much easier."

But Prudence, when pressed to do something, usually turned intransigent, and this situation was no exception. "Easier for everyone but me," she said tartly. "I'm sure I don't know how to reply to such a letter. He's probably even forgotten that he's written it." Returning her attention to the looking glass, she applied a touch of rose petal salve to her lips.

How very beautiful Prudence was, with her heart-shaped face, her brows thin and delicately arched over round green eyes. But how very little of a person the looking glass reflected. It was impossible to guess what Prudence truly felt for Christopher Phelan. Only one thing was certain: It was better to answer, no matter how ineptly, than to withhold a reply. Because sometimes silence could wound someone nearly as badly as a bullet.

Later, in the privacy of her room at Ramsay House, Beatrix sat at her desk and dipped a pen nib into a little well of dark blue ink. A three-legged gray cat named Lucky lounged at the corner of the desk, watching her alertly. Beatrix's pet hedgehog Medusa occupied the other side of the desk. Lucky, being an innately sensible creature, never bothered the bristly little hedgehog.

After consulting the letter from Phelan, Beatrix wrote:

Captain Christopher Phelan
1st Battalion Rifle Brigade
2nd Division Camp, Crimea
17 October, 1854

Pausing, Beatrix reached out to stroke Lucky's remaining front paw with a gentle fingertip. "How would Pru start a letter?" she wondered aloud. "Would she call him darling? Dearest?" She wrinkled her nose at the idea.

The writing of letters was hardly Beatrix's forte. Although she came from a highly articulate family, she had always valued instinct and action more than words. In fact, she could learn far more about a person during a short walk outdoors than she could by sitting and conversing for hours.

After pondering various things one might write to a complete stranger while masquerading as someone else, Beatrix finally gave up. "Hang it, I'll just write as I please. He'll probably be too battle-weary to notice that the letter doesn't sound like Pru."

Lucky settled her chin beside her paw and half-closed her eyes. A purring sigh escaped her.

Beatrix began to write.

Dear Christopher,

I have been reading the reports about the battle of the Alma. According to the account by Mr. Russell of The Times, *you and two others of the Rifle Brigade went ahead of the Coldstream Guards, and shot several enemy officers, thereby disordering their columns. Mr. Russell also remarked in admiration that the Rifles never retreated or even bobbed their heads when the bullets came flying.*

While I share his esteem, dear sir, I wish to advise that in my opinion it would not detract from your bravery to bob your head when being shot at. Duck, dodge, sidestep, or preferably hide behind a rock. I promise I won't think the less of you!

Is Albert still with you? Still biting? According to my friend Beatrix (she who brings hedgehogs to picnics), the dog is overstimulated and afraid. As dogs are wolves at heart and require a leader, you must establish dominance over him. Whenever he tries to bite you, take his entire muzzle in your hand, apply light pressure, and tell him "no" in a firm voice.

My favorite song is "Over the Hills and Far Away." It rained in Hampshire yesterday, a soft autumn storm that brought hardly any leaves down. The dahlias are no longer in stem, and frost has withered the chrysanthemums, but the air smells divine, like old leaves and wet bark and ripe apples. Have you ever noticed that each month has its own smell? May and October are the nicest-smelling months.

You ask if there is a peaceful place in the world, and I regret to say that it is not Stony Cross. Recently Mr. Mawdsley's donkey escaped from its stall, raced down the road, and somehow found his way into an enclosed pasture. Mr. Caird's prized mare was innocently grazing when the ill-bred seducer had his way with her. Now it appears the mare has conceived, and a feud is raging between Caird, who demands financial compensation, and Mawdsley, who insists that had the pasture fencing been in better repair, the clandestine meeting would never have occurred. Worse still, it has been suggested that the mare is a shameless lightskirt and did not try nearly hard enough to preserve her virtue.

Do you really think you've earned a place in hell? I don't believe in hell, at least not in the afterlife. I think hell is brought about by man right here on earth.

You say the gentleman I knew has been replaced. How I wish I could offer better comfort than to say that no matter how you have changed, you will be welcomed when you return. Do what you must. If it helps you to endure, put the feelings away for now, and lock the door. Perhaps someday we'll air them out together.

Sincerely,
Prudence

P.S. Went sketching with Beatrix yesterday. Enclosed is a drawing of a brown hare foraging through the apple *orchard at Ramsay House. Unfortunately the subject would not hold still and insisted on running off with a stem of thistle. Clearly these low-minded Hampshire rabbits have no respect for artistic endeavors.*

When Beatrix was done, she folded the sheets of paper and tucked in a sketch of a rabbit in the orchard.

She had never intentionally deceived anyone. She would have felt infinitely more comfortable writing to Phelan as herself. But she still remembered the disparaging remarks that he had once made about her. He would not want a letter from that "peculiar Beatrix Hathaway." He had asked for a letter from the beautiful golden-haired Prudence Mercer. And wasn't a letter written under false pretenses better than nothing at all? A man in Christopher's situation needed all the words of encouragement one could offer.

He needed to know that someone cared.

And for some reason, after having read his letter, Beatrix found that she did indeed care.

MINE TILL MIDNIGHT

*'All men, no matter what their situation, occasionally succumbed
to their lower natures. What attracted Amelia's notice was the third
man, the would-be peacemaker, as he darted between the drunken
fools and attempted to reason with them. He was every bit as well-
dressed as the gentlemen on either side … but it was obvious this
man was no gentleman. He was black-haired and swarthy and exotic
in appearance. And he moved with the swift grace of a cat, easily
avoiding the swipes and lunges of his opponents.'*

Amelia Hathaway is the oldest of four sisters and has only one
brother to drive her mad. They live a genteel but impoverished life
until they come into an unexpected inheritance. Amelia tries her best
to rein in her colourful and unmanageable siblings to match society's
expectations. Until the mysterious, extremely wealthy half-gypsy
Cam Rohan appears.

The irresistible attraction between Amelia and Cam poses a huge
problem for both of them. However, as Amelia deals with a multitude
of problems, including trying to save her alcoholic brother Leo from
ruin, she finds herself turning to Cam Rohan, whose friendship turns
into a passion that neither of them can deny…

978-0-7499-3855-0

SEDUCE ME AT SUNRISE

*'I love you,' Winifred said wretchedly. 'And if I were well, no power
on earth could keep me away from you—"*

London, 1848 – for the last two years, following an attack of scarlet
fever, Winifred Hathaway has been an invalid. She's been told she can
do nothing but succumb to her illness, but her bright and optimistic
nature means she will not accept such a fate. She has too much to live
for, namely the handsome Merripen.

A part of the Hathaway family since they took him under their wing
– after he was wounded and left for dead – the gypsy-bred Merripen
will do anything to protect Win, even hide his true feelings and break
her heart. However, nothing can stand in the way of true love…

978-0-7499-0885-0

TEMPT ME AT TWILIGHT

Engaged to the very sensible Michael Bayning, Poppy Hathaway is
content with her lot – having longed for a life of normality. That is,
until she meets a mysterious hotel owner, Harry Rutledge – the most
complicated and dangerous man she has ever met.

Harry is wealthy and powerful, a collector of secrets, with hobbies
more dangerous than Poppy could imagine. What Harry wants, Harry
gets – and Harry wants Poppy, like he has never wanted a woman in
his life.

So when Michael breaks off their engagement and Harry makes his
move, Poppy quickly learns that her life is destined to be anything but
normal – filled with wild, passionate days and steamy nights …

978-0-7499-0958-1